The Eighth Hero

By Lucas Olson

Map Artwork Done By: Cassandra Lynn of Oakleaf Arrow Studios

This book is dedicated to the 40 long years it was lodged in my brain.

1

"Now, where did I leave my book?" The figure of the old woman spoke, her voice very old and very wise. "It is always difficult to keep track of things when reality will shift without warning."

The old woman fumbled through a small bookshelf. It held no more than maybe ten books, but the books were always changing. They shifted in size, shape, and color constantly.

"Ah, here it is." She seized one of them, and it settled. She held the now extremely ancient tome in her hands as she made her way to the large stone plinth. It made a heavy thud as she laid it down. "Now, this story has not been settled yet. I can feel it in the pages. Gods can never stop in their schemes, apparently."

She shifted through the pages to find the correct page. "Ah, here it is. Maybe this time you will succeed. So it begins again…"

*****

A story once spoke of ancient Gods. The Gods did not care for their creations. They would feed off of the worship from their creations. Some Gods would create entire worlds for people to live and thrive. Only to bring calamity upon them. The Gods would feed upon the death and strife of their creations. When their creations were desperate and brought to their knees, the Gods would reveal themselves and appear to save them from the very calamity the Gods themselves had wrought. Then feed off the praise and worship.

This went on for eons; time means nothing to a God. Nothing but atrocity after atrocity, a timeless age of maleficence and brutality. Worlds created, then torn asunder by the evil Gods. Gods would play trivial games with their creations. To promise salvation from the oncoming darkness, only stand aside and laugh as their creation died.

The question you must ask yourself is, can something be considered a God if they only demand worship, instead of earning it?

A small group of Gods, the Twelve, grew tired of the slaughter and wanted to be worthy of worship. The Twelve created our world, Sýna, in an act of defiance to the Outer Gods. This angered the Outer Gods. That anger spawned a war to consume all of creation. How do Gods war? We do not know. We do know that to save us, the Twelve created the Wall and placed the Towers and Runes of Blessing around it to protect us.

That is why we make the Pilgrimage to the Twelve Towers and pay our respects. Worship the Twelve to give them the strength so they may fight for us. Two of the Gods have fallen in battle. We know this because their towers have gone dark, and no one is blessed with their powers.

The Ten remaining still fight to this day...

Excerpt from The Sacrifice by the Twelve, yr 256

"What happened to the Gods, Khet?" the small boy asked.

Khet stooped down and looked at the boy. "Well, Ty, what does the book say? You will never learn to read it if I have to tell you everything."

Ty looked up at Khet. "It doesn't say spit about 'em, Khet. Just there outside the Wall fighting evil. This book is boring."

Khet reached out and ruffled Ty's thick, dusty-colored hair. "Well, all we know about the Twelve and their battle with the evil Outer Gods is in that book. We should be thankful that they are out there trying to protect us."

Ty made a face. "OK, I will try to be more thankful for the Twelve's sacrifice." His tone held a mild sarcasm.

"I was the same when I was your age, head full of questions about the Twelve. As it says in that book. It is fine to question, but never question the sacrifice of the Twelve. Or you might be considered under the influence of the Outer Gods and named Arankai." Khet gave Ty a wink.

Ty's face soured. "Never! The Temple will put an end to the Arankai."

"Boy!" A voice bellowed from outside.

"Khet, come on time for work!" the loud voice carried on. "Let's go!"

Khet straightened up. "Well, Ty, Tarin sounds like he is ready to get some work done. You should go see Kase about chores."

"Fine, ruin the fun, why don't ya? She scares me a little, all the scars on her arms." Ty grumbled.

Khet and Ty left through the door into the fresh air of daylight. Both Khet and Ty were contracted workers. A total of five contracted workers serviced this small homestead and smithy. All of them, except Khet, were sold on contract by their parents at a really young age. Khet was sold by his father when his God blessing started to show. A child that could wield a God's blessing was a valuable thing. Poor families would sell the blessed children and normal children into a contract for money, goods, or maybe to be rid of them.

Khet's father was a drunk. As soon as Khet started to show his Rune of Vulcan at the base of his neck under his chin, his father sold him to Tarin for drinking money. Maybe it was for the better, Tarin didn't strike Khet like his father did. From what Khet could remember, all his father did was drink and strike him. Khet did not have any good memories of his father.

Khet made his way towards the blacksmith and owner of his contract, Tarin ve Drast. Tarin was a mountain of a man. Taller and wider than most men with bulging muscles from years of forging steel and iron. His hair and beard were the color of wheat and were braided in the northern fashion. He stood out in the south, but as he explained, it kept his hair away from the flames. What folks thought about his hair didn't matter much anyway to him. Tarin only cared about what they thought about his work.

"Light the forge, boy. We have work to do." Tarin's voice was like a mountain grinding a stone.

Khet walked over to the forge that was in the center of the smithy. A big, monstrous thing blackened by centuries of use. He placed his hands in the cool coals and closed his eyes. He cleared his mind. He called on Vulcan, the Forge Lord.

"Come on, boy. Light the forge." Tarin was always impatient when he wanted to work.

"I am, it's just-" It was never easy for Khet to call on Vulcan's blessing. A chorus of voices assaulted him whenever he tried. He had to sift through them to find Vulcan. "There." A glow appeared in the forge. The deep red light spread as the heat began to build.

"I tell you, boy, I should find your father and beat him until I get my money back. You are the slowest Forge Blessed I have ever seen. How much longer is your contract?" Tarin didn't mean it in a negative way; he just said it as he saw it. He never wanted to sugarcoat anything when it came to his smithy.

"Three months, sir. I was sold to contract on Sol Anum 10 years ago." There was an excitement in his voice. A hope for freedom and new beginnings.

"Well, settle down, you're not done yet. You better make it worth the gold I spent on your hide. Now go grab those swords we are repairing for the Temple. They need 'em repaired and sharpened by next week." Tarin may have seemed like an angry man, but Khet thought deep underneath all the bellowing anger, he was kind and cared for Khet.

Khet grabbed the bundles of the Temple's swords. He separated them by the amount and type of work that was needed to repair them. After they were sorted, Khet and Tarin were set to their task.

Blessed with Vulcan's forge fire, Khet was perfectly fit to work a smithy. Vulcan's Blessing gave him the ability to summon fire hot enough to set a forge ablaze. Fire did not burn him. The brightest glowing steel only felt warm to the touch.

So, the rhythm of the work began. BANG...BANG...BANG. The sound of the hammer strikes rang through the farmstead. Like a heartbeat made of iron, the rhythm was steady. Khet and Tarin worked in sync. Each other's hammer blow was timed to strike just as the other began to rise. This went on for several hours until Tarin called for a break.

"Let's break for water and some food, boy. Fetch me a tankard of water." Tarin was slightly winded from the exertion, though nowhere near tired.

Khet left the cover of the smithy and walked into the sunlight. The light of the stationary sun shone down. It made him glisten with sweat. The breeze was cool on his skin. In the almost 10 years of Khet's contract with Tarin, Khet had grown stronger. Hard work and good eating had added a great deal of muscle to his frame. He was nearing his 19th year and ever closer to the end of his contract.

At the water barrel, Khet grabbed two empty tankards from the wall nearby and plunged them into the cool water. He brought one to his lips and took long, deep pulls of the cool water. Khet could feel the coolness slowly seep down into his chest. He refilled his cup and made his way back to Tarin.

Tarin sat on a bench enjoying the cool breeze outside the smithy when Khet made it back to him. Tarin took a deep pull from the tankard. Water dribbled out of the sides of his mouth and trickled down his beard as he drank.

"That was good, thank you for that. So, what are your plans when your contract is over?" Tarin brushed the water from his beard.

"I want to walk the Wall. Visit all the Twelve Towers. I have read about them, and I want to make the Pilgrimage." They both looked towards the ancient Wall. It was a three-day walk to the Wall, but it still took up the entire southern horizon. Stretching out of sight in either direction. The slight curve in the wall was hardly noticeable.

"Plan on honorin' the Gods, huh?" Tarin half-chuckled. "Plan on becomin' an acolyte of the Temple of the Twelve? I thought about it when I was your age. I never made it far; maybe two months of traveling the Wall. I met Kase, and that was that. Neither of us is God-touched, so we found some land and started this farm. I've been here since." Tarin paused for a moment, an awkwardness to him. "You could stay here and work for me, you know? You're good with a hammer. I can start a campfire quicker with my piss than you can light the forge, but I can work with that. You will get paid fairly and have a room in the house."

Khet stood there for a moment in shock. He never thought about staying. For years, he planned to complete the Pilgrimage of the Twelve Towers and find adventure in between. "Sorry, sir. I want to feel the road under my legs for a while, see what is out there. It feels like something is calling me to adventure."

"Is that from one of your books? Or would it be that pretty-read-headed light bringer that came through about five weeks back? She was just starting her Pilgrimage. You think you could catch up to her? She was mighty cute." Tarin chuckled, only as a man that has chased after something pretty before chuckles.

Khet blushed slightly; was he that obvious? "No... I just really want to see the Towers...that's all."

Tarin still held a broad smile on his face. "All right, boy. Time to earn your keep. Back to the forge." Tarin stood and stretched. He shook out the tightness that had started to form in his muscles. Soon after entering the smithy, the iron heartbeat sounded through the farmstead again.

Time moved by with the rhythm of the hammer strikes. Eventually, a voice called out. "Are you guys hungry? I have a pot of beef and potato stew, and I baked a couple of loaves of bread. Also, Calli found a monger at the market and purchased some soft cheese." It was Kase va Drast, Tarin's wife. She radiated strength in the way she carried herself. Kase had a medium build and long, dark brown hair. Unlike Tarin's tight braided hair, Kase's hair was let to go wild. The only thing trying to control her hair was a small blue ribbon. She was always like a mother to Khet and the other contracted. Scars covered her hands and arms, that spoke loudly of a past life long left behind.

Tarin and Khet shared a look. "It sounds delicious, women. Be there in a minute. Khet, you go wash up. I will clean up here."

"Are you sure you don't need my help, sir?" Khet asked.

"No, go and wash up. Clean well around your collar. There is a lot of suit buildup on it. I have a couple of things I need to do here. I will join you after."

Khet left the smithy and walked to the stream nearby. He could feel the buildup around his collar now that Tarin had pointed it out. Khet idly touched his collar. It had been placed around his neck 10 years ago when he was sold to contract with Tarin. A collar magically sealed by a Sidierion Priestess. Runes marking the terms of the contract etched into its metal surface.

When a contract is formed, a Sidierion Priestess carves the terms of the contract in runes into the collar. She then takes a special type of stone and carves a binding rune into it. The collar is placed on the contracted worker, and the stone is given to the owner of the contract. The stone can be used to inflict pain, to force submission, or it can be used to locate the contracted if they were to run.

At the end of the contract, the rock and collar shatter on their own, leaving the contracted to go free. The owner of the contract can also end the contract early by breaking the stone. Doing this will free the contracted.

Khet washed himself in the small river. The water felt refreshing in the constant sun. He used a small bar of lye soap that was left there for contracted workers to wash with. All the while, the massive Wall loomed in the distance. Khet was always drawn to it. When he was first contracted, there was a small group that came through the farmstead that needed Tarin's services. One man stood out in the group. He was tall and lanky with a long, grayed beard but intense blue eyes. Khet thought he looked like the wizard from the old stories. He was a Storm Wielder; according to legend, the strongest ones could summon great, catastrophic storms and gales. But this old man, according to his companions, could barely summon a breeze. Ulric was the old man's name, and he was full of stories. Stories of the Gods and of heroes that fought alongside them in the battle before the Wall was built. He said he knew a legend of how the Wall was forged and why it had to be built. He spoke of many tales of what was outside the Wall. Ulric was full of them. He and his group were on the Pilgrimage to the Twelve Towers. Ulric boasted that he had been to six of the Towers. He spoke of the God Shards. The ancient crystal shards that held a sacred power. At the top of each Tower sat a shard. Anyone could see the power that radiated from a shard. Our prayers and sacrifices were absorbed by a shard. This would give the Gods strength to keep up the fight. We know two of the Twelve Gods have fallen because their towers have gone dark and their names lost from memory.

All the stories of Gods and heroes that Khet had heard filled his mind as he sat by the river. He wanted to live those stories, be a hero, and he was determined that he would. "As soon as this damn collar is off," he mumbled to himself.

2

After he was finished daydreaming and his stomach could no longer be ignored, Khet made way for the barn. The smell of the stew and bread made Khet's mouth water and his stomach growl. Almost everybody was there already except for Tarin. He must still be in the smithy tending to what he needed to tend to.

"Sit down, Khet, and get yourself some food. There is plenty, so eat your fill." Kase always had a motherly air about her and would treat the contracted, especially the young ones, as her own children. Kase and Tarin didn't have any children of their own. "Tarin tells me you want to do the Pilgrimage. You know you are more than welcome to stay here. It has been nice having you live with us." Her smile was warm and loving.

Khet looked at Kase and thought for a moment. It had been nice here, but the call of the road was too strong for Khet to ignore. "Sorry, the Pilgrimage is something I want to do. I want to honor the Gods for their sacrifice and pray they keep fighting." The more Khet said it, the whole idea of his freedom and the Pilgrimage became more real. Like each utterance made it come into being.

"OK, I understand. But you realize that we can't let you go unprepared, right?" Kase's look almost bore through Khet. She always has a way to see right through someone and get to the heart of the matter. It made it really hard for Khet to lie to her when he was young.

That look always unsettled him, as if he had done something wrong. "Uh, no…ma'am"

"Do you know how to handle a sword?" Kase's tone changed; her normal motherly affect was gone. A bit of fear swirled in Khet's gut.

"Uh, not really, I mean I handled some to test them out, but-" Khet bumbled.

"OK, show me. Come here and show me." Her words, her posture, all changed. Her body seemed to stiffen. Her words and movements sharpened. She resembled a weapon, not a person.

Kase stood and walked to grab 2 thick sticks, the kind that children would use to play fight. "These will do, now come." She threw Khet one of the sticks. Khet caught the stick and lifted his head to face Kase. She struck. The blow was to the side of Khet's face. Not hard enough to cause damage but hard enough to punish him for not blocking it.

"Rule 1, always be ready or you will be killed. Now come at me." Her voice was cold as a freshly plucked river stone.

Khet raised his stick and stepped towards Kase. Another blow came across the other side of Khet's face. This time it was harder, more punishing.

"Rule 2, hesitating can get you killed." Kase drilled. "Now come at me!"

Khet lunged at Kase. His frustration was high. His mind raced as Kase lazily brushed off his attack. Pain erupted across Khet's back and then his legs were thrown out from underneath him. The wind forced out of him as his back slammed into the ground. His vision swam. Seconds passed before the stark realization that Kase stood over him with the stick pointing to his neck.

"Rule 3, leaping without thinking will get you killed." Kase was made of iron, her voice cold. She reached out and offered her hand to help Khet. He took it and she pulled him up. Kase walked around him, checking for injuries. "Good, you are not bleeding. Tomorrow before breakfast, meet me behind the house, on the west side. We will start your training. Now brush yourself off, finish your food, and go get some rest. Tomorrow may be hard for you, but you will learn."

"Yes, ma'am." Is all that Khet could say. He bowed his head and walked to the table. As he ate, his jaw ached and his body hurt. Hidden deep down inside of him was a flicker of excitement. The excitement of a new path to be taken.

After the meal and his first lesson, he made his way back to the hut where the contracted slept. Khet couldn't wrap his mind around what had happened. *How did Kase become so good with a sword?* His thoughts raced, one question being overshadowed by the next. The door creaked as he entered the hut. The mixture of excitement and confusion made his head hurt. Sleep would not come easily for him tonight, for there was too much to think about. He closed his eyes and lay there until hours later, sleep finally took him.

3

"Khet," a voice roused him from his deep sleep. Khet slowly opened his eyes. Vision still blurred from sleep.

"Khet, get out of bed. I have somethin' for you." As Khet's vision resolved, he saw a mountain of a man, Tarin. He stood over his bed. "Come outside." For a man of such size, Khet marveled at his ability to move and speak so quietly.

Khet started to shift, and pain ran through the welt in his back and the bruise on his face. He moved with great care to avoid any more pain. When he was up, he realized that everyone else was still asleep. *How early is it*, he thought. He slowly shuffled his way outside into bright sunlight; it made him squint until his eyes finally adjusted. Tarin sat on the bench outside the smithy. Khet stiffly walked over to see what Tarin had woken him for.

"I hear Kase has decided to train you?" There was a softness to Tarin's voice now. As if the boulder of a man had grown a soft layer of moss.

"Yes, sir." Sleep still muddled Khet's mind and his words.

"It is not right for a contracted to strike the owner of their contract or his wife. I can't have that." Tarin stated flatly. Reminding Khet that he was still a boulder, even if there was moss.

"But, sir... Sorry, sir." The grogginess of sleep evaporated in an instant. Khet bowed his head, afraid he was about to be punished.

"No... no, Khet, you misunderstand." Tarin placed one of his large hands on Khet's shoulder. The weight of it pulled Khet slightly off balance.

Khet raised his head just as Tarin reached into his pocket. A small stone with runes carved into it appeared in his hand. It was Khet's binding stone. Tarin brought the stone to his lips and mouthed something to it. With minimal fanfare, he crushed it in his big hands. The collar around Khet's neck started to glow and crack. Then it shattered and fell to the ground. The pieces made a hollow ring as they hit the ground. Khet stood there stunned.

"I am releasing you from your contract. You are free to go, if you want. You can stay here until you are done training with Kase. It will be hard, but if you want to travel to the Twelve Towers, you should know how to defend yourself." Tarin's eyes seemed misty.

"Sir... I... what..." Khet was at a loss for words. It had been so long he had forgotten what the breeze had felt like on his neck, the warmth of the sun. Khet slid his hands around the freshly exposed skin around his neck. It was foreign and beautiful to Khet at the same time.

Tarin raised his hand to quiet Khet. "First, you are a free man. Call me Tarin, you have earned it. According to the contract, once the contract ends, you are entitled to 3 months' earnings." Tarin reached down on the bench and grabbed a leather pouch. He handed it to Khet. He took it from Tarin as if he was just handed a newborn child. The coin bag felt heavy in Khet's hands; he could feel the coins inside shift. "That is yours to keep; you will need it for the Pilgrimage. A room has been made up in the house for you, and you are welcome to use it while you are here. Also, I have something for you in the forge." He gestured for Khet to follow.

Khet stood there for a moment, still in shock from all that had just happened. He stood there with his mouth agape. The sound of the smithy door shook Khet from his daze. He gathered himself and followed Tarin.

Khet entered the smithy. The windows were closed, and only one lamp was lit. It took several seconds for his eyes to adjust. On the table was a set of leather armor.

"It is yours. It was made not long ago for you. I hoped you would stay with us, but as soon as I saw the way you looked at the redheaded Lightbringer, I knew you were leaving. Well, don't just stand there; put it on. You will need it for your training this morning." Tarin grinned.

Khet was still stunned, no words came to his mind, nothing but awed numbness in his head. *Can this be real*, he thought, as he reached for the armor. It was smooth and firm in his hands. The craftsmanship was of a quality Khet had rarely seen. He slipped it over his head. The welt on his back was like fire as the armor slid across it, a reminder of Rule 3.

"Sir... Tarin.... I don't know what to say." Khet was still lost in the emotion of the moment. "Thank You" he choked, his eyes filled with tears.

"No thanks needed. Kase and I have spoken at length about this, and we think it is the right thing to do. And don't get too choked up yet, you still must train with Kase. You may want to change your mind after a round or two" Tarin chuckled. "Now tie on your bracers and go. Kase is waiting for you. I will put your coins in your room."

"Thank you, Tarin" Khet exhaled.

They exchanged a look. Tarin nodded and Khet went out the door. The elation that Khet felt washed over him. He almost felt intoxicated. How it felt to be a free man was so foreign to Khet, but he liked it.

4

Khet walked towards the west side of the house. A figure leaned against a tree. He froze. It was Kase. Not the normal motherly Kase, in her dress and apron. No, she wore armor, a mixture of leather and chain-link armor. It looked so natural on her like she was more comfortable in the armor, and the dress was a costume.

"I see my husband has given you armor. I am going to see that you earn it." It was a statement with no malice or hate. Like the Wall, just a stated fact. This was the real Kase. The woman that earned the scars the crisscrossed her hands and arms stood before him now. She threw him another stick, this one heavier, weighted more like a sword. Before he could properly grab ahold of it, she was on him. The first blow was across his stomach, not enough to wind him. Enough to make it hurt. Pain blossomed in his ribs as he was thrown from the impact of her kick. "Rule 1, always be ready."

Khet lay sprawled on his back. His side throbbed. He looked up and Kase slid in for another strike. This time Khet rolled and just missed the hit. He scrambled to get to his feet. Before he could manage, Kase planted her boot to his ribs again. Khet rolled across the ground, wind forced from his chest.

"Rule 4: No mercy. Your enemy is down, you strike." Kase's voice was cold, uncaring.

Khet gasped, trying to draw air into his lungs. He rolled to regain his footing. She was there as soon as he stood up. Kase drove her fist into his face. Pain erupted, everything became a blur, and his body collapsed. It all went black.

Khet floated weightless in the void. Something dark stirred below him. He could hear a woman humming. *Am I dreaming?* As an answer to his question, the sudden icy cold of the water brought him screaming back to reality. He couldn't breathe. Panic kicked in. He thrashed and thrashed. His head broke through the surface of the river. Kase stood on the bank, a grin forming on her hardened face.

"Dead boy lives!" Kase said with an icy mirth. "Come to the shore, dead boy. You are getting your new armor wet."

Khet swam the short distance to the shore and crawled out. He hacked and spitted between deep gulps of air. After he coughed, half of the river came up from his lungs. Khet collapsed on the bank, completely confused about the situation. Too many things had happened that morning. He was given freedom to live his life, and a couple of hours later, a woman, that he almost thought of as a mother, tried to kill him.

"That is enough for today. You did well for your first day. Start again tomorrow." Kase spoke to the soggy lump of bruised flesh that lay on the shore. "Wash yourself, stow your armor in your room, and come eat breakfast."

Kase left him there. Khet slowly brought himself to a sitting position. All the pain made him dizzy. Old and new bruises sang in a chorus. Khet had never been this miserable. He tried to stand, but his legs betrayed him. He rolled onto his back and stared at the sky. The sound of footsteps drew his attention.

"I see you survived your first day. She said you did well. Here, let me help you up." Tarin hid a grin under his beard, but you could see it around his eyes.

"Good? I couldn't defend myself at all. She kicked the crap out of me." Khet whimpered.

"You didn't die. It was a good day. Now come, let's go to the house and get that armor off you." Tarin practically carried Khet up to the house. Everybody took notice. Ty had a look of surprised concern and came over to Khet.

"Khet, are you hurt?" Ty said worriedly. "Wait, Khet, where is your collar? Are you done with your contract?"

"He will be alright, little one. He and the missus just had a little disagreement. He didn't want to do his chores before breakfast." Tarin smirked.

Ty paled, like he had not finished his chores yet. With a flash, he was gone to complete them.

"That will keep him on the straight and narrow for a while." Tarin chuckled. They had made it almost all the way to the house when Kase stepped out into the light, dressed in a dress and her cooking apron. Not a single sign of the woman that beat him a little bit ago.

"I found this by the river." Tarin really enjoyed this. Khet didn't see the humor.

"I will fetch some water to clean him up, take that armor off of him." Kase wore her motherly costume. Khet now knew the full extent of Kase. Fear crept through his body.

"Come on, son, let's get that off of you." Tarin peeled the armor off and took off Khet's shirt. He tried to be as gentle as a mountain could be. Fresh bruises were forming over Khet's jaw and ribs. The pain was indescribable.

Khet had come back to his full senses by the time Kase returned. He stared at her as if she was a predator that had come into the house. A predator that now carried a bucket of water and a sympathetic guise.

"Here, wash up with this." Kase tossed a rag at him and pointed to the bucket. She reached into her apron and pulled out a vial. "Drink this first, it will help with the pain."

Khet took the vial, inspected the contents for the barest of moments, and swallowed it. The liquid tasted awful, but it did refresh him. He took the rag and plunged it into the bucket. Khet cleaned himself with such care that he tried to avoid all the tender patches. It was a slow process. Soon, though, the mixture that Kase had given him must have started to work. His head didn't pound, and his ribs ached less. He started to feel like a person again. Every moment that passed, he felt better and better. He was energized, almost like he had just gotten a long rest on a featherbed. Khet, in astonishment, tested all of his injuries with short jabs of his finger. His bruises didn't seem so severe, and his jaw now felt fine.

Tarin brought a new shirt and a pair of breeches. "These are for you. Give me your old clothes. I will dispose of them."

"Why would you throw them away? They are still good. And wow, what did she give me?" Khet buzzed with energy.

"Oh, she gave you some nectar, didn't she?" The look on Tarin's face was that of one who had said too much.

"What is that?" Khet said with a puzzled look.

"Yeah, she doesn't like to talk openly about it. She is a Grun, and a

16

damn good one." Tarin had pride in his voice. "She doesn't like everybody to know because then you have everyone and their brother here begging to heal the smallest wound. She will help those who really need it, but she does it in a way that doesn't draw too much attention. Remember when you first got here and we were straightening out that shield? You didn't have your rhythm and you crushed my hand with the hammer?"

"Yes, I thought it just wasn't as bad as it looked." A new world had been opened to Khet.

"No, you crushed it, completely." Tarin held up his hand, flexing it. "I went to Kase and she gave me some nectar. I was right as rain the next day. A little stiff but workable."

Khet stood there, his mind sent spinning again at the latest revelation about Kase. It all made sense, he thought. When the contracted were sick, Kase would come around with medicine that worked a little too well. And that time that traveler was here, and he fell off his horse. Everybody thought he broke his arm, but after Kase looked at it, it was fine.

"Close your mouth, son. You're going to catch flies. And I shouldn't have to remind you not to mention it to anyone," Tarin leaned in and made eye contact with Khet. "Correct?"

The memory of this morning flooded back into Khet's mind. "Yeah, yes, I won't say a word."

"Good. Let's go eat." Tarin said as he turned and walked toward the barn. Khet followed his body, moved like this morning's events never happened.

5

At breakfast the other contracted noticed that Khet did not have a collar. Some looked in shock others shared the joy. Khet was never close to the other contracted, only Ty would come and talk to him. Maybe because he was the only God Blessed or maybe he had the shortest contract. Khet didn't know. Ty was young though and full of questions. In the year and a half that Ty was contracted to the farm he always wanted to be around Khet. So Khet would try to be his older brother. Khet taught Ty how to read and write, not fully but enough to understand. Khet shared some of the tales that travelers would tell at night while they laid in their bunks. Khet would miss Ty.

"Khet, is it true? You are free? You have no collar!" Ty said eagerly moving towards Khet.

"Yeah, just this morning. Still trying to get used to it." Khet rubbed his bare neck. It still felt odd with no collar.

"Are you leaving? Today? Where are you going to go?" Ty's own words tripped on themselves.

"Whoa, slow down, Ty. I am not going anywhere just yet. Tarin and Kase say I need some training before I go walk the Pilgrimage." Khet ran his hand through Ty's hair.

"Much needed training from what I saw this morning" Tarin said with a grin, seated at the other end of the table, mouth already full of breakfast.

Khet blushed a little.

"When you go who will be there to read me more stories?" Ty stood higher and half covered his mouth to whisper. "The others are so boring. They don't tell good stories."

"You will have to find your own stories. And I will come as visit after I am done." Khet tried to reassure Ty.

"Enough talking everyone hurry up and eat." Kase walked up to the table, she made direct eye contact with Khet. "After breakfast you light the forge, and you meet me on the road. I have more things to show you."

Khet's inside twisted. "I thought we were done for today?" He squeaked.

"This morning you died a lot. If you want to live, you will meet me at the road." Kase's statement was something Khet couldn't ignore.

Tarin stifled a chuckle as he watched Khet buckle under the pressure.

"Yes, ma'am…. Should I go put on my armor?" Khet was full of dread.

"Rule 1." is all Kase said.

After breakfast Khet lit the forge. Vulcan was still hard for Khet to summon. But eventually he was found, and the forge was lit. He went to the house and collected his armor. The armor was still wet from his swim earlier. It was cold and uncomfortable. The leather chafed him as he made it down to the road.

Khet stood there beside the road for an hour. A constant state of anxiety was his only companion. Every shift in the tall grass, every whisper of sound was Kase preparing for an attack. At least now he knew she could heal him quickly so that made it a little better. The tension eased out of him slightly when he saw Kase at a distance. She exited the house clad in her armor. He eased his muscles a little now that there was no surprise attacks in store. Khet was relieved that she didn't carry any weapons. All she had was four water skins.

"Here" she handed him two full water skins and pieces of leather cord to tie them to his belt. "Do you have a knife on you?"

"No." Khet said.

With a swift movement she produced a blade that was hidden on her. Fear and awe filled Khet. *Where did it come from?* Nothing in her armor gave away a the hidden blade. *Could there be more?* Khet wondered to himself.

"Take it." Kase offered.

Khet reached for the blade in the way you reach out to touch an animal that you don't know if it is dangerous or not. Once he had the blade, he had no idea where to put it. He searched his body for a good place to store it, but he could find nothing.

Kase noticed the confusion and held up her arm showing the underside of her bracer. "Put the blade here."

Khet looked at where the bracer met her wrist. An iron ring, same as the ring on the knife he had, slightly stuck out of a pocket. He glanced at the same spot on his right bracer. There was a small built in sheath, it fit the blade perfectly.

Kase reached up and slapped Khet on the forehead. "No, you are right-handed. If you only carry one blade, carry it in the left bracer."

Khet didn't hesitate and followed the instructions. He placed the blade in the sheath, he marveled at the simple but useful design.

"Let's go." Kase prompted.

Khet looked up and Kase was already sprinting down the road. Khet jerked into motion. His feet struggled to catch up to Kase.

Her pace was relentless. Within minutes sweat soaked his shirt, and his breaths were hard. They ran south toward the Wall. Khet tried to focus on the Wall to take his mind off the pain of the run. But he couldn't, he had to be present. On top of that Kase's Rule 1 was ever present in his mind.

Time slowly ticked by, Khet's legs screamed for a break. Finally they stopped at the edge of a forest. Winded, Khet grabbed a water skin to quench his thirst. Kase barely looked tired at all. She went off the road to look for something. "Boy come here." She sounded much farther away than she should have been.

Khet stoppered the water skin and went towards where her voice sounded. Ever wary of her next attack. Khet crept through the forest. Almost a perfect ring of trees appeared before him. Kase stood at the center holding two thick arm-length branches.

"We train now." She tossed him the stick. This time he kept his guard up, but she was still too fast for him. She blew past his guard. Slipped around to his back and struck him. The leather took most of the impact. "Better, not good, but better. Again." She came at him directly and to Khet's surprise he was able to block a blow, but she slid into his block and drove her elbow into his jaw. He tasted blood, and his mouth throbbed.

Kase danced back, light on her feet. "Again." Her tone was cold. Khet raised his stick to defend himself. Again, she was too fast. Kase made her way past his guard with ease. She wedged the stick under his arm and pried upward. Khet heard a pop and pain flared in his shoulder. He cried out. His weapon and arm fell useless to his side.

"Rule 5, if you take away your enemy's ability to wield their weapon, the fight is over." Kase's voice had a brutality to it.

Khet laid on the ground, it took a great deal of effort not to whimper like a struck child. Kase walked over and placed the tip of her stick to Khet's throat. "You're dead, boy" She stated as a fact. "Now give me your arm."

"I can't move it!" Khet said with pain in his voice.

As Khet spoke, Kase reached down and took hold of his wrist, placed a foot on his chest and pulled to reset his shoulder. Khet screamed and the world started to spin.

"Get up, we need to go now." Kase reached down and pulled him up by is uninjured arm. She set off into the forest and Khet stumbled after.

Khet's head was swam in pain. He attempted to focus on where Kase was going. His vision blurred.

"Why are we doing this? Can I get a break? I am hurt really bad." Khet whimpered.

Kase slowed but did not stop. "Do you think your enemy will slow when you are hurt? Do you think they care if you get a break?" The sound her voice made was like a sword drawn across stone.

"But you haven't taught me anything, you just beat me up. Can you heal me?" Khet wined. Suddenly Kase stopped and clotheslined Khet with such force it was like she threw him at the ground instead of to the ground. With the impact Khet's vision went black.

6

"Boy, wake up." Kase nudged his ribs with the toe of her boot.

The pain forced open his eyes, his head throbbed, his whole body hurt just in general. Kase sat in front of him on a tree stump. The world was not in focus. Everywhere seemed smudged. Even Kase's form on the stump was smudged. The brightness of the world made his eyes feel like there was sand in them. "OK, I am up." His voice was weak.

"You want to know why I do this to you? Training you like this? Let you feel the pain instead of just healing you?" There was a fire in Kase's words.

Khet just lay there and looked at her for a while. A battle between fear and rage warred inside him. Fear lost. "Yes, tell me why you just kick the shit out of me and not actually teach me anything! Do you know what the fucking teaching means?" The rage he held deep down bubbled to the top.

"Here, drink this." She handed Khet a small vial filled with a greenish liquid. She totally ignored his tantrum. "Good, now come and I will show you why I train you this way." She stood and waited for Khet.

The way she dismissed him as his rage. Extinguished the fire in his chest. He took the vial of nectar and did as she told him. It hit him quicker this time. Before he could get up, his head stopped pounding, and his vision had lost its dark edges. He stood for a second, tested his limbs, his balance, and everything seemed to work fine. His anger and rage were still there. He just pushed them farther down.

"Follow me." Kase moved off into the woods.

With every step through the forest, a question nagged at Khet. "Where did you learn to fight like that?"

"What, you think I have always been a good little housewife?"

"No...I just thought..."

"That Tarin was the fighter?" Kase turned and looked at Khet.

He froze, "Well...yeah." Immediately, he regretted saying that. Khet's bowels threatened to loosen as he waited for her reaction.

Kase turned back to walking. "Tarin is good with a hammer but not a fighter. Did he ever tell you how we met?"

"No," Khet said a little more relieved.

"He never liked talking too much to the people we have a contract with. He said he didn't want to get too attached. He always does, though. We are unable to have children, so we always try to contract kids from parents that don't want them." She pushed her way through the brush with a practiced ease. "We would have more, but contracts can be expensive. Then we try to raise them to become their own people. Doing it this way is highly frowned upon in general society and would probably affect work at the smithy, so we have to keep up appearances. Did you know that?" Kase glanced at Khet.

In Khet's mind, pieces fell into place. He never realized how well they were treated. Nobody on the farmstead was ever beaten or punished severely. "No." Is all he could manage.

"Yeah, there are other people like us out there, but they are few and far between. Most treat the people they have contracted as slaves. If it is in the contract, that is the excuse that they use. Or they use the Temple as an excuse for their cruelty." She went on. "Enough of that. Now, what were we talking about? Oh yeah, how I met Tarin."

Khet's mind still reeled from the revelation. The fact that Kase acted like the mother again, not the fighter, made the ground not feel as stable as it should.

"I met Tarin on his pilgrimage. We were just outside of Forst, it is a small city on the east side of the Dragon's Spine. He was by himself, just a young blacksmith. I was a mercenary looking for work. I would get hired by travelers and protect them on their pilgrimage. We met at a pub and became fast friends. We traveled together for a while. He never hired me, but I was having fun so I stayed with him. We made it all the way to the Spine and the path to Vulcan's Tower was blocked. We were enjoying each other's company enough. So, we decided to walk the 30-day journey north to Drake's Pass. We had a couple of scraps with animals, bandits, and the like. During the quiet parts he talked about what he wanted to do after the pilgrimage. First it was talk of joining the Temple and serving the Twelve. After a couple of weeks it turned into, settling down, building a smithy, raising some animals, and maybe some children. Once we made it through the pass, he convinced me to join him in his dream. We found an old abandoned smithy. We just decided to build the rest of the homestead around it and have been there ever since. Well in the beginning I would take mercenary jobs to help fund things but after 4 or 5 years I quit that life. So, that is how we met. I learned to fight like I do from the Mercenary Guild outside the University of Valkai. Any questions?" Kase looked at Khet.

Again, "No." is all he could say. It was so much information for him to take in. Kase was a trained mercenary. Tarin's plan to work for the Temple made sense, he always seemed devout.

They walked through the woods for hours in silence. It gave Khet time to wrap his head around the revelations. Kase raised her hand to stop and motioned him to stay quiet. Her body tensed; she waited for something. The icy hand of fear gripped Khet's heart. An explosion of leaves and sticks erupted to the right of Kase. In the blink of an eye, she had another larger blade out, and it was buried in a creature's neck. She wrenched it free; gore and black blood sprayed across her face. "Where there is one, there is more!" She shouted. Explosions of debris were everywhere around them. Khet fumbled for his blade. Kase shoved him to the ground just as one of the creatures swiped at him with its claws. Kase severed its arm with her large knife. The creature howled in pain. Before the creature could finish its cry of agony, Kase rounded and separated its head from its body.

Khet's heart pounded in his ears. The sounds of the fight around him were distant. There was movement out of the corner of his eye. One of the creatures lunged toward him. This one was larger and looked different from the others. Khet froze, unable to move; fear wouldn't allow it. His rage could not overcome his fear. His body betrayed him. Kase barreled into the side of the creature. Both she and the creature tumbled over the ground. A snarling pile of limbs twisted chaotically before him.

Kase kicked free of the creature. She charged back into the beast's arms with her weapon held high. Kase's battle cry rang thunderously as she plunged. Kase thrusted her blade to the hilt through the screaming mouth of the beast. Its body spasmed violently before it fell limp.

Mournful howls erupted in the forest as the creatures scattered. Kase freed herself from the tangle. "That is one of the reasons why I train you the way I do."

"What were those things? Why did they run?" Khet shook; panic and fear flooded his senses.

"They are called galins, stupid, nasty creatures. They were put here by the Outer Gods. If the Temple is to be believed. The damned Dodecahedron, those immortal bastards, are to be the ones to take care of these." Kase explained calmly, like nothing had happened.

Khet had heard about the Dodecahedron from the stories of travelers and books he had read. The immortal army of the Temple of the Twelve. Created by the Twelve to keep the Outer Gods from causing chaos within the Wall. The Dodecahedron hunted and destroyed all the Outer Gods' creations.

"Why did they run, and by the Gods, are you hurt?" Khet still shook.

"What?" Kase looked at her arm. Blood flowed freely down it. "This isn't bad, have you seen the other guy?" She chuckled as she wavered and fell to her knees. With her good arm, she pulled out a glass vial, pulled the cork out with her teeth. She spit the stopper to the ground and raised the vial high. "To my health." She swallowed the contents and passed out.

Khet panicked; his head was on a swivel. He rushed over to Kase. "She is still breathing, thank the Gods." He rolled Kase on her back to check her wound. The blood had stopped flowing, mostly. *That nectar worked well,* thought Khet. He sat there and waited for her to awake. With his blade out and ready, he prayed to the Twelve that she would wake soon.

7

A long, agonizing hour had passed before Kase awoken with a start. She shot to her feet, another blade drawn.

"They haven't come back." Khet said to her, relieved she was conscious. The tension in his shoulders eased slightly.

"They won't, galins are pack creatures and that one over there" Kase said as she pointed to the big one, "was the leader. Kill the leader and they will scatter. Remember that."

"I will" Khet said as he looked at one of the galins. The skin was the color of mud with patches of wiry fur. Its head was bird-like with a large, curved beak. The body was human in shape except for the exaggerated limbs and the addition of an extra joint in the arms. "Why do those Outer Gods send them here? Where do they come from?"

Kase walked around to collect her blades and checked her armor. "I don't know where they came from, but I have heard stories. I know how to kill them though. The Outer Gods want to kill us off so we can't pray to the Twelve. Our prayers give the Twelve the power to keep fighting. Can you fight when you are starving?"

"No. I guess I couldn't. Is that what you wanted to show me? That the woods have these galins in it?" Khet hoped they were done in these woods.

"No, what I wanted to show you is up ahead." Kase pointed in the direction of the Wall, south. "Come, we must move quickly; we have been gone too long and I have run out of nectar."

Khet followed and a short while later they came to a ruined village. The Wall was much closer now. Its blackened, ancient surface took up most of the horizon.

Kase turned to Khet. "This is what I wanted to show you." She pointed to the village. "Yes, there are evil creatures lurking out there, but some of the worst are men. This was a nice, quiet village until a group of God-touched bandits raided, raped, and burned it to the ground." Kase's eyes teared up. "A mother and a child, an infant, escaped. Both were badly beaten and bloodied when they made it to our home. I tried to heal them, but they were too far gone." Tears freely flowed down her cheek. "I was too weak. The bandits had to be stopped. I tracked them. For three Gods damned weeks, I tracked them. I caught up to them near Dragon's Spine, and I killed them all... one...by...one." She spoke in an agonized whisper. "But their leader survived. What I did to him took days. Did you know, a good healer can heal a severed limb? And with every bit I cut off, I proved that I was a good healer. When I was done, I left him there fully healed with one arm and a dull knife." Kase took a long, slow breath. The strength came back to her voice. "That is why I have all these scars. I could have healed them, but I keep them as a reminder of what is out here. Now do you understand?"

"Yes," is the only thing Khet could say.

"Remember this, Khet. Animals and beasts will kill for food or territory. A man will also kill for those things, but a man will also kill for fun. It is a hard world out there. You need to be ready for it." Kase put her hands on Khet's shoulders. "You will be a good man, like Tarin. I see a lot of him in you. I want you to live and be safe out there. Now let's leave this place. No good memories are left here." Kase turned and started for the tree line.

Khet struggled to focus on where he placed his feet as he followed. The day had been too much: he was freed from contract, beaten unconscious twice, learned that Kase was a Grun, found out that Tarin and Kase are just good people trying to help kids out, attacked by creatures he had never heard of, and the revelation that Kase was a mercenary that killed an entire bandit camp. All these thoughts clashed in his head. His breaths were hard and fast, and he struggled to keep pace with Kase.

Eventually, they made it to the road. Khet was breathing hard, so he slowed to a stop.

"Drink some water; we will rest for a bit." Kase instructed.

Khet collapsed on the road; exhausted, he reached for a water skin. The water tasted delicious. He almost finished one skin when he noticed Kase had hardly sweated.

"Why are you not tired? I can barely walk. How do you look so refreshed?" In between gulps of air, Khet complained.

"I am a Grun, remember? I can replenish my own strength. Eventually, I will tire and be forced to rest, but I can run for days before needing to stop."

"Can you replenish me? Maybe give me some nectar?" Khet asked; his breath slowed a little.

"Nectar can be dangerous if you take it too much. When you are injured, that is fine, but if you are not, it can become addictive. The craving will grow so intense that people will go insane. You have only had a watered-down version." Kase stressed with caution. "Once somebody is addicted to nectar, it is a hard road back; some don't make it."

A question came to him. "Back in the forest when you were wounded, you drank some of your own nectar, didn't you?"

"Yes, the wound was bad, and I would have healed on my own, but that would have taken a long time, and I didn't want to lie there vulnerable for too long." Kase made a vague gesture to the forest. "If you are still feeling exhausted, I could go find some herbs that would give you energy to get home, sound good?"

"Yes, please, thank you." Khet was excited to hear she could help him.

Khet sat in the road, the breeze cooled his sweat-soaked skin. The sound of the breeze through the leaves relaxed him. Not long after she left, Kase came out of the trees with two flowering plants.

"OK, this one," holding up the plant with the blue flowers, "is called Bell Fairy. It will help with the pain. And this one," she holds up a plant with a flower that was orange on the outside and faded to black towards the center, "is Dragon Thistle. Pull the flower's head off, chew them really good, and swallow them down with water. Now it will taste like dog piss, but it will give you the energy you need."

Khet plucked the blossoms off and chewed them. Kase was right; they tasted awful. After they were properly chewed, he washed them down with plenty of water.

"OK, let's get going. The effects will take a couple of minutes, but we can start running now." With that, Kase ran north towards home.

In the short time that they had rested, Khet's muscles had tightened.

He struggled to get back into the rhythm, but after a couple of minutes, things loosened back up. Energy flowed to his limbs. He felt lighter and refreshed. This pace would not be a struggle for him to maintain.

With the added energy from the herbs, they made it back to the homestead rather easily. They stopped at the gate. Khet breathed hard, but he was not tired. "Thanks for those herbs; they really worked."

Kase turned to him with a sheepish grin on her face. "They were just weeds."

"What? But I feel great. You got to be joking." Khet said, confusion across his face.

"Nope, not joking. Rule 6, you are stronger than you think." Kase smiled fully. "Now go clean up; dinner will be in a little while."

Confused, and exhaustion not far away, Khet made his way to the river to wash up. He stripped, grabbed the soap on the rock, and submerged in the water. He couldn't really get a grip on all he learned today, all that had happened. He thought he knew so much. Just to find out he knew so little.

He stayed in the cool water for a while. After a good soak, he washed himself and got out. His muscles disagreed with him putting his clothes back on. Each movement ached. Khet made his way to the smithy to see if Tarin needed anything. He found Tarin sitting on the bench smoking his pipe.

"I hear you learned a lot today." Tarin said.

"Too much I think." Said Khet, "I didn't know that I didn't know so much." Khet collapsed on the bench next to Tarin. He pushed his face into his hands.

Tarin reached up and clapped him on the back. "Yeah, I had the same reaction. That is why I settled here and chose the quieter life." He took a puff from his pipe and slowly blew it out his nose. "Kase did say you show promise."

"She did? She kicked the crap out of me twice and then had to save me because I froze." Khet was a mixture of bewilderment and frustration.

"But you could have run away. You are free to go and do what you want. You stayed and you kept going. That is something most won't do." Tarin had a fatherly tone.

Khet pulled his head out of his hands. He knew Tarin had a point, and he was set to see this through. He looked at Tarin, "You're right. Is dinner ready?"

"It was done an hour ago. We tried waiting. There is still some food left. Go eat. We left two plates of food out for you." Tarin clapped him on the back again. "Go eat, then rest."

Khet made his way over to the barn. Sleep called his name. He sat down at the table and Tarin was right. There were two plates made for him. Khet was so hungry and tired he just ate until it was gone. Not even taking notice of the taste.

He drank down a glass of ale and with a full belly, made his way back to his room in the house. Coming through the doorway, he saw Ty asleep in a chair by his bed. A book leaned against his chest. Khet took the book, gently lifted Ty up, put him in bed, and covered him up. Khet laid down on the floor so tired he didn't care. Sleep took him fast that night.

8

Khet woke early; he thought he heard somebody come into his room. His eyes adjusted, and there was Kase dressed in her armor. She gestured for him to follow her. Stiffly, he got up. All of his muscles ached with the strain from the prior day. Khet grabbed his armor by the door and went out of the room.

Out in the bright sunlight, Kase waited for him.

"Are you ready to learn?" Kase said.

"Yes," Khet tried to loosen his shoulders and back. His back muscles ached more than anything else.

Kase turned her head to the west. "There is a storm coming from the west today. It will help with your training today, I think."

Khet looked up at the dark clouds headed their way. He knew the storms from the west were bad. All southerners knew Arc Storms were some of the worst. Normally, storms in the south come off the Dragon's Spine mountains to the east. Generally, they were gentle rains, a few thunder showers maybe. Storms from the west were strong. The Towers of Arcanus and Bast were to the west. Arcanus, the Storm God's Tower, with massive thunderstorms that churned outside. The area around it is nothing but craggy rocks stripped by the ferocious storms, called the Blasted Plains. Bast, the Lightbringer, is the Sun God. The Dunes of Bast that surround his tower are nothing but a heat battery. When the heat builds on the dunes. It spills onto the Blasted Plains. All the extra energy feeds the Arc Storms, and they spill out across the south. It is going to be a rough day.

"Normally, when we see an Arc storm coming this way, we close everything down and bring in the animals. Shouldn't we do that first?" Khet worried.

"Tarin and the others can handle that. You need to worry about being prepared." Kase gestured away from the house. "Follow me."

Kase led Khet into the middle of a field next to the farmstead. There were 3 large stones lying close to each other on top of a large hill. Each stone was roughly waist-high and had somewhat of a flat top. The craggy stones looked ancient, surrounded by the abundance of the fresh green grass.

"You need to go pick up those logs over there and bring them here." Kase pointed to a stack of 5 large logs in the distance. "Hurry."

Khet set off at a run, his tight muscles resisting the movement. He made it quickly to the logs and noticed that their size wasn't as big of a concern as he first thought. *This will be manageable*, Khet thought. He reached down to wrap his arms around the first log and discovered these weren't ordinary logs. The logs were iron wood, much denser and heavier than oak. Iron trees were a rare tree in the south. Think veins of iron ore impregnated the trees. Khet breathed deeply and prepared himself. He shouldered the first log, the days in the forge really paid off. With effort, he made his way back to the stones. Khet dropped the first log with a thud. Winded from the strain, he made his way back to the other logs.

The second log was not any easier. Khet placed it on his shoulder. There was a low rumble in the distance. He looked to the west towards the dark clouds. "Still a ways off, but I should hurry." Khet tried to reassure himself. He made it back to the stones and dropped the second log. The whole time, Kase watched the Arc Storm, with her back to Khet.

Khet breathed hard as he made his way over to pick up the third log. For a moment, he glanced at the last two logs that were half sunk in the mud with dread. Khet pushed those thoughts from his mind. He had to focus on the current problem at hand. This log was more difficult to shoulder. Each step back to the stones was more difficult than the last.

Khet dropped the third log with a thud. The sound of the impact drew Kase's attention. "Khet, come here. I want to ask you something."

Khet, grateful for an excuse to take a break, walked over next to

Kase.

"Do you know anything about the Arc Storms?" Kase asked.

"Besides that they are dangerous, not much else." Khet said between heavy breaths, too tired to really want to explain everything he knew.

"Well, to the east there are two God Towers, Arcanus and Bast. The heat from the dunes of Bast sometimes feeds the Arc storms on the Blasted Plains. Once the storms grow strong enough, they break free from their borders and come east. You understand that, correct?" Kase stood there with her hands on her hips as she questioned her pupil.

Khet, half distracted by the storm, nodded his head.

"Have you heard that the University of Valkai has been working on ways to keep them from happening? From slipping loose from their borders?" Kase asked.

Valkai the Knowing, God of Knowledge and Curiosity. Khet remembered travelers speaking about the University that surrounds Valkai's Tower. A vast city made of nothing but different schools of thought. Schools for every God Blessed to learn how to use and improve their abilities. Also, abstract studies into the how and the why of things. A vast library is there, holding all the collected knowledge of the Sýna. It was customary for a Scholar of Valkai to transcribe everything they had learned into books before they died. Then the next Scholars could learn from their experiences. Khet wanted to visit there someday on his pilgrimage.

There was a rumble of thunder in the distance. Khet snapped out of his deep thought. "No, I didn't think it was possible."

"The Scholars of Valkai believe so. In fact, they sent a Storm Wielder and a.... What was the name of the people touched by Ferun? Frost something or others?" Kase asked.

"You're thinking of Frost Slingers, but I think they actually like to be referred to as Cold Adepts." Khet was happy he knew something she didn't.

"Yes, because they don't throw frost or ice, just make things cold." Kase continued to explain. "Well, a Storm Wielder and a Cold Adept are in the City of El right now. Hired by the University to test their idea."

Khet loved to think and speculate on God powers; this was the first time in a long time that he could learn more about them. He leaned forward, all attention focused on what Kase was saying.

"The idea is if the Cold Adept could cool down the storm, it would weaken it. The Storm Wielder would create wind to push the cold into the storm, taking the heat out of it. Once the Arc Storm weakens enough, the magic of Arcanus Tower should pull the storm under control. That is the idea anyway. I heard about it when I was at the market in El a couple of weeks back."

Burning with more curiosity than Khet could handle, a question filled his mind. "Do the Scholars of Valkai know what is outside the wall? What happened to the two nameless Gods?" More questions bubbled up, but Khet stopped himself.

"I don't know." Kase said, "I attended the University when I was young. I studied at the School of Gruenive the Healer to learn to use my healing skills more effectively. After a year of that, I wanted to chase adventure in the mercenary guild. I didn't think I would make a good member of the Hand. So I became a mercenary. Maybe you should go there to learn more before you start your Pilgrimage. There are schools for all the God-Blessed and others that just deal in the theoretical. I know there were people trying to answer your questions when I was there. That was years ago; maybe they have figured something out by now. Or you could join in on digging up all the strange and weird artifacts."

Khet was conflicted; he wanted to go and visit the God Towers, but the chance to learn more about the questions that burned inside his head. To get them answered, then carry out the Pilgrimage tempted him greatly. He knew of the University, but he had no idea that there was so much there. He was very curious; "I don't know what I want to do right now. I did, but now I don't," Khet said frustratedly.

A gentle breeze formed at their backs. Kase was the first to notice it. "I think we are about to witness something. Did you feel the wind shift?" There was excitement in Kase's eyes as she spoke.

Khet noticed it now as well. A sensation of awe shot through his body. The City of El was maybe a five-day walk from the farmstead. For the Storm Wielder to move that much air, Khet realized, they had to be extremely powerful. The wind never lessened, just steadily grew stronger. When the wall of cold air hit the storm, it was not a gradual shift. A massive hole formed like the Arc Storm was pierced with a giant invisible spear. Like a great beast that was wounded, the storm retreated and then slipped out of view. The wind died down and everything was calm. Khet and Kase stood there awestruck. Khet knew he had to go to the University. His mind yearned for answers to his burning questions. The Pilgrimage will have to wait.

"Let's change our training a little today. At the University, we were taught how to use our abilities. I am not an instructor, and I don't know much about Vulcan, but I might be able to help you a little." Kase paused for a second. "Tarin told me you are slow to light the forge. Why is that?"

Khet, still excited to finally have a real plan of what he wants to do, tried to slow himself down to respond to Kase. "I don't know. When I try to find Vulcan and use his power, there is a chorus of other voices, and it is difficult to find his voice. Sometimes it is easier than others."

"A 'chorus of voices' I have never heard of that. Maybe one of the Valkai scholars will know of this and can help you." Kase thought for a second as if to mull over this information. "Since I can't really help you with that problem, maybe we can just work on your speed by practicing. When you draw your rune, do you draw it on your hand, or do you draw it on what you are heating up?"

"I have never used a rune." Khet answered as a matter of fact. He had never used one and did not know that it was something that he needed to do.

Kase looked at him stunned, mouth agape. "What, that doesn't make any sense. Everyone must use their rune; that is how it works. You use the mark on your skin to access your power. You see, I have my runes tattooed on my body in different places so I can use Grunaive's healing on myself." Kase pulled her armor away from her shoulder to show one of her tattoos. "I have 7 more around my body so I can heal myself or replenish my strength."

"No, I have never needed a rune. I just find Vulcan within my mind and poof, forge fire."

"Show me this. On that log there, show me how you do this. I want to see it." Kase was now the curious one. She watched with great intrigue.

Khet felt almost insulted for not being believed as he walked over to the log she had pointed out. But still kind of special for not needing to use a rune. He pushed those thoughts to the side as he reached down and laid his hand on the log.

When Khet would call upon Vulcan, a door would appear in his mind. The door would be a part of a massive ancient temple. In his mind, he would climb the stairs to the entrance and walk through the door. This time, like every other time, there was a chorus of voices in the massive darkened temple. Black voids shifted in his mind. Each one emitted a sound that confused Khet. He made his way to the back of the temple. Through the shifting blackness, he could make out glimpses of Vulcan's radiant golden armor. Khet pushed through and grabbed hold of Vulcan's outstretched hand.

Vulcan's power poured through him as his mind was brought back to his body. The warmth radiated through his chest, into his arms, and hands. A red glow formed where his hands contacted the iron wood. The surface of the iron wood yielded. Small sparks shot off as he pushed deeper.

Kase stared, dumbfounded by what she saw. Khet was almost elbow-deep by the time she spoke. "OK. Stop."

Khet stood up and pulled his arms free, letting Vulcan's power fade. His new armor was discolored by the heat. He had never owned armor before, and now after two days, he had already damaged it.

Kase had a look of confusion on her face. "Now try it with a rune. I noticed that your rune is a little different than the other forge-blessed, maybe that is your problem. Draw it on the palm of your hand. Use some of the already-burnt log to make it."

Khet did what she asked. He placed his hands on the log in front of him. As he closed his eyes, he tried to summon Vulcan. The surge of power that erupted through him overwhelmed Khet. Jets of magma shot from his palms. His whole body glowed a hot white as everything around him started to melt. Khet had lost control.

Kase screamed as she threw herself to the ground away from the heat. She scrambled and clawed her way to cover behind the rock as the metal on her armor started to soften from the heat. "STOP!" she screamed once she found cover.

Khet couldn't hear her though; he was lost in a rage that was not his. It consumed him. Lost in the flames, lost in the rage, Khet howled. "Everything will become ash!"

The entire hilltop had become liquified. Molten slag poured down the side. Khet's guttural wails echoed off the surrounding land. Everything was burning, all was consumed by his white-hot rage. Something heavy struck Khet in the head. The blow was so great that Khet was made unconscious. The infernal rage had been brought to an end as quickly as it had begun.

9

Khet woke, his head throbbed, he lay on something hard and uncomfortable. Unsteadily, he brought himself to the seated position. He couldn't understand why his head throbbed and why he was outside. Khet surveyed the area around him. It was foreign and strange. *What happened?* he thought. Nothing made any sense to him; he was in a blackened crater. A voice in the distance drew his attention. For a second, he couldn't make out who it was, but Tarin's distant figure came into focus.

"Are you okay?" Tarin yelled.

Confused, Khet gave a thumbs up. He made a failed attempt to stand. Every motion made the pain in his head worse. His limbs were slow to obey his commands. Reality was not connecting with what surrounded him.

"Can you stand?" Tarin cupped his hands around his mouth as he called out. "Come here, and I can give you some water." He held a water skin in the air.

Khet dug deep and forced his body to move. His body rebelled, but Khet was determined. His vision swam if he moved too fast. So he took a great deal of time. Once he stood all the way up, he could see his immediate surroundings. Blobs and solidified puddles of blackened slag covered the ground around him. Small whirlwinds of ash swirled about his ankles. Confused and disoriented, he stumbled his way to where Tarin stood.

"Damn, Khet, you gave us a fright! I thought I killed you! How did you do that? What the hell was that?" Tarin handed him a water skin and backed away ever so slightly. Fear tinged the edges of his voice.

"I… what… are you talking about?" His head pounded harder than a forge hammer.

"That!" Tarin pointed to the black scar that was once a hill. "You did that!" Panic now mingled in the large man's voice.

The charred mass that was once a hill came into full focus. Confusion and fear swirled as Khet attempted to understand what Tarin spoke of, then reality hit him. His memory flared in violent crimson. The rune, how Vulcan's power raged, all the fire, the hate for it all, Kase's scream, and then pain. "Oh, shit…" he mumbled to himself. The weight of it was too much for him, and he collapsed again. Unconsciousness took him.

10

He startled himself awake. Khet lay in bed, his bed. Each movement took a massive effort. Memories of fire and pain played in his mind. Brief, intense flashes of infernal rage mixed with righteousness. A horrible need to render all in his wake into slag and ash. *I haven't had a nightmare like that in a long time*, he thought. Movement in the corner drew his attention.

Ty sat in a chair by Khet's bed. "He is awake! He is awake! He is awake!" He screamed as he ran out of the room.

"Hey, wait, Ty, I'm fine! You don't have to go yelling like that!" His voice was weak, like it hadn't been used in a long time. Khet moved to get out of bed. His body didn't agree to his movements. So he stayed where he was. He was weak and famished. *What happened?*

"There you are, about time you wake up. You had Tarin worried that he killed you." Kase moved stiffly as she entered the room.

"What happened? What are you talking about?" A slight panic crept into Khet. *That was a dream, right?*

"You don't remember?" Kase used her motherly tone, but something else was mixed with it. "You lost control yesterday, in a way I have never seen or heard of before. If Tarin wasn't such a good throw, I would have been burned to a crisp." She nonchalantly put down a small tray on the table next to him. She avoided making eye contact with him. "It has been five days, and we still can't get near where you melted the hill." Stress and fear were in her voice, Khet could feel it. "The heat is still so intense. We had to hire a Saphite to keep watering the trees and that side of the house. We fear if we don't, they would catch fire." She handed him a glass of opaque liquid.

It washed over him, all that had happened. His body broke into a cold sweat. "I am sorry. I never meant to hurt you or anybody." Khet pleaded. His voice trembled with remorse. He never wanted to hurt anyone. "It was an accident. Did I hurt anyone?" His question was more a prayer to the Twelve.

"Everyone is fine, bit of a scare though if I am honest. Enough of that now. We can talk about it more later. You drank all of that glass, it is kind of a nutrient-rich nectar. You haven't eaten in five days. We could barely get you to drink water. This will help get your strength. Sit back in bed and drink it all. I will go and get you some real food and water. I will tell Tarin that you are awake if the sound of Ty's wailing hasn't made everyone aware. He hasn't slept much since then." Kase slowly guided him to sit in his bed.

The taste of the nectar was sweet. With each sip, he felt a little more like himself. Relieved that Kase was okay, he sat and just looked out his window. *Why did the rune change my ability that much? Why was Vulcan so easy to connect to, and how can I control his ability so that nobody else gets hurt?* Thoughts just swirled in his head until he heard footsteps at his door.

Tarin stood there, he took up the entire doorway. His eyes teared. The smile on his face was the largest Khet had ever seen. "I thought I killed you. When you didn't wake yesterday, I thought you were too far gone by the time Kase could get to you." He sniffled and wiped away the tears that had fallen. "I am happy you are okay. Try to forgive me. I didn't mean to... I just reacted."

"Please, Tarin, forgive me. I am the one who lost control. Forgive me, please. You did no wrong." Khet fought back tears of his own. In the almost ten years he had lived with Tarin, he had never seen the man cry. It was hard for him to handle now.

"Well, you forgive me, and I will forgive you. How is that?" His voice regained some of its strength. Tarin always took responsibility for his own actions, and sometimes that meant he would share in the blame.

"Deal." Khet rubbed a sniffle in his nose. He knew it would be impossible for Tarin to forgive himself at all if Khet dismissed the split of the blame. He felt like it was all his fault though, Tarin just reacted the way anyone would have.

Tarin bowed out of the doorway, walking off into the house. *Hopefully, he was gone to rest*, Khet thought.

Khet sat in his thoughts when Kase came into the room. The tray she carried was full of food. Ty followed with a big pitcher of water. His eyes refused to meet Khet's.

"Eat and drink your fill, Khet," Kase instructed. " I have new clothes for you at the end of your bed. You burned off all your armor and clothes when you lost control. So, I got you some more."

Khet blushed as he remembered that he was naked when he walked over to Tarin the other day. "Did everyone on the farm see me?" Khet admonished himself at the thought of being nude; embarrassed by what he had just done.

"More than everyone on the farm, sorry to say. Tarin tried to go find a Cold Adept, but all he could find was Saphite. Not a very powerful one. All the water she pushed towards you would just evaporate." Kase said.

"She? Don't tell me it was Evira." Khet had a doomed look. Evira was such a beautiful thing that no matter what they wore, heads would turn. He had always wanted to catch her eye, but it never seemed to happen.

"Yes, Tarin was panicked. He even ran halfway to El to get another Forge Blessed. He could get closer than the rest of us, but he couldn't make it to you. The heat was too intense." Kase went on. "You did something that nobody has ever seen or heard of in memory. People noticed from all around. Everyone is more than a little frightened."

"I didn't mean to. It was an accident. It won't happen again, I promise." Again, he pleaded. Tears pooled in his eyes.

"I am sorry, Khet, but there has been a messenger sent to the Temple of the Twelve. They have people that investigate this kind of stuff. I am sure everything will be alright. They will probably just want to ask you some questions."

"How long will that take?" Fear settled into his spine. *Could they see me as a fiend sent by the Outer Gods?*

"I don't think it will take longer than a week or two. There is Temple garrisoned just north of El. I am sure everything will be fine." Her voice didn't sound like everything would be fine. "Now eat up and if you're up to it, come outside. I am sure everyone would like to see that you are okay." Kase's left the room before Khet could respond. Her mask of calm slipped, and Khet could see fear underneath.

There was something else in her tone that unsettled Khet. Could he have been mistaken? *Was that a weapon in her shirt?* Khet thought, *It couldn't have been a weapon. I am no threat to them. It was an accident, that is what happened.* His thoughts swirled until the smell of the food in front of him pulled him out of the spiral. Khet shoveled food by the handfuls to his face. Each bite tasted better than the last. He made quick work of the entire tray. Afterward, he downed the last bit of nectar and half the pitcher of water. He laid back for a moment. While his stomach settled, he gazed out the window.

Khet didn't want to face everyone right now, but he had to at some point. With his body mostly recovered but his mind still a maelstrom of thoughts and emotions. He slid out of bed. His new clothes fit him fine. After multiple attempts to prepare himself for the scrutiny he would be under. He steadied himself and set out the door.

11

The light of the day was bright in Khet's eyes. He used his hand to shade them while he looked for Kase. Out near the barn, she was talking to the other contracted. At the sight of Khet, they all stopped and turned towards him.

Kase turned back to them and continued to speak; the contracted moved away quickly. She made her way towards Khet. Kase now carried a blade on her hip. Never had Khet seen her openly wear a blade in her motherly costume. But there it was in broad daylight, a sign of how much things had changed.

"Khet, we need to talk." Kase's posture was tense, her voice tight.

Khet stood there, not ready to hear what he thought she would say. "What about?" He wanted to appear harmless, but how could he do that now?

"About that." Her hand pointed off to the distance.

Khet knew what she pointed to before he turned to look. The once large hill next to the farm was now a blackened crater. Everything around it was now charred ash. Heat poured off it. The intensity of it distorted the air. Flashes of fire exploded in his mind. Vulcan's rage boiled under his skin. A need to burn it all, burned in his gut. His breath became heavy.

"Khet?" Concern was in her voice. "Are you okay?"

Her hand was moved to her knife on her belt. "I am fine, just a headache." It was plain that she didn't believe him.

"Okay, you looked unwell for a moment there. Here, have a drink." Her hand came off the hilt of the knife, but it did not stray far from it. She handed Khet a water skin.

Khet accepted the water skin awkwardly; he tried not to look like a threat. "Thank you." Even with the gentle movements, he could see it in her eyes and hear it in the edges of her voice. She was afraid of him. He looked out at the others in the farmstead. They all looked at him with fear. Ty even hid behind a barrel and stared at Khet. "I am not a threat."

"After what happened, you can't say that." Kase stated flatly. "You are now."

Khet's frustration exploded. "I AM NOT A THREAT!" Kase's fist slammed into Khet's jaw and sent him flying. Before he could recover, she was on top of him. She violently shook him by his shirt.

"YOU ARE A THREAT!" She shouted into his face. "YOU WIELDED THE FULL POWER OF A GOD!" Fear and rage echoed in her scream. Before Khet could react, a blade was in her hand. She pressed it into Khet's shoulder. He let out a scream of pain, it was cut short by another blow to his head from Kase. "I TRIED TO RUN! TRIED TO HIDE FROM THE HEAT!" Kase howled inches from his face. She twisted the knife, slowly. "MY ARMOR MELTED TO MY SKIN! TARIN ALMOST DIED TRYING TO GET TO ME!" Khet bucked and spasmed underneath her. He wanted it to stop."YOU ALMOST KILLED MY FAMILY! I CAN'T LET YOU LIVE! YOU ARE DANGEROUS! YOU NEED TO DIE!" She spat.

Khet struggled to free himself. Kase wrenched the blade free from his shoulder. "YOU'RE A FIEND SENT BY THE OUTER GODS. YOU MUST DIE!" Kase shrieked. Fear gripped Khet, he couldn't move. A large hand grabbed ahold of her and lifted Kase off Khet.

It was over before anyone could stop it. Blind fear and rage fueled her. Kase held the hilt of the blade that now pierced through the neck of her husband. Blood poured from Tarin's neck. A look of panic and confusion filled his eyes as he fell. The light left him before his head touched the ground.

"NO!" Kase screamed and fell to her knees. She grabbed ahold of her husband's neck. "NO! NO! NO!" Her eyes glowed green as she called upon all of her healing power. "I am sorry! I am sorry!" She repeated again and again. She tried to pull back together the flesh of his neck. "You can't die! You can't die! Please!" She cried.

When her power had no effect. She howled with searing pain. The sound in her voice changed as her mind broke. A guttural shriek marked the point when madness took over. She ran away from the farm. Away from her family that now lay dead.

Khet lay there in shock on the ground. He had to move, he had to get out of there. Fear and panic took over as he looked into the Tarin's dead eyes. He started to run in no particular direction, just away. Confusion, fear, and guilt were his only guides. He just ran until he couldn't run anymore. Then he walked, he did not care the direction as long as it was away. When he couldn't walk anymore, he crawled. Khet just wanted to get away. Either from blood loss or from exhaustion, he collapsed.

12

Khet felt movement; he shot up, pain seared in his shoulder. He couldn't move his arms. His wrists were bound. He looked around, panicked; he was in a cage. Two other people were in there with him, bound just like Khet.

"Hey boys, our little Forge Blessed is awake!" A bald man said as he was walked next to the cart. "OK, pay up!" Groans came from all directions.

Men and women half-dressed in armor, the other half in dirty home-spun, surrounded the cart. Some rode fine horses while others shambled along on foot. He was in a cage, on a wagon as it moved down a small forest path. The woods pressed in on either side. Most of the group pulled a small bag from some hidden place on their person and threw it at the man laughing next to the cart. Khet could hear the coins jingle as the bald man caught them.

With a big grin on his face, "You made me a good amount of money by waking up. All the others thought you were dead the way we found you. Now you are going to make me even more when I sell you for a contract. A man your size and Forge Blessed, I will be rich indeed." The man gloated. "Name's Alen, what's yours?"

Khet stared, confusion and fear still controlled him. He jerked his head around. He hoped to find a way to escape. There was none; he couldn't move.

"Well, that's fine. No matter anyway. In a couple of days' time, you will just be coins in my pocket. Coins that will be turned into ale and whores." Alen laughed. A few chuckles could be heard from the others.

Khet sat there. It had to be a dream. He would wake up in his bed at his home. The horrors that transpired over the last several days swarmed in his mind. His home was no more. Tears spilled down his face.

"Now don't you cry, my precious. We have a healer at the camp that will get you all fixed up." Alen said with mock concern. "You will be our guest of honor at our humble camp. We will have you all clean and spiffy for when we bring you to market." His rotten grin pressed between the bars of the cage.

Khet needed to do something. He had to escape. Weak and desperate, he racked his brain to form a plan.

"Hey, there, my little precious." Alen pressed his face to the cage. Khet could smell the rot of his teeth. "Before you go and get the idea in your head that you can escape, I want you to look at that ugly fellow next to you with the flatbow." Khet turned his head, and yes, there was a man with a flatbow pointed directly at him. A smile was on the bowman's face. "Well, that ugly fucker's name is Barnt. And Barnt is an Arbiter, blessed by the God cunt herself, Sidierion. Have you had much experience with Arbiters, my precious?" Khet sat there with contempt on his face. While fear and rage swirled in his gut. "I will take that as a no, not surprising being a southerner. You see, Barnt can see into your intentions. So, if you think a little too hard about escaping or calling on your friend Vulcan. You will get a bolt through that pretty face of yours. And if you don't care about your life, think of the two in there with you; they would die as well, and you don't want that on your head when you traverse to the afterlife. So, sit back and enjoy the ride. It is beautiful out."

"Alen, would you shut up? I am tired of hearing you yap." A man on a horse said as he rode up beside them.

"Sorry, Gillian, are you the one in charge here?" Alen's temper bloomed out of him.

"Uh, no… I just thought." Gillian stammered. "Someone could hear us, and we could be ambushed."

"Good thought. Oy Barn-!" Before Alen could finish Barnt's name, a flatbow bolt buried itself into Gillian's head, to the cheers of those around.

"Remember that precious, I am in charge here. You breathe because I allow it." Alen said with a wink. His face was hard set. His grin was full of malice.

Khet wished there was an ambush so he might escape. He snapped his head toward Barnt. Barnt just sat there on his horse with a knowing smile, the flatbow reloaded and aimed at Khet. He desperately tried to think of other things. He didn't want to give Barnt a reason to kill him. His thoughts haunted him though. Everything that happened in the last few days. He was freed, learned more about his adoptive family, almost killed his family, Kase almost killed him, and Tarin dying. He sat in deep sadness wishing Kase would have just killed him.

What felt like hours later, could have been days. Khet would fall in and out of consciousness so time meant nothing. A group of men on horses rode up to join the group. They talked with Alen for a while, Khet couldn't make out what was said. The newcomers handed Alen a small bag and looked at Khet. Worry came over Khet, *why are they looking at me?* He thought.

Alen swaggered back to Khet and fished two vials out of the bag. "Here is some nectar to heal you right up." Alen stuck his hand through the bars, both vials in hand. "Now our healer says you need to drink both. So, drink them and I don't want you fucking about, alright."

Khet didn't say a word, just nodded in agreement. He was thirsty and he knew how nectar would refresh him. So, he did as he was ordered and drank the vials as Alen poured them into his mouth. The taste was odd, not like the nectar that Kase had given him. A pang of guilt came over him when he thought of her.

"Sorry there precious, you are going to need to be asleep for this next bit." Alen smiled his putrid smile. "One of those vials was a knockout drug. So nighty night." Even his laugh was wicked. It was full of a venomous mirth, that made Khet feel cold.

Khet could feel the drug pull him down into unconsciousness. All the things around him slowed, his vision blurred, and finally blackness. The last thought that crossed his mind was hope of never waking again.

13

Discomfort is all he could feel. Khet was groggy, the drug still heavily affecting him. His hands were still bound, but they were out to his sides now. A great pressure was on his waist and shoulders. Khet tried to move his legs. They were sluggish and numb. Through the haze of the drug, he understood he was in a standing position. So, he pressed his feet down and the pressure in his shoulders and waist was eased mostly.

"Hey, everyone one, it looks like my little precious Forge Blessed is waking up." Alen's voice still sounded like a knife's smile even through a drugged haze. "Gret, I told you, that you drugged my boy too much. If you fucked him up where I can't sell him, I will sell your ass to a pleasure house."

Hands were on his face, the sensation was distant. "Ay, wake up there precious, let me see those beautiful blue eyes." Khet tried but his eyelids were heavy. "I told you Gret, you fucked him up! Wake up! Rathen, could you use a little of that cold bullshit of yours to rouse him."

Cold stabbed into him. Gasping for air, Khet's eyes went wide. Things were blurry, but shapes and colors took form.

"There we go! Thank you kindly Rathen." Alen grinned from ear to ear. "So, my boy, we must talk a little. You know, before your big day tomorrow." Khet remained silent but looked at Alen. "So, my precious, do you have a name? Or do you want me to just make one up for you?

49

You will sell for a lot either way."

Khet pushed against his restraints to no avail. His body was still affected by the drug, and he was bound tightly. He was defeated. "Khet."

"Khet, what? Do you have a family name? Are you vo?" Alen's smirk made Khet hate him even more.

"Just Khet. No family name." Contracts weren't allowed family names. Even after the contract is completed.

Alen lifted Khet's chin. "I see, you, my friend, are one unlucky man." Chuckles came from Khet's blurred periphery. "Alright, Khet, what is with your rune? It looks like the rune of Vulcan but only slightly different. Generally, you, forged fuckers, have a mark with two legs on it; yours has three. Also, where did you get that wound? You were half dead when we found you."

Flashes of Kase beating him and Tarin's throat ripped out hit Khet. "My mark has always been like this. I was told by my father that it was a cursed mark. I was still Forged Blessed, so he sold me when I was young to be rid of me."

"How about your mother? Didn't she not want to keep you?" Alen's voice was full of so much fake sincerity. He giggled through the question.

"I don't know." The weight of it was heavy on Khet. "Never met her, and my father never spoke of her."

"What about the wound? A wound like that isn't normal for a person to have. Did you kill somebody? Are you hunted?" Alen brought his face close to Khet. "I am trying to be reasonable here. If you are hunted, you need to tell me." His breath smelled of spoiled ale.

Khet's mind raced to make up an answer. "I was attacked by a galin, managed to burn it, and run away."

"Well, you're lucky to be alive, not lucky in general." Alen seemed to believe Khet. "Now I can sell you to a much better class of folk. If you were hunted, I would be forced to sell you to the much less savory types."

Khet's vision cleared. Several tents were near him. Cages that held other people were on top of a small rise; nobody was tied up like he was. In the distance, he could make out the wall to the camp. "You're slavers." His words dripped with malice.

"We prefer, labor organizers. We facilitate a workforce for people who have the money to use our service. It is how the world works, my boy." Khet glared at him with disgust. "It's fine if you hate us;

tomorrow we will take you and the rest to Tarsis. The biggest flesh market this side of the Spine. The gold I will make from you alone will line my pockets for months. You Forge Blessed are few and far between nowadays. Maybe one of the Temple higher-ups needs a new blacksmith or a fuck toy; you are pretty enough. That would make me a sweet fortune."

"The Temple? The Temple doesn't buy slaves."

"Oh yes, they do, and they pay a lot. This whole system of contracted slavery is a part of their religion. If Sidierion wasn't a thing, the whole slave trade would be much harder."

Khet's disdain went icy numb. *How could the Temple of the Twelve allow this to happen?* He was almost out of it; he was free, just to be brought back to it. He never even had a chance to miss the collar.

"Oh, it's fine there, my sweetness. Everyone holds us folk in contempt for the same thing they laud the Temple for. We are used to it." He smiled like he was empathetic to Khet's plight. "Now I have other things I have to get done 'fore our little trip tomorrow." Alen called back as he walked away. "You remember our ugly friend with the flatbow, Barnt? He is right behind you; so behave yourself." Barnt chuckled behind him. Khet was stuck, and his hope was depleted.

The hours dragged on; Khet grew exhausted. His muscles cramped and spasmed from being bound in one position for so long. He tried to listen to conversations throughout the camp, to maybe get an idea on how to escape. Nothing ever came of it. Either he was delirious, or the slavers were speaking in code; he didn't understand anything he heard.

"Hey, you don't look too good there, Khet." Alen approached. "Have you been given any water? Hey, Barnt, have you given my payday any water?" There was a guilty pause from Barnt. "You ass! I need him healthy for tomorrow. Don't you worry, Khet, I will get you something." Alen walked off shouting for water and the healer.

Khet was hot. His vision swam. Gret, the healer, came to him with a vial. "Drink this, and you will be right as rain." The nectar had a strange taste to it. "What is this bruising on your neck, boy?" Gret's voice sounded like somebody gargling sand. "Looks like somebody branded you with the letter V. Maybe you got some parasite from the wound? Well, if that nectar I just gave you doesn't cure you, I don't know what will."

Khet felt better, but something was wrong with that nectar. He heard a figure approach; they hummed a strange tune. The voice was soft and feminine. Nothing that should be in this camp. It was faint now in his ear, and it didn't come from any particular direction.

"Here is some water." Thoughts of the humming evaporated from Khet's mind. He recognized her. The woman that offered him water. It was the red-haired Light Bringer that he had met weeks ago. The one that he was going to find after he was free. But she wasn't the same bright-eyed and full of dreams girl he had met at the homestead. Darker things had happened to her, and now her light was diminished.

"I know you." Hope grew in his chest. "You came through my farmstead weeks ago."

"No, you're mistaken." She was beaten down. The light gone.

"Khet, my boy, do you know our little Kariit here?" Alen appeared from behind Khet. "We found her sweetness about three weeks back. Something this nice we had to keep to ourselves for a while. We won't use her all up though. When we get our fill, we will sell her to a pleasure house." A smirk formed on Alen's face. "You had a thing for her, didn't you? Don't lie, I can see it in your eyes."

Khet pulled at his restraints, he snarled with murderous intent. "I will kill you!" Barnt struck him in the back of the head. Khet's world flashed white.

"Listen here, you little forge bitch, I own you. The only reason I don't just put a collar on you is the fact that I am selling you tomorrow. I have been nice. I have been kind even. I could break all the bones in your arms and legs and leave you in agony all night. To just have Gret heal you before the market." Alen viciously grabs a handful of Kariit's hair. "This is mine! You are mine! I can do what I want with what is mine!" His words were acrid and full of rage.

The humming returned, a sweet melody.

Alen, full of rage, threw Kariit to the ground and began to rip off her clothes. "I will show what I can do! After I am done with her, I will let everyone in the camp have her, and you can watch!" There in front of Khet, Alen made true his promise.

Khet strained against his bonds. All attempts to call upon Vulcan failed. Something blocked him. The melody in his ears grew louder.

"

"I have to stop it!" His mind screamed.

Another person was getting hurt because of his weakness. Khet raged at his bindings. More beast than man now. The melody deafened him. His rage and the melody came together and spun a thread. The golden thread of rage uncoiled from Khet. It slithered its way to everyone one throughout the camp. Nobody was aware of the thread, but it pierced all of them through the neck. No slave or slaver was spared. The end of the thread came up through Kariit's neck and ended with Alen.

Power swelled within Khet. It felt good, he drank it in. He could feel the thread woven through everyone. Khet relished the power, he would not be weak anymore. The moment hung in the air. Time seemed to slow. The need filled him. Khet felt the gentlest touch on his shoulder. She whispered into his ear "Do it." Power surged through Khet and into the golden thread.

There were no cries of pain, no calls for help. Just bright flashes and the sounds of corpses hitting the ground. Khet came out of his rage breathing ragged and weak. The scene in front of him was pure horror. The bodies of Kariit and Alen lay in front of him with a fist-sized hole burnt through their necks. It hit him, he did this, again he did this. He frantically looked to see where the voice had come from, where did the humming come from. He was alone in a camp full of corpses. He screamed until he passed out.

14

Time had little meaning, tied as he was. Khet woke to the same gory scene that he passed out to again and again and again. By now, though, the bodies had voided their bowels and had begun to bloat.

Racked with pain from the bindings and guilt from what he had done, Khet would scream in between fits of dry heaving. He was delirious from thirst and hunger. It had been days since he last ate or drank anything.

He struggled to break free. Flies swarmed everywhere. They tried crawling in his eyes and mouth. He tried to call on Vulcan to burn his bindings, but he was too weak to focus. He would beg for a quick death even though he knew he didn't deserve it. The crunch of leaves brought Khet out of his delirium. The sound of steps moved closer.

At the mouth of the camp appeared a large creature that Khet had never seen before. Its head was a grey mass of fur and teeth. Long grey-brown hairs covered its head. The creature was lean with short brown fur on its body. Blood soaked the fur around the creature's mouth, probably from eating the sentries' bodies. It sniffed the air. Khet froze; maybe if he held still, the beast wouldn't notice him and leave. Mind and body betrayed him. Thoughts of " *When was the last time you cleared your thoughts?* And *You need to cough now.* Punished Khet. There was no fighting it; he was too weak to resist. He forcefully coughed. The dryness of his lungs racked him with pain. Laughter erupted from Khet. He couldn't stop.   An acceptance that he was screwed and the relief of a quick death bubbled through his laughter. At least he would now pay for all that he had done.

A whistling sound came through the trees. Three arrows struck the beast in the side. The beast whelped and tried to turn to run. Before it could turn and retreat, another two arrows buried themselves into the beast. It slumped to the ground and ceased breathing with a groan.

Khet laughed hysterically as men came through the gate. He was delirious and didn't know if they were real or not. So he just kept laughing. Robbed of his quick death, all he could do was laugh. One hunter came down the hill from the gate, noticed all the gore that was at Khet's feet, and covered his face in disgust.

"Friend, calm yourself, we mean you no harm. Here, let me help you. Let me cut you free." The hunter severed Khet's bonds. As each one was cut, Khet just slumped further and further, not strong enough to hold his own weight. When the final bond was cut, he collapsed and fell into the two corpses that lay at his feet. Khet flailed weakly to get himself away from Kariit's dead, bloated face.

Hands firmly grabbed him and pulled him away. "Ease, my friend, we are of the Hand, we mean you no harm." Khet still struggled, but it was pointless. These people had him, and he was a prisoner again.

"Raine, he needs aid, come quickly." The hunter waved for another to come help.

"Poor thing, he must have been tied up there for days. Abner, go get my bag and bring me clean water. Hurry!" Raine examined Khet quite thoroughly, which was easy since he only wore a loincloth. Her hand felt both cool and warm as she ran it over Khet. Raine was using her ability to heal him or to examine him; Khet did not know. He didn't know what to think at this point.

Abner came back with Raine's bag and three water skins. "Is this enough? I have to go help Grim and Trip to cover the area. Waraik never travel alone. Call if you need anything."

"That should do it. When you are done, could you find him some clothes? There must be something for him in these tents." Raine never looked at Abner. She focused all her attention on Khet. She dug through her pack. "You're going to be okay, friend."

She took a variety of crushed, dried plants, placed them in a vial with water, and shook it up. Raine inspected the vial for a moment to see if it was to her satisfaction. She placed a small bit of cloth over the opening. "Drink this, I need you to drink all of this. It will ease your pain. Then I will need you to drink at least one of those skins of water.

Do you understand me?"

"Do you have nectar? Just give me nectar." Khet was weak and just wanted relief.

"Yes, I have nectar, but you can't have any. Your body is showing signs of a sweet tooth." Raine dug again through her bag and pulled out a salve for Khet's wounds.

"Sweet tooth, what is that?" His entire life on the farmstead, he had never heard of this term.

"Sweet tooth is what we call nectar addiction. Slavers like to get people hooked on it to keep them compliant, fucking bastards." Raine had a distant look in her grey eyes. "You are going to have to heal the long way. Lucky for you, we will help." After the salve was applied, Raine went to a nearby tent and grabbed a blanket. "Not the best, but it doesn't have fleas or lice. Let me cover you, and I will find out what Abner wants to do with you. You can't stay here."

She left, and again Khet was alone. He drank down one water skin and was slowly sipping on the second. Every movement brought agony. Muscles would spasm, and his body would shake violently. *Must be the nectar withdrawals.* The water made his body somewhat better, but not by far. He finished the second waterskin. He tried to stand up to maybe get his bearings. When he sat fully up, his world began to spin. He couldn't maintain any balance. He just laid back down, too weak to do anything.

Khet played through the events of the last couple of days. *What was that humming and who was that woman that whispered into his ear? Raine said I was addicted to nectar. Could it have just been a side effect? That doesn't explain the golden thread.* The moment played in his mind. He saw the thread weaving through everyone's neck. He realized with horror that he had a choice at that point. He controlled the thread, where it went, and who it affected. He made the choice to go through all their necks. He wanted them all to die. Guilty or innocent, he did not care; they all had to perish. A dark need stirred within him. Just for a moment, he was glad for what he did. The echo of Vulcan's rage stirred within. The feeling left him. Alone with the guilt, Khet started to sob uncontrollably. Guilt and an unbearable sadness burned in his chest.

"Friend, calm yourself; you are safe now. We will take you with us and see you to a safe place. Calm, my friend." Abner was there by his side. Khet didn't know where he came from; he did not hear him approach. "My name is Abner, leader of this group. We are members of the Hand." Abner held out a small leather patch that had a Hand embroidered into it. "Do you have a name, friend?"

"Khet."

"Well, Khet, we have been looking for these slavers for months now. The Hand charged us with finding them and ending their operation. We came across the waraik tracks and followed them to here. They are usually drawn to the dead, and we happen to come across the camp as well." Abner surveyed all the bodies. "What happened here, Khet? We counted 30 slavers and 20 captured, and they all had the same wound. A fist size hole in the neck. What did that? Did you see what it was? Hear anything?"

"I don't know. I didn't see anything. I did hear a loud humming before it happened." Khet panicked. *Did they know?* "Somebody was humming a song really loud, and then small flashes of light, and they fell dead. That's all." His sobbing returned.

"Grim, come here. I need to ask you a question." There was a noticeable sense of urgency to his voice. "Have you heard of any creature that hums a song and can burn a hole through 50 people's necks at once?"

Grim put his fingers on the bridge of his nose. "Not to my knowledge. Maybe the Outer Gods have sent another fiend? Or maybe an elemental beast? We had heard a report of something burning a hill to a cinder weeks ago. Maybe something from outside the Wall? I am just guessing here."

"Elementals haven't been seen for centuries. Just fairy stories now. Use the stones and contact the University and see if anyone has heard of something like this?" Abner looked around the camp. "Hey, Raine, have you found any clothes for Khet?"

"Yes, Sir. It took a little while, but I found some. Not much of a selection though." Her voice came from somewhere distant.

Khet lay there, his heart thumping. *Am I a fiend sent by the Outer Gods?* It was too much for him to handle right now. His body began to spasm. He shook violently. He couldn't control it. His body revolted against him.

"Raine, come quick! He is having a fit!" Abner pulled away any debris to clear an area for Raine to help Khet.

Khet felt Raine press on his chest. Her voice was far away. Her voice retreated to an echo. Khet heard humming, the same melody he heard nights before. His body shook violently as the melody filled him. It washed over his limbs, soothing him. His body and mind relaxed. The shaking subsided, and his muscles went slack. A voice whispered in his ear, the same voice he heard before. It was her.

"Go with them. The Arankai will find you."

15

Khet woke to movement. Again, he was in a cage. He scrambled for a moment.

"My friend, be calm. You are safe." A blurry figure sat in the back corner of the cage. Khet's eyes were dry, his eyeballs were rough as stones. A wrung-out rag would be a good way to describe his current state of being. Nectar withdrawal was horrible. "Raine, our friend is awake. Come and attend him, please." Khet remembered the blurry figure's name, Abner. These were the people who saved him.

"You made it through, good one." Raine entered the back of the cage. "Here is some water. Please drink, but not too much or too fast. It has been a rough couple of days for you. Take it slow." Raine did a brief check-up on Khet while she spoke. "No fever, and your pulse is much stronger. I think you are past the worst of it."

"Where are we?" Khet's throat was sore like he had spent hours swallowing broken glass.

"We are about..." Raine glanced at Abner for clarification. "Two days from Drake's Pass. Is that about right, Abner?"

"If the weather and horses hold, maybe we will arrive late tomorrow." Abner straightened himself. "Sorry for the accommodations, Khet. It appears those slavers only had three usable carts, and they all had cages. A lot of supplies, though. We took what we could and burned the bodies. Even told some local folk where to find the camp. We left a lot behind. We won't have to stop and buy supplies for a while." Abner caught himself mid-story. "Sorry, my friend. I do enjoy talking to a new person. Now, where was I? Oh, yes, you are free to get out of this cage when you are able to walk. I must tell you, though, we are under orders from the Hand to bring you to the University. So, I need you to stay with us."

"I have always wanted to go to the University." Khet really didn't want this to be the circumstances that brought him to the University, though. Too weak to even attempt a fight, Khet decided to see where this goes.

Raine handed Khet a large waterskin that was very full. "This is a mixture of herbs and goat's milk. Drink it slowly; you haven't eaten in a while."

"How long...?" Khet's brain was still foggy. Thoughts and memories were sluggish.

"We left that slavers camp 7 days ago, and you were not asleep the entire time." Raine waited to see if Khet would have a reaction. "Good, you don't remember. It was a bad time for you. Getting out of nectar addiction is a nightmare." The look of relief and concern on her face was all Khet needed to see to understand he shouldn't question it anymore.

"Alright... How much longer till I am back to normal?" Khet worried if there would ever be a normal again.

"Should be a day or two, maybe a week tops. Depends on how well you keep that down and if you can eat food tonight when we camp. Just rest for now. Grim has a lot of questions for you anyway." Raine gave Khet a once-over check one more time before she left the cart.

"Grim and I have some questions for you, more Grim really. Since we will be traveling together for the better part of a month, we might as well get to know each other. Are you feeling good enough to have a chat?" Abner waved his hand out of the back of the cart to get somebody's attention.

Grim came into the cart holding a pack of clothes. "Here are some clothes for you. They should fit fine."

Khet, now made aware of his nudity, quickly grabbed the clothes and slid them on as fast as he could. He tried and failed to hide his embarrassment. "Thank you."

"No shame; during your recovery, you kept soiling yourself, so we just kept you naked instead of changing your clothes constantly." Abner overshared. "Trip might not want to be around you much. You damn near broke his jaw the other day. As I said, no shame though."

Khet felt horrible for what he did to Trip. Almost horrible enough to forget the fact that he was just told that he kept soiling himself. "I am sorry... I didn't mean to."

Abner raised his hand to quiet Khet. "Don't worry, you can tell him tonight at camp. He has already forgiven you." Abner made himself comfortable on the bench. "Now my only question is how did you end up like we found you? Why were you the only one left alive?"

Khet was not ready to answer this question. He needed to lie. His brain raced to think of something they would believe. "I was contracted on a farmstead to the south near the Wall and I was recently released." Truth. "I was walking through the forest starting my pilgrimage and I was attacked by a beast, I think it was called a galin. I managed to burn it and run away. I was wounded fighting it. I eventually collapsed. Then I woke up in a cage. I don't know how many days it was before I made it to the slaver camp." Not completely a lie.

Abner made a face. "They had you tied up like that because you are a Forge Blessed, okay I understand. You fought off the galin by burning it... that was clever. It was all by itself? Strange galins are pack hunters. Grim aren't galins only in the north?"

Khet didn't think it was going to be this easy. "Yes, I guess I was just lucky it wasn't a part of a pack."

"Mainly they stick to the north, reports have mentioned galins in the Spine. So, it could have been one. I will log it and see if anyone else has had similar encounters." Now it was Grim's turn to question. "What happened? Please explain everything after you were captured."

So Khet explained everything. Minus the fact that he was the one that killed everyone, and the truth that deep down he wanted to do it. This time he added something. "As he was raping her in front of me... I heard a scream... not a human scream...more like a falcon but sounded much deeper." Khet needed them off his trail. If they knew he did it they would have killed him or worse given him to the Dodecahedron. "And then flashes and everybody collapsed. Then I blacked out and woke up not too long before you showed up and saved me." *Please believe me.*

Grim continued questioning, "Abner said you mentioned something about a humming? Or a song?"

Khet tried not to look as panicked as he felt. "I was delirious from dehydration and nectar withdrawal. I don't remember hearing anything like a song."

Grim nodded his head in acceptance. "OK, that is understandable. If you remember anything new, just tell me, okay?"

Khet flooded with relief. "I will."

Grim was just about to leave the cart. "One more thing. Did the people who owned your contract tattoo or brand you with an odd, shaped V and an X? The X is really faded though, like an old scar. I have never seen a God Rune like yours either. It looks like Vulcan's, but the shape is off."

"Yes, it was a tattoo, and that is just an old scar from when I was younger, yeah," Khet didn't know what they talked about, but he tried to play it off the best he could. *Maybe the V is another God Rune? What about the X? Three marks, do I have three abilities? Is that even a thing that is possible?* His mind jumped over itself with questions, all the while he tried to look relaxed.

"Tattooing your contracted, simply barbaric. Well, if you remember anything else, please tell me." Grim spoke the questions while he stepped off the cart.

"Just rest, it will be a while before we camp. Say something if you need anything." Abner left Khet alone in the cart.

Khet was relieved that the questioning was over. He had never been a very good liar, but he couldn't tell them the truth. He didn't even know what was going on. His life had changed so drastically in the last couple of weeks. Everything just kept happening to him; he had no control. At least now it seemed he was safe. He had a month to figure out what the University wanted with him and if he needed to run. *Where could I run? If I am a fiend sent by the Outer Gods, would I even know it? Would the Temple of the Twelve send their immortals after me?*

Khet had to stop his mind from spiraling. He was exhausted, too weak to do anything about it. So, he shoved his thoughts aside and just tried to focus on the here and now. Khet drank his goat milk mixture and tried to look at the mountains of the Dragon's Spine.

Khet relaxed as much as he could. The smell of the cool breeze that came down from the mountains calmed him a little. He remembered stories he had heard about the Dragon's Spine. Inside those mountains is the Tower of Vulcan. Khet had never seen it in person. He was told from the top of the Tower that raw molten ore spills forth and cascades down the sides. A ceaseless torrent of fiery molten iron. The cascade pools into a molten lake. The Tower sits on an island in the middle of the molten lake. At the base of the Tower of Vulcan lies a grand anvil where a great hammer, named Ending, rested upon it. It was not a hammer made for forging but for destroying. The Ending is a God killer made by Vulcan for his battle against the Outer Gods. The Twelve were attacked before Vulcan could wield it. Now he is out there beyond the Wall fighting with his molten fists. Legend says that only the strongest Forge Blessed can cross the lake to retrieve the hammer. Nobody, to Khet's knowledge, has made it even halfway across the molten lake.

Khet did love the god stories, and he wished he could have those adventures he wanted when he was younger. Things have changed and now he is on a different path.

16

By the time they made camp, Khet was more himself. His body still ached, but it was tolerable. They had found a large shaded spot to get out of the sun. It was nice to be out of the direct sun for a little while. It reminded him of the times he and Ty would play games in the river and dry off near the large tree next to the smithy. They would look at the Wall and wonder what was on the other side.

Things had been so intense that Khet didn't have really any time to think about it. *What happened to Ty and the others?* Tears started to run down his cheek. There was nothing he could do now to help him or the others. Khet quietly sobbed to himself. He was only ever close to Ty, but what happens to contracts if there was no one left to hold them? Khet did not know.

"Are you okay, my friend?" Abner came up beside him. "Are you in pain?"

"No." Khet rubbed the snot that threatened to drip from his nose. "A lot has happened, and I don't know how to handle it."

Abner sighed as he made himself comfortable against the cart. "Sometimes the only way is through. You just have to push through and take the hits as they come."

"What about the friends you leave behind? The ones who die?" Khet just wanted a path out of this.

Abner's eyes went out of focus like he was viewing something that only he could see. "Sometimes you just have to keep going. Honor them by keeping moving forward. Use the memory of their beautiful, sweet time in your life to keep going. Use it as fuel. Would your friend or loved one want you sitting here sad? I think they would want you to move on."

He thought about Abner's words. The important people in his life would never want him to suffer like this."Okay, I'll try." Khet stiffened his spine. He had to keep going. He had to see this through. Whatever this is.

"Good, now can you walk to the cooking fire, or do you need my help?"

"Let me try." Khet stepped down slowly, testing the weight on his legs. Everything ached, but he felt like he could do it. He stood there for a moment as strength returned to his body. The ache faded till he hardly noticed it.

"That's my boy! Hey, Raine, look at Khet here. Your milk stuff must have worked wonders!" Abner shouted proudly, as if Khet standing was his own child taking his first steps.

Raine sat by the fire, a question written on her face. "You were steps from death two days ago. Grim, have you heard of anything like this? Somebody recovering from a sweet tooth so quickly."

Grim closed his book and thought for a second. His eyes had a blue sheen. Grim was a Scholar of Valkai. Touched by Valkai the Knowing. "There are reports of people recovering quickly from nectar addiction. Maybe Khet's simple southern lifestyle or the fact that he is Forge Blessed has something to do with it?"

"Oh, you might want to find yourself a cowl or something. It looks like you have gotten too much sun. The scar on your neck has gotten a lot darker. And since you seem well enough to walk, and we are pretty close to the Drake's Pass, I will kit you up properly. That can be a dangerous area, don't want to leave you helpless." Abner left to go find equipment for Khet.

Khet made it to the fire, quite well and famished. "What's for dinner?"

Raine studied Khet. "Trip got us a fox and a hare today. We have some potatoes and carrots from the slaver camp still. Are you hungry?"

Khet's mouth watered. "Yes, very much so. And where is Trip? I want to apologize for striking him."

"Right here." Trip was sat against a tree away from the fire. A black eye and bruised cheek stood out on his pale face.

"I am sorry for hitting you. I was not of my right mind." Khet bowed his head to try to show how sorry he was.

"Your punch was impressive. Did you train to fight?" Trip spoke; his accent was foreign to Khet.

"No, I spent 10 years working in a forge. I mended a lot of steel and iron." Khet explained with pride.

"Like Vulcan himself, nice." Trip's voice had a tinge of sarcasm.

"Well, Vulcan, I don't have a hammer for you to wield, but I found this sword. You know how to make a sword. Can you swing a sword?" Abner came to the fire, arms full of gear for Khet.

"No, I never learned how." Thoughts of Kase's training and then her attacking him filled his mind. Emotions began to well up again; he forced them down. He had to keep it a secret.

"Well, if you are feeling up to it tomorrow, I can start teaching you." Abner had a grin on his face. "Finally, something more to do than just walk all day."

The weight of the sword in Khet's hand felt good to him. He made a couple of practice swings. The only time he got to swing a sword was playing in the back of the Tarin's smithy, and his opponent was a tree.

Abner almost hit by Khet's practice swings. "Slow down there, Vulcan. Put away the sword before you mortally wound us all." Chuckles erupted from everyone around the fire. "Try on this armor I found. It looks in good condition and is about your size."

Khet removed himself from the sight of the campfire to have some privacy as he undressed. To his surprise, the chain mail was a lot more comfortable than it looked. The muscle he developed in the forge filled out the armor quite well. Most important, though, was the cloak with a hood. It wasn't a heavy weight, but it was of a sturdy construction. The best thing was the clasps started high so he could hide the runes on his neck easily. Khet wasn't sure what was going on with him. The supposed runes on his neck must be a part of it. So, he thought it wise to keep the runes hidden until he could learn more.

Finally, he felt that he might have some control over his life. The weight of armor gave him more confidence. He walked back to the others at the fire. A question tickled his mind. "So, Abner, why do I need to go with you to the University? What do they need me for?"

Khet could see the thoughts as they formed on Abner's face. "You have possibly been a witness to a new type of fiend. The University wants to find out all you know about it so they might be able to defend against it. Also, to keep you away from the Temple and their

Dodecahedron. They will just torture the information out of you. We don't want that." The lie was obvious in Abner's eyes, but Khet had no idea what that lie was.

"I thank you for that." The runes around Khet's neck prickled, making him very aware of their existence.

"No, problem, friend. The Hand does not support how the Temple does things. Destroying entire villages to stop a fiend is too much. We are not at an open war yet with the Temple, but I believe one is brewing. Look, you are hungry, and these topics are heavy. Just eat, and we will talk more some other time." Abner handed Khet a large bowl of the stew.

Khet's stomach shouted for food at this point. The smell of the cooking fire and the food was intoxicating. He didn't even wait for it to cool; he was a Forge Blessed and could handle the heat. By the end of his feast, he finished three bowls of the stew and two small wedges of crumbly cheese. Full and now relaxing by the fire, sleep called his name. He hadn't been this comfortable in a while.

Everyone sat next to the fire, their bellies full and eyes heavy. Abner had to ruin the moment. "OK, I guess that will be all for today. Trip, you stand first watch. Grim, you take care of the fire and clean up after dinner. Raine, you tend to the horses. Khet, come with me and help with the tents." Everyone nodded and set to their given task.

The tents were not that large, but there was more than enough room in each for a person and their gear. The task made more laborious by a full stomach, Khet sweated profusely. With the tents erected, Khet had his heart set on some sleep. Abner came to him before he could lay down.

"I am sorry to say this, my friend. You do not seem like you are a threat to us, but we still don't know you yet. So, I ask you to give me your sword for the night. I will place it in my tent, and I will give it back to you in the morning so we can train. But return it to me after, okay?" Abner was a leader through and through, and he cared for his people. "And because of where we are, I would keep your armor on. Fiends like to live in the remote areas of the mountains and sometimes come down looking for food."

Khet was a stranger in a strange place, so he handed over his sword. "I understand, it makes sense." Khet smelled the cool breeze coming off the mountains. He had never been this close to Dragon's Spine. He could see them looming in the distance. Still in awe that somewhere in them is a sat lake of molten iron with Vulcan's Tower in the middle.

Maybe he will see it someday.

17

There was a tapping on his tent. He had slept significantly better than he thought he would. It was a dreamless sleep. He was thankful for that after all the nightmares he had had and lived through. Honestly, he was happy he didn't wake up in a cage again or tied up.

"Khet, up you go, it is time for some training 'fore we break fast. Go to the trees, relieve yourself, and then meet me by the wagons." Abner's footsteps retreated before Khet had the wherewithal to respond.

Khet crawled out of the tent a little stiff. His muscles complained with each movement. *It is a new day*, he thought. *Things will be better.* Khet relieved himself near the trees and walked over to where the wagons sat. He had his guard up, ready for an attack, Rule 1.

To Khet's relief, Abner leaned against the far wagon, eating an apple. "Good morning, so how do you want to start this? Do we warm up or just go at it? I am ready for either." Khet attempted to sound more casual about it, not nervous like he truly was.

Abner grinned. "Good, I am glad that you are." Abner handed Khet a dull practice sword. "OK, come at me and let us see what you know." Abner slid into a low pose with his sword at the ready. It was more playful than threatening.

The way Abner trained was definitely different than the training that Kase put him through. It started with a couple of simple sparring matches so Abner could assess his new pupil's skill level. Then it moved to some basic blocking and striking techniques. Even though Khet was not a natural with a sword, he felt that he was getting better at it. That was until Abner called for a pause to the training.

"I am sorry, Khet. I don't think a sword is a good choice for you. Your movements are brutish, almost clumsy. When you wield a sword, you need to be fluid." Abner flowed like water over rock around the training area. His sword tip flowed smoothly through the air. "You're swinging the sword like it's a hammer and your opponent an anvil." Abner rubbed his chin. "Today, we should reach the pass. I am friends with a smithy that lives in the village before the pass. I say we stay there for a day or two. We can find you a better weapon to use and maybe sell off some of our goods. Carrying less through the pass will make us less interesting to any bandits that may be hiding in there." "Is the pass that bad, that I have to be good with a weapon?" Khet was slightly concerned.

"Usually not, but there is always a chance, and I don't want to leave you defenseless. My wife would never look at me the same if I let you go into the pass without a proper chance." Abner took the sword from Khet and smiled. "If you are lucky, maybe we could find Vulcan's hammer. A hammer would work better with your heavy blows. Maybe a shield as well. With your strength, you could always bash your enemy with a shield."

The small group broke camp after a breakfast of hard sausage and cheese. The wagons were reloaded, and they took off toward Drake's Pass. Khet drifted in between the carts. He struck up conversations to help the miles pass by. Thoughts nagged at him constantly. The woman's voice whispered in his mind, " *The Arankai will find you.*" The Arankai, according to the Temple of the Twelve, are a cult of Outer Gods worshippers. He didn't want anything to do with them.

When the well of conversation ran dry among the group, Khet focused on the mountains and the ground under his feet. It was a slow, steady march. The gentle wind from the mountains chilled his skin. He grabbed a small blanket from one of the carts and wrapped it around his shoulders. It kept the cold mostly at bay and allowed Khet more time to think about his situation.

Khet was taken out of his thoughts as a rider approached. Trip had returned from scouting ahead. He rode up to the cart that Abner drove. Curiosity drew Khet closer so he could listen.

"The Temple and those bastard Dodecahedrons are blocking the pass. Inspecting everyone that goes through. They are looking for information about a new fiend in the area." Anxious worry was thick in Trip's voice.

Khet's blood froze. The Temple was looking for him.

"Damn, they move fast. They came all the way down from Iridam. Well, fall in with us. We will move on to the village and see what we can learn. Maybe they will leave in a day or two."

"If it is all right with you, I will ride on to Graven's and tell him to prepare for us." Trip had a mischievous look.

Khet could hear the smile on Abner's face. "Tell that old goat that I am coming for the silver he owes me and to warm the forge. I have work for him. Our Khet needs a weapon that fits him."

Khet's blood thawed a little. Abner didn't show a lot of concern for the Temple being there. The Temple's presence was still a large stone in his gut. The runes on his neck felt like they were shining. A beacon pulling the Temple ever closer.

"Since you are dropping those eaves, you might as well come have a seat." Abner had a good set of ears on him.

Khet climbed up beside him, a little embarrassed for being called out.

"Don't you worry, Khet. I would do the same if I was in your situation." Abner patted Khet on the back. "The Temple may be a problem here. If they find out that you may have seen this fiend, they will snatch you up and question you until you break. We don't want that. I know they will have at least one Arbiter with them at the pass and probably another one hidden in the town." Abner became serious. "My job is to get you to the University, and I am good at my job. Graven's smithy is on the edge of town. When we are there, I need you to stay there and not to talk to anyone that you don't know. Do you understand?" The last bit was more of an order, not a question.

Khet nodded his head. "Yes."

"Good," Abner reached into his pocket. "Here, take this. It is a badge of the Hand. You are not a member, but if somebody gets too nosy, you can just show them the badge and tell them it is business of the Hand. That should hopefully make them leave you alone."

Khet took the badge as if it were the most precious thing. He had seen these badges growing up, only once or twice. Travelers would come into the farmstead brandishing the badge of the Hand. Tarin would help them for free. When somebody showed the badge of the Hand, Tarin would never charge and would forgo sleep to finish the job. Now he had one in his hands. "OK, I will do my best to stay out of sight."

"Ride with me until we get to Graven's. He is a good, trustworthy friend of the Hand. We will be safe there until we make our decision on what to do next." Abner grew quiet in thought and stayed silent for the rest of the way into town.

18

They arrived late to Graven's smithy, indeed as Abner had said, Graven was a true friend of the Hand. The smell was the first thing to draw Khet's attention. A whole pig slowly roasted on a spit over a large fire. Trip stood unsteady beside it. By the look of Trip's posture and grin on his face, he was already several cups into his celebration. He hollered and raised a toast to us as we stopped the carts.

"See you have started without us. Where is the old man?" The joy Abner had at the sight of his friend warmed Khet.

"Who are you calling old? I have hammers in the forge older than you and twice the smarts." Graven stood in the doorway of his house. He wasn't a large man, but what was there of him was all hard muscle built up over decades of iron and steel work. His bald head and a short-cropped grey beard gave him a wisened appearance. Scars covered his hands and face; it happens when you handle blades a lot.

"I am calling you old, old man. The reason you have hammers older than me is because you have been doing this longer than most people have been alive. Now, the fact that you talk to your hammers and think they are smart is a sign of metal poisoning. You should see a healer." A smile split Abner's face.

"Remind my niece, Varith, that I still disapprove of her marrying a dunce like you." Graven struggled to hold back his laugh. "Come here, Abby."

"You know you don't have to call me that anymore." Abner walked over to Graven and embraced him as friend and family.

"You didn't tell me he was your wife's uncle." Khet said, enjoying the familial scene as it unfolded.

"Graven, this Khet, he is our friend we are taking to the University, the one Trip told you needed a weapon." Abner walked Graven over to Khet.

"So this is the young Forge Blessed that needs a weapon. I also can see from Trip's face that you pack a punch." Graven reached out to shake Khet's hand. Graven's hand was a vice, unyielding. Khet didn't want to back down from a test of strength and squeezed back. Graven was completely unfazed by Khet's attempt. "He seems to be strong. How long have you worked in a forge? Your grip tells me you're not some normal lunkhead farm boy. You have spent your time in a smithy."

"Ten years, I was contracted for ten years working in a forge." Khet puffed his chest out with pride.

"Contracted? That's a pity. Fucking Temple and their slave trade." Graven spat on the ground. "A person should never own another."

"That is why the Hand does what it does." Abner clapped Graven on the back. "Now let's celebrate this reunion."

"OK, tonight we feast and share stories. Tomorrow, I want Khet to come and work in the smithy with me. I will see what he has learned in those ten years. Now come, I have ale and food. You all must be tired from the road." Graven was a solid-built man from years in the smithy, but tonight his heart was soft to the returning of family and friends.

"Where can we put our tents and wagons?" Abner asked Graven.

"Around back with your tents. Your carts leave them right where they are, and your horses you can put them in the field across the road. They should be fine there. I have never seen you traveling this heavy before. Is the Hand setting up a merchant's guild?" Graven had a curious look.

"No, we were hunting a group of slavers, and they happened to have a well-stocked camp. We thought we might sell a great deal of it before we go through the pass." Abner gave Graven a look of, "We will talk later."

"Sounds like a great plan. Now you go take care of what you need to. Trip and I will handle things here." Graven walked back towards his house. His step never showed any signs of his age.

Abner looked around to develop a plan. "Raine, you take care of the horses. Grim, you set up our tents over behind the smithy. Far enough away that we don't get covered in suet. Khet, I need you to download that cart. It has all the weapons we gathered from the slavers. Take everything and place it inside the smithy. Graven will tell you where."

All of them set to work. Khet removed the tarp from the cage on the cart. The cart was filled with armors of all types. There were even some bits of dented plate armor, like the type Temple knights wore. The swords, axes, and shields were in various states of disrepair. Khet took to the task of unloading the cart. Armful by armful, he made trips to the smithy. It was a sizable smithy from Khet's guess. Free-standing a good distance from the house. One side was charred from a past fire but still looked solid enough.

The inside was impressive as the outside. It was all well stocked and organized. He placed all the items in an opening at the back of the smithy, where Graven had indicated.

Even with the cold breeze coming off the mountains, Khet worked up a sweat. He removed his cloak and stripped to the waist. The mountain wind was cool on his skin. On one of Khet's last loads to carry into the smithy, Graven stopped him.

"Those markings on your neck, what are they?" Graven stood there, not drunk but a good deal in that direction.

"One is Vulcan's mark, this is a tattoo the owner of my contract gave me, and this one is a scar." Khet was not a good liar, but he was getting better.

"The former owner of your contract, who was he? Why did he tattoo that mark on you?" Graven had a look that he knew that the story he was trying to pass on to him was not the full truth.

"I don't know why he did it, all of us contracted had one." A chill tickled Khet's spine, not from the mountain air but fear of being found out.

"I have seen markings like that on people that come through here from time to time. I was just wondering what they meant, that's all. Now finish up, food's ready." Graven left Khet to finish his task.

Did Graven know something about what these markings are? What they mean? Khet hadn't even been able to see them for himself yet. Maybe while they work together in the smithy, Khet could ask him some questions. Anyway, about it, Khet had to finish unloading the cart.

"Here you can wear these. No need to wear your armor around here. Also, you being shirtless is distracting Trip. He likes strong farm boys a little too much." Raine had a sheepish grin as she handed him a set of clothes made for the cooler climate and a jacket.

Khet blushed, slightly embarrassed, "Oh… um… I will have to tell him I am not like that."

"Oh, it's fine, Trip maybe a little heartbroken when he finds out, but that is all a part of living life. Some people just don't like playing with the same toys as you do. Nothing to be shy about. I will go tell him for you, save you the trouble and awkwardness." Raine had a way that made Khet feel relaxed.

Khet never thought about it that way, but it did make sense. So Khet cleaned himself up and changed into his warmer clothes. He never had clothes for the cold. Life in the south, the hot sun never really let it get cold. Sometimes a storm would cool things off but not enough for a jacket.

Khet walked out of the smithy. The celebration was well underway. They all sat at a long table between the house and the smithy. A large cooking fire was burning bright not too far away. Khet sat at the table, Abner handed him a plate, and Graven handed him a pint of ale.

"Khet, have you had much experience with ale?" Graven slurred his words.

"Not a lot, why?" Khet didn't like being treated like a child.

Graven grabbed a pitcher of water. "Here, water down that ale, it is strong. You don't want to be hung over when the hammers start ringing tomorrow." He chuckled there at the end.

Slightly offended, "I can handle myself, thank you."

"HERE! HERE!" Trip shouted from nearby, a flirtatious smile on his face.

Graven grinned. "All right, handle it yourself then."

As an act of pride, Khet tipped the pint back and drank it all in one go, slamming the pint on the table. "I am thirsty tonight, another!"

Cheers erupted around the table. Abner slapped Khet on the back. He mentioned something about regretting that later, but Khet couldn't get much past his slurred speech. Khet piled all the food he could on his plate. Pork, potatoes, tomatoes, and carrots. Raine ripped him a large hunk of bread and put a gob of honeyed butter on it.

The aroma of wood and pipe smoke mingled in a delightful fragrance. Khet loved it, all of it. This was the type of life that he always dreamed about. A group of friends that feasted together, drank together, and shared stories of past adventures. In between mouthfuls of food, Khet would take sips of Graven's ale. It was sweet and hoppy, unlike anything he had ever drank before. This was the life.

The feast carried on, and stories were shared. Abner told a story about when he first met Raine. An all-out brawl had broken out at a tavern near the University, and Abner was sent to stop it. He met Raine outside the tavern. Where she gave first aid to an injured person. He questioned several drunk patrons and made the discovery that Raine only healed the man because she wanted to fight him again. The story sent drunken laughter around the table.

Grim had a story about a mission to help a village repair a damn that had broken during a heavy rainfall. It had taken months and months to repair the damn. The very last day, the damn was finished, and they were just cleaning up. A mob of angry wives came down from the local village. Rocks and anything that could have been thrown were directed at them. Turns out Trip made himself too acquainted with their husbands. At that point, Trip blurted out something close to, "The heart wants what the heart wants!" But nobody could really hear him over all the laughter.

Khet's head swam from the ale, and his face hurt from all the laughing. More tales were told, and laughter was shared. After a rather good story about Abner's proposal to his wife Varith, a quiet lull settled over the table.

"The Temple is waiting at the pass, you know. An Arbiter is questioning everyone quite thoroughly from what I hear." All the joy in the air disappeared at Graven's mention of the Temple. "There is talk of a new fiend. It killed an entire farmstead and burned a hill to cinders. Down to the fucking nub they say. The fiend howls with madness and strikes down anyone it comes across. It has been a long time since I have seen the Temple like this. Do you have a plan?"

Abner sighed. "I am forming one. I want to shrink our load amount. Sell the cart and horses, all the armor and swords we don't need, and anything else we can't carry on our backs."

"We are not keeping the horses?" Raine sounded concerned. "I really enjoyed not walking everywhere."

"You have to feed a horse, and it will be harder to slip by the Temple." Abner responded.

"You could always take the small trail through the mountains. Not many know of it, and you can just slip by, and the Temple would be none the wiser. I heard stories that the Arankai used it to get around." Graven said.

"Not this Arankai nonsense again. I told you they are not real. Just something the Temple made up to scare us into submission." Abner drunkenly spat.

"You listen here, boy. They are real. They came through here once about twenty years back. I shoed a couple of their horses. I paid me a lot to stay quiet." Graven's anger was clear as he pointed in Abner's direction.

Abner was drunkly irritated as well. "That was just some rich folk pretending. You can't prove otherwise."

"What are the Arankai?" Khet asked, raising his hand. " The only thing I have heard about them is what the Temple has said. They worship the Outer Gods and are trying to bring down the Wall."

"Don't get him started." Abner said.

"You shut your mouth, boy, 'fore I shut it for you." Graven leaned in, drunken tempers flared. Everyone sat quietly and waited for the explosion that never came. "All that bullshit that the Temple spouts is exactly that, bullshit. The Temple just wants to keep you scared because scared people can be controlled easily. The Arankai, the real Arankai." Graven raised his hand to silence Abner. " The Arankai believe the Twelve Gods of the Temple are false and the Temple created all of this to maintain control. They also maintain that the Temple lies about the why the Wall was built." Graven had to stop for a second to stabilize himself. "Keepers of the truth, people say. The Arankai are from the Shaded Vale in the Forest of Dusk. They hide in the shadows, biding their time until they can take down that Temple and their bullshit immortal bastards."

"Alright, that's enough. Your drunken ass is not making any sense. Everyone to bed. We have a long day tomorrow. Now go." Abner stood and stumbled to his tent. The others groaned in dissent but did as their leader ordered. Khet wanted to hear more about the Arankai, but he was too drunk to do anything about it. Khet rose from the table, his world started to spin and tumble. He made it three steps before he hit the ground, passed out. Through the cheers and laughter at Khet, Graven commented. "Sure looks like you handled it."

19

"Up, boy!" Graven yelled.

Graven's boot nudged Khet's ribs. His head throbbed, and his body ached. "What was in that ale?" He muttered before he wretched on the ground.

"Ale was in that ale. Now get yourself together; we have work to do." Graven sounded so loud in Khet's head.

Khet struggled to his feet. The entire world swung this way and that. No matter how Khet tried to hold it, the world would not hold still. He made it four more steps before completely emptying his stomach on the ground. "Ugh, I don't like this."

"Next time you think you are a big man and can drink with the adults, remember this." The volume that Raine was speaking was icy daggers behind Khet's eyes. "Here I made you a little something to rehydrate you and help with the headache. It should help with your stomach as well."

"Can't you just give him a couple of sips of nectar? That would fix him up." Graven asked from the table.

"No, I don't think I should." Raine studied Khet for a second as if thinking about it. Khet got a little excited that there might be an end to his suffering on the horizon. "This one had a bit of a sweet tooth when we found him. Don't want him to get hooked again." Turned out the end to the pain was just a mirage.

"Well, Khet, today you are going to learn a hard lesson. In two hours, we start in the smithy." The enjoyment was plain on Graven's face.

Khet stumbled to the tree line to relieve himself. As he fumbled to undo his pants, he felt nothing but dampness that smelled strongly of piss. "Fuck." Disappointed and embarrassed, he walked to a nearby creek. Standing at the muddy shore, he thought about taking off his clothes and washing them separately. Maybe he was still drunk, or he just didn't care at this point. Khet jumped in the water. As soon as his head went beneath the surface, his mistake was evident. This was a mountain run-off stream, freshly melted snow, just above freezing. The shock was so intense that he inhaled deeply underwater. Khet thrashed and thrashed, coughing up the water and throwing the remnants of what was left in his stomach up. When he made it to the shore, he was uncontrollably shivering. He had to get warm. Khet scrambled to a nearby boulder.

Shivering on the boulder, all he could think about was calling on Vulcan. Maybe then he could heat the boulder, and that would warm him. Khet closed his eyes and tried to find him. The door appeared in his mind, the same as it always had. Inside the temple, it was different. There wasn't a chorus of noise; it was quiet. Five figures stood at the end of the massive ancient temple. Three were visible in bright light, and two were obscured in shadow. He approached the one he recognized as Vulcan, wearing his flaming golden armor.

"Vulcan, I need your power to warm myself. I am going to freeze to death." Khet looked down at his body; it wasn't his. "What is going on here?"

"Calm, my child. All will be explained in due time." The God in flaming armor reached out his hands. "My name is not Vulcan. It is Magnus of the Eternal Flame." Magnus gestured with his hands again.

Khet hesitantly reached out to grab hold of Magnus's hands. For the briefest of moments, searing pain shot through his hands. Khet jerked away and inspected the palms, where the pain was most intense. A rune was burned into each of his palms. It was the same rune that was on his neck.

"I am sorry, my child. That is all I can do for you right now. It should be much easier for you to use the gift I have given you and to be able to control it as well. But you must go now." Magnus stood powerful in his golden splendor. A rage Khet recognized burned inside his eyes.

"But I have so many questions. Who are you? What is this?" Khet talked so fast that all his questions piled on top of each other.

"All will be explained later. Just know the Temple of the Twelve is evil, and their twelve gods are not gods. You must go, know." Magnus raised his hands. A force knocked Khet from his feet, and he was hurled through the air out the door of the temple.

Khet's eyes shot open. He was back on the boulder near the stream. He opened his shivering hands, and he could see the runes as they faded to nothing. He called on the power that Magnus had given him. The warmth slowly moved through his hands into his arms. Khet pulled the warmth into his chest and pushed it down to his legs. A knowledge came with it, an understanding of the power. His rage deep down called to it, like a long-lost love.

The shivering subsided quickly. He pushed his rage deep down, back where it belonged. Khet sighed as he rolled onto his back. His head still throbbed from the hangover, but he was warm now. The sky above was so blue that he just wanted to lay there and stare at it, but he couldn't. Khet sat up and looked around to see if anybody had witnessed what happened. To his relief, he was all alone. Only the sound of the gentle breeze and the stream had witnessed his poor decision.

An idea came to him. He pulled more power into his body, gradually heating himself up. The clothes that he wore began to steam. In short order, his clothes were dry. Khet slowed the intake of power. He just wanted a trickle of power for right now to keep himself warm.

Now warm and dry, Khet grabbed the water skin with the mixture that Raine had given him for his hangover. Alone in the forest, Khet attempted to make sense of all that had just happened. His visit to the temple was completely different from other times. For one thing, it was quiet as a tomb. The walls were completely covered in shadow. The one that Khet now knew as Magnus actually spoke to him. In none of the stories that Khet had heard did the Gods talk to someone. And who were the others? And why were his hands not his hands in the temple?

The only solid conclusion that made sense was that the temple was dangerous, and he needed to avoid it. Khet was glad that Abner had tried to stay away from the temple as well. He did not want to become the next thing the temple hunted. If they were not hunting him already.

With the mixture finished, Khet's head felt a little relief; at least it didn't look like he had pissed himself anymore.

20

Khet made his way back to the smithy. The air in the forest and the deep green of it was a fresh breath to him. The crunch of the pine needles, the soft carpet of the forest floor relaxed Khet more and more. All this went away when he saw Graven as he leaned on the side of the smithy.

"About time. I said two hours, not three. Now get in here so we can work." Graven apparently didn't give a shit if Khet felt better or not. "Before we get into making anything for you, I want to see your skill. Take this ingot and fashion a blade out of it. Impress me, and I will let you look at my schema, and we can forge you a weapon." Graven folded his arms and waited for Khet to start.

Khet walked around the old smithy, collecting the tools he needed. The age of the smithy showed proudly throughout. Finely forged weapons adorned the wall. Well-worn tools all had their place. Even the pieces of ore and scrap steel had their place. Khet was at home in Graven's smithy.

He stopped in front of the forge and paused for a moment. Now that Khet had a grasp of his power, he wanted to show off a little. Maybe it was his youth, or for a moment of his life, he felt in control. He wanted to impress Graven. Khet held the cold iron ingot. Instead of starting the forge, he called on his power and slowly poured heat into the ingot. Within seconds, the ingot glowed a dull orange. He couldn't hide how smug he felt from his face.

"OK, fire fist, the metal is ready. Now what?" Graven did not look impressed.

Spurred on by the barbed comment, Khet grabbed a hammer and started to shape the metal. The sound of the hammer strike was like a spike driven into Khet's eyes. Apparently, he was still hungover. He pushed through it. Khet let the muscle memory take hold and just let his body react naturally to the rhythm of the strikes. Bang...Bang... Bang... Bang sounded throughout the smithy. The movement of the hammer falls cleared Khet's hangover with each strike. His place was here in a smithy between the hammer strikes.

The rhythm of the hammer carried on for over an hour. Khet's muscles were taught from exertion. Finally, he placed the forged blade into the quenching oil. The sizzle was a beautiful song to Khet. One he had enjoyed many times. He leaned back against the cold forge to catch his breath, his head now perfectly clear.

Graven pulled the blade from the quenching bucket. "Work is not done. You have to see if it will hold an edge."

"I wasn't ready for that yet." Khet picked up the blade and poured heat into the handle. Once glowing, he twisted it into a spiral. Before the metal could cool, he took copper wire and worked it into the handle, giving it a spiraling finish. He held the handle aloft. Khet couldn't douse the handle because of the two different types of metal. It had to be cooled gradually.

Once the blade cooled enough, he went to the grinding wheel and shaped the edge. At this point, sharpening blades was like breathing to him. Hours upon hours, days upon days, he spent in Tarin's smithy sharpening blades of all kinds. After the grinding wheel, Khet found the whetstone. He took some fresh, clean water and poured it on the stone and began to refine the edge. It only took Khet part of an hour before he was done. He took a piece of cloth, cleaned the blade, and then he put a light finish of oil on it. When it was done, the long knife was five hand spans in length and had a slight forward curve with a wider blade at the top. He presented it to Graven.

"What type of blade is this?" Graven tested him.

"It is called a Kukri."

"What is it used for? It doesn't seem good for stabbing."

"In the south, we use it for hacking and slicing. Most hunters carry one to gut their kills." Khet was confident in his work, and it showed in his voice.

Graven rubbed his thumb over the blade. "Well, it took an edge.

Let's see if it holds its edge." Graven chopped away at a log sitting in the corner. After many hard hits, he stopped and tested the edge again on his thumb. "And it is still sharp. Good job. I am impressed. This blade is yours now. Keep it on your side as a mark of your skill."

Khet took the blade. Pride swelled inside him. He had never been able to make a blade for himself. He would cherish this blade. "Thank you."

"Abner tells me you need a weapon. What type of weapon do you want?" Graven asked.

Khet looked around the room at the different weapons on the wall. None of them really spoke to him. "I don't know. Abner said I was no good with a sword. All my swings were too much like hammer blows on an anvil."

"Okay, follow me to the house. I think I have something that may suit you better." Graven was out the door, and Khet followed close behind.

Graven's house was modest for a blacksmith, more function over form. Where one might have a table that would be big enough to seat guests, Graven had a table for one. A small fireplace in the corner and a single bed near it. On the walls hung a menagerie of trinkets. Many Khet had never seen before and couldn't explain them if he had.

"Oh, I noticed my collection. Sometimes people passing through who need my services can't pay in coin. So I trade them for odd things." Graven walked into the only other room in the house, still talking. Khet was too distracted to hear him.

"Here is what I wanted you to see." He slapped the book down on a large drawing table, the only oversized thing in the house. "That mark under your chin, your odd Vulcan mark, I thought I recognized it from somewhere." Graven flipped through the pages and found the schema he was looking for.

The schema was of a pair of gauntlets with the mark of Magnus engraved in them. On the sides, there were notes and dimensions, temperature requirements, and mixture ratios to create an alloy of metals. Written across the bottom, "Hell Hammer, is that the name of these? Where did you find this?"

"Yes, that is the name; painters name their paintings. So do blacksmiths. I do think Hell Hammer is dramatic, but the design seems solid." Graven was looking through a book by his bedside. "Here, I found that schema in this book."

Khet held the book like it was a precious artifact. Thumbing through the pages, he couldn't understand a word in it. He had never seen this language before. "What language is this? Some kind of code?"

"Remember the story I told you about the Arankai last night? After I sorted their horses, word came that the Temple was on their way. So those Arankai left in a hurry and forgot a bag." Graven stared off to the middle distance. "I feared the Temple would come and find the bag, so I hid it in the mountains. Eventually, my curiosity got the better of me, so I went and grabbed it. Inside was the book, that schema, and two pieces of ore."

"What was the ore? Did you try to make the gauntlets?" Khet buzzed with excitement. This kind of thing only happened in the tales that travelers told. Stories of the heroes he wanted to be.

"No, I could never get the forge hot enough as per the requirements in the schema. Not enough of the ore; I didn't want to waste any."

"Do you think the ore is only meant for the inlay of the runes? There is not a lot here." Khet wouldn't let this die; he wanted to make these gauntlets. This was meant for him. It tugged at his guts.

"I don't know; that inlay is so fine you would be hard-pressed to do it with tools." Graven's thoughts flew across his face. "You could do it with your hands; can you make it hot enough?"

"I am willing to try."

"Hot damn! My boy, you have convinced me. Come with me to get supplies. I am going to need more copper and tin. I know a man in the village that should have some." For an old man, Graven could move quickly out a door when properly motivated.

21

The edge of the village was only a short distance from Graven's house. Deep set into a forest surrounded by mountains on all sides, it was a new experience for Khet. He had never been this far north. At this distance, the Wall was barely a smudge low on the horizon. Even with a cloudy sky, Khet had an excitement in his step.

For a nameless village, Khet was impressed with the quality and quantity of the homes. "Why doesn't this village have a name?"

Graven looked around as if he had never thought to ask that question. "I don't know. I guess nobody got around to naming it."

The further they walked, the more impressive the buildings became. Glassed widows with images painted on them were almost on every shop. Some of the paintings were descriptions of what was sold inside. Others were landscapes of beautiful vistas or scenes depicting the Twelve and their endless battle.

All of this was nothing compared to the market. Nothing could have prepared Khet for the assault on his senses. The smells of food cooking, the sound of vendors clamoring for a sale, colors of every hue displayed, and the amount of people. Sent Khet's world spinning.

"This market is amazing." Khet slack-jawed at the size and intensity of it.

"You should see the other side of the pass. From what I am told over the last couple of years, it has gotten bigger." Graven moved through the crowd like a veteran. Khet struggled to keep up. "Khet, there is a

Temple around here. We need to just get what we came for and get back to the smithy."

"OK, I understand. I just have never seen something so impressive." Khet wanted to see as much as possible, take it all in. The fear of the Temple extinguished by the excitement. Hands grabbed Khet and roughly pulled him behind a stall.

"I told you to keep out of sight." Abner had a finger in Khet's face. His tone was a hard whisper.

"Graven and I are going to make something together, so I came with him to get supplies." It came out weak. Khet knew he was in the wrong.

"Turn and look over there." Abner pointed to a group on the other side of the market. They were dressed in fine robes made of twelve different colored vertical stripes, two of them grayed out. All to symbolize the ten known Gods and the two forgotten slain Gods. Khet's heart froze; behind them stood four of the Dodecahedron, soldiers of the Temple of the Twelve's immortal army. Clad in their flawless silver and gold armor, each one carrying a sword with a blade that glowed ever so subtly. It is said the blade contains the fury of all twelve of the gods. No one dares to cross blades with an immortal. "You must leave now. Trip will go with you; I will talk with Graven."

Khet nodded and pulled the hood of his cloak tight. Trip leaned in just so only Khet could hear. "Act natural, like we are just two friends out to find drinks."

Khet relaxed his posture and tried to look like he was having a good time. Anxiety danced through him. *Had the Dodecahedron seen him? Were they now moving closer to kill him?* His heart thumped threatening to burst out of his rib cage. Out of the corner of his eye, he saw something. It was a woman with a blue ribbon in her hair; was that Kase? Trip called to him, then the woman was gone. *Could it have been her? Just nerves, had to be. She wouldn't be all the way up here.*

Trip and Khet meandered their way back to Graven's house. All the while, Trip prattled on about nothing Khet could follow; he was distracted. His mind was a jumble with self-doubts. Did he see what he thought he did, or was it just his mind playing tricks on him? Did the Temple notice him? Are they looking for him or something else? If that was Kase, will she tell the Temple that the one who burned a hill to cinders is here? Graven said that the fiend burned a hill and killed everyone on the farmstead. Khet knew he didn't do that. *Kase wouldn't have done that, would she?* Khet thought it was just an exaggeration, as most stories are. *Was Ty okay?* Khet wanted to run back to them, but he knew he couldn't. He had to stay the course and find out what all this was.

"I suggest you better listen to Abner when he tells you something." The sound of Trip's scolding brought Khet out of his thought spiral.

"I… just wanted to see the market." Khet was ashamed.

"You need to understand something: the Temple and the Hand don't get along." Trip was serious in his words. "If they found out that someone that had witnessed a new type of fiend was here. The Temple would destroy this village trying to find you. And the fact that the four of us are wanted by the Temple doesn't help much."

"Wait, you're wanted by the Temple, why?" This caught Khet off guard.

"I will let Abner tell you when he is ready. Leave it at that." Trip's tone was final. Khet was not going to get any more out of him.

They walked the rest of the way to Graven's house in silence. Khet was fine with it; he had a lot to think about. Also, there was the excitement over forging Hell Hammer gauntlets. That made him feel better and less worried about the things he couldn't control and focus on the things he could.

22

Khet sat on a stool in the smithy, anxiety gnawed at his gut. He didn't know who was going to show up first, Graven or Abner. He would probably get scolded by either, so he decided to just focus on other things. The smithy had racks upon racks of weapons and bins full of different ores. A thin layer of dust coated everything except for a few weapons hanging on the wall. Even in the low light of the smithy, the weapons had a strange, unnerving shine to them. Khet was uncomfortable when he looked at them. A dread filled him like water into a cup.

Khet shook his head to get his mind off such dark things. A distraction was needed. He poured through his memory to remember the ingredients for the Hell Hammer gauntlets. The bins had the ores he needed to make one of the alloys in the schema, so he decided to have a go at it and see what happens.

He called upon his power; it poured through him. All three pieces of the ores started to glow and grow soft. Using his hands, he pushed the ores together all the while pumping more and more heat into them. The metal was more like a firm clay at first. He worked it more, as he pushed more heat into the alloy. Now the glowing blob was more like a good baker's bread dough. Khet pushed and rolled the alloy in his hands. Glowing almost a bright white now, he shaped it into a hammer head. He pushed his thumbs through to make the hole for the haft. Now struck with inspiration, Khet moved with great purpose. He grabbed an iron bar, he heated one end of it till it glowed, all the while he kept the head of the hammer at a high temperature. He forced the head onto the iron rod. He twisted the haft to ensure the two metals fused properly. He inspected his creation. Satisfied, he put it in the quenching oil bucket.

"You should be glad Abner is paying me a great deal. Wasting my supplies to make a hammer. I have ten hammers in the smithy and more in the house. Why did you do that?" Graven was quite irritated.

Khet was so involved with what he was doing that he didn't hear Graven come in. "Sorry, I just remembered the schema saying that I had to make it hot enough to make an alloy out of iron, tin, and zinc. So, I wanted to try, and I found I was able to."

Graven walked over to a box in the corner. He grabbed a dull grey container from inside and walked over to pick up the still quench hammer. Khet made a move to stop him from touching the hammer; the quenching oil was still sizzling. Graven warned him off with a look. With the dull grey container in one hand, he reached for the hammer. The sizzle stopped, and the temperature in the room dropped.

"You're a Cold Adept, aren't you?" Khet asked in awe of what he just witnessed.

"Yes, I know it doesn't make sense that a blacksmith is a Cold Adept. Everyone always focuses on the heat of the fire to work the iron. Never giving a single damn about the proper cool down." Graven took the hammer and let it fall on his anvil. It bounced perfectly off with the most excellent ring to it. "Khet, I think you just made my favorite hammer."

"Really? Thank you." Pride of his work filled Khet.

Graven held the hammer aloft like it was a sacred artifact for his collection. He let it fall again on the anvil, a perfect ring again. He handed Khet the grey container while he marveled at the hammer.

"What is this?" Khet could feel that some kind of thick liquid sloshed inside.

"Oh... It is a salt battery, made by the University. I use it to store the heat I pull from items I am cooling down. Rather ingenious, really. Cold Adepts don't make things cold; we just transfer the heat. Before the batteries, we would generally just force it into the ground. Caused a great deal of fires." By this point, Graven had grabbed another hammer and compared it to the new one. Khet's hammer strikes made the anvil sing. The other was a muddled ping compared to it.

"So that is how it's done." Khet was impressed with the ingenuity of the University. He spun the container in his hand. The weight shifted with each turn.

"Do me a favor and put some more heat into it. The contact point is the disk on the top. I want to forge something with my new hammer. After you're done, go help the others prepare supper. Abner wants to talk to you anyway." Graven, now lost in his own pursuit to make something, left him to it.

Khet did as he was ordered. He injected more heat into the salt battery. The salt inside became runny and sloshed about. Not really knowing how much to put in or where to put the battery. He placed it in the forge and left.

Outside sat Abner at the table near the cooking fire. "What you did today was reckless. You put yourself at great risk." Abner looked more disappointed than angry.

"I am sorry I..." Abner raised his hand to cut Khet short.

"I don't want to hear your reasoning. We got lucky today. Don't do it again and let us leave it at that." Abner had an amazing ability to get his point across with few words. Khet found it odd for a man that talked so much.

Khet didn't say anything, just nodded.

The rest of the day went on with Abner, Khet, and Grim prepping some of the meat from last night's dinner. They roasted more vegetables. Raine sat off to the side and puffed on her tabac pipe while she played her lute. The smell of the tabac smoke was sweet and reminded him of times on the farmstead. He lost himself in thoughts of the others he left behind. He had focused on it for so long already that it didn't hurt as badly this time. It was hard for him to admit it to himself. Khet had to move on, and he had to accept the things he could not change.

When they all sat down for dinner, Raine was well into her cups of wine and played a rather raunchy tune. Laughter erupted around when she hit the dirtier bits in the verse. Some she announced with more emphasis than others. Khet was trying to hide his inexperience from the topics she sang about, but his face still reddened.

With no need to repeat last night, Khet stayed away from the ale and kept to the water. The food was good, and the laughter was better. Graven displayed his new cooking knife that he had just made with his new favorite hammer. Cheers and compliments were all around.

23

In the morning, Khet rose before everyone else. Pretty natural for that to happen since he was the first one to bed, and by the looks of it, the others celebrated a great deal more. At least another three bottles of wine and a half barrel of ale more in celebration. Khet busied himself with cleaning up after the ravelers.   He washed the plates and silverware, disposed of all the rubbish, and cleaned the fire pit. After all the noise of cleaning, not even one of them stirred. He could hear Graven's snore from inside the house. Khet walked back to where the tents were set up. He wanted to make sure his new friends were okay. Both Abner's and Raine's tent flaps were wide open, and he could see them peacefully asleep. Khet did notice that Raine had half of her armor off and left herself exposed. Khet quickly turned and walked away, face red.

Khet made his way to where Trip and Grim put their tents. Trip's was empty. Grim was sound asleep in his. Curious, he searched for Trip. After several minutes of a worried search, he found Trip passed out and completely naked in the back of one of the carts. *It must have been a good night.*

With nothing else to do, Khet set himself to making some breakfast. Starting the fire was a simple task now that he had more control. Khet cooked some thick oatmeal and several rashers of greasy bacon. The smell of the bacon cooking roused his still somewhat drunk comrades.

Khet finished his second bowl of honey-buttered oatmeal by the time Abner made it to the table.

"You guys had a fun night last night?" Khet knew this already by the state of everything.

"Maybe, a little too much fun. When Raine gets to playing her lute, things kind of get out of hand." Abner tried to rub the hangover out of his eyes. "Where's Trip? I noticed his tent was empty."

"He is passed out in the cart over there." Khet pointed to the closest cart.

Abner gave a still drunken grin. "Is he naked? I bet he is naked. Hey Trip!"

Trip launched himself to the standing position, fully exposed. "What? What's going on?" Trip looked down at his nakedness. "Again! I have to find my clothes."

"Yeah, Trip was talking about being too hot last night. This isn't the first time this has happened." Abner grabbed a bowl of oats and a big dollop of butter. "Thanks for breakfast."

"What's with all the yelling?" Graven stumbled outside. "For gods sake, where is that Grun woman? I need some nectar."

Around the corner came Raine, fresh and bright, like last night never happened. "Right here, you old goat." She fished out a couple of vials of nectar, handed one to Abner, and another to Graven. "Where is Trip? He probably needs one."

"Looking for his clothes, over by the carts." Abner pointed in the direction Trip might be found.

Abner and Graven swallowed the contents of the vials.

"So, who made breakfast?" Graven chewed on a fatty piece of bacon.

"I did." Khet was glad he didn't stay up with them last night. He didn't want to swim in the river again.

"Gods Damn! Trip, your arse is white. Put some clothes on, you are blinding me!" Apparently, Raine found Trip, and Trip has yet to find his clothes.

Chuckles came from around the table. Khet heard a shuffle from behind. Grim drunkenly hobbled to the table. "Way too much ale last night." The intensity of the hangover was plain on his face.

"Raine has some feel-good stuff. Go find her." Abner said with a more sober tone.

Grim shuffled away, moaning, looking for relief. Khet sat at the table, enjoying the sight of his new friends, and felt alright. At this moment, everything is good.

Graven grabbed a bowl of oats and sat down. "Abner, did you think at all about what we talked about last night?" Graven took a big spoonful of oats and shoveled it into his mouth. The serious comment kind of deflated Khet's joy a little.

"Yeah, I think we are going to have to, sooner rather than later," Abner said with a sigh. The weight of their discussion still heavy on his brow.

Khet perked up. "What did you guys talk about?"

"Whether we take the small hidden path through the mountain or we backtrack and go around to the north of the Spine or maybe even the northern pass near Sarin's Reach. There is no getting through the Temple at the pass, and they are not leaving until they find what they are looking for." Abner explained in between spoonfuls of oats.

"I tell you the path may be trickier, and you will have to go with only what you can carry, but if you go north, I guarantee the Temple will be up there as well." Graven ate a spoonful of oats as a way to put a button on it.

Khet could see Abner's reluctance. "Are you sure the path goes all the way through, and it will only take a week?"

"Going all the way through, yes. How long it takes I am not sure of; a man that I know lives on the other side of it. He told me he would hike through it for fun sometimes. Weird guy, that one. He did tell me it took him only a week and two days one time, but I don't see how. It takes almost a week on horseback to get through the pass. I don't remember his name though. If you see him, tell him Graven sent you and he will take care of you. His farm is at the eastern entrance to the path."

"I will think about it more." Abner said.

The others joined the table and ate breakfast, and Trip was fully clothed. They ate in silence until the nectar took full effect. Khet just sat there and thought about a hike through the mountains. What they would discover. He almost wanted Abner to just say that they were going to hike the mountains. He wanted to see them now; no more stories about them; he wanted to have his own story about them.

Graven finished his bowl of oats and made his way back to his house. Khet could tell by the way he walked that the nectar had done the trick.

"Raine, how easy is it to get addicted to nectar?" Khet asked.

Raine sat there for a moment, chewing on a piece of bacon. "Depends on a lot of things. It varies from person to person. If someone has an addictive personality, they can become addicted rather quickly. Also, it depends on what is mixed with it. Why do you ask?"

"Because I have seen you guys drink it several times since we have been together, and you guys are not addicted. I didn't drink it much, but I became addicted."

"Oh, that is simple. The nectar we have been drinking is diluted in pure water. The nectar the slavers fed you probably had Cray Flower in it. It is highly addictive. When you combine the two of them, it can be dangerous. Does that answer your question?"

Sound came from the doorway of the house. "Khet, let's get to forging those gauntlets. Abner, could you run to the market and pick up supplies for me? I have a list inside and maybe get rid of all these carts. If you take the cages off, I could use the steel." Graven was almost giddy to work in the smithy today. An odd sight for Khet to see an old man practically skipping with an armful of books.

"I will be right there." Khet answered him, but he was not done questioning Raine. "The Cray Flower, why would they use that?"

"Withdrawal from Cray Flower can cause lethargy and confusion rather quickly if not given constant doses. Slavers put in everything given to the slaves. So if the slave runs, it won't get far before they start to go through withdrawal and collapse. Pretty disgusting practice but effective."

Khet more and more is coming to grips with the fact that his life on the farmstead was sheltered from the rest of the world. Things like this made him miss it. "Thank you for answering that. I don't know if I really wanted to hear something like that though."

"You will learn those facts and many others at the University. The motto is Question Everything, Never Stop Learning." Raine said with a smile.

Khet made his way through the yard to the smithy, excited to deal with things he is familiar with and not slavers or Cray Flower.

24

"Done running your mouth out there and ready to work?" Graven had it all prepped. The schema was on the wall for reference, the forge fire was lit, and a couple of tools were set at the edge of the coals warming up. "I have weighed out each of the major components so there is little waste. And I was thinking you work on smelting and forging the basic shape, I can make the fine-tune adjustments and assembly."

"Sounds great, how long do you think this will take?" Khet was impressed by the organization. Memories of Tarin's haphazard way of organization played in his mind.

"Well, if you don't stop talking, three days. If you actually get to work, the better part of today." Graven had a playful yet admonishing smile. He wanted to work.

So the work started. Graven went over the plans with Khet. He was very detailed in his approach. Khet was not really accustomed to Graven's methodical nature, but he had never worked from a schema, so he trusted Graven's process. Khet could tell from how Graven explained how things were going to flow that he had studied the schema and gleamed what he could from the book.

Bang... Bang... Bang... the heartbeat of the work echoed through the area. At the beginning, work was slow. Khet was only shaping small pieces and then waiting for Graven to do his part. Constantly heating, cooling, and then reheating the pieces in accordance with the schema. This was all foreign to Khet, but he was intrigued by the experience. With each bang of Khet's hammer came the ping of Graven's. The back and forth carried on into the afternoon. Piece by piece, the gauntlets came together.

"Khet, all that is missing now is the inlay of the runes. Grab those pieces of ore and heat them. According to the schema, they must be heated quickly, so give it your all." With that, Graven took a couple of steps back.

"Worried it might get too hot for you?" Khet said with a sarcastic smile.

"No, I don't know that ore, and some rocks have liquid trapped in them. Heating them causes them to explode." Graven said in a tone that wiped the smile off Khet's face.

Khet braced and pushed heat into the ore as quickly as he could, careful not to overdo it. Khet and Graven were both surprised and relieved that it worked as nicely as it did. The ore glowed white hot. Khet began to fold and stretch the ore like it was bread dough. After several minutes, Graven told him to pull it into a thread and push it into the inlay carving. The metallic thread sparked and sizzled as it was being pushed into the gauntlet.

After it was done, Graven put an arm around Khet as they stared at their creation, like two parents proud of their child. "Well, they should be good to put on. Try them out."

Khet's hands fit perfectly into the gauntlets, like they were designed for his hands. Something deep within him stirred. The gauntlets called to something. It vibrated deep in his chest. He could almost hear it, a deep and low whisper of the word "Yes". Khet stood there for a moment. Maybe it was the heat, or another side effect of withdrawal. The not knowing scared him.

"The schema says you should be able to use your forge fire with them, and they won't melt or deform." Graven was excited to see their creation in action. "Just in case though, go outside. I don't want the smithy to burn down again."

Outside, the gauntlets felt good on him. The weight made Khet feel stronger, more in control. He liked it. Moving far enough away from anything flammable, Khet turned on the heat. Since Magnus visited him, his forge power was so easy to summon. All it took was a thought. The gauntlets glowed a dull red. Heat waves distorted the surrounding air. Khet felt good. He had power. Confident, he took several swings, striking the air in front of him. Small thuds were sounded with each swing.

"OK, that is enough. Don't want to draw too much attention with the Temple nearby." Graven had a massive grin.

"Looks like we did it, they work well." Khet mirrored Graven's massive grin.

"Let's have a cup and celebrate our creation."

"I will take mine watered down, please."

"Learned your lesson, did you?"

"Yeah."

25

Khet and Graven sat at the table to enjoy their celebration drink. With each sip, they marveled over their craftsmanship. The cold breeze from the mountain hardly bothered Khet anymore. If he got cold at all, he would just use his power to warm himself. The gauntlets sat there inert on the table. The blackened iron had a slight shine. The shine called to him. It wanted him to wield his power. To burn down the world.

The sound of footsteps brought Khet out of his thoughts. "Khet, tonight you need to pack your things. We leave first thing in the morning." Abner carried several bags with the others close behind him.

"Why so quick? What happened?" A slight panic seized him.

"There is talk that the fiend, the one the Temple is looking for, has been sighted near town. I fear if we stay past tomorrow, we will be found. Graven, tonight we need to talk about that pass. I want us all there and sober."

Khet followed the others back to his tent to make sure what little he had was packed. After a quick look through his meager things, he found the badge of the Hand that Abner had given him. "Hey Abner, since we are leaving, do you want the badge back?"

"I talked with the others, and we think you should hold onto it for now. Maybe I could put a request into the Hand to make you a member when we get back to the University, if that is okay?"

"Yes, I would very much like that."

"Now, no promises. We have a long way to go still before we reach the University. Then there is the training and acceptance into the ranks. But I, as well as the others, think you would make a good fit. You seem like the good type." Abner handed Khet one of the bags he had carried. "Here are all the supplies you should need for the journey through the mountain trail. I want you to pay attention tonight when we go over the plan. Just in case we get separated up there, I don't want you to get lost. Understood?"

Khet felt a warmth inside, like he had found a new home, a new family. He wanted to make them proud. "I will do my best."

It took Khet several hours, and the assistance of Grimm and Trip, to get everything properly arranged in his pack. He put on the pack to get a feel for it. Everything fit snugly and was well balanced. All set up perfectly for the morning. The plan was to leave the tents they were currently using for Graven to keep or sell. They were too big for them to carry by pack anyways. After he checked and rechecked a half a dozen times, Khet joined the others at the dinner table.

There was a large map placed out on the table of Drake's Pass and surrounding area. Everyone was studying it intently. Noticing that Khet had joined them, Abner began. "Okay, here is the plan, everyone. We are leaving in small groups tomorrow first thing. Khet, you will come with me. Grim will go with Raine after us. Trip, I want you to leave after dinner and see if there will be any problems. Meet at the trailhead in the morning. Graven tells me there are several farms between us and the trail. Try to avoid encountering anyone, especially Temple. If you run into someone, just act like you're lost and looking for the smithy. Understand me so far?" Nods from around the table. "Graven has told me that there are supposedly caves all along this route. So, we should be good for protection if the weather gets bad enough. There will be no campfires; we don't want to draw attention." Abner's tone became serious. "Graven does not know of this plan. I told him we are going up and around the Spine, so if an Arbiter asks him, he won't need to lie. Oh, I got ahead of myself; the trail starts here." Abner left his finger in place for all to see. "If we get separated at all, I want you to keep going and wait for us at the other end of the trail. Wait three days and, if nobody else makes it. Head for the University and report what happened to the Hand. So, is this understood by all of you?" Abner made eye contact with each one of them and waited for their nod of understanding. "Okay, Trip, burn the map."

Trip took the map and threw it in the fire. Before he returned to the table, Abner had another copy of the map with a route marked on it going to the north of the Spine. "Remember, this is the path that Graven knows, so don't speak of the other. This isn't my first time dealing with the Temple."

Khet couldn't stop himself from asking. "Why are you so worried about the Temple?"

The tension in the air grew so thick that Khet could feel the weight of it. "I killed three Arbiters after they killed a family for hiding a runaway contracted." Abner locked eyes with Khet. "And I don't regret it."

"Alright, enough of this humdrum. Let's eat." Trip made an obvious attempt to change the subject. "Hey, old man, where's the food?"

Graven came out of the doorway with a bundle of meats and cheeses in his arms. "Right here, ya dandy shite house!"

"Dandy shite house! HA!" Trip's blurted laughter was infectious and lightened the mood for everyone.

"I wish you would change your mind and take the mountain trail. There are going to be even more Temple bastards up there." Graven peered over the map.

"Look, the trail is unknown, and I think we can move along here and cross right at the tip of the Spine. It is the safest route. If the northern pass is clear, we might take that." Abner had made his decision; his tone had a finality to it.

"Well, fine, just be careful and take care of my niece."

"I will, and you too, old man." Then, men shared a glance of familial love.

The night went on, and they all indulged themselves in the food. All of them stayed sober, of course, not wanting to be hungover for their early morning travel.

26

That night, Khet had had vivid nightmares of people dying by the dozens. A great fissure had opened in the Wall. Warriors in dull black armor and creatures of all shapes poured through in a destructive torrent. They ravaged the land and slaughtered everyone. The dark shapes were hard to see in the low light. In the sky above, a pale shining disk shed a dull glow. Small specks of light could be seen all over the sky.

Khet stood there frozen to the ground and watched the carnage from a cliffside. A woman approached him. She wore a fine blue dress and jewelry that sparkled in the dim light. She did not match the scene that was taking place below.

"Khet, I am Arrinia. The others do not know I am here. What you are seeing is what will happen if you let them win. You must wake. You are in danger. Use my gift. It will help you." Arrinia grabbed Khet's hands forcibly. Her grip was iron. Khet struggled to free himself. Pain seared into the backs of his hands as tiny golden threads wove a symbol. It was the shape of a V. Khet's mind swirled as if the threads wove an understanding of what the V meant into his mind. It meant control. "You must wake. Go!" She raised her hand, and Khet was forced off the cliff.

Khet woke in his tent with a start, his breath hard and sweat gathered on his brow. He examined the back of his hands. A golden V shape slowly faded. This was the same golden thread he used at the slaver camp. It was different now. He understood it. Focused, he summoned a thread and moved it around his tent.

The sound of a scream cut short him, bringing him back. Cold fear grabbed him. Arrinia said he was in danger. Khet slid on the gauntlets and bolted from the tent.

The air was still. Something was wrong about it. He glanced at the tents. Attached at the top of his tent was a blue ribbon. The same type of ribbon Kase would wear. He ran towards Graven's house, screaming the alert, but before he could finish the warning, he rounded the corner and beheld the gruesome sight.

Bodies of his new family with their throats cut, all were there except for Abner and Trip. Abner was sprawled on the ground nearby. A figure covered in blood with wild, dark hair sat on the edge of the table; it was Kase.

"You're early. I was hoping to have them all set up for you." Kase slowly slid a blade down her face, just letting the blood run a little before healing it. Hundreds of scars covered her body now. "Your new little family is cute. Too bad you killed them." A wicked smile split her face. His adoptive mother was gone, replaced by something dark.

"Why?" It was a whisper.

"Just like when you killed Tarin!" Kase drew the blade along her arm. "Just like you killed Ty and the others! Ty did scream a lot when you killed him! It was horrible!" Her sick giggling stabbed at Khet.

"Why!" Rage flooded Khet. Not just his own rage, another's rage mixed within his own.

"Your new family didn't cry much. You killed them in their sleep, nice and quiet. Like the demon you are." Kase stood and pointed the blood-slicked knife at Khet. "Now I am going to get my revenge for all the death that you have brought upon me. All the innocents you have murdered. All the families you have destroyed. DIE YOU FIEND!!"

Time slowed and the golden thread of rage unfurled. This time was different; this time Khet was in control. He saw the blade in her hand. He didn't think she needed that. A golden thread wound around her wrist. Rage ran freely through the thread. Her hand and blade fell to the ground.

Shock and pain rippled across Kase's face. She howled as she reached for another blade. A viscous smile appeared on Khet's face. "Remember rule number one, or is this number two?" Three threads seized Kase's remaining limbs. He pulled the threads tight, hoisting her up in the air. "No, this is rule three, definitely rule three." She went into a frenzy. Kase fought feebly against her restraints. Khet let his fiery rage flood the threads. He wanted to cauterize the wounds. He wanted her to live through this. Kase's body and limbs separated in flashes of light. He was in control now.

He walked over to her torso. She coughed blood. "Die, you fucking fiend." It was a weak whisper.

"WHY!" Khet brought a Hell Hammer down on her face, with a sickening thud. "WHY!" He screamed again as he brought down the other. This time, he heard her skull crack. That didn't stop him. Thud. Thud. Thud. Khet could feel the ground through what was left of her face. Thud. Thud. With each blow, he put more heat into his gauntlets. With each blow, the mutilated flesh that was Kase's face sizzled. The rage consumed him in fire.

Khet sat there, the embers and ash of what once was Kase's body, a woman he would have called mother at some point. He felt no regret. He felt justified in his rage. He felt powerful. The sound of coughing snapped him out of it.

Abner lay on the ground with a massive wound in his stomach. He was beyond help. Khet ran to him.

"Abner, hold on. I will find some nectar." Khet checked his wound. He didn't want to lose another friend.

"No, I am done. You need to run. The Temple would have seen that. Take our badges and go to the University. Tell Scholar Creshing that you are the one he is looking for." It was barely a whisper.

"No, I can help you."

"Go... now... run... they are coming." The light left Abner's eyes.

27

Khet's heart slammed against his ribcage. He knew he had to act quickly. Again, his life, his place in the world, was stripped from him. The packs, that were once his friends, were in their tents. Frantically, he raced to the tents. Sadness rang in his heart as he grabbed each badge. In everything, Khet forgot Trip was not there. He went to the mountain trail last night. He needed to know what happened. Tears of rage and deep sadness welled in Khet's eyes.

The sound of armored footsteps snapped him out of his spiral. "Fuck." Khet grabbed his bag and made a run for it. Heart threatening to burst out his chest, he ran for the trail. Not looking back, he couldn't; the pain was too sharp. He had to survive this. Out of the corner of his eye, a single silver and gold figure charged at him with a sword that glowed menacingly, an immortal.

The Dodecahedron warrior was on him inhumanly fast. Khet barely had time to react. More of a stumble than a dodge, the blade sailed within an inch of his head. Khet never stopped, and the warrior came after him. He knew that there was no way he could outrun the immortal. He had to think. Rule 2. Khet poured all the heat he could into his gauntlets and turned to face the warrior. The immortal was not ready for someone to turn and fight; his sword was not yet raised. Khet caught the warrior off guard. He struck him in his armored chest plate. The plate couldn't withstand the heat and shattered. Khet's white-hot fist melted through the chest of the immortal. A shockwave of energy thundered in the valley. The momentum of the warrior sent them both tumbling to the ground. Their limbs were tangled like branches in a flood. Confused, Khet struggled to free himself. Pain erupted in his arm as he wrenched it clear. He stood and stared at the motionless figure. A fist-sized hole was through its chest. The immortal was dead.

Khet heard other armored footsteps in the distance. More Dodecahedron stood at the edge of the clearing. They did not charge. The armored figures stood there, their posture was one of caution. Khet took the moment they had given him and made for the mountain path. In the distance, a horn sounded. Dread filled his belly.

There was no sound of armored footsteps closing in. Khet did not waste any more thoughts on it and ran until he could see Trip.

"What happened? Where are the others?" Trip asked as panic spread through his face.

"Temple... Others dead... Temple coming!" Khet said in between gulps of air. An arrow grazed Khet's shoulder and buried itself in a tree.

On the edge of the clearing were three Dodecahedron archers knocking arrows. Trip and Khet turned and ran. Arrows sizzled through the air, so close Khet could feel them. Desperate to defend himself and Trip, Khet called upon the golden thread, time slowed and the threads unfurled out of his body. Each thread moved to wrap itself around an arrow. With a thought, Khet knocked them out of the air. He looked back in triumph, only to be met with another volley of arrows. Not enough time, not enough thread, he was done. A hand gripped Khet's bag and wrenched him to the ground.

"Are you stupid!" Trip breathed hard. "Let's go before they fire more arrows."

The mouth of the trail was insight, it would be a lot harder for their pursuers to shoot them when they were in the rocks. Trip was right in front of Khet yelling something he could not understand. He ripped his badge from his pocket and forced it into Khet's hands.

"Go, I will only slow you down. I will try and distract them and buy you time. GO!" Trip ran back towards the archers. "Don't stand there, GO!"

Khet turned and made for the path. He had to make it, somebody had to tell the University what happened. Khet couldn't let their sacrifice be for nothing. He made it to the narrow opening of the path and into the shelter of the rocks.

The rocks formed a deep, narrow path. The sun did not reach down there. Patches of ice slowed Khet as he continued to maneuver through. His breaths came hard. He did not have any kind of experience on this type of terrain. Each step was urgent and haphazard in the dim light. The sound of armor scraping on rock hit his ears. They were right behind him. Khet turned to fight. No one was there. The narrow passageway amplified the sound. He had another moment to think.

He placed his hands on either side of the path and pushed as much heat as he could into the wall. Khet hoped what Graven had told him was true. If there is water in the rock, it will explode. The only thing he could hope for at this point was a cave-in. The side to his left cracked and crumbled. Soon followed by the right. A deep vibration shook him as the rock started to move. Khet turned and ran. There was a flash of silver and gold as the walls of the path collapsed. Dust enveloped Khet. The sound of the collapse roared in his skull. Everything was black with thick dust. It made it difficult to breathe. Khet covered his mouth with his shirt and pushed forward as quickly as he could.

28

The thunder of the collapse subsided quickly. Khet paused in his retreat. It was quiet, not a sound of the Dodecahedron in pursuit. Khet held fast and waited for the dust to settle. He was lucky that he hadn't hurt himself more as he escaped the collapse. The only thing he could do for now was sit and wait for the dust to clear. There were no sounds of further pursuit.

It was eerie in the dark. A light wind would push the dust around as it settled. The air had a cold bite to it. Khet pushed more heat into his body as he sat on the cold stone floor. *How could this happen again? Why did Kase do what she did? Am I to spend the rest of my life hunted by the Temple?* Thoughts swirled in his mind. One thought pushed its way to the surface. "What am I?" Deep within Khet something stirred. A voice reverberated within him. "Retribution." The voice answered.

The sound of metal on rock pulled his attention away. Khet jumped to his feet, ready to fight. Most of the dust had already settled, and Khet could clearly make out an immortal halfway buried in the rubble. Once it noticed Khet, it thrashed violently, not in anger but fear. The trapped warrior screeched as it attempted to flee from Khet.

Khet cautiously drew closer. One arm was missing, and the other was trapped. It could do no harm. "What are you?" Khet spoke to the armored warrior. It just thrashed like a wounded animal caught in a trap. The sound it made was like a muffled shriek. Khet could feel the fear coming off of the warrior. He relished it. An immortal warrior that everyone knew to fear was afraid of him. A smile spread across his face. The smile was full of menace and did not feel like his own.

Now more at ease with his situation, Khet noticed a faint glow near his feet, half-buried. He made quick work of the rocks and dirt. A soft, glowing sword, the immortal's sword, shone brightly in the dim light. He lifted it out of the rubble to inspect it. The trapped warrior thrashed harder and harder. "Dropped something?" Khet toyed with the warrior. It feared him; he didn't have to fear it. The sword had strange runes that covered the blade. The stories Khet grew up with told him that the Dodecahedron's swords carried the fury of the Twelve. The runes on the blade and hilt were not of the Twelve. They were different. Khet could feel a connection to them. The power the sword called to him in a way that made Khet nervous.

The rubble shifted. With no hesitation, Khet brought the sword down on the immortal's head. The blade split the head into two as the body went limp. Khet stared at the insides of the creature. There was no blood or bone. No exposed flesh. A strange metallic sponge made up the immortal's head. There was no body inside the armor, just the almost honeycombed metal. He reached out to touch it. "Just what are you?" The metal had no give, just a rough cut edge. "How are you alive?" The eyes of the creature were a dull, metal grey. The skin of its face still looked like a person's skin. It even had the give of flesh as Khet prodded it.

More rocks shifted, sending a fresh cascade of dust. Khet sprang backwards and watched as the rocks covered the warrior. He decided it was time to get away from the area and make way for the other side of the Spine.

Now not in a rush, Khet made his way through the narrow path. Every couple of minutes, he would pause to see if there was anyone or anything that followed him. He stopped briefly to wrap the sword in a spare shirt and strap it to his back. Somebody at the University would probably want to study it.

All he had to do was stay on the path; that is what Abner told him. He had their badges packed tightly in his pack. There was a mission now that he must complete. The University must know what happened to his friends. He must find this Creshing. They had to know that the immortals can be killed.

29

It was over a day's hike through that narrow mountain path before Khet tasted the open air. The moment Khet was free of it, he was blinded by the patches of white snow. Khet had never seen snow up close before, and now it was everywhere. Nothing but ice and snow-covered rocks awaited him. The massive rocky peaks dominated the skyline. Jagged like horns down a dragon's back. The smaller mountains, that were in no way small, surrounded the peaks. The scale of it all was hard for Khet to take in. The air itself had a dry bite to it. That would make him cough if he tried to breathe too deeply.

A small cave was not too far from the opening. Exhaustion came on to Khet quickly now that the hope of rest was in sight. Between the hunger and the need for some rest, he trudged on down the path to the cave.

The trail was not narrow nor was it comfortably wide. On the right, it was a mountain. On the left, there was a steep drop-off. Not the type that would kill you, but it would take hours to climb back up from the bottom. The wind would bite at his exposed skin. With each gust, Khet surged more heat into his body to try and dull the cold's teeth.

By the time he made it to the cave, he could barely stand; he was so weak. He made a quick survey of the cave and promptly dropped his bag and fell asleep.

Khet awoke later, half frozen to death. He pulled on his power to warm his body. He had a problem when it was this cold. He wasn't able to use his fire to keep him warm while he slept. Abner said, "Don't make any fires." What was he going to do? He needed to sleep. After not coming up with anything, he decided he would eat a little first and check more of the cave.

Now that he was a little rested and fed, Khet could see that the cave was more spacious than he would have thought it would be. Inside, there were signs that small cooking fires were made. Whoever made those fires must have carried the wood up here with them. There were no trees or anything burnable within the valley. Luckily for Khet, he didn't need a fire; he could make his own. He moved around the cave and found a couple of large stones that were blackened by fire. Behind a larger rock, there was a small, neatly stacked pile of wood. Somebody must have come up here a lot to leave a pile of wood; maybe it was the guy Graven spoke of. Khet didn't want to think about it, but he had to deal with it. They were all dead, and he couldn't have done anything to stop it.

He brought out the small cooking pot from his bag and filled it with snow to melt down and refill his water skins. Khet wrestled with his thoughts. Every person he had ever cared about was dead. It wasn't the thought of them dead that bothered him. It bothered him that he didn't feel anything about it now. Khet tried to feel something about their deaths, but that well was dry. *Am I broken? Or just numb to it?* Either way, Khet needed to eat more and prepare for the rest of the path through the mountains. Maybe later, after he is done with all of this, he will grieve them, but not now.

Khet heated the pot to get the snow to melt and pulled out his bag of rations. Nibbling on a piece of hard sausage, he noticed writing on the wall.

"Hello friend, there is a stack of wood and a cooking pot in the back of the cave. Also, I have three large stones you can heat to help keep you warm while you sleep. Help yourself to it. You have about a day's walk to the west side of the mountains or about thirteen days going east. Sincerely, Luke." So that must be the guy Graven talked about. What a weird thing for a person to do. Khet didn't understand this person's kindness. To be this kind to someone you could possibly never meet, that is a rare thing indeed.

Maybe inspired by the stranger's kindness, Khet grabbed a piece of charcoal and wrote his own message below. "Turn back passage at the west end blocked by cave-in. Khet." As he said the words, Khet did feel a little guilty that a person would make it this far just to find out that the path is blocked. It gave him an idea. Khet went to the back of the cave and dug through the pile of sticks and grabbed the thickest one. He used his power to blacken one end. Khet would use the stick to make warnings for travelers to turn back. A simple gesture but something that could save somebody a lot of hurt or even their life. Feeling better about his situation, Khet decided to rest a while. He took a couple of the larger rocks from the back of the cave and slowly warmed them. This would keep him warm while he slept.

When he woke later, Khet was decidedly warmer than he was last time. He took the stone and placed them back where he had found them. And made his way out of the cave.

The path didn't change too much throughout the morning, winding up and down the sides of a couple of mountains. Only ever traveling a quarter of the way up. The biting wind was always a constant companion. The mountains of Dragon's Spine still loomed in the distance. With every step, it seemed as if the mountains never came any closer, just grew in size.

Halfway through the day, Khet came across a small outcropping of rock with a message written on it. "Perfect place to rest and warm up. If heading west, easy trail ahead. If heading east, trail becomes steep with loose rock. Be sure to rest a little. Your legs will thank you. Sincerely, Luke."

Khet did as Luke suggested and had a seat. It was a spot that wind did not touch. The seat was perfectly situated out of the wind. He sat there and relaxed a little and let the heat in his body settle down. The view was amazing as well. Three separate mountains formed a valley. At the very bottom was a large lake completely frozen over. The beauty of it gave Khet a little joy.

The next half of the day lived true to Luke's message. Steep uphill with loose gravel. It seemed like every two steps he would gain. He then would slide three steps back. A constant battle that took him a couple of hours to win.

At the top of the last treacherous inclines, out of breath with his legs burning, Khet was greeted by another message. "Heading west, be careful you can easily lose your footing. Heading east, way to go! Pretty easy for the rest of the day. Sincerely Luke."

"Thank you for the advice, Luke. Really helped with resting my legs back there." Khet caught himself after he responded. It was weird for him to be talking to the writings, but what the hell. He had twelve more days to the other side of the trail and nobody to talk to, except for

Luke of course.

Khet pulled out his charred stick and wrote his warning. "West path is blocked due to cave-in. Turn around. Khet."

During the next couple of hours, the trail indeed was easy. Fast clouds from the east began to fill the valley below. The clouds grew thicker and thicker until they completely swallowed the trail. Obscuring everything except for maybe two feet ahead. Khet had to slow his pace. The left side of the trail was a steep drop-off to a grey void.

Step by step, he pushed on. His own footsteps were muffled in the fog. The rumble was low and muffled when Khet heard it. He feared a landslide, so he paused and listened. It came on again, this time there was a muted flash. A storm was headed his way. More flashes, and the thunder rang through the valley. Khet pushed ahead; he needed to find cover before the storm was on him.

The louder the storm became, the faster he moved. Almost reckless in his movements down the rock-strewn path. First, the wind began to pick up and pushed the fog away. As it cleared, Khet saw a message written on the wall. "Cave just ahead, you did it! Be careful, steep downhill can be slippery in the rain. Your friend Luke."

A blinding flash and the very air exploded in front of him. The spray of rock threw Khet to the ground. Disoriented, he lay there for a moment and waited for the afterimages to clear from his vision. "What was that?" As he sat up, it was plain to see. Part of a rocky outcrop smoldered. A lightning bolt had struck within an arm's length of Khet.

A fat droplet of water smacked him out of his moment of awe. Then another and another hit him. Urgency filled him; he needed to get to shelter. Khet moved as swiftly as he could as the rain came pounding down. It was dark and getting darker. Bright flashes of light would leave Khet momentarily blinded. He couldn't stop. He needed to find that cave.

Rain came down so hard Khet struggled to breathe. Mighty torrents of water fell off the mountain and threatened to wash Khet away. The slope of the trail now was steep and slick, as the water flowed down it.

The wind ripped at Khet's clothes. It threatened to send him tumbling. With every slip down the trail, his heart would seize in his chest. The constant battle with the wind and slick rocks punished Khet. His legs burned. His body wanted to run away. Away from the storm. Away from everything. He wanted the safety of Tarin's farmstead. He wanted to be home.

An explosion of rock and light sent him careening down the path. His world went upside down, and pain assaulted him as he slid. Dumbstruck, he flailed. Desperate, he tried to grab onto anything, but no firm purchase could be made. It was done; he would fall and be lost.

It ended almost as quickly as it began. The deluge of water engulfed him. He had slid to the bottom of the path. He was still on the path. Khet forced himself up. His world swayed, but he fought to keep himself upright. The wind pulled at him. A bright flash of lightning revealed the cave to be just feet ahead. Khet threw himself towards the opening.

Water filled the bottom of the cave, but there was a high spot in the back. Khet sloshed through the thigh-deep water to the dry rock. Khet collapsed. In the dark, he pulled off his pack and placed the sword next to him. His head hurt. His body ached everywhere, but at least he was out of the rain.

Khet poured heat into his body. It relaxed his aching muscles. He pushed more in to dry his clothes and to warm the rock he lay on. After being sufficiently dried, Khet let sleep take him as the storm raged on outside.

30

Khet opened his eyes. He was cold again, but he was alive. He rolled over to check his surroundings. Most of the water had left the cave except for a puddle or two. The bright sun shone on the beautiful mountainside. Hard to believe that just hours ago the outside tried to kill him.

Shakily, he sat up and tested himself for injuries. No major injuries were evident. Just small cuts and bruises covered his body. Maybe some bruised ribs on his right side. A hand-length cut down his right calf. It wasn't deep. Fucking lucky, he was.

"Let's not do that again." Khet said to himself as he stood. His boots squelched as he put weight on them. He wasn't about to let that ruin his day. Everything in his bag, minus the rations he kept in his dry bag, was soaked through.

Nothing could be done but to separate it all and dry it. He laid everything out on any dry spot he could find. A message on the wall drew his attention from his work. "Careful, the cave can flood. Sleep in the back on the raised stone. Storms in the area can come on strong and fast. Two more days if you are going west. Going east, you got at least 10 days. A hard two days of hiking are coming up. So be ready. Your friend, Luke."

"I wish you had said something about the storms before I came into this valley." Khet hung his head for a moment. He knew it wasn't Luke's fault. "I am sorry. I know you couldn't have done anything...

and I am talking to nobody." Khet's face reddened from embarrassment.

With everything laid out, he pushed heat out of his hand. Slowly, he drew his hand over his gear. He took great care not to burn or singe anything. The process was slow, but Khet would fare better on this hike if his gear was dry.

With all his gear dry, he repacked everything. Not as well as he should have, but it worked all the same. The pack now didn't feel as comfortable as it did before. Khet shifted his shoulders a lot after he put it on. The odd lumps that pushed into his back will just have to be something he needs to deal with today. He needed to be out of the valley before another storm came in.

He made sure to write his warning underneath Luke's message. "Turn Back, West Path Closed. Khet."

There was a chill in the air back on the trail. Khet kept a weary eye out for any clouds that might threaten a storm, but the sky was crystal clear. Minus the small clouds that lingered on the peaks of the large mountains of the Spine.

The ground and air were scrubbed free of dust in a way that only a hard rain could do. Small little ravines were formed from the hard rain, now just laid empty and damp. Khet's sore feet welcomed the softer ground.

So far this morning, Khet had not really come across any rough hiking conditions. Just some rolling ups and downs. The only part that made his breath hard was the switchback trail out of the valley.

The view at the rim of the next valley floored Khet. A vibrant bowl of green moss surrounded by sheer cliffs on all sides except for the entrance and the exit. Which Khet could see clearly. "Luke, you said this would be hard." Even to Khet's own ears, that sounded smug.

A glance to his right on one of the flat walls. " Good Luck! Or Way To Go!" Khet ignored the message and set off down the path.

Three strides into the vibrant bowl of green, Khet sank to just above the knee in sticky mud. It was cold and slimy. The mud stuck to everything. The smell was the worst of it. With each hard-fought step, the mud would belch a rotten odor. This wasn't normal mud like from his home. This was years upon years of dead, rotting plants.

Each time Khet would wrench his leg free to take a step. The mud would threaten to take his boots. Just then, to press it back down into the pile of squelching decay.

The smell of the rot was made worse by Khet. As he pushed heat into his legs to keep them from freezing in the icy mud, it would warm the rot and make the smell even worse. He had never heard of anything like this in any of his stories. Fuck, he wanted to be home.

The weight of it all bore down on him. Every step made him want to just lay down and quit. Let the rot have him. Every breath burned in his lungs. He must be almost to the end of this hell.

"Fuck!" His voice echoed off the walls. He was only a little past a quarter of the way out. He broke down and sobbed to himself in the stench for several minutes.

It was one of those moments that he needed to have. He screamed and howled his frustration and pain. He let it all out for no one to hear except for the cold mountains, not judging and not caring.

He cleared his eyes after he'd had his moment. He had to think. "How did you get through this, Luke? Graven said you were weird, not part mountain goat." Scanning the valley, Khet saw it plain as day on the shadowed wall. "Stay in the shade. The ground is frozen." He read it out loud.

Hope lit a fire in his heart. Khet threw himself towards the shadow of the cliff. His heart hammered and lungs burned, but there would be an end to this hell. Sweat made his clothes stick to his chest.

Now each step closer was more solid. Khet stepped up out of the mud onto hard, frozen ground. His laughter echoed through the valley. Collapsed on the hard ground, Khet felt relieved. "Not dying today." He chuckled.

The mud and stench still held fast to Khet, but at least now he could stand. The solid moss-covered ground was still slick to walk on. Not to mention all the rotten mud that still clung to Khet. Progress was still slow but much easier.

Two or three times, Khet tumbled and almost ended back in the thigh-deep mud before he made it to the other end of the valley. A small victory, but it was still a victory.

On the other side, Khet was greeted with a message from Luke. "Way To Go or Good Luck." And a note on the side that stated, "Stick to the shadow; the ground is firm there." Khet looked across the valley and could almost make out the same phrase on the other side. Maybe next time, he will pay more attention.

31

Khet walked on with all the mud that clung to him. The extra weight made every movement of his legs more difficult. The sound of flowing water lightened his mood a little. A chance to clean all the rot and stink gave him a small amount of joy in a day he needed more joy.

The water flow wasn't a great flowing river but enough for Khet to clean himself. Khet stripped completely. And stepped into the small waterfall. The water was ice but Khet just pulled more heat into his body. The whole thing reminded him of the times he washed in the warm rain storms back home, minus the warmth.

It took some time to get all the mud off of his clothes. The cold of the water just made the mud stick more. After a time he gave in to the frustration and decided to just put on his spare pants and strap the dirty ones to the outside of his pack to clean them later.

Khet inspected for any more injuries that he might have gotten from the hike through the rot. No new injuries but the cut on his leg looked awfully red and puffy. He would have to keep an eye on it.

Fully dressed and only partially refreshed he walked on down the path. The large mountains of the Spine were much closer now. The heights they reached boggled Khet's mind. He hadn't seen the Wall for days. It was foreign to him to not see it. It was always a constant companion, that he now missed the sight of.

The small cave was a welcomed sight. The amount of exertion Khet put in at the muddy valley left him drained. His movements were weak and sluggish. He needed food and rest. First he had to melt more snow for water. The process did not take long but in Khet's state everything was an effort. With full water skins Khet did a quick survey of the cave to see if Luke had left any warnings or supplies. The only thing in the cave was a positive message from Luke and a mention of a better cave not much farther up. Khet was too tired and didn't care.

He ate a couple of bits of hard cheese and some dried sausage and fell asleep. A deep and dreamless sleep.

Searing pain peeled Khet's eyes open. His leg with the large cut on it pulsed. He pulled up his pant leg to reveal a greenish purplish gash that was oozing a thick, sickly yellow puss.

"No, no, no, no." Khet knew what this meant. The leg was infected, badly. Dark veins could be seen under his skin all up and down his leg. His foot was a dead purple. The infection had spread far and fast. Stories played in his head about people removing arms or legs to keep infections from spreading, if there was no Grun nearby to heal them.

Khet didn't have anything. He couldn't remove his own leg. Desperately, he tried to come up with a plan. There was no way out of this that he could see. There were no messages from a friendly stranger that would help. He was alone in the mountains, and nobody left alive knew he was here.

The only chance he had was to keep going, and maybe he would either find someone or make it out of the mountains. He had to try.

"Agh, Fuck!" The pain in his leg was too much. Any weight or movement on his leg made him dizzy and nauseous. His clothes were soaked with sweat. His skin was hot and sensitive to touch. Everything that touched made his skin burn.

In an act of desperation, he called out to Magnus. He had helped him that time in the creek, maybe he would help him here.

32

"What did you do?" A voice boomed.

"Ahg... You're out of control."

"This is the only way!"

"Your thirst for power has blinded you!"

Khet's eyes flew open; the shock of it all made him stagger. Blurry figures stood to his left. A golden figure shouted at a blue figure. He tried to rub the blurriness from his eyes. The hands were dark, almost black, that rubbed his eyes. His vision became clear.

The room was dark. Torches lined the wall of the massive room, but there was very little light given off by them. Magnus stood in his full, blazing armor, like the sun in human form. "Weak words from a weak mind!" He struck the woman in blue.

"You will fail, you always do!" It was Arrinia. Two massive golden spikes pinned her shoulders to the wall. Dark blood oozed down her suspended body.

"Norona said the same, and where is she now? She served her purpose, and so have you. So why don't you join her?" Magnus raised his hand toward Arrinia. A golden spike matching the two in her shoulders flew from his open hand into Arrinia's screaming mouth. The spike crunched against the wall. A wet, gurgling noise that came from Arrinia as her life left her made Khet feel faint.

"What is going on?" Khet said the words, but the voice was not his. It was deeper, more ancient.

Magnus spun. "You dare question me, Calver…" His eye lit up like he had just noticed something. "Khet is that you? Why are you here?"

Khet collapsed to the floor. "I need help. I am dying. My leg is infected. Help." The voice was weak. Khet could feel himself slipping.

"Rafir, give him your power!" Magnus pointed to someone in the darkness.

"But Sire, if I do that, I won't have anything." Rafir came out of the shadow. He looked every bit as pathetic in his green garb as he sounded.

"Khet is the one that will free us from this prison, so I can get my revenge. Do as I say or join the others." Magnus's words dripped venom. There was a finality to them that turned Khet's blood cold.

"Yes… Sire." Rafir knelt next to Khet. Rafir pressed his hand deeply into Khet's shoulder. "You better not fail us, you little shit." Rafir whispered into Khet's ear. "I have helped save your pathetic life in the past. Now I have to relinquish it all. If you fail us, I will personally flay your skin from your body."

Sensations flooded through Khet. A mixture of warm and cold filled every limb. It filled every nook and cranny of his body. It was intense; every part of his body felt renewed and refreshed. It was gone quicker than it had arrived. Khet opened his eyes again; he was back in the cave.

There was no pain. He was cold from lying on the cold cave floor. "OK, I am alive." Khet checked his legs. The infection was gone; in fact, there was no sign of the cut either. All of his scrapes and bruises were completely gone. His body was stiff from the ground, but everything else was fine.

He tested his limbs as he walked around the small cave. No discomfort of any kind bothered him. Minus the scene he just witnessed, that bothered him. *Could it have been the fever? Maybe a state of delirium.* Khet heard about people who could go crazy if their fever got too high. *All of his wounds were healed, though.*

He will just have to accept the mystery for now. His mission was to make it to the University; failure was not an option. Before he left, he made sure to write his warning under Luke's message.

The trail went as rough as Luke said it would be, pretty rough. Nothing like the rotten pit of green death he crawled through a day ago. This was a lot of steep and narrow passages. It wasn't all that strenuous for a refreshed Khet. The switchbacks were monotonous and slippery. Other parts were covered by rock slides, which forced Khet to do some tricky climbing.

The snow cover did get thicker and started to cover parts of the trail as he came closer to one of the large mountains. The crisp air bit at Khet's throat if he breathed too deeply. But the sky was crystal blue without a cloud in sight.

Khet marveled at the large mountain. When he first saw it days ago, it looked smooth and wind-worn. Now, as he has moved closer day by day, he could make out all the cracks and boulders. The mess of it looked like a child piled massive grey play blocks in a jumble. Not smooth in the slightest until you get three-quarters away from the top. That is where the Dragon's Spine gets its name. Sheer rock, the color of ancient bone, rose from the grey rock to a point far above. In the sunlight, there was a soft reflection off of it. It was unlike any of the rock that surrounded it. As if a giant beast had fallen there, or as the legend states, fell asleep guarding Vulcan's Tower. As Khet stood this close to the out-of-place rock, he could almost believe the legend.

Another cave appeared on the trail ahead. Khet's stomach gave a low rumble at the thought of a break and food.

The cave entrance was quite small compared to the inside. As usual, there was a message from Luke on the wall of the cave. "Good job. It was a rough hike coming from either direction. If you are hungry, I have a storage of dried food in the back on the raised shelf. Enjoy, but please leave a little for the next person. Your friend, Luke."

His stomach growled hard at the thought of something else than hard tack, sausage, and cheese to eat. He made his way to the back, hope filled his chest. Luke had not let him down yet.

In the back was a large bag stuffed full with food. Khet sifted through the contents. A bunch of dried beef and pork packed in a bag of salt. Over half the bag was rice. Khet's mouth watered, and his stomach let out a growl that probably echoed through the mountains.

He had never made rice himself, but he had seen Kase do it a time or two. Rice was rare on the western side of the Spine. From his best recollection, he washed the rice and added water to his first knuckle in the cooking pot. As the rice cooked, he placed some pieces of the beef and pork. The smell was beyond belief.

Every bite filled Khet with warmth that only a hot meal could. He scraped the pot thoroughly and leaned against the cave wall. His belly was full, almost too full. "Thank you, Luke. That was delicious."

Tired was in his bones now. He gathered some of the charred stones and warmed them up. Khet placed them in his clothes and under his legs. Sleep took him fast.

33

The sky was bright with small wisps of clouds the next morning. The gravel crunched underfoot as Khet made good progress down the trail. A stiff, chilling breeze blew heavily into his face. It didn't bother him at all. The feeling of being well-fed and the weight of the extra serving of rice and salted meats in his bag improved the mood.

It was a steady downhill section of trail. From the angle of the descent and the distance to the larger mountain of the Spine, it seemed like Khet would be at its base soon.

Before him appeared a massive frozen lake. It was a large lake hidden away amongst the mountains. It was so secluded away from the rest of the world that Khet wondered how many people had seen it or even knew of its existence. The ice was blueish-grey with striations of white. No snow was left on the lake save for the northern shore. There it was piled quite deep.

At the frozen shoreline sat a large boulder with a message on it. "The ice is safe, just watch your step. Trail is easily seen on the eastern shore as you get closer. Your friend, Luke."

Khet made good effort to see if there was another message off to the side. "OK, Luke, if there is nothing else." He paused for a moment as if he waited for Luke's response. None came, so he pushed on.

The ice had a rougher surface than Khet could see from the shoreline. Large rocks sat in bowl-shaped holes. The wind had carved deep ripples in the ice. Giving the look of a wave frozen in place. It was an odd sight out on the thick ice.

The large mountain loomed high overhead. Khet had to crane his neck to see the top. Memories of monstrous dragons tickled his thoughts. Travelers would share tales about them while visiting Tarin's homestead. The dragons they spoke of were nothing compared to the creature that left these.

The eastern shoreline and the continuation of the trail were in sight now. Khet picked up his pace. He knew the ice was solid, but he felt vulnerable out there exposed.

The first steps on solid ground were a relief. Another boulder met him on the other side with the same message that was written on the opposite shore. He glanced back across the ice and thought for a moment. He had come so far. Never had he dreamt of this being his life. Is the adventure he wanted? Yes, but not in this manner. Khet wrote his warning with the weight of the world heavy on his shoulders.

With thoughts darkly clouded, he carried on. The path wound its way around the base of the giant mountain. It just kept going. Just a gradual curve that went on forever. Khet's stomach growled, and his feet ached as the next cave came into sight. It wasn't so much a cave but more of an overhang that cut into the mountainside.

"This is the halfway point, congratulations!! If you are headed east, you have an easy 6-7 day walk. If you are heading west, get ready, it will be a difficult 6-7 day hike. But you can do it. Your friend Luke."

"I hope when I get out of here, I can meet you, Luke. Shake your hand and thank you for the help." Khet pulled out his burnt stick and wrote his warning to turn people around.

Inspiration came to Khet. He wrote,"This is for the people that were family that I have lost along the way. Let them be remembered for the good that they have done to save my life.

Tarin

Kase

Ty

Abner

Raine

Trip

Grim

Graven

These were my family and friends. I miss them dearly. Khet"

Tears stung his eyes. Kase might not have belonged up there on the wall, but there was a time when she was a lovely person. She loved her husband and her adopted children. It was Khet's actions that made her react the way she did, and it broke her mind. At the end, she wasn't the same person. That is how he wanted to remember her.

A somber weight lay on Khet while he rested. He missed them right now. He wondered what Ty would think of all this. He missed Ty.

34

The next several days passed by with little trouble. The sky stayed clear, and the trail was mostly level. The scenery after the large mountain was mainly smaller mountain after smaller mountain. Some were partially covered in snow, while others lay bare and jagged.

Throughout it all, there were messages from Luke. Attempts at humor and general encouragement. The man must have been bored as Khet when he hiked these valleys. Every message and every joke gave Khet the motivation to push just a little harder.

He tested himself with the power Rafir had given him. Cuts and scraps would take time to heal, but they would heal. His stamina was easily refreshed. Khet, ever fearful about an addiction to it, used it sparingly.

Khet was lonely at this point. It had been, by Khet's calculations, thirteen days without talking to another person. Only the interaction with messages written on walls and long diatribes to himself to make sure his voice worked.

On the fourteenth day of hiking the mountain trail, Khet came around the last mountain. The air was clear and crisp on his skin. The sight of the plains made Khet grin from ear to ear. Looking to the southeast, Khet could barely make out the shimmer of Lake Saphos. Saphosi's Tower and the eternal waterfall were too far away to make out. By his judgment, he was maybe a day's hike to the plains at the base of the mountain.

Khet was not surprised when he found the next cave. A message from Luke read, "Good job! That was a hell of a hill to climb. Or only a day's hike left. Rest your legs here for a while; it is steep all the way down until the last bit." Khet pulled out his charred stick, now just a nub, and wrote his warning. Sad to think this was the last one. Eager to finally be free of the mountains, but sad for its end.

He ate a little bit of his rations and melted some snow to fill up his water skins. The same routine he had done for the past fourteen days. He felt a lot better today than he had felt in a long time. Excitement for the change in scenery made him want to forgo resting, but he knew it was a bad idea.

After he rested for several hours, he decided to take off down the mountain. Khet was glad he listened to his new friend, Luke's, advice. The hill was steep. He breathed   heavily with effort. The muscles in his thighs burned. The excitement to have this lonely leg of the journey complete pushed him hard.

The trail became a narrow path with high walls. Each step echoed as he made his way down the path. Once the trail leveled out, Khet nearly sprinted to be free. The final stretch, daylight at the end of the long hike, appeared around the corner. Halfway up the trail was a figure sitting on a chair next to a small grave. The figure stood strong and leveled a spear at Khet. The tip of the spear a very short distance from Khet's throat. To close for Khet's liking.

"I mean you no harm. I am just passing through." Khet put his hands up. "My name is Khet. I am just passing through." His breath made a puff of steam around his face.

The woman stood there in her leather armor. Her eyes studied every inch of Khet. He started to feel nervous. She was obviously capable of defending herself. The confidence in which she held the spear, she had been trained. Her dark skin made her look even more fierce in the low-lit area of the pass. "She said you would be coming out of the pass today." Her shoulders relaxed, and so did the spear.

"Who said I would be coming out of the pass?" A slight mixture of fear and apprehension stirred his guts.

"A woman, I don't know her name. She was good friends with my mother and father." She never fully relaxed. Khet could sense her tensed muscles.

"How?" Khet dropped his hands, and the spear came back as a warning. "Sorry, I mean no harm. I am just tired from the hike. Do you by chance know a man named Luke?"

Her shoulders dropped slightly. "Yes, he is my father. I guess you saw his messages." The woman lowered the spear tip fully. She seemed to relax more.

"Your father is Luke?"

"Yes, he is."

"His messages possibly saved my life. I am grateful for the supplies as well."

The woman chuckled a little. "He told us about those all the time. None of us in the family ever saw all of them. We made it up the first hill and then said that was enough. Oh, I am sorry, my name is Ayla."

Khet understood the pain of that hill. "Where is your father? I would like to shake his hand. The messages he left helped a lot. The jokes were not funny, but they still made me laugh."

Ayla's shoulder slumped a bit. "He is right here." Pointing at the small grave marker. "He died about a year ago. He would be happy to hear that his messages did you some good. He always did love that trail. We always thought he was a little crazy, but he loved it."

"I am sorry to hear that."

"It is okay. My family and I are at peace with it. Are you the one the Temple is looking for?"

"Er…" A slight fear tickled his spine.

"It is okay. We are not friends of the Temple. If it weren't for my family, I would introduce every acolyte I could find to the tip of my spear." A deep anger burned in her eyes.

"Why?"

A tear ran down Ayla's cheek. "They are the reason my father is dead. They killed him because he stopped a Temple acolyte from beating a contracted child to death." She sobbed at the pain of the memory. "We didn't even know what was going on. My father came home with a look on his face. He gave us all hugs and said he was proud of us. He kissed my mother and left. Days later, we found him hanging near Balin's Bridge. An Acolyte stood there proclaiming his guilt. They wouldn't let us near his body. We don't know what happened to his remains. We couldn't bury him, so we made this grave marker in a place he loved."

The silence was deep. Khet couldn't force himself to form a word. Anger and rage stirred within him.

She regained her composure. "Are you a part of the

Arankai? Are you going to destroy the Temple like they are saying?"

"I am sorry, I don't know. I don't know what the hell anybody wants from me. All I know is that I have to deliver these badges to the University, and the Temple wants me dead."

"Alright, that sounds pretty shitty, sorry for asking. The woman wanted me to give you this bag. It has supplies and a change of clothes. I guess so you wouldn't look so southern."

"How did she know I was coming through here today? And southern?"

"I told you she is a friend of my mother and father, don't know her name, and I don't know how she knew. And yes, you look like a farm boy from west of the Spine. Am I wrong?"

"Well, you're right. I did grow up on a farmstead."

"OK, well, I have to get going. I have chores to do." Ayla locked eyes with Khet. "Promise me, if you are Arankai, I want you to burn the Temple down."

Khet swallowed hard at the intensity in Ayla's eyes. The rage within him grew hotter. "I will." And another log was added to the pyre that will burn the Temple to the ground.

She nodded and left Khet alone on the path.

35

With the weight of Luke's fate burning in his gut, Khet changed his clothes and pushed on ahead. He had to see the end of this.

The world on this side of Dragon's Spine was like a dream. Colors and smells that were completely foreign to Khet assaulted his senses. In the south, there were rolling hills of green with small dots of flowers here and there. On the east side of the Spine, the colors were so vibrant, that it hurt to look at.

His head was on a swivel as he made his way down the small path to the main road. Flowers of every color bloomed on either side. Fields of vibrant green were everywhere in sight. Row upon row of vegetables were ready for harvest by farmers.

Carts lined the field as they awaited the day's harvest. Bored drivers dozed in the soft sunlight. The blue of the sky was softer. Clouds lazed about in small clumps. The air had an earthy sweetness to it that made Khet's mouth water. He really was a bumpkin from the south. The mountainous path was more like his home than this.

The main road was wide. A lane made of stones big enough for three carts was at its center. With hard packed dirt lanes half as wide on either side. Carts moved with ease. The heavy carts loaded with goods stayed on the stone road. While the lighter, empty carts kept to the outside.

Khet stayed as far as he could to the side, out of everybody's way. Not trying to draw attention to himself.

"Not from around here are you?" A kind old farmer called to Khet from the back of a cart. His face was full of grandfatherly warmth.

"No… That's obvious."

"Pretty much. Just stay to the sides as far as possible. Those carts will run you over if you're not careful. Where are you headed?"

"I am going to the University. Do you happen to know the way? I am pretty lost."

The old man gave a warm chuckle, like he had had this conversation before. "The University, eh? Just keep heading toward the Wall. There will be a turn to the left, a big turn you can't miss. That will lead you to Balin's Bridge. Then just follow the signs. A couple of weeks, maybe, depending on if you dawdle or not."

"Thank you." Half embarrassed, half still overwhelmed by it all, Khet moved on.

"Be careful, son. The Temple is wondering about something has them buzzing about like somebody kicked their hive."

"Thank you. I will."

It was difficult for Khet to maintain focus on where he walked. Everything was new, and he wanted to drink it in. All the people wore bright colors. Very few faces seemed to be angry or sad. Just people living their lives. Nothing back home could have compared to this. The road to the City of El was wide back home, but never this busy.

Khet forced himself to just keep his eyes focused on the road ahead and kept walking. All the hustle and bustle swallowed his presence.

The crowded road thinned out to nothing after Khet found himself away from the fields. A thin forest surrounded him now. Even the forest was vibrant and colorful. The trees looked so alive. Maybe it was the influence of the Tower of Grunaive and the waters of Sophis making everything so vibrant. Khet heard that the God Shards would affect its surroundings, but he never thought it would be like this.

His attention was drawn to the distance ahead. A large group of people marched down the road. They were not dressed in the same vibrant colors of everyone else he had seen. No, this was a dull grey mass. Lifeless in its shape and color.

By the time Khet could understand what he was looking at, it was too late for him to hide. It was a group of about one hundred contracted in two columns, shuffled along. Guards, in their mixture of plate and chainlink armor, were on either side of the group. A Temple Acolyte dressed in his robes of the Twelve stood upon a cart in the back of the convoy.

The contracted's faces were dirty and dour. All the color of life just drained from them. Khet's heart yearned to help them. He couldn't risk a confrontation with the Temple. He was alone in a strange place.

Crack! A contracted man cried out in pain. "No time for rest! We are already late!" The acolyte driving the convoy bellowed, a whip held aloft as a sign of power. Crack! Rage surged through Khet as if a bolt of lightning had struck him. "Our grand leader, his Eminence the Eye of the Twelve, will not be pleased if we do not arrive on time." Crack! The whip struck another contracted. The sound of their cry stabbed at Khet's heart.

Khet strained to control the rage burning in his heart. The rage burned in his blood. All the evil he had heard about the Temple was on display before him. Crack! Another cry. No remorse could be seen on the acolyte's face. Just a cold face of stone. For all the punishment, the contracted did not move any faster. They just shuffled along at the same speed. Crack! The man split the scalp of a contracted right next to Khet. The contract screamed and fell to the ground.

Khet dove to catch her. He stared murderous intent at the man with the whip.

"That is Temple property. Back away, you filth!" The acolyte wore a mask of anger.

Khet ignored the man and helped the woman to her feet. Crack! Pain exploded on his shoulder. Khet flailed backwards from the impact.

"Do you dare defy a sworn acolyte of the Temple of the Twelve?" Khet's hood had fallen back, leaving his runes exposed for all to see. The mask of anger turned to shock, then a vile smirk took over his features. "You have the runes of an Arankai. You dare attack members of the Temple! You filth! Your kind will not win! Guards! Kill him! Kill the Arankai!"

Rage flared inside Khet. His blood boiled in his ears. Everything seemed distant, detached from himself. His body just reacted without Khet's bidding. Two golden threads shot from his arms and anchored themselves around the cart. Khet used them to launch himself towards the acolyte. The acolyte's face, that was once full of pompous indignation, was now full of shock and terror as Khet's knee drove into his nose with a sickening crunch. Both of them tumbled off the side of the cart. The contracted just stood there with faces that were a mixture of confusion and fear.

Khet managed to regain his feet quickly while the acolyte

whimpered as blood poured from his nose. Three guards fumbled with their weapons, not the least bit ready for what had just happened. Khet seized the opportunity and sent two threads around a guard on either side and launched himself at the middle one. It didn't work as planned, though. The two guards he anchored to stumbled, and this sent Khet tumbling into all three.

It was a twisted pile of limbs as every man grunted and screamed as they tried to free themselves. Icy hot pain seared down Khet's thigh as one of the guards swiped at him in the tangle. Once freed from the mess of limbs, the guards quickly surrounded him. Khet was outnumbered by trained warriors. He couldn't just fight them. He had to think.

He slid on his gauntlets and let the rage slip its binding. Khet glowed with white-hot fury and threw himself at the guards. The guards panicked as Khet burned like a forge fire. They screamed as their armor became soft and their lungs were seared with every breath. It was over before they could react. The three guards were now just charred lumps with patches of soft glowing metal.

Three other guards witnessed the massacre and ran for safety. But there was no safety from Khet's rage that day. He reached out with his threads and launched himself at them. A fireball of rage and retribution. Their bodies were left just as the other three, smoldering piles of slag.

The acolyte with the whip crawled away in terror. The blaze was extinguished, now replaced by cold revenge. Khet stalked toward the cowering man. He reached out with his threads and pulled the man towards him.

The acolyte snarled at Khet. "You will not win. You filth! You fiend! You who was sent by the Outer Gods!"

"Free them." Khet gestured to the contracted.

"No, you evil scum—AGHH!" Khet drove his fist into the acolyte's gut. The acolyte heaved and struggled to regain his breath.

Khet lifted the acolyte by his collar. "I said free them." His voice was full of fury. A fury that would burn cities.

"Fine, this will not end the way you want it. You Arankai filth." The acolyte reached into his robes and produced a large stone covered in runes. "Die," he whispered to the stone.

Khet dropped him and stood in horror as all one hundred of the contracted soundlessly collapsed dead in the road.

The acolyte burst with sick laughter. "Their contracts were for life!

Now they are free! Way to go, hero!" He just kept laughing. "Go ahead and kill me; you still lost. You filth. You dark fiend, you will lose."

Cold fury burned inside Khet. "They were people."

"No, they were property. Bought by the Temple in accordance with the vows of Sidierion." The acolyte spat, a sneer still on his face.

Among the bodies of the contracted, Khet could make out the shape of young children. The horror of the slaughter detached him from his own actions. "I want you to listen to me." Khet was so close to the acolyte's ear that he whispered. "When they find you, and they will find you alive." His breath, his voice were full of hatred. "You tell them I will bring an end to all of this. I will bring the Temple down on their heads. I will burn it all to cinders." With a rough hand, Khet took the acolyte by the feet and severed the tendons on the backs of his ankles. The acolyte shrieked in pain. Now he will never walk again, and he will remember.

Khet retrieved his bag and made his way down the road. All the while, the acolyte whimpered in agony.

36

Once Khet could no longer hear the screams of the acolyte, the rage drained out of him. A hollowness replaced it. The colors of the world now subdued. His thoughts and actions reconnected. Panic filled his chest.

Now the Temple will know he is on this side of the Spine. Now they know what he looks like. "Fuck." He sprinted off to the left side of the road into the trees. Pain flared from the gashes in his thigh, neck, and shoulder.

He called on his healing power he took from Rafir. The pain subsided enough he could move faster, but the wounds were not quick to heal. He had to find some shelter quickly. He needed to slow down so his body could heal.

A dense grouping of trees was not far. He dashed to them. The trees hid a small clearing that opened to the river. On the shore, Khet could see Balin's Bridge. It was still a good way off, but it was in sight.

Still bleeding more than he would like, he rummaged through his pack to see what he could use. There were a small set of cloth bandages, but not a lot else for treating wounds. Khet didn't want to waste them, but a bleeding man can draw a lot of attention. He had to think. His healing ability was slow; he needed more time.

A solitary horn sounded from the direction where Khet left the acolyte. Someone must have found him. He was out of time to think. The opposite shoreline was only maybe twenty to thirty feet away.

Khet was confident he could swim that. But the weight of the sword, gauntlets, and his pack would weigh him down. Not to mention the current seemed strong enough to give him trouble.

No time to come up with a well-thought-out plan. Khet decided to keep it simple; he would just have to throw his stuff across. He was strong enough; it should be no problem at all. The gauntlets and the sword sailed across just fine. The pack landed short and splashed in the shallows of the river. Luckily, it was close enough to dry land that the current did not sweep it away.

The water sparkled as Khet waited in it. The clean, clear, coolness refreshed him. The current pulled at him. The pull of the water grew with each step deeper into the river. At about waist-deep, he plunged fully into the deep water. The current was too strong for him to fight, so he just angled himself to the opposite shore and pushed on. A pleasurable tingle washed over him. All the fatigue that had hounded Khet before just melted away, like it amplified his healing ability.

The opposite shoreline had no tree cover, so Khet grabbed his belongings and sought out shelter. More horns sounded in the distance. His wounds did not bother him in the slightest anymore. He glanced at the slice in his pant leg and could see that the cut was now just a pink scar. Could the water from Lake of Saphos have healed him? Another horn sounding pushed him on; this time, it was closer.

The only serviceable cover was on the southern side of the road. Only one or two travelers could be seen, so Khet slowed and tried to act naturally. The grassy field upon which he walked made him extremely exposed. As he was, he was a beacon for the Temple to follow.

Three steps onto the road, another horn blared, too close. Khet could see just on the other side of Balin's Bridge, Temple guards, too many for Khet to count. They covered the far side of the river. Khet had to fight every instinct to just bolt for the trees. His body shook with fear as he slowly slid into the cover of the forest.

Among the dense trees, Khet moved as fast as the terrain would allow him. Only stopping on occasion to drink water or listen for pursuit. The main danger of Khet's plan was the fact that he couldn't stay far from the road. He did not know this area, and he was told that the road led to the University. So he always kept it in sight.

The hours passed, and from time to time, Khet would have to dive into the brush as a Temple guard mount rode by or a patrol talked to travelers. At three different nerve-racking points, Khet had to cross clearings in the forest.

Exhausted from the stress and the strain of being on the run, Khet's body begged for rest. Either his healing power was at its limit or his mind was too exhausted to command it. He turned and traveled farther into the forest. Deep enough that he wouldn't be seen and anyone looking would be heard far out.

He found a tree that had a deep bowl at the base. The area was quiet, only the sound of the wind blowing through the trees could be heard. Light from the sun did not penetrate the dense canopy. Only small patches of sunlight reached the ground. This was a perfect spot to hide. He grabbed some fallen limbs and built up one side to give him some more cover. Satisfied, he collapsed and fell asleep instantly. Too tired to even set up his sleeping roll.

37

Dreams came to Khet while he slept. Not horrific dreams of armies or monsters. Not dreams about Magnus or the others. No, these dreams were about his life on Tarin's homestead. All the fun times he had laughing with Ty. The times Tarin would give him fatherly advice or try to make him laugh. Kase, being the great woman she was. The love of a mother he'd had never known.

The sound of a footstep brought him out of his dream. Another step, this one was closer. Khet froze; he barely dared to breathe. His body betrayed him once at the slaver camp. It was not going to happen again.

"Look, Khet, I was told that you would be out here today. The day is getting late, and I have other things to do." The woman's voice sounded not far off. Her footsteps grew closer. Khet's old friend, panic, made a home in his chest again. He moved to grab his gauntlets.

"There you are." A smiling face popped around the brush that Khet had piled up. Khet scrambled up and out of the bowl and prepared for a fight. The sight that greeted him, he was not ready for.

A small woman stood with her arms raised to show she was not armed. Her hair was a silky golden color tied into a long single braid. Her clothes were as bright and vibrant as the farmers he saw when he first came through the mountain path. Everything from her posture to her smile proved that she meant no harm but was capable of it. "Hi Khet, she was right; you are handsome. My name is Clair, and I am here to show you to the cave."

"Who told you I was here? And what cave?" His body remained ready to fight, Rule 1.

"OK, OK, first, I don't know who she was. But I do know she is important enough that my boss took me off of what I was doing to find you. Second, the cave that will lead you to the City of Passes. There is a pub called The Restless Crow. People will be waiting there to get you to the University. You must be pretty important. My boss's services don't come cheap." She had a smile that made Khet uneasy. How relaxed she was did not fit in with the situation.

"And who is your boss?" Khet wanted answers. His bones were getting weary of all the mystery bullshit.

"Best to not ask questions that I will have to lie to, okay. All I can say is that she is a serious person that does serious things." She leaned against a tree so casually, but underneath it all Khet could feel it was a lie.

"Finding me and getting me to this cave, is a serious thing then?"

"Must be. We had spent the better part of yesterday leading the Temple away from you. So you're welcome for that."

"Thank you, I guess."

"You're welcome. Now follow me. It is a short walk to the entrance. There are some funny-looking stones that surround the entrance. They will make you feel like running, but once you're on the other side it clears up pretty fast." Clair turned and walked deeper into the forest. "Don't just stand there, come on."

His body just reacted to her call like he was a puppet. "What are you doing to me?" His voice was full of panic as he struggled.

"What?" She turned and looked at him, a playful surprise on her face. "Oh, I am sorry. Force of habit."

The strings were cut and Khet stumbled, now free. "What the hell was that? How did you do that?"

"Again I say, don't ask me questions that I will have to lie to." Her smile disarmed his anger.

"Okay, just don't do it again."

"Can't make too many promises, but I will try. Now would you please kindly follow me? The entrance to the cave is just over this rise." She held her disarming smile like casting a magic spell.

He didn't make a comment as he followed after her.

The trees pressed in as they walked further on. Their numbers didn't grow. They weren't growing closer together, making the path tighter. It was the trees' presence that grew. Pressure began to build in the back of his skull.

"Do you feel that?" Clair's voice sounded like she was speaking through a thick fog.

"What is it?" The pressure grew with each step. In his own ears, his voice was distant.

"The stones, we are close now. Keep going. Don't stop." It sounded like they were underwater now.

The weight of it all grew immensely as they stepped into the clearing. Pressure bore down on Khet, as the panic and anger in him rose. He couldn't feel her hand in his anymore. She pulled now, and Khet tried to resist. He tried to run, but something made him lean into it.

Fresh, clean air flooded his lungs. The pressure and the panic disappeared in a flash. Khet felt like a man that had almost drowned. Panting, he noticed a small cabin stood before them.

"What a rush, huh? Never really get used to it." She said with an almost playful smile.

"What was that? What is this?" Khet pointed to the small wooden structure that didn't look over a day old. All the wood was freshly cut and clean. The grass and flowers around looked odd in their freshness as well.

"That pressure, like you are almost drowning? That is the stones. Don't know why they do that, just that they do." She gestured to the scene before them. "I don't know anything about this really. It is different every time I come here. But it is the entrance to the cave."

Khet gawped. "This is different every time you come here? That makes no sense."

"I know, right. Magic can do some weird shit. Well, you can't change what was or what is, am I right? So you might as well move on, right? Wow, using right in three different sentences in a row. Those stones really do a number on me. Well, the entrance to the cave should be right through the door, and good luck." Clair turned on her heel and started to walk away.

"Wait! What now? You're not coming with?"

"Oh, sorry, I forgot. The cave will lead you to The Restless Crow. People will be there to meet you. You see those fucking stones, scrambled my thoughts."

"How long will that take, and how will I know when I am there? Can you please show me?" Khet was angry for being thrust into another situation where he would be left on his own.

Clair made a pouty face. "Sorry, Khet. I only do what I am paid to do. Nothing more, nothing less. Judging by the distance, though, maybe three days, five days tops. The path is pretty obvious."

"How will I see? It's got to be pitch black down there."

"Just wait, you're going to love it." Clair slipped out past the stones. Her exit left Khet with a sad look of confusion.

Khet stared at the spot she exited through. Frustration churned his stomach. "Fuck!" He shouted loud and long at the cabin.

38

Khet stared at the small cabin and just waited. What did he wait for? He didn't know. Maybe somebody else would come out the door and lead him to where he needed to go. Maybe it will be the mystery woman that always knows where he will be before he does. Or maybe the magical house that is never the same thing will fucking explain it! Khet's mind hurt from all the questions. Never had he thought magic would be like this.

"Well, looks like I am just going to have to do this one on my own." Just for a moment, Khet looked for a message about what to do from Luke. Nothing was there, of course, but he hoped there was anyway.

The door glided on freshly greased hinges. The one room inside the house was pristine. The floor was pristine hardwood, not a speck of dust was on the floor. "Sorry, but I am leaving my boots on. Sorry for the mess." He said to no one. Nothing was in the room except for a stairway that went down. No other options available, he made his way down the stairs.

The stairs were a fresh-cut stone. No sign of age or use. Like Khet was the first to step upon them. Each section repeated itself. Ten steps down, then a left turn. Ten steps down and a left turn. This repeated and repeated. Ten or eleven turns in, Khet realized it wasn't getting any darker and there was no source of light. *Did a Light Bringer infuse the entire staircase?* Everything was just evenly lit. Walls, steps, and ceiling all lit. Khet didn't even cast a shadow.

On he went. Ten steps, turn, ten steps, turn, ten steps, turn. A slight breeze could be felt as Khet made his way downward. The air changed to a nice, cool, damp air. It smelled like soil after a fresh rain. And still ten steps, turn, ten steps, turn. A doorway appeared at the bottom of one of the sets of the ten steps.

The door looked old, ancient in fact. Made of a strange metal that Khet did not recognize. A symbol of a swirling eye was embossed at its center. The door gave off a chill Khet could feel in his bones. The door almost sang as Khet slid his hand across it. "No other option." He turned the handle and slowly pushed the door open.

The creaking door echoed in the darkness beyond. Khet could make out a dimly lit pathway laid out before him. He cautiously stepped onto the pathway.

Blackness spread in all directions. There was just enough light from the small glowing stones that Khet could see his path but nothing else. The door closed with a gentle click behind him. Khet's heart froze. He turned and ran back to check the door. It opened freely, still with the loud creak. The fact that he had another option instead of being trapped down there made him relax a little. He closed the door and turned back towards the path. The unknown darkness lay out before him.

Khet summoned all his courage. His first step was the hardest. Just a small glowing path trailed into the black. He put steel in his spine and pushed on to the City of Passes and The Restless Crow. His eyes adjusted slowly to his dark environment. More and more things were noticeable as he walked. Above him was a massive mosaic of tiny pin pricks of light. Like a Light Bringer took handfuls of tiny stones, imbued them with light and scattered them in the sky above.

The vastness of the cavern was made more apparent when Khet could see the dull blue glow that covered the walls. The path wound around and through dense clusters of glowing plants. Some were mushrooms, others were trees. Khet was at a loss. Never would he have imagined something like this. A structure that looked to be man-made loomed in the distance. The now well-lit path led directly to it.

The structure grew and grew with every step. Small features of it became visible. A balcony, windows, and a doorway were all plainly visible as Khet came closer. In his eyes, it looked like an inn. *An inn down here?* Khet didn't know what to think. On the other side of the path were stacks of barrels. They were stacked three high and maybe fifty or so deep. They all had a weird shimmer to them. A couple of the barrels sat off to the side as if they were awaiting being stacked with the others.

He opened one of them and found it was full of fresh apples. "How?" Khet reached in to grab an apple. An odd pressure on his hand gave a slight resistance. He inspected the apple; nothing seemed amiss. "Why not?" he said to reassure himself. The taste was so extravagant that Khet let out an audible moan. Apples were a rare treat in Khet's life, and this one was the best he had ever tasted. He savored every bite of its crunchy sweetness.

He grabbed several more and placed them in his bag. The other barrels contained dried meat; another had cheese. There was one that was nothing but carrots. The stalks were still green as if they were freshly harvested. Everything looked fresh and delicious. Khet loaded his pack and his belly. Now with his stomach satiated, he continued off down the glowing path.

More buildings appeared out of the gloom. Some were small wooden structures; others were the size of barns. Nothing was in a state of ruin. Signs of use were apparent. A half-finished repair on the siding of a house. A well-loved chair sat on a porch. A thin layer of dust was on everything. Like somebody stopped cleaning it a month ago. It was all very strange. *Why was all this down here? How did all this get down here? All the material to build these couldn't have come down those steps.* His mind had a thousand questions.

The hard-packed path turned into a wide stone road. Buildings crowded in on either side; all of it had a glow that came from nowhere but everywhere at the same time. His curiosity got the better of him, and he walked off the path to investigate one of the buildings. It had a familiar shape to it that drew his attention.

It was a smithy, a well-appointed smithy at that. The door was a solid hard wood with well-oiled black iron hinges. There was no rust, none anywhere. In a damp cave, rust would be a nightmare for a smith. All the hammers, clamps, anvil, hooks, and nails were not rusted in the slightest. A pair of thick leather gloves lay atop an anvil, still supple like they were worn yesterday. None of this made any sense.

Wariness crept into Khet's mind. The kind that makes a person want to leave a place because it doesn't feel right and they don't belong. He made quick work back to the path. He attempted to ignore all the questions and kill his curiosity. This place was full of too many questions Khet could not answer. *Maybe one day I will have answers to this, but not today.* He thought.

He passed side street after side street. He had to keep reminding himself to just focus on the path. The strangeness of it all was too grand to resist. The more time he spent walking those empty streets in a cavern too large to comprehend. Khet's eyes would make out more and more of his surroundings. There was a breeze down here. The air was fresh and not wet and dank like a cave should be.

An intersection, to a much larger road, appeared in front of Khet. To the right, Khet could see the road go on out of sight. Buildings crowded either side. What he saw to the left gave Khet even more questions he could never answer. At the end of the wide causeway lined with large statues. Which in the darkness Khet couldn't see their faces, but their postures were imposing. A palace sat at the end, unlike anything Khet had seen. No story told by travelers or a book he read described anything close to its majesty. The small pinprick lights slowly swirled above it. Like lazy fireflies doing patrols around it. Khet could easily make out the high wall and the large towers that surrounded it. Gardens could even be seen from this distance, all giving off their own light. The domed roof at the center was a collage of muted colors given off by a radiant internal light. The glow of some half-remembered dream.

His curiosity burned, but he couldn't give into it. The mission he had was too great. When he got to the University and found this, maybe he will get some answers. Then there is the matter of the score he needs to settle with the Temple. He forced himself to turn and continue on, saddened by being forced to leave it a mystery.

The faint sound of flowing water made Khet uneasily aware of the fact that besides his own footsteps and breath, there was no sound in this city. A gentle stream flowed through this part of the city. Several water wheels soundlessly turned up and down the stream. All of the water wheels were connected to small mills. *This city was alive once. People lived their lives here. Where did they go?*

Further down, the road was less maintained. Small weeds and grass grew between the stones. He was tired from all the walking. The hours he had spent through the city and all the questions wore him down. He didn't want to leave the path, but he also didn't want to sleep out in the open. A richly appointed house sat on his left. The porch had a small wooden slatted railing that could hide Khet rather well if someone were to walk by. He stood there for a great deal of time with his head on a swivel. Nothing was out there, and Khet didn't know if that was a good thing or not.

39

Khet had a dreamless sleep when he actually slept. He wasn't comfortable in the strange city. He gave up on trying to get more rest. The hard floor and the quiet made it impossible for Khet to get comfortable. "Well, might as well get moving." He fished an apple and a piece of hard sausage from his pack for a quick bite of food. Then he was back to the path.

The more he craned his neck to look up at the tiny lights above, Khet could see a slight motion to them. Farther out from the palace, their motion was sluggish. From time to time, Khet thought he could make out a rocky roof to the cavern. Though he could never be sure, though, at these distances.

The stone road turned back into dirt eventually, and the buildings and side streets slowly tapered off. A wall with a massive gate made its way into Khet's view. Torches hung dark on the wall. There was no need for them to be lit because the wall gave a faint glow itself. The gate was raised halfway, and the black of the iron was well taken care of, not a single spot of rust. The spikes at the bottom had dried dirt on them from being closed in the recent past, but the rest was clean.

Beyond the gate, it was much darker. A slight bluish glow in the distance, the tiny pinpricks above, and the lighted path were the only sources of light. He readjusted his pack and kept moving.

The path led up and over rolling hills. At the crest of one of the hills, Khet turned back to view the city. It was just a faint fuzzy glow with no defining features. In the other direction, the trail continued on and eventually split in multiple directions.

The road upon which the path was laid narrowed gradually. Now only wide enough for maybe two carts to pass each other comfortably. Grass grew along the edges of the road. It was healthy and looked to be green in the low light. The grass rustled in the slow, gentle breeze. The sound of wind through trees came from the darkness on his right.

Now that he was out of the city, Khet was more comfortable. This was still a strange, darkened landscape to him. He had never been without sunlight this long, but out here made him feel less stressed. He was more familiar with the sounds of the countryside. All he was missing was the sun on his back, and he would be home. He did miss it, his home.

A gate on the left side of the road appeared from the darkness. Across the top, there was writing of some kind. A language that Khet did not know. It was obviously the name of the farm it belonged to, but what it said, Khet did not know.

More farms and houses appeared along the road as he went. Each one sat as empty as the next. Again, nothing was in ruins or old, only slightly weathered. He couldn't see any trace of footprints anywhere except for the ones he left.

At the top of the next hill, Khet was met with another worry. The glowing path branched out in three separate directions. *Which path was the right one?* The thought nagged at him. "Nothing to do but go see." He muttered into the black.

A signpost greeted him at the crossroads. Three of the arrows bore words that Khet couldn't make heads or tails of; the other was completely different. "The Restless Crow" in bold, blackened letters almost shined in the dark. Relief swept through Khet; he had made the right decision. For a moment, he turned and looked down the other paths. He hoped to see a glimmer of where they led, but nothing but blackness greeted him.

The path to The Restless Crow led into another ancient-looking forest. At least that is all he could tell by the sound of the wind in the leaves and the occasional dried leaf on the ground. The trail wound through the dark forest. Up and down small hills. It would switch back and forth up steep hill sides. Just to repeat itself going down a hillside. Time and direction were completely lost to Khet. It felt like he had walked for days in the forest. He only stopped to take small naps and to eat some food when he needed to. At moments, the sound of something walking through the forest could be heard from the distance. It was always just beyond his ability to tell what it might be. This just made him push harder and rest less.

After he crested another large hill, he was met with another sight that would never leave him. A lake that stretched as far as he could see. Colors of every hue shimmered on its surface. The surface was calm, but the colors rolled and tumbled under the glassy surface. In the center was a small island blackened in shadow. A pillar of black rose from its center. *Must be the stairway out; the path leads directly to it.* His heart filled with excitement.

On the shore, the colorful blooms spilled and splashed underneath the surface. Colors swirled together but never combined in an eternal dance. Khet could have stood on the shore forever and watched the display.

The path led to a bridge of cold black iron. Solidly built and anchored strongly into the ground. Possibly over three hundred feet long. In the shadows, small runes were etched into the bridge's surface. Khet ran his fingers over them as he walked. It never swayed or bowed as Khet made his way across. All the time beneath him, the colors danced.

Not twenty steps from the bridge stood the black pillar with an ancient iron door. The same swirling eye embossed on its surface. Khet turned and looked one more time at the magical lake and soaked it in. With a sigh, he turned the handle and opened the door.

The same stairs that he came down greeted him again. Ten steps, turn, ten steps, turn, ten steps, turn...

40

After the long climb, Khet came to another door. It was wooden and showed its age. He half-held his breath, not sure of what was on the other side, turned the handle, and pushed.

It was a cellar Khet found himself in, barrels lined one wall while a rack of wine was on the other. The cellar was blinding with how bright it was. He squinted as he moved forward. A sound came from one of the corners. A disheveled-looking man not quite in his middle years slept fitfully in a chair.

Khet decided to just throw caution to the wind. "Excuse me... sir."

The man acted like he was in the most restful of naps, opened his eyes, and grinned. "About time, young one. We have been waiting for you ever since Elesia sent us word you were on your way." The man stood and let out a long yawn while he stretched. "Names Cornelius and Trundle. My friends call me Nell."

"My name is Khet, just Khet. Do you get a lot of people coming into your basement?" Khet was a little thrown off at the nonchalant posture Nell had.

"It has been a while. The Arankai would come through and get some ale and whatnot from me. Nothing large, mind you. They have other tunnels for that."

"Did you know there was a city down there and the forest and a lake of colors?"

Nell sat there for a moment, like he was chewing on his thoughts.

"Aye, I have heard of the city. Apparently, there is more than one. When I was younger, I would play in the forest but haven't done that in years. The lake was just a lake last time I saw it." In the light of the cellar, Khet could tell Nell studied the runes on his neck. "So you're the one? It's about time then, eh?"

"The one what? What is about to happen?"

"The one the Arankai need to fulfill their big plan or prophecy. Whatever you want to call it. Nobody has told you this yet?"

"No, who are the Arankai? And what do they want from me?"

"Look, I am nothing much in the whole plans of the Arankai. I do believe in what they are doing, though. Somebody has to stop the Temple and their slave trade." Nell spat on the floor. "No one has the right to own another person. And those bastards at the Temple prey on the weakest among us."

"So they are trying to stop the Temple?"

"That is the plan as I hear it, but I am not the one to be telling you all this. I will be sending you in their direction soon, though. Follow me. I have a room for you and a much-needed bath." Khet followed Nell up the creaky wooden stairs. The sounds and smells of everything made Khet nauseous. It was all so bright that he had to use the walls to feel his way through the glare.

"I forgot how difficult it can be once you come back up. For some reason, the people of Passes enjoy having their buildings be all white and have a lot of windows." Nell led Khet down a long hallway lined with windows on one side. His head pounded from the intensity of the light.

Thankfully, the room set aside for Khet had the shades drawn. It was a large room with a high ceiling. The furniture was sparse. Not the highest quality but better than anything Khet had used. A bed in the far corner, a small table and chair, and a set of screens hiding a wash tub and a wardrobe. Incense burned on the table. It gave the room a pleasant spiced smell.

"So what now?" Khet asked.

"Not to be too unkind, but you could start with a bath. Over there is a wash tub and fresh clothes. Elesia said you would need a wash and where you're going next. Being filthy will draw attention, so you will want to clean up."

Khet's stench became apparent. His face was reddened slightly. "Where am I going next?"

"To the University, of course. Now clean up and put on those clothes in that wardrobe. Elesia picked them out. You have to look the part of a rich merchant's son." Nell looked at the well-worn pack and sword wrapped in clothes on Khet's back. "Will you be needing to take all your belongings with you?"

"Yes, do you have a case I could put my sword in?"

"I might have a sheath you could put it in. We also put on plays and the like, so we have a lot of different costumes that carry a sword. Might I ask what type of sword it is?" Nell's fuzzy eyebrows raised in peak curiosity.

Khet exhaled and braced for Nell's reaction. He unrolled the sword and let it clatter on the table. The blade glowed dully in the room.

The blood drained out of Nell's face. "Fuck me, boy, is that what I think it is?" Nell inched toward the sword in Khet's hand like it was a snake about to strike.

"Yes, I was being chased by the Dodecahedron through a path in the Dragon's Spine. A landslide happened, and it trapped the immortal. I had to kill it. Its sword was in a pile of rock at its feet."

"Gods be damned, those immortal bastards are not immortal. That explains why the Temple is trying so hard to find you. If those immortal bastards can die. They are not all powerful, and the Temple's tyranny can come to an end. Fuck, son, you might actually be the one."

"I had a run-in with the Temple on the way here. Pretty sure I have given them a better reason to find me." Regret of his brash actions tinged his voice.

"Don't fret, boy. You killed one of their most powerful tools. You bring hope; you really might be the one that puts an end to them." Nell slapped Khet on the shoulder. "I will find a case for the sword. Even if we found a sheath for it, that hilt is too recognizable. Wash up, and I will bring you a new bag as well and some food."

"I have plenty of food. There are barrels of it down there." He hefted his bag to show how full it is.

"By chance, do you have one of those apples?" Nell asked with hope in his voice.

"Yes, here, have two."

Nell bit into one of the apples, and a nostalgic joy spread across his face. His smile was so big it made the man squint. "I haven't had one of these in years. Thank you."

"You're welcome. Thank you for helping me."

Nell nodded and left the room, enjoying his apple.

41

Alone in his room, Khet set to the task of washing himself. The heavy, spiced smell of the room just made his stench more pronounced. His clothes were stiff with sweat and covered in stains, some of them were blood. All the repairs he had done in the stitching were on the brink of failure. He was glad to be rid of them.

The tub, a deep copper basin with a dimpled pattern, was filled with hot, scented water. Khet had never seen this much copper in one place. The outside of the tub had a dark green tarnish from age. While the inside was polished to a shine. A hard bar of soap lay on a wooden stool next to a soft towel.

Khet lowered himself into the large tub. The heat of the water melted away the soreness in his feet and muscles. The soap did its job as he scrubbed away all the filth. By the end, the water looked like a muddy brown soup. He used a small bucket nearby to rinse himself completely. The grit in the soap made his skin pink from the hard scrub.

Clean and refreshed, Khet made his way to the large wardrobe. The clothes inside looked like something out of one of his books. The rich, dandy son of a merchant they screamed. All high-quality stitching, extra panels of cloth that served no purpose, high-polished buttons placed where there were no pockets, and frills. There was one not as ostentatious as the others. A somewhat plain green pants and shirt. Leather cords were used for the belt. The fabric had a durable feel to it, like it was meant to be traveled in, and the others were meant for parties. So the plain green outfit was the only proper choice.

A thud came at the door. It was Nell with arms full of items. "Ah, good, I see you are dressed. Sorry for not knocking." He dropped everything onto the bed in the corner. "I have a case for your sword. It was my nephew's, a big artist that one. It is full of sketches and supplies. I am thinking we can place the sword underneath just in case some guard wants to open it. They usually don't bother the richer merchants, but who knows in this day and age. Also, here is a new bag for your belongings."

"Thank you for this, all of this. Do you want this stuff back? I am sure your nephew would want his case back." The wooden portfolio was exquisitely made. Dark-stained hardwood with small splashes of color. The handle was iron wrapped in a soft, buttery leather. He could tell it meant a great deal to someone.

Nell lowered his head like a great sadness was laid upon his shoulders. "The Temple hanged him for heresy several years ago. He made some art they didn't like, and they hanged him for it... I really hope you're the one to put a stop to all this." His voice hung heavy in the room.

Khet didn't know what to say. The story was just another piece of kindling he would use to burn the Temple down. "I am sorry, and I thank you for your help."

"Not a problem at all, Khet. I will go get you some food. But please don't leave this room. Temple knights and other people friendly to the Temple will come to the pub and drink. I don't need that kind of trouble." Nell shuffled out of the room, the weight of his nephew's memory pressed down on him. The sight of the man's pain made the rage in Khet burn a little hotter.

Khet transferred all his belongings to his new bag as well as two of the outfits in the wardrobe that didn't make him feel gaudy. The sword fit perfectly in the large artist portfolio. He strategically organized the supplies around it so the sword wouldn't move about inside it.

"That fits you quite nicely, stunning would be a better word to use." A richly dressed woman stood in the doorway. Panic hit Khet, where was his weapon? "Oh relax sugar, I am your ride for tomorrow. I am playing the part of your mother. You can call me Elesia, or Mommy." The smirk on Elesia's face made Khet uncomfortable.

Realization rolled on Khet like thunder. "I have seen you before? I have seen you before! You came to Tarin's smithy. You gave me that strange candy that fizzed in your mouth. How did you know I was coming here? Were you the one that told Luke's family that I was coming through the pass?" The questions tripped over themselves in Khet's mouth.

"You have quite the memory, Khet. As for your other question, I am afraid you will have to wait. Don't worry though, we can discuss that and many other things when we leave for the University." Elesia lounged in a chair at the table. Her outfit accentuated every curve of her body. Her hair was long black ringlets that reminded Khet of the beautiful pinpricks of light in the cave. The glow of her almond skin made Khet almost forget himself. She cleared her throat with a raised brow to bring him back from his distraction.

Khet tried to recover. "Ah... How quickly will that happen... our leaving that is... for the University?" He failed.

"In such a rush to get me all alone? Are you planning something lurid?" The mischievous smile made the blood drain from Khet's face.

"No...I"

"Enough playing with him, give him a break." Nell walked through the doorway with a tray filled with food and drinks.

"But he is so cute, look at him." She gently caressed his cheek. Khet's face was redder than the radishes that Nell had brought.

"Now if you're done fooling with him, let's talk out the story for tomorrow. The Temple has their panties in a twist looking for our boy here, so we have to play this well." Nell talked sternly to both of them, but a majority of it was pointed at Elesia.

"Alright, enough having fun for now, but later." Elesia eyed Khet like a predator eyeing its prey. "Who knows?"

Khet's face turned a deeper shade of red. He tried in vain to drink the glass of water in a relaxed fashion. His hand trembled too much to convince anyone.

"There, we don't need that right there. The Temple would see right through it." Nell's temper came through in her words. For a man who looked to Khet as a kind man, there was a threat behind his words.

"Why can't I be the sex-starved wife of a merchant, and he can be my artistic lover? You know how the Temple loves infidelity. We would be swinging by noon." Her laughter was intoxicating. Khet laughed along with her until he met Nell's eyes. To describe the look on Nell's face as unpleasant would be an understatement. Noticing the icy glare, Elesia rained in her humor.

Nell let out a tired sigh. "Now that you are settled. What is the story for tomorrow?"

Elesia, disappointed at the end of all the fun, said, "My name is Pearlem va Elance, wife of Marek ve Elance, and this is our son Gale. We are traveling to the University to meet up with my husband and possibly get Gale into the University."

"Now, Khet, if anyone asks what you are going to the University for, just say art." Nell was to the point. He looked tired behind his eyes. "No need for an elaborate backstory, keep it simple."

Khet just nodded and ate his food. The other two sat there in silence as the weight of the situation slowly pressed on their shoulders. When the meal was finished, Nel and Elesia rose to leave the room. To just torture Khet a little, Elisia gave him a flirtatious wink as she exited. That made Khet's heart skip a beat.

Khet lay on his bed that night, his brain was mush. Today was too much for him, in a long line of too-much days.

42

Khet opened his eyes. He stood on the edge of a massive precipice. The sky was dark with small pinpricks of light. The scene was quite alien to Khet. A soft glowing orb hung in the sky.

"It's called the moon." Arrinia's voice startled Khet. It was ethereal, dreamlike in the way it flowed in and out.

"What is this? Where am I? Wait, I saw Magnus kill you."

"Arrinia knew that her time was short. I am not the one you knew. I am just a fragment given to you when she gave you her power. We don't have long. You are on top of a cliff outside the Wall. She thought you needed to see this."

"What? What are you trying to show me?"

"Look down there. Do you see it?"

Khet looked in the direction Arrinia's fragment pointed. In the dim light of the moon, Khet could just make out figures moving, thousands of them. Khet's heart jumped into his throat.

"It's an army, waiting for you to bring down the wall."

"How? Why? Who are you people?" Khet shouted. His voice was a hollow shriek.

"Sorry, I am fading. I must go. You can't let them get away with what they are planning."

Khet shot up, breathing heavily and covered in a sheen of sweat.

"Calm there, sugar. It was just a nightmare. Elesia is here. Calm now." She spoke in a soothing tone that made Khet settle slightly.

"I am sorry. I am having a lot of those lately." Khet was a little embarrassed, but her presence put an ease to his mind.

"Do you need anything? There is water and food on the table. Once you have some food and gotten dressed, you can meet me downstairs. We are almost ready to go."

"OK, I am good. I will be down in a couple of minutes." Khet tried not to notice her lingering scent after she left the room. Elesia was dressed more modestly today. Khet did notice how much her neckline plunged though. He shook those thoughts from his mind as he dressed himself while trying to shove food in his mouth. All in a hurry to get to the University and maybe answers.

Downstairs, Elesia, or Pearlem, was waiting in the cart for him. The sky was overcast, making the white architecture of the town a dull gray. The street had a sullen look to it. Not a lot of people were on the street, and those that were didn't look like they wanted to be there.

"They are inspecting the people and carts on the way in and out of town. So remember what we discussed." Nell reminded them. "And behave." That comment was pointed directly at Elesia.

"In the city, most definitely, outside the city wall, a woman can get pretty lonely." Elesia gave a wink to Khet. Khet just turned forward. He tried and failed to look like her comment had no effect.

Nell walked away and threw up her hands in defeat. Khet could hear him mumble something, but the sound of the moving cart drowned it out.

"Don't worry, I like giving Nell a hard time. We can talk more once we are outside the city. Until then, just relax. Hopefully, your pretty face doesn't attract too many guards." A playful smile showed brightly on her face.

Khet's posture was that of a coiled spring. He tried to relax and look like the bored son of a merchant. "OK, I'll try."

After a couple of turns, the cart made it to the main thoroughfare of the city. It was a ghost town. Spots for stalls were empty up and down the street. Merchants that were there just sat quietly. Nobody was at their stall to buy or sell. Hardly a soul could be seen on the street. Everyone that was there looked skinny and not well. A lot of hungry eyes on miserable faces. Were the only things to be seen.

"What is going on? I thought the city would have more going on. Everyone seems so miserable."

Elesia leaned close to Khet. "The Temple has a grip on the city. This isn't the first time in recent memory that they have harassed Passes, and everyone knows it won't be the last. The people are beaten down. They try to carry on, but it is getting hard. Whenever this happens, people starve because the Temple won't allow all the food to get in."

"Why does the Temple do that?"

"For control. To make people fear them so the people will submit. This has been going on for years now. The Temple is taking food and diverting it to their army and their own personal stores."

Another log to add to the pyre, is all Khet thought.

"Hey, look alive now we are nearing the Northern Gate. It looks like there is no line either for us to get out, lucky day for us." Elesia straightened herself to appear a proper lady of higher station.

The gate had been barricaded to only allow one cart through at a time. About twenty of the Temple's guard stood watch at the gate, dressed in simple chain mail with their twelve-striped tunics. Each carried a spear like a person who knew how to use it. Several Temple contracted milled about, one was actively being beaten by a guard. A man stood among them dressed in metal plate armor that shined like a beacon of authority, even on this drab of a day. Khet struggled to remain calm. The sight of the contracted being beaten stirred the rage inside.

"Another log on the pyre, you bastard." Khet mumbled to himself. Every part of him wanted to kill them all. His fists clenched tight. His blood began to boil. A voice deep down called to his anger.

"Khet!" Elesia whispered. "Khet, calm down. There is nothing we can do right now. You will get both killed. Hey!" She slapped him in the back of the head.

Khet snapped back to reality. "What?"

"Calm down. I need you to look annoyed and bored. Not a seething killer. Understand?"

He felt the tension in his body. His anger simmered and then cooled. He took a deep breath and played his part. "Sorry, I am good now."

Elesia transformed herself in voice and posture to Pearlem. "Excuse me, sir! Excuse me!" Pearlem waved her hand at the guards very daintily with mild distress. One glanced her way but then returned to his duties. "Excuse me, I have to get going. I have business at the University. Urgent business!" Pearlem turned on the pouting merchant wife charm that always gets her way. "I said my husband, Marik ve Elance, needs me at the University as soon as possible."

The mention of the name Marik ve Elance got the attention of the Temple Knight on duty. The knight walked over in his armor, swaggering like a peacock. Khet had two thoughts at the sight of the cocky knight. One thought was he sounded like pots and pans clanging about. The other idea was more about if it was possible to melt his armor off while he was still alive.

"Excuse me, Miss. Did you say your husband is Marik ve Elance?" The Temple Knight had an air of arrogant authority that rubbed Khet the wrong way.

"Yes, I did, and if he hears that you kept his son hostage and not allowing him to pass through, there will be consequences." Said as only a rich, entitled woman would.

"Yes, ma'am, sorry, ma'am." The knight turned to the guards working the gate. "Let va Elance through." The open threat worked.

The guards scrambled to clear the way. They tripped over one another to obey the knight. An absurd rattle of armor and shifting of the barricades. Even the guard beating the contractor paused to follow the orders.

"Tell your husband I am sorry for the delay, ma'am." The knight respectfully moved aside. His face still had the cocky grin that Khet just wanted to burn off him.

Ever playing her part, "What is your name, good sir? I will tell my husband what you did for me and his son today?"

"Captain Danton, my lady."

"Well, Captain Danton, my husband will hear of how you helped me today. Thank you." Pearlem gave the most fake, sincere bow.

The cart creaked as it rolled through the gate. Elesia or Pearlem was sure to smile and say her thanks as they rolled easily through the barricades. Khet, on the other hand, stared daggers into the guard that had beaten the contracted. Every bone in his body wanted to attack him, attack all of them. But his hate subsided as they rolled from view. Khet leaned back with a sigh and just stared at the grey sky.

43

The line to get inside the city stretched on for miles. Some of the merchants selling food and drinks made sales to the people while they waited. The two of them rode along silently in the cart until they were well out of anyone's ability to hear them.

"Well, that went much better than I hoped." Elesia almost sang with relief. "And you played the despondent son quite well. Minus that moment you looked like you were going to kill them all."

Slightly ashamed of her last comment, Khet ignored it."Who is Marik ve Elance?" Khet asked, not fully understanding what he witnessed.

She leaned in so nobody could overhear, even though nobody else was around. "He is a wealthy merchant with a lot of pull in the Temple, and he is not a part of the Arankai, but he does feed them information."

"So, he is playing both sides?"

"No, Marik has been helping before he became a wealthy merchant. It was his idea to use the power of his influence to get his way into the Temple. There are many of us in the Temple now, just waiting."

"You are one of them." Khet leaned in to whisper. "You are Arankai?"

"Yes and no. You see, the Arankai are the leaders, and I am one of the members. Kind of like the Temple and its followers. It's just the Arankai are about protecting the people and giving them freedom to live as they want to live. The Temple is about control and worship."

"What more can you tell me about the Arankai? All I really know is what the Temple has said; they even accused me of being one."

"I can't go into it too much here; it is not my place to tell you. I can say that the Arankai is ancient. Older than the Temple of the Twelve."

That statement made Khet's head hurt. "How can it be older than the Temple? The Temple was here before the Twelve forged the wall."

"Look, I can't go into it here. Just know the Temple lies. Knowingly or unknowingly, it's all lies."

More confusing thoughts rampaged through his head. He took a breath and tried to sigh the headache that was growing away. "OK... were you the one that told Luke's family I was coming out of the mountain pass? Did you tell Clair where to find me?"

"Yes on both accounts. Who met you at the pass? And did they tell you about what happened to Luke?"

"Ayla met me and yes she told me what happened to her father. How did you know these things?

Elesia's eyes became distant like she was reliving a memory."Oh Ayla, I always liked her. It is a shame what happened to Luke. He will be missed. Always had a bad joke to tell or a story to share. Good memories."

"How did you know?" There was a slight frustration in his tone. He had so many questions and received so little answers.

"Not my place to tell you, Khet. At least not yet, sorry"

Now Khet was just annoyed now. He wanted answers to something. "OK...OK... something else then. In town you acted and spoke differently around Nell, and then it seemed so natural when you were being Pearlem. And now you are different again. Are you an actress of some kind?"

Elesia leaned back on the bench. "We all have a role to play. I am not a trained actress, but I found that I can mold my behavior to keep life easy. Nell on one hand thinks a woman should be proper and lady-like. When I act more sexually aggressive around him it keeps him uncomfortable, and I find he is easier to deal with when he is unbalanced. With that Temple Knight I played the pampered wife of a rich and powerful merchant. You saw how unbalanced he got when he heard the name Elance?"

"Yeah, they were practically tripping over themselves to open that gate."

"Remember how you were when we first met. I set you off kilter from the start. Sorry about that. Sometimes I just like to act a little sultry to make myself feel good."

"Are you like this with everyone?" Khet asked innocently. Never had he met a person that could change almost everything about themselves at will.

Elisia slowly sucked air through her teeth. "I am a spy, smuggler, saboteur, and I have even been called upon to be an assassin. I have played more roles than any person should have. It is not easy, but I am still alive."

His mind reeled again; people like this are only in his books. "Is this you, know, the real you?"

She let out a tired sigh over an old subject. "I think about that sometimes; who am I? I don't have a good answer for that. Do you? Do you know who you are?"

"Well..." Khet really had to think. Who was he? He wasn't the contracted boy anymore? What is he now? This chosen one people talk about? He doesn't feel like the one. And what was the chosen one supposed to do? Nothing made sense, nothing at all. "I don't know." A hollowness absorbed him, and it ached. A sadness for all that has happened to him flooded the empty void inside.

Elesia placed a hand on Khet's shoulder. "It is okay; we all have moments like this. We all have moments when the weight of it all gets too heavy. Sometimes you just have to put the burdens down and give yourself a rest. Just rest for now. The burdens of the world will still be here tomorrow."

44

After a night of much-needed rest, Khet felt better. All his problems weren't fixed; the hollow ache was gone. It also made things easier because he recognized he isn't the only one with burdens that get too heavy sometimes. With lighter shoulders, he carried on with his life.

It was another overcast day. A slight breeze blew through the trees; it carried the smell of smoke. Not a campfire kind of smoke or a forge. This smelled like a home was burning, a lot of them.

A temple guard stopped them before they came back on the road.

"Ma'am, I need you off the road. The Temple asks you to keep off the road." The guard had a tired look in his eyes. By his look, it seemed like he had already told twenty other people the same thing.

"How come? I have business at the University that is most urgent." Elisia evoked her best Pearlem impression.

"The Grand Inquisitor is coming; the Arankai have set half of the City of Passes on fire. Now move or get moved." The guard commanded.

"Sorry, we will go back to where we were camping and wait there." Elesia sounded almost panicked to Khet.

Once they reached the alcove where they camped, Elesia made her way to the back of the cart.

"What's going on? You smell the smoke; did the Arankai do that?" Khet asked as he followed her.

"No, couldn't be. Maybe it was an accident? Or the Temple is trying to instill fear? Either way, it is bad news. The Grand Inquisitor controls the Dodecahedron. He never travels anywhere without his immortals and always twelve squads of twelve."

It was a thought that would chill any person, with sense in their head, to the bone. A single immortal would make people quiver in fear, and Khet was about to see 144 of them. Even as the fear gripped him, he hid in the brush next to the road so he could see them pass by.

It was the sound of distant thunder as they approached. Armored gleamed in the distance. A shiny wall of silver and gold came down the road. Each step was in sync with all the others. The very ground shook under Khet's feet. His stomach tied itself in knots.

He almost shat himself out of fear when Elesia appeared beside him. "I wanted to see too." She whispered.

The first wall of silver and gold passed by. The sound of the armor was like a landslide of steel plate. Khet could feel the anger stir within him. *How much damage could that many do?*

The road cleared and now there was a man on a horse trotting by. His robes showed his level of authority. It was the Grand Inquisitor, his uniform carried the same twelve stripes as other Temple members but his was twelve shades of black. Not a single piece of armor. His face was carved from cold gray stone. He looked like a man who has never smiled unless it was at another person's pain. There was a vibrant red jewel set into a golden chain around his neck.

"That jewel is what allows him to control the Dodecahedron." Elesia dared to whisper.

Khet's rage flared almost beyond control. He could deal a massive blow to the Temple. Kill the Grand Inquisitor, take the crystal and turn the Dodecahedron against them. The rage pooled in him. The voice came again. "Do it. Kill. Burn it all." It whispered. The rage poured fire into his veins.

Khet moved to stand. Hot rage surged into his hands. A mortified Elesia grabbed Khet by the hand. The heat seared her skin. She yelped in pain, but she pulled him down anyway.

The sensation of falling snapped Khet out of it. His mind cleared as he witnessed Elesia cradling her hand in agony as the next formation of Dodecahedron thundered by.

"I am sorry. I don't know what happened. I just lost control." Khet pleaded.

"Fuck that hurts!" She made her way to the back of the cart. "You need to learn to control that. What the fuck were you thinking! What, were you going to attack the Grand Inquisitor and take his jewel and turn the Dodecahedron against the Temple?"

That stopped him in his tracks. "Yes, how did you know?"

"Look I can't go into it right now, but that crystal won't work for you. You would have just gotten yourself killed."

Khet just dumbly stood there and watched her salve and wrap her hand in a bandage.

"You had a good idea, but it has been tried in the past. Never works though." She tested if she still had some flexibility in her hand after she bandaged it. "We need to get going, get in the cart."

Khet was a scolded pup, the way he crawled back into the cart. He slunk down low and dared not to look in her direction. The tension was heavy.

"Look, Khet, I am sorry for snapping back there. Your heart, even though it was foolish, was in the right place." Her shoulders seemed to relax a little. "We still have a couple of days until we get to the University anyway, and I don't need you hiding from me."

He righted himself; he didn't need to hide anymore. "I am sorry for losing control of my temper. As you know, I was contracted…"

"I know, Tarin and Kase were good people. It is sad what happened."

The wheels of the wagon creaked and complained in the uncomfortable silence that grew. That wound was still pretty fresh. "I feel like that whole thing was my fault. If I didn't lose control, then none of this would have happened."

"Hey, I know this won't fix things, but that was not your fault. You had no idea of what would have happened. You can't change that." She placed her bandaged hand on his shoulder. "There will be other times out there when you will have to learn the hard thing the hard way. We all stumble, we all fall; just keep standing back up and keep moving."

"That is easy for you to say. You didn't get all of your family and friends killed."

"I have more bodies at my feet than you know. I have seen and done things that you couldn't imagine. One thing that has gotten me through it. Is the idea that you have to accept the things that you cannot change. Focus your strength, your force of will, that anger, that rage towards the things you can change. No mercy for those who stand in your way."

"How do you know the difference between the things you can

change and the things you can't?"

"In your case and most people's cases, for that matter. It is the amount of effort you want to put into it. That decides which is which."

45

The days went on with light banter and good spirits. No more incidents with the Temple. No bandits were seen. Just the wide road with the last ribbons of farming from the Fertile Plains on their left and the dense Forest Valkai on the right. When the road would venture far enough away from the trees, Khet could see the Tower of Valkai and the Wall looming over it. This would be the first Tower he had ever seen close up. The whole University surrounded the Tower. The excitement in Khet made him fidget like a child before Yule.

When they finally made the turn down the road that goes straight into the University, the Tower stood out and the faint blue shine from the God Shard could be seen. Khet's skin prickled at the sight of it. The blue shine pulled at Khet.

A man in a blue robe stood with an air of great authority. He stopped them before they could travel far down the road. "I am sorry, ma'am, but the University is conducting a test. No carts are currently allowed to travel down this road." His voice was reedy and had the arrogance of the overeducated about it.

Pearlem appeared. "But I have business at the University. I am expected by Prelate Creshing." Khet's ears perked up at the name Crashing. That is the person Abner wanted him to see.

The man's thin mustache was as smug as the man himself. "The Prelate is the one who gave the order to stop all cart traffic. You may travel on foot if you need to."

"How long are you going to make me wait?"

"The test is scheduled to run for the next eight hours and twenty-two minutes. You are free to wait or free to walk. Now I have to go, ma'am. Can't waste any more time speaking with you." He spun on his heel and stiffly walked back to his post on the edge of the tree line. Khet and Elesia stared daggers into his back.

"Give a weak man power, and that is what you get." Elesia resigned herself to just wait. No good reason to just leave the cart.

"Is it okay if I just walk it?" Khet was halfway out of the cart before she could even respond.

"I guess so. It may take you a couple of hours to get there, but if you really want to. You are looking for Prelate Creshing, and when you find him, tell him I am stuck out here." He had his bag and the art portfolio out and was ready to walk before she could finish.

A grin spread wide across his face. "OK, I will tell him." He turned heel and set his shoulders to walking. He was finally going to be at the University of Valkai. All the stories he had heard about it, and he is finally going to see it for himself.

A couple of hours of a hard march later, Khet could see a massive gate in the distance. The dense forest abruptly ended, followed by a major clearing of trees. The clearing was covered in odd-shaped boulders laid at odd ends and deep ditches. Closer to the wall of the University, the rocks became smaller, and the holes deeper. Turrets evenly spaced went along either side of the dark grey wall. The wall of the University was not nearly as impressive as the Wall. But it was still impressive. On top of each of the turrets sat an oversized flat bow. Khet had never seen anything like that before. He found himself standing there with his mouth hanging open as a worker on the giant flat bow noticed Khet staring. Khet hurriedly left before somebody questioned what he was doing there.

Three rows of what Khet could only describe as trebuchets greeted him on the other side of the wall. Large stacks of dark gray boulders stood behind each, with a larger pile further behind. *Why does a University have all this weaponry?* Khet didn't know.

Next came barracks, where people in different colored uniforms came in and out of them. Small groups of them were clustered together. Khet could hear laughter drift from a couple of the groups and stern words from others. Everyone there, though, seemed to have a purpose, and they did not pay any attention to Khet as he walked by.

The sound of clanking hammers and the smell of coal smoke from the forges reached him long before he could see them. Many smithies, laid out in an odd arrangement, were there. Khet could count seventeen with multiple blacksmiths in each. Young apprentices sharpened swords, wrapped leather around hilts, and fletched arrows. All faces were smudged with grime and coal dust. Their faces set to the serious task. Racks of swords, armors, and shields looked as if the University had an army to supply, and they were preparing for war. *With whom?*

Small fields where farmers grew a variety of crops spread out before Khet once he was cleared of the smithies. Some had big tents over them, and others it looked like they were flooded. It was a smaller version of the Fertile Plains. Farmers and people dressed in green-colored robes worked the soil and harvested the plants. Some had scales for weighing, others carried large jars of liquid. All had a purpose; what it was, Khet was oblivious.

Large buildings that looked to be for storage huddled near a large inner wall. A massive gate stood open in front of Khet with the University's motto emblazoned across it.

"NEVER STOP QUESTIONING, NEVER STOP LEARNING"

Beyond the gate, the University sprawled out. Stone buildings seemingly to have sprouted out of the ground. Wooden buildings on stilts looked like a large insect frozen in place. Every stone that made up the pathways and the buildings was cut different sizes and shapes, but all fit together perfectly. One domed building looked like it was just a pile of boulders with a door on it. Large and small courtyards, some with stone, others with flowers of different colors, went in every direction.

Students moved everywhere like ants on a sweet roll. They clustered in groups, with what looked like a professor lecturing. Students ran in formation, others did exercises. On the far left, Khet could see fighting drills. A small, official-looking man approached Khet with an irritated look about him.

"You're three days late for admissions. Before you tell me, I don't care who your father is. You must come back next month between the first and the fifth of the month." The man obviously has said this to many students in his career. He wore his uniform with practice and pride. Every crease, every fold of fabric looked impressive. His shoes had a shine that sparkled in the sunlight. His hair had a masterful part. All of this professionalism and impressive clothing, Khet still wanted to punch the man in the face.

"I am not a student. I am looking for Creshing. I have business with him. Where can I find him?" Khet tried to sound as official as possible, but he was not pulling it off well.

The official man's face took a sour turn. "You have business with the Prelate of the University? Whatever, at least you came up with something original. He is in the grand building on the right side of the Tower. Good luck, hopefully the Hand isn't too gentle on you when they toss you out of here." He spun on his heel and left, probably on to ruin somebody else's day.

Khet ignored the rudeness and made his way to Creshing's office. The main entrance square was overwhelming in size. Khet figured he could have fit at least three of Tarin's farmsteads inside of it. More students walked this way and that. Very few even spared Khet a glance. He felt out of place in this large of a place. His heart ached to be home.

The Tower of Valkai stood before him now. No massive gardens, no massive display of majesty surrounding the garden. A waist-high stone wall made up the perimeter. The inside was made up of a grassy field cut short with a shade of trees spread throughout. Under most of the trees, Khet could see students reading or conversing. The Tower was a simple twelve-sided stone structure with nothing much in the way of decoration. The stonework was masterful, and the size made Khet's brain ache when he tried to comprehend it.

To the right of the Tower stood a grand building indeed. Each piece of stone that made up the walls was cut in irregular shapes. When standing back and looking at it as a whole, Khet could see the beautiful picture it made. It was a forest scene with students and teachers sharing knowledge. The whole wall face didn't have a single window. At the center above the entryway doors, the stones displayed a message. "We Only Gain Freedom Through Knowledge". The entry doors themselves were just plain heavy wooden doors. They stood out in their simplicity. But why would you want to complicate a door?

Inside the entryway, there was a small room with very little to get in the way of its function. A woman dressed in a blue scholar's robe sat on the corner of a small desk. She was in a deep conversation with the man that sat behind the reception desk. They paused their conversation as Khet approached.

Khet fished the hand badges from his bag. "I was told I need to deliver these to Prelate Creshing."

"You were, hmmm." The woman eyed Khet questioningly. There

was a look in her eye that made Khet uneasy. "Paul, tell the small counsel I am indisposed for the afternoon." She waved for Khet to follow. "You come with me."

They walked down many a long corridor, in silence. Khet, not knowing why, but had a strong feeling that he wasn't supposed to speak. The pair entered a large room at the end of one of the hallways. She closed the doors behind them. It was a large empty room with a couple of soft chairs and small tables in the corners.

"Where did you get these?" Tearing the badges from Khet's hand. She flipped through them. Her face became more distraught with each one.

"I need to talk to Prelate Creshing; he is the one I must get those to." Khet reached for the badges.

The woman pulled her hand away. "Where did you get these!" She shouted, tears pouring down her face. "Is Abner alive? Is my husband okay?"

"You're Abner's wife? Graven's niece? Varith?" He met Varith's tearful gaze. There was no hope in her eyes. Khet's heart sunk like a stone. "I am sorry." Khet lowered his head. "I am sorry… Abner and Graven are both dead." It was a whisper, all that he could muster at that moment.

Varith collapsed to the floor and wept at her loss of her husband and uncle. The empty room now filled with her sobs. Khet didn't know how to comfort her, so he just stood there with his head down.

It took time for her to collect her voice and ask the question Khet didn't want to answer. "How did they die? How did it happen? Was it some stupid act of heroism Abner likes to pull off?"

Khet wanted to spare her the pain as much as he could, so he lied. "I was held in a slaver camp on the west side of Dragon's Spine. They rescued me. We thought we lost them by the time we made it to Graven's. They attacked while we were sleeping. Abner killed five before he had fallen. Graven died from wounds he got in the attack." Sometimes a lie is more kind than the truth.

Varith sat on the floor for a couple of moments absorbing the story Khet had told her. "Do you have his wedding band, by chance?"

"No, sorry."

"OK, that is okay." Varith stood and straightened her robes. "Thank you for telling me about Abner and my uncle… I must go… I will let the Prelate know that you are here." She quickly left the room.

Khet stood there in that room full of sadness and thought about the friends he had lost. The sadness rooted him to the spot.

46

Hours passed in that empty room. Khet just stood there staring at his shoes. A mixture of sadness and anger filled him. Sadness for Varith's loss and anger at himself that he couldn't be more of a comfort. Abner was a good man and deserved to be honored.

"There you are." An older man stood in the doorway. "Sorry for keeping you waiting. I was speaking with Varith, sad business that, really sad business. Abner was a lovely man. Varith and Abner were such a loving couple." He looked wise and weathered like a man that had seen too many wars. His robes were a scholar's blue like Varith's but were trimmed in silver and gold.

"I am sorry I am forgetting myself, I am Prelate Vagner ve Creshing, and you are Khet? Am I right?" There was the light of knowing in his eyes. Khet had heard of the Scholars of Valkai, the ones that contain the power of Valkai the Knowing, can retain all knowledge that they have learned. It is said that before a Scholar dies, they must copy all their knowledge into books, so future Scholars can learn from them. That ability manifests itself as a blue shimmer in the eyes.

Khet was confused; he never told anyone here his name. "Yes... How did you know my name?"

A slow grin grew across Prelate Creshing's face. "Khet, I am glad to finally meet you. Come with me; I have something we need to discuss and bring the sword with you." The Prelate had a smile like he knew something that Khet didn't.

Dumbfounded that the Prelate knew about the sword as well as his name. He apprehensively followed. It was another journey that twisted down long hallways with just the sound of their footsteps to keep them company.

The room they entered was grandiose in its size; windows and a massive stained-glass roof lit the interior in an awe-inspiring array of colors. Sunken into the floor was a vast map of Sýna. At the location of every Tower, there was a chair and a thirteenth chair in the middle for the Gods' Spire.

"Impressive, is it not? Made almost a thousand years ago to give us at the University a better understanding of the world. Took many years and many surveys to complete this. If you look over here, you can see where you lived with Tarin and Kase, correct? In the south, just northeast of the Tower of Sidierion? Where you turned that hill to ash." The Prelate wore a smile like the wise men in Khet's stories. A smile full of mischievous wisdom.

Anger, frustration, and confusion swirled in Khet's head. "How do you know that? Who are you people? Why do all these people know so much about me, and I know so little?" Khet was frantic.

"I am sorry, I know you are frustrated. You will get your answers shortly, but first, I must explain a few things. Is that alright?"

"No, I want answers!" His shout filled the massive room. Heat filled his body like a forge fire come to life. The floor beneath where he stood blackened and began to smoke. The room seemed so far away right now.

The Prelate didn't flinch. He stood powerfully and spread his arms out wide and shouted something at Khet. Instantly, the fire and rage left Khet, like a candle blown out by a strong gust of wind.

Khet stood there confused and his body weak. "What was that? What did you do?" Khet's breath wheezed like all the air had been pulled from him.

"Some knowledge is not meant for sharing. Have a seat; the weakness will pass shortly." The Prelate reached into his robes and held out something for Khet. "Here, have some chocolate; it is quite delicious and will help you feel better."

Khet propped himself up in Grunaive's chair and put the chocolates in his mouth. The rich, creamy texture and the gentle sweetness flooded him with pleasure. His fatigue just faded away as he enjoyed the chocolate.

"Well, I would have savored that a little slower than all at once. But to each their own, I guess." The Prelate slowly wandered around the giant map of Sýna, enjoying a small piece of chocolate while Khet pulled himself together.

Khet sat himself straight in the chair. "I am sorry for losing control."

"Oh, it is fine. You have been through a lot. A weaker man would not have survived everything you have been through. So all is forgiven." The Prelate's tone turned grandfatherly. "And you can call me Vagner."

"OK Vagner, how do you know all this about who I am and what I have been through?"

"OK, OK, fair enough of a question. But I have to ask you one first. What do you know about the Tower of Alfir?"

"Not much, Alfir is the God of time. Three mountain peaks surround it, each one represents the past, present, or the future."

"Yes, the mountains are called the Norns. Urd represents the past, Verdandi the present, and Skuld the future. I am more interested in the Timeless Plateau. What do you know of it?"

"Nothing really."

"OK that is where I will start." Vagner's eyes lit up with a light that shimmered the faintest blue. "On the Timeless Plateau there are these bubbles of distorted time." He waited to see if Khet would speak up but Khet's face just waited for more information. "These bubbles of distorted time, we at the University, believe are windows to different time periods in Sýna's history. We have found several pieces of evidence that point to that conclusion. One of those pieces of evidence is a book. A book with your name in it Khet."

"What?"

"That is why we know so much about you. We think portions of your story are written in your own hand. Many different people in many different languages have written in the book. One of them is in a cipher that I designed when I was younger and I have never taught it to anybody. It has many truths in it, that we have verified and have been verifying it as things came to pass after it was found over two thousand years ago. We call it The Book That Fell Through Time."

Nothing made sense to Khet. "I haven't written in any book?"

"You haven't yet. You will... This book is from a future

time."

"That doesn't make any sense and who is we?" Khet was getting irritated again.

"We are the Arankai. These chairs are for each leader. We have been looking for you, Khet. We weren't sure when or exactly where the sign was going to come from, but we have been vigilant and preparing."

"What sign? And why me?" Khet struggled to keep his composure.

"The sign was you turning that hill to ash. The reason we need you is that you are the one to end the enslavement the Temple enforces or at least start the revolution. According to the book, the war will be long and many will die. In the end, we will be free."

"Free from what? I agree the Temple needs to be stopped, but I don't want to start a war. Why me?" Khet was shouting.

Vagner raised his hand in an act to calm Khet. "Khet, the Twelve are not real gods. The beings that gave you your Runes are Gods, of sorts. I think it is time for you to read the book. It will help you understand what I have just explained to you." Vagner moved to a wall next to the chair for Alfir. With a wave of his hand, the wall slid aside. "This way to the truth, Khet. Follow when you are ready."

Khet wanted to run and just escape all of this, but the people that have sacrificed themselves to help him would not be honored if he just quit now, and he had a score to settle with the Temple.

The doorway led directly into a small room. The book Vagner spoke about lay closed on a stone plinth. It was large and bound in ancient leather, covered in scars and worn patches. Khet placed his hand on the ancient cover. Vagner spoke. "Most of it is written in different languages, but the very beginning is written in our common writing. And we don't know why."

Khet took a deep breath and turned to the first page.

47

From The Book That Fell Through Time, as translated from the Stone Tablets of Dunmar, as translated from the Fenris Bone Carvings, as written on the Living Wall.

Nothing is known about where the Gods came from. All that is known is that there are two separate tribes that lived at one point in balance. One tribe was the Thane, they knew many things and had deep knowledge of all things. The other tribe was the Thune, they could make the things that the Thane thought. Both tribes lived in a symbiotic balance.

The balance was maintained for eons, until a single Thane, known by Malak, craved more power. In secret, Malak gained the knowledge to craft a collar that would bind a Thune to his will.

Malak searched for a Thune to forge his collar of binding. All of them could see through Malak's deceitful plot and refused. His obsession with power drove him to darker thoughts. Malak turned to his own tribe and corrupted three others to believe in his twisted schemes. Each of the converted followers worked with a Thune to create a piece of the collar.

Now with all the pieces of his collar, Malak searched for his victim. His scheme required a powerful Thune, the most powerful in fact. Nox, the very creator of night, became the one that Malak bound and enslaved.

The very first thing the enslaved Nox was forced to create was of a forbidden design. A weapon that could kill and absorb a God's power and knowledge, all the things Malak craved.

At the first discovery of the weapon, an open war began to consume all creation. Beings that once held themselves in perfect harmony turned to chaos and bloodshed. Entire societies were created and then destroyed to feed off the anguish to fuel the God's power. All of this was according to Malak's plan.

He slaughtered his fellow God's. He absorbed all of their essences for his own. This only fueled the war that now burned the very stars. Explosions of light could be seen from all corners of creation as the war raged.

Malak used his new power and that of Nox to forge a prison for the remaining gods. Under the false flag of truce, he brought them into his trap. Before they could realize, the prison slammed shut.

Malak knew that the other gods, even imprisoned, were still a threat to his plans for power. His need to be free of them drove Malak to even greater feats. He feared that one day the others would be free and bring their vengeance upon him. A plan was set to destroy them forever.

Sýna was forged out of the rock and the dust. The remnants of the battles throughout creation. Nox created it all with his own hands, from every grain of sand to every mountain peak. Malak placed the prison with great effort in the shadow of Sýna so he could keep a watchful eye on his captives.

Malak forged the Gods Spire so he could glower over his creation. He placed a crystal of creation at the top of the spire. Where it would collect the life and death energy from his creations. Nox was used to forge all of the living beings on Sýna. His creations flourished, and the crystal fed upon them.

The gods trapped in their prison were patient and planned in the shadow of Sýna. They found a flaw in their prison, a small crack that allowed them to project influence onto Sýna. Disease and famine moved swiftly through the land. It warped and killed Nox's creation in a way the crystal could not absorb the energy. Enraged by Nox's failure to create perfect beings that were incorruptible, Malak slaughtered Nox and absorbed his power. The very act shattered the god-killing blade, sending shards all across Sýna.

In desperation, Malak seized the power in the crystal and reforged the entirety of the world. He buried it all with his new creation. The power he needed to wield taxed his body and mind. So Malak slept while his creation lived and fed the crystal.

The peace lasted for centuries before the trapped Gods could exude the influence to corrupt Malak's creation again. A type of magic was created that fed off the crystal itself and was given to those that turned against their creator. By the time Malak awoke from his slumber, his creation was almost completely corrupted.

He used the nearly depleted crystal to reforge his creation yet again. Malak buried it all and started anew with different creatures that could not wield magic. Again exhausted, he collapsed into a deep sleep.

The peace did not last; the trapped ancients were patient in their plans. The corruption took hold deep in Sýna. When Malak finally awoke, the entirety of his creation was dead. Rage and vitriol fueled him as he remade it all again.

The cycle of peace and corruption repeated over and over again. All life on Sýna would be buried and remade. Each time it left Malak weaker and weaker. Each time he would wake to find his creation ruined.

In a desperate act to save his plan, Malak forged twelve great towers with the power to hold the sun in place. At the top of each was placed a shard of the great crystal. He created a temple for his creation to worship in and make sacrifices. The shards atop the towers would feed on this worship. Then he tapped into all the power locked inside the great crystal and forged a Great Wall to protect his creation.

All of this was written on the Great Living Wall.

"So, the Twelve Gods are false? Is it all a lie?" Khet mumbled to the room.

"Yes, that is a core tenant of the Arankai."

"How could this story have been written with everything being remade again and again?"

"The Great Living Wall, of course. Now, what that is and where it is located, nobody knows that I am aware of, but in our digging, we have found the Stone Tablets of Dumar and remnants of the Fenris Carvings. Those were found deep underground, to the north if my memory doesn't deceive me. All that and more further on gives this book credibility." Vagner opened the book to another section. "You see here." He pointed to a passage written underneath a drawing of a city. The large structure at the center of the city looked the same as the palace Khet had seen when he was underground. "This passage told us where to go to find the Stone Tablets of Dumar. That city, according to this text, is Tel Afurn. Once an island said to be created by a god in order to honor the sun. In Tel Afurn, there are temples worshipping the sun. A lot of it seems correct. Although we can't know if it is all true."

"I have been in that city, Tel Afurn, on my way here. I have seen that palace." Khet's mind spun. How could this be? It was all too much.

"I know, you wrote about it." Vagner flipped to a page about three-quarters into the book. Khet stood in a mix of awe and terror. A full five and a half pages were written in his own hand. The story was of Khet's life from his first memories to where he stood in front of the book. All straightforward, none of the lies he has told others or himself. Stories about private moments that he never told a soul about. Even words that he commonly misspelled were scratched out and corrected.

"OK, so what does the rest of the book say?" Khet believed it, but he looked for a reason not to. He wanted to hide from it like it was a bad dream.

"The rest are accounts of what has happened and what will be. A person that worked for the University found the book over two thousand years ago near a time distortion on the Timeless Plateau. When she discovered its impertinence, she gave it to the Prelate of the University at that time, Prelate Gorsk if I am not mistaken. Every Prelate since then and some of the lead scholars have studied and deciphered a lot of it." Vagner dug deep into his pocket and fished out a chocolate. He popped it into his mouth and relished it for a moment.

"A lot of knowledge is there, and it has led us to many discoveries. The most important is instructions on how we defeat them, Malak and the others, and free us from the Temple's tyranny." Vagner closed the book with a finality that just piqued Khet's interest more.

"Why defeat the others, the trapped gods? Malak imprisoned them. When they become free, won't they just leave us alone? We had nothing to do with their being trapped."

"You see, my boy, the book details what happens after Malak falls. Those trapped gods have been busy building an army in the shadow outside the wall. The book details their wrath comes down on us after the fall of Malak. Some of us are kept alive as slaves to keep the power in the crystal growing. The one called Magnus has a great lust for power and wants to wield it himself."

Khet's heart froze at the mention of Magnus. "What do I have to do with any of this?"

"In the book, you are the one who defeats Malak, and Magnus betrays you. In the fight, a large portion of the western wall collapses, and Magnus's army invades. Centuries of war begin, and eventually, another hero will rise to defeat Magnus. Then the war will end, and we all will be free."

Khet's head throbbed. "So I am to die? I don't want to die."

"Khet, we have studied this book for centuries, and we think we have found a way to end this without the war ever starting."The old man's voice became solid as stone. "We believe with the right planning, we can change what has been written."

"How?" Khet's voice sounded small in that tiny chamber.

"It is too long to go over now. The rest of the Arankai will be here tomorrow. We will go over the plan more then. I suggest you rest. We have rooms for you and Elesia vi Danes. Quite cosy, and your dinner should be there shortly. Follow me if you could, and tonight try to get some rest."

Khet followed Vagner out of the small chamber with the weight of the truth bearing heavily on his shoulders.

48

The walk to his rooms was a sullen one. Revelation bared down and made it hard to breathe. His feet shuffled as if great weights were tied to them. He just followed Vagner's back and wished he would wake from all this in his bed at home. The home that was no more.

Hallways went on, students and teachers that passed like vague shadows. Once bright courtyards were muted in their grandeur. Vagner spoke of a chance to end this without a war, but he never mentioned a way that Khet lived through it.

Vagner led Khet to a small cottage set on the far southern side of the University grounds. Even though the design was completely different, all he could see was Tarin and Kase's home, his home. The memory struck him hard.

Inside the cottage, Khet's spirits lifted slightly at the sight of Elesia. She had changed from her Pearlem costume to something much more comfortable and form-fitting. Even with the burden of everything on his heart, just the sight of Elesia eased his worries. Light from outside gave her smile a glow.

"Vagner, how good is it to see you again? It has been ages since we last spoke. How are you doing?" Elesia flashed the warmest smile Khet had ever seen.

"Oh, I am feeling my age lately, and look at you. It has been an age since we last shared company, and you haven't changed in the slightest. How do you do it?" Vagner's eyes shone a deep blue.

"I spend a lot of time in the healing pools of Grunaive, eat clean, and I wear a lot of hats to shade my skin from the sun. I will take the compliment though, thank you." Elesia noticed the sullen look on Khet's face. Her smile sagged under its weight. "Khet, are you okay? You look like a man that has just lost his best friend."

Khet let out a deep sigh. "My world just got a little heavier, that is all."

A bell sounded in the distance, its drone just added to Khet's misery. "Well, I'll be. I am late for a class. I am sorry, but I must be on my way. Khet, please join me for breakfast in the morning. I will send someone to come get you. Good day to you both." Vagner didn't wait for either to respond. His hurried footsteps echoed in the room until the door shut.

"You wanted to learn the truth about everything, so how did it go? Was it all you wanted?" Elesia sat at the table, the soft light from the window framed her in a dreamy haze.

Khet wanted to tell her everything. He wanted to fall into her arms and unload all of his burdens. With the revelations he was just given and everything he knew growing up is now a lie, Khet didn't know if he could trust her. So he lied.

"I didn't really learn anything new. Sounds like a tale from an overactive imagination." Khet's frustration with the situation came out in his tone. The conflict inside him was a problem he didn't want to deal with right now. "I don't even know if I can trust these Arankai."

Elesia's face showed the slightest bit of surprise and knowing. "That is my motto, don't trust anyone." Her tone became icy, her glow faded. "The Arankai have a bone to pick with the Temple, so do I. Enemy of my enemy is my friend." There was a deep hatred in Elesia's eyes. "I want to see the Temple burn."

"Besides everything they do, why do you hate the Temple so much?" Khet regretted the words as soon as they left his mouth.

Elesia's eyes went cold. Khet's skin prickled at the intensity of her stare. "My adoptive sister was sold into contract when she was thirteen, just because a powerful man from the Temple thought she was pretty. Her parents didn't want to do it, but their belief in the Twelve ran deep. So, they folded under the pressure of their belief and sold her." Malice dripped from her words as the corners of Khet's vision darkened. "For three months, he abused her. For three months, he raped and beat her. Then, he released her from the contract. We tried to take care of her and make it better. We tried to piece together what was broken." Tears full of hurt and rage fell down Elesia's face. "Four weeks later, my parents found her hanging from a tree."

His head felt like it was in a vice. "I am sorry..." The words sounded muffled.

"Everyone was fucking sorry!" Elesia erupted. A pressure built on Khet's chest, like a large stone crushing him. "Her parents were sorry, but did they do anything? No, they fucking didn't because of the Temple." She leaned into the rage, her voice swallowed the room. "Do you know what? I did something. I got revenge for my sister." Elesia reached into her boot and produced a long knife and buried it into the table. The name Kala was carved into the handle. "With that blade, I hunted him. I stalked him and his beautiful little bride out for a ride in the woods. With that blade, I separated him from his manhood, and I made him choke to death on it. With that blade, I made sure as he died, the last thing he saw was his wife's throat getting cut over the top of him." Her voice was ragged.

Khet couldn't speak. Couldn't breathe; the pressure crushed him.

Several long moments passed. Elesia wrenched the blade from the table. The pressure that crushed Khet evaporated. "Sorry about that. Maybe I should work on control myself." She slid the blade back in her boot. "After that, I was on the run for a while. The Arankai found me and gave me a home and a purpose. They accepted me for me. And as long as they are all about bringing down the Temple, they will have my loyalty." Elesia's eyes were now red and puffy. "Well enough about my shitty past. Do you want to go get some air? I can show you around the University a little."

"OK, that sounds great." Khet really didn't care where they went; he just wanted fresh air.

49

Elesia led them through a couple of small courtyards that were littered with members of the Hand and students. Each group they passed by stopped talking and just watched them pass. Khet could feel their eyes on him. *Does everybody know about me?* Their faces were a menagerie of emotions. Some were faces of awe. Some held fear in their eyes. A couple of the Hand members showed outright disdain.

She pulled him down a path that wound down in a slow curve to the left. The high walls reminded him of the mountain pass. He almost missed his time in the mountains. Back before he learned about the book and his part in it. Life was simpler then. When his purpose was just to deliver the badges.

The narrow path opened up to a wide hole in the ground. A hole lined with a chest-high railing. Several stairways worked their way down, deep down. No end to them could be seen. Deep caverns dotted the side walls. Khet could only guess at the size of each. Tiny figures moved about within them. Buildings and other structures showed the vastness of each cavern.

"Yeah, it's pretty crazy, right? I remember when they first started digging it. Everybody thought the scholars were off in the head. But when they found the first cavern, everyone joined in to support." Elesia breathed in the cool air. "When the first city was found, the University devoted an entire branch of learning to excavation and ancient history."

Khet's brain stuttered for a second. "Wait, you were here when they started digging this? It looks like they have been doing it for a long time. And where does all the rock they dig up go?"

"Khet, are you asking a woman her age? Tisk tisk, young man, I am allowed my secrets." A playful smirk danced on her face. "As for the rock, the outer wall and many of these buildings were made from it."

"I have seen one city underground. Is there more?"

"Yes, I don't know how many there are, before you ask." A soft breeze swirled from the depths. The scent in the air was sweet, almost fruity. "You smell that? That is from the orchard. They must be harvesting today."

Khet had walked through a forest for days underground. It would make sense that there be fruit trees. In a world full of Gods warring with each other, buried cities, and underground forests, pretty much anything should make sense. "What else have they found?" Khet's curiosity peaked.

"I don't know everything they have found. I have heard talk of great temples to different Gods. Farmland that is still fertile and stretches on for days. Rivers flowing out of solid rock. And not a single person alive or dead."

Khet stared down into the seemingly bottomless pit. Lost in complete confusion. His world had been turned upside down and set to flame. *What else don't I know?*

"You look pale. Let's go this way. I have more to show you." Khet followed Elesia down a narrow path around the rim of the hole. A short side path led to the backside of a courtyard full of random bits of what Khet would describe as junk. Everything in the courtyard looked like organized piles of rubbish.

"What is all of this?" Khet moved closer to study one of the piles. It was junk covered in grime and dirt. Pieces of metal in strange shapes made up the bulk of the pile.

"It's some of the things they find in the underground cities. I don't know exactly why they do it this way. I think the scholars and workers sort it out here and then break the piles down further over in that large building over there." Elesia pointed off into the distance at a group of nondescript buildings.

"Out in the open like this, what if the Temple sees this? They would send the Dodecahedron for sure." Khet could imagine the immortals swarming the university, slaughtering everyone. The thought stirred the rage within him. He would not let the Temple get away with that.

Elesia was quiet for a moment, seemed to be lost in thought. "All this stuff is junk found down there. Think about it for a minute. Wouldn't it be more suspicious to keep digging even though you don't find anything? I think this is all just for show. The rest is processed in a cavern underground, hidden away from prying eyes."

"How do you know all this stuff?" Khet is ever at a disadvantage because of his sheltered life in the south.

"I have been a part of the University and the Arankai for a long time now, longer than most probably." She had a look that said *don't ask.*

"OK… So, what else have they found down there?" Khet's curiosity ate him.

"The scholars don't let me in on everything. I have heard rumors." Elesia smiled conspiratorially.

"What rumors?" Khet was a fish that had been hooked.

Elesia's smile widened. "Khet, my sweet innocent farm boy, I am a spy. I can't tell you all my secrets. You know too much already." Her smile had a mischievous glow to it.

Khet's mouth dropped open, he knew he was being played by her, but he enjoyed the melody of the tune. "Fine, you can keep your secrets." It sounded so much more impressive in his head.

"OK." Is all Elesia said. With her impish grin, she turned and walked out of the courtyard.

Dumbfounded by her response, Khet stood there, after several heartbeats and the hard realization that he tried and failed to flirt with Elesia, swiftly moved to keep up with her.

They walked through a couple of other courtyards all filled with things Khet could never even dream of when he lived with Tarin. His emotions were a mix of awe and bewilderment at all the structures and odd metalwork. Khet saw a man with a metal leg made of gears, his gait only had the slightest limp. Small blocks of metal no bigger than a man's head were hauled aloft by a team of horses that strained under the weight. His new world made little sense. It was all so much.

"Khet, are you okay?" Elesia stood several feet away with a concerned look on her face. "Looks like you were lost there for a minute. Do you need to sit down? You look flushed?"

Khet snapped back to the moment from his thoughts, noting that he was so deep in thought that he stopped following her and almost walked into a wall. "Err… Yeah, sorry, I got distracted. It has been a lot for me to handle."

"Come with me, you are stressed and it looks like you could use some good food and even better drink. There is a tavern outside the inner wall called the Lost Thought. We can relax a little. You look like you could need it." Elesia reached out for Khet's hand.

Her hand was warm and comforting. Khet felt like he could relax around her, just for a while. He could lay down his burden.

The time of day must have been late. The courtyards were practically empty except maybe for a few more dedicated students. Most of the workers seemed to have gone home as well. It was just the two of them, hand in hand.

After the food and drinks, the air was light and lovely. Khet felt as if he floated along the pathways back to the cottage. He had left his burden behind for a short while and was feeling great.

"You are a breath of fresh air, my friend. Tonight was something I think we both needed." She sat down on a secluded bench near their cottage. "Too many folks out there trying to fuck or fuck over one another. It gets so tiring. You come from good folk and it shows. Don't change who you are?"

"But who is that? Who am I?" The joy Khet was just filled with fled. The question made him face his reality. His anger flared at it.

"You are you." Elesia smiled. "People will try and define you. Make you fit your identity into a little box that they have created to make themselves comfortable. I say fuck that and you be you." Her strength came through her words. "Don't let those fuckers define who you are. You get to decide, not them. Do you understand that?"

Khet averted his eyes; he had never experienced this. The thought of something so simple, yet so profound in its nature. Told to him in this way, overwhelmed him. He couldn't make eye contact with her. He wanted to run back to the moment before. To that moment of happiness. But before he could run, she embraced him. Khet lost complete control of his emotions. He felt every emotion surge through him all at once. He broke down and just sobbed in her soft embrace. He felt safe to feel what he needed to.

50

The next morning, there was a knock at the door to the cottage. Khet, feeling refreshed, emotions a little frayed from the night before, untangled himself from his blankets. At the door stood a stranger, a small wisp of a man dressed in a fine set of blue student robes.

"I am sorry to wake you, but Prelate Creshing has requested your audience in the Great Hall." His voice was thin like the last gust of air from a broken bellows.

"Alright, tell him I will be there soon. I need to get dressed and maybe a bite to eat." Khet yawned.

"I was told to escort you there as soon as possible. Food and drink will be there waiting for you."

"OK, could you wait outside while I get dressed?"

"Yes, sir." He closed the door with an indignant thud.

"Who was at the door?" Elesia yawned deeply.

Khet almost startled out of his skin. He struggled to act like he remembered that she had her own room in the cottage and he hadn't forgotten. "Just ah…" The light caught her form perfectly; he had to focus. "Just somebody… to take me to see Vagner… He wanted to share breakfast this morning."

"OK, have fun. I am going back to bed. I haven't slept in a bed this nice in a long time." She sleepily trudged back to her bed and hid under the blankets.

As Khet was getting dressed, he couldn't wipe the smile off his face. That moment last night with Elesia made joy fill his chest. His steps were lighter, and he stood straighter. Sunlight sparkled as it filtered through the window.

Khet met the man just outside the door and followed him to the Great Hall. It wasn't all that long of a walk. Just down several flights of stairs. And through a great set of double doors. The Great Hall did indeed live up to its name. Colors from every hue rained down on the tables and chairs that covered the floor. A bookcase covered the entire left side wall, three tall men high. His head swiveled back to the ceiling. All the colors shimmered and blurred shapes moved across it in varied patterns. It only took him a moment to see that those shapes were people. His jaw truly dropped when he connected that the Great Hall's ceiling actually was the Grand Courtyard he walked through yesterday. Khet stood there in complete awe.

"This way, sir." Said the man, the comment knocked Khet out of his stupor.

Khet could see Vagner at a table off to the side near the bookcase. A warm smile spread across his face as Khet approached.

"Good morning, Khet. Have a seat. I ordered some breakfast if you don't mind."

"Thank you. I am a little hungry this morning." Khet's mouth watered at the sight and smell of the food.

"Thank you, Ulrich. That is all I need. See you at classes tomorrow afternoon." Vagner barely looked at Ulrich as he dismissed him.

"The students are servants here?" Khet was confused by their interaction.

Vagner gave Khet a puzzled look. "Oh, no. When students are disciplined, they must pick up extra duties. And that Ulrich has a hard time controlling his drink. Speaking of which, are you a morning wine drinker?"

"No, thank you." Khet replied.

"Oh, I enjoy a glass in the morning, to oil the hinges a little, if you catch my meaning." Vagner raised his glass to Khet before downing it whole. "I noticed the look on your face when you came into the hall. Impressive, isn't it?"

"I have never seen anything like it. I walked through that courtyard yesterday and had no idea." Khet marveled at the colorful ceiling.

A grin spread across the scholar's face, always happy to teach. "We call it translucent stone. We discovered it ages ago when the University was first built. The process to reproduce it still eludes us, but we are making progress. The Great Hall and the rest of the structure below it were here before the University was founded."

"Elesia has told me you have found many strange things while digging." Khet bubbled with curiosity.

"I bet she did. She has helped us a lot over the years. Oh, that reminds me, the rest of..." He scanned the area to see if anyone was within earshot. "The Arankai have been delayed for a couple of days. The Temple is slowing down travel. You have kicked over a beehive, my boy. They are looking for you really hard. No worry though. There have been sightings of you near the town of Dusk heading into the Shadowed Vale." He gave Khet a wink. "We have planned this for a long time. We will keep them busy and off your back. Now, where was I... ah yes. First, I have a task for you, that I think you are uniquely suited to complete."

"OK, what task?" Khet's body vibrated with intense curiosity.

"That sword you brought with you. I have a schema that is referenced in the book you read yesterday. It speaks of how to reforge the sword into a weapon you can wield against them. You are going to need it in the upcoming quest of yours. We can talk more about it later with less prying ears around. I am sure you have more questions weighing on your mind."

"When I was traveling here, I traveled this cave west of the City of Passes. There was a massive storage of barrels of food down there. How did it get down there?"

"Oh yes, that was us. We have been storing supplies all around to prepare. It's quite impressive actually. There are hidden entrances to the cave system all over. You see, in the book, it detailed many of the locations and helped us track down several of the Alfir blessed before they accidentally fell through time. That is what we believe happens when they unknowingly use their ability."

"Did the book ever explain how people became marked with runes and have these abilities and why only one ability and..."

"Slow down, slow down, not all at once, my boy." Vagner chuckled like a loving grandfather to his grandson. "You asked a very interesting question. A question nobody really knows the answer to. It could be a product of the shards atop the towers. Another idea is that we were made by Malak this way. Or maybe all the different ways Sýna was remade, the magic warped and changed in unknowable ways." Vagner paused for a moment to see if Khet had any follow-on questions; none came. "Alright, where was I? Yes. We used the book and taught them to control their abilities. Nothing grand or dangerous, mind you, just use it to slow time to almost a standstill on an object like a barrel. That is why the barrels seem to shimmer. And they are reusable. Empty one out, and you can just reload it with fresh produce, and it will keep for years. It takes an extreme amount of concentration to shift their moment in time properly. Only three were able to control it; the others were sadly lost."

Khet knew what the answer was going to be, but he wanted to ask anyway. "If you think I will stop them, the gods, why prepare like this?"

"To be honest, we, the Arankai, are not willing to risk all of humanity on your success. This is completely uncharted waters we are moving through. We are off the edges of the map, if you catch my meaning. The main goal is to protect as many as we can. The Arankai believe you will succeed." Vagner ran out of assurances. "I am sorry, Khet, we must wait for the full counsel to arrive before we can discuss more. Sorry I brought it up; sometimes I just get carried away. They should be here in two days. I am sure you have other questions."

"Yeah, I have another one. What can you tell me about these, and why do I have them?" Khet pulled back his collar to reveal the runes on his neck.

Relief came to Vagner's face for the change in topic. "Most of us are not for certain. I have an idea though, not particularly supported by my fellow scholars." He looked around to see if anyone could be listening. "I believe the trapped ones, that is what we call them, have had time to study their situation and they have observed what Malak has done. Basically, they have made a champion of their own."

A piece of food fell from Khet's gawped mouth."Wait, are you saying they made me?"

"I have no tangible proof that they created you. It is just a hypothesis I have. You see, reading your written part of the book over and over again, I see coincidences that I can't shake. Now, you can't just build your knowledge off of coincidences. You will never find the truth that way. The fact that you never knew your mother, your father never talked about her, and in your words, he never cared about you. I see a possible justification that your father found you and tried to raise you. Not to mention how your runes and abilities are unique gifts from the trapped ones. Now, I can't find demonstrable proof to support my claim. That is why it is just an idea."

Khet sat there for a moment and mulled the idea over in his mind. Vagner's idea did make sense, but Khet could easily find several other reasons for his childhood. He had to settle for the idea that even if he knew the truth, there was no changing his past. Elesia's words rang in his ears: " *You are you.*"

The rest of the meal, Khet kept it to just small things. No more large revelations about his past because there was no reason to really stress about it if you can't change it.

51

Khet's belly now comfortably full, he followed Vagner back to the cottage to gather the sword. He entered the cottage with a new vigor in his movements. The excitement over the mysterious task that involved the sword made him buzz. His small, simple room was undisturbed from when he left in the morning. His modest-sized bed was pushed into the corner. The art portfolio folio that held the sword leaned against the small bedside table. An aroma lingered in the air. Faint and light, it caressed his face. It was the scent of Elesia's perfume, fresh in the air.

What was I doing? He lost himself for a moment. On the table out in the common area was a small note. "Hope your breakfast with Vagner was good. How about dinner again at the Lost Thought 8th bell?" The note smelled of her delicate perfume.

A wide grin spread across Khet's face. A great friend, great food, and great drink is exactly something Khet could use more of these days. With high spirits, he grabbed the sword and met Vagner outside.

Vagner led Khet to a small, secluded workshop. It was a smithy tucked behind a massive building. Several trees and bushes almost obscured the entire thing. The area was far enough from the main area of the campus that it looked as if it had been abandoned for years.

"This is a special workshop where the University's more advanced students work on certain projects that need secrecy, and it is yours for the next three days. I don't think you will need all three days, though. I just wanted you not to feel pressured." Vagner spoke loftily as he walked around the workshop, opening shutters and vents.

"What is it you want me to do?" Khet inspected a tool set up that made no sense to him. All the tools in there were unlike anything he had ever worked with.

"Hold on one second... Ahh, here it is." Vagner squeezed between two of the benches near the far wall. He reached up and twisted a small bracket that looked mangled to hold anything. A soft click followed by a low grinding noise came from the wall. A seam appeared and continued to grow. The newly revealed doorway yawned back at them. Khet could see stairs led down into a deep blackness. A chill breeze came from the depths that made him shiver.

"Don't worry, my boy, a strapping lad like yourself will be fine. For me, this will be slightly unpleasant; there are a lot of stairs." Vagner reached into a small glowing box on the wall. "Here, you will need this." He threw a small light stone to Khet. "Follow me, and be careful; the stairs can become steep, not to mention slippery due to the dampness."

Khet followed Vagner down the long stairway into the inky blackness. "As you can see, the glow stones become less effective the deeper we go. It seems that the darkness becomes thicker, for the lack of a better term."

Indeed, the darkness started to overcome the small glow stone with every step. The blackness had an oily texture to it. "How will I be able to see to do my work?"

"It will be fine; you will see." Khet couldn't see Vagner's face, but he could hear his smile in his voice.

The stairway ended after a long descent at a small landing. Khet and Vagner both breathed hard. The darkness was thick, stuck to Khet. The glow stone in his hand barely registered to him at all. Panic at the thought that he would never see light again gripped his innards.

"Give me your stone, please." A hand grabbed hold of Khet and removed the stone from his hand. Vagner placed both stones in a small box on the wall and pushed the box into the wall. The room ahead of them flooded with light. Khet braced his eyes against the glare. "Watch your step." Vagner warned.

The brightness stabbed at him, painful and sharp. His skin prickled at the heat the light gave off. Then it all faded like it was a dream. Khet stood at the entrance of a large room, the largest anvil Khet had ever seen sat in the middle. The metal it was made from had a slight shimmer. The light around them almost danced like it does around a fire.

A pathway to the anvil, about three strides wide, led to the base of the anvil. The rest looked to be covered in an inky black cloth. Khet walked closer to get a look at the cloth that covered the floor.

"Don't!" Vagner reached out and grabbed Khet. " You don't want to fall down that. We would never be able to recover your body."

Khet's bowels threatened to loosen. Most of the room was a deep chasm. "How deep is it?" His fear apparent in his question.

Vagner rubbed his chin. "We don't know. Several times we tried to find out. We have dropped coins, metal bits, and even a stone imbued with so much light you couldn't look at it directly. Once we lowered a man by rope. We used all the rope we had available. When we gave up and brought him back up, he said he didn't see or hear anything. Watch this." Vagner grabbed the hammer that lay on the top of the anvil and hurled it into the blackness. Within seconds, the hammer appeared back on the anvil. "Amazing, isn't it? We don't understand how. It just happens. Something with the magic used to create it, I assume."

"I guess I don't have to worry about dropping my tools. Anything else does this?"

"No, just the hammer. Everything else we have thrown down there never came back. So be careful with the sword."

"You haven't explained what I am doing here?" Khet had almost forgotten.

"There is your schema." Vagner pointed to the wall opposite the anvil.

Khet didn't notice it when he entered the room, because who would look there for a schema across a void? But there it was in all its glory. A massive drawing of a hammer bound to the haft by coils of golden threads. Notes and measurements scrawled all along the sides and the bottom. Underneath it all, there were three symbols. The runes for Magnus, Arrinia, and Rafir. "How?... How old is it?"

"We don't know, Khet. As you can see now, I think this is a job only you can do." Vagner looked to be enjoying the profound moment of wonderment on Khet's face.

"I don't know what those ores are on the schema. What are they?" Two markings, foreign to Khet, were displayed on the wall.

Excitement jolted through Vagner's features. "This is the beauty of this room and invokes a deeper mystery. One is referencing   blood,

blood of the weapon as it translates."

"I am a weapon?" Something woke inside Khet. It was ancient and full of rage. He pushed against it to bring it back under control. The rage settled for now. Khet swallowed hard and relaxed slightly. "How do you know it says that?"

"One of the cities that are underground, Risala, I believe, had a temple that referenced this forge. That is how we found it, actually. In the temple, it says 'The living weapon will give their blood to forge a god killer on the anvil of living iron.' Now I don't know this magic, if it is actual magic that has survived all the recreations of life on Sýna. It could be referencing your actual blood, or you are the only one that can forge the hammer. Other places have been found deep underground that reference a spear and a sword. I believe that is what was on the other walls."

Khet tore his eyes from the hammer and looked at the other walls. There were remnants of other schemas. A little bit here and there, but no clear image or instruction. "What is this place?" Khet asked the room.

Vagner just shrugged his shoulders. "We don't know what it was originally called. We have found it referenced as Telos, Dagsátr, Dies Irae, Dysis, and more. We have just called it by the hammer's name Skrið, it translates as war."

Khet stood there, mouth agape. The weight of it pressed on him. He fought back against the pressure. With this hammer, he could end all the unnecessary suffering brought by the Temple. Strið could bring about a new age. An age free of the Gods and their schemes. Determination stiffened his spine. He had a way now. A clear path to walk. He would forge Strið and bring an end to Malak. Bring an end to Magnus. Then burn down the Temple and free all the contracted.

Vagner could see he was at the end of his usefulness. "Well, I will leave you to it. If you need anything, I will be in my study." He pulled a light stone from his pocket and headed towards the stairs. "Sorry, almost forgot. When you leave this chamber. Pull the box from the wall and retrieve the two light stones and place them in the box upstairs. Also, one other thing, do not mention this to anyone. This is a closely guarded secret, and I want to keep it that way."

"Yes...yes...of course." Khet only half listened; his mind was set to his task.

"OK then, don't forget to eat and drink water. Don't want you passing out and disappearing down the hole." Vagner chuckled to himself at his attempt at humor and left the room.

Khet stood there transfixed by the schema. Everything had been pointing to this. All the random bullshit that had happened in Khet's life led to this point. The rage, ancient and wise, stirred again from its slumber.

52

Khet set himself to the task before him. He pulled the sword out of the case and studied the runes on it. This was the first time he really looked at it since he took it from the immortal in the mountain path. Faint lines crisscrossed the blade. Strange runes were pressed into the spaces between. None of the lines or runes made a discernible pattern.

He scanned the notes and measurements on the side of the schema. All of the schemas that Khet had seen were almost like a recipe. He remembered as Tarin had taught him. "Every schema is a recipe. You mix a little bit of this with a little bit of that at this temperature, pound it to shape, and let cool." Khet chuckled to himself as he tried to imitate the large man's voice. This schema was different. There were no percentages of metals to combine. No indicators on how many times the metal needed to be folded. The measurement for how much blood is needed was not exact either. The symbol Vagner said was blood of the weapon appeared throughout the schema.

He had to think. He only had one sword. The thought of attempting to acquire another did not seem like a great option. Khet rested the sword on the anvil. The surface of the anvil rippled and shimmered like the surface of a lake. Runes on the blade glowed and the forge filled with blinding light.

Khet shielded his eyes against the glare. The fragrance of freshly bloomed flowers filled his nostrils. He lowered his arm as the light faded. A figure slowly came into view, it was a woman with golden iridescent hair. She had a warm, comforting smile on her face. Her eyes were a piercing blue, that glimmered. The green dress she wore did very little to hide what was underneath. Khet glanced around, he was no longer in the forge nor was he in the temple where he met Magnus and the others. He stood in a room that was sparsely decorated. Columns lined the walls that let the open air easily flow through. The air smelled crisp and slightly damp. The sun hung low in the sky.

"First time you've ever seen the sunrise." The woman's voice was luxurious; it caressed Khet ever so gently.

"No, but I have heard of it." He was used to this game. The way she carried herself radiated godly power. He was getting tired of this ploy. So he tried to act like he was nonplussed about this situation.

The God laid down on one of the several couches. "It is a beautiful time, the cool of the nighttime air mixed with the gentle light of dawn."

"What is this? Why am I here? Who are you?" Khet tired of being manipulated by Gods.

The God's face shifted ever so slightly, apparently taken aback by Khet's bluntness. "This is a place made for myself long ago before I was imprisoned. I am here to help you end Malak and Magnus's petty schemes. The others don't know I am here. I am the one called Norona; I created you."

Khet was at a loss. "Created me? You're my mother?"

"Oh no, your birth mother died shortly after you were born. I am the one that made you inside your mother." Norona spoke like it was a trivial fact. "I tried many times before, and few succeeded. You are the eighth and final one."

"What do you mean eighth and final one?"

"It took many tries to even get one of you born. Those beings that Malak created may look like us, but they are very different. Only eight of you lived. Of the eight of you, you're the third to come to me."

"OK…So you're my father then?"

Her laugh was intoxicating; it washed over Khet. The softness of her eased his frustration. "You could say that if you wanted to, but that doesn't really matter. There are more dire issues at hand."

As she spoke, strange sensations enveloped Khet. Almost a need to please Norona, to do whatever she says. He fought it. "What are you doing to me?" His rage burned the need away, leaving anger in its place.

Norona looked surprised. "You found me out. I am not like the others. I am a Thune. And if you could please forgive me for my tricks, I am dying or dead already and just wanted to have a little fun."

"What, you're dying?" Khet wanted to trust her. But she is a God, there is no trust left in him for Gods.

"You know before the war that trapped us, I would come here, my lover and I. It was beautiful. I just wanted to feel that again. And yes, I am dying, I was the last of my tribe and Magnus does not need me anymore. Magnus killed us all, in his plans for power. Only Arrinia, Rafir, and Calver are still alive." The light in Narona's face had left her.

"Arrinia is dead. I saw Magnus kill her. I have her and Rafir's power now."

"Well, that was expected. I always thought Magnus's would kill us all."

"So why all of this?"

"When we were first imprisoned, we still carried on the war Malak had started. As time passed it became clear that we needed to get free. A peace was struck, and we came together, but the balance was gone. We threw everything we could at that prison and slowly we wore it down. It took many ages to finally produce a single crack." With the wave of her hand a small table with a glass of wine appeared in front of Narona. She scooped up the glass and relished a sip. "First, we watched Malak and Nox, we thought they were both traders. Quickly we could see through the crack, that Nox was Malak's slave. So again, we attacked the walls of our prison weakening the cracks further." She savored the wine. "After a time we could push our influences now, but only in the shadow of the star. So, as Malak's creations would come into the shadow we would corrupt them and turn them against their creator." Another slow sip of wine. "We witnessed Malak murder Nox with that blade of his. We watched the shards scatter all across Sýna. We watched your world be remade again and again. With each iteration we would find new ways to corrupt Malak's plan. Until he built that damn Wall and kept the world from turning." Another deep pull of wine.

"So, the story about the Wall's creation was only a partial lie. It wasn't evil beings kept out, it was Malak's enemies." The picture of the truth of things became clearer.

"Depends on your definition of evil. Magnus is just as bad, if not worse." Norona finished the glass; the glass refilled itself. "After the Wall was first built, we almost gave up. But we worked together, and a plan was formed. We created an army and attacked the Wall. We tried everything, but nothing could scratch it. The army is still out there now, waiting."

"That doesn't explain why you made me or what the plan is." Irritation was plain in his voice.

"I was getting to it, slow down. We came across a perfect opportunity. A long time ago, we were able to make a spy for us. In this new world Malak created, there exist rifts in time. Something in the old magic he created corrupted the new magic of your world." She took a slow sip and let out a long sigh. "We, or I at least, could reach through it and affect the past. I took all of the knowledge we had gained and gave it to one of Malak's creations. I found a woman that was injured badly, and a healer was pouring all his energy into her to save her, and this made an opening for me. With a mixture of old and new magic, I brought her back to life. I gave her information, and she would spread our influence. One purpose she was given was to search the many levels of creation to find the shards of Malak's weapon."

"How many did she find?" He could feel the answer before she even said it.

"Well, I know she found at least eight of them." A half-drunken, playful smile spread across her face.

"She found eight. Wait, what are you saying?" Khet could feel his irritation begin to simmer.

"I am saying, my sweet, sweet boy. The shard of the blade that can kill us runs through your veins. Two of you have come here and forged their weapons. Also, they were kind enough to indulge me in my fun. I don't know what happened to them." She had a playful, drunkenness to her that rubbed Khet the wrong way.

"What do you want with me!" His frustration boiled over.

No reaction at all to Khet's shout, she went on. "Well, I say we. It's just Magnus now. When you were born, you were our last chance. Factions were formed on how to use you."

Khet's eyes lit up. "Magnus won."

"Yes, he killed all who opposed him. I was the last of the opposition to fall." Norona violently coughed.

"What is the plan? What does he want to do with me?"

She coughed again; her complexion paled. "He wants you to restart the spin of your world. So, he can kill Malak." She coughed again. Blood dribbled from her mouth. "You will need to forge the hammer, Skrið. Use it to defeat him and destroy the creation crystal atop the Gods' Spire. There is a crystal in the anvil; take it, keep it with you. The crystal will protect you from the moment that is coming." Her body heaved with coughs; blood splashed on the ground. "Rin will find you. Use the hammer to destroy that crystal atop the spire… then kill him… kill that bastard."

"Who is Rin? What moment?" Blinding light flashed, and Khet was back in the forge.

53

Questions, more questions, is all he had. Rage, ancient and wise, burned in Khet's chest. It smoldered like a dull red piece of hot iron. Determination moved his hands to work. He placed his hand upon the anvil. The surface flowed and reacted to his touch. It whispered to him its secrets, knowledge of what needed to be done.

Khet pressed the tip of the sword to the anvil. He drove the blade into the rippling anvil. Arcs of energy peeled off the anvil. The sword fought him; he felt the sword's fear. The farther the blade sunk into the anvil, the harder it fought. Khet could almost hear it scream. He let the rage fuel him, and the blade sunk further. Silence filled the forge as the hilt touched the anvil.

Khet took the hammer, and with a mighty swing, he broke the hilt from the sword. A shower of sparks flew in all directions. The anvil's surface rippled and flowed. A great wrenching noise emanated from it and vibrated deep in his chest. The rage blossomed within Khet. The last remnant of the sword was pulled into the anvil.

He waited for the anvil to give him its secret. What was whispered earlier now revealed. A small shard of a dull grey steel surfaced from the anvil. It was only the size of a man's palm, but power radiated from it.

The shard had knowledge in it. Khet did not understand it, but he knew it in his blood. He pushed all the heat he could into it. Then he struck it with the forge hammer. Again and again and again, each impact was thunder rolling off of a cliffside. The heartbeat of a God killer shook the forge.

He called upon his golden threads. The ancient rage slipped its bonds and poured through them. He wound them tightly around the shard. Then he hammered again and again and again. The entire forge trembled with each impact. Skrið breathed in the fury to end Gods.

Now he summoned his healing ability; the shard glowed a hot white. The intensity of the light forced Khet to squint. Then he brought his hammer down. Great waves of energy arced. Bolts of lightning struck the walls, blasting pieces of rock into the void. Howls of defiance and rage echoed through the forge.

He grabbed the white-hot hammer head with his hands. He used every ounce of his strength to hold it in place as he pushed all of his rage into the hammer head. All of his hate flowed into every piece. Golden threads wrapped and twisted as it pulled the hilt of the sword into the hammer.

Then it was done. The hammer Skrið, the one to put an end to the God's plots for power, had been forged. Khet took Skrið into his hand. His blood ignited with power. It surged through him. It filled every fiber of his being with it. He felt as a God.

He released a breath, slow and smooth, as he lowered the hammer. Skrið was a part of him now. They were one and the same.

The anvil shimmered and boiled. A large yellow crystal floated to the surface. It shined dully in the light of the forge. As Khet took hold of the crystal, the ground shifted and crack underneath him. He launched himself towards the doorway.

He turned as he made it to the doorway, just in time to see the anvil disappear into the blackness. Its fate complete.

54

He strode back to the cottage. The power of Skrið pulsed in his hand. His skin prickled with heat.

A bell chimed. Bong...Bong...Bong...Bong...Bong... Khet was pulled from his thoughts. Bong... How long had he been down there? Bong... "Please let it just be the eighth bell." Bong... Khet held his breath and braced for impact. Bong... "Shit." Khet ran, weaving his way through students and scholars. Bong...Bong... He slowed to a walk, his shoulders slumped in defeat. Elesia would not be waiting for him at the Lost Thought, not for this long. Bong... Khet glared in the direction of the bell. Defeated, he made his way back to the cottage.

Elesia was his first real friend since he left Tarin's. He didn't want to disappoint her. He needed a friend now in his life more than anything right now. His heart and feet were heavy as he shuffled through the door.

"Hey there, sugar, did you forget about little old me?" Elesia was seated at the table with several empty bottles.

Khet was a mixture of hope and despair. "I...ugh..." Words failed him. "Iam sorry. I was working on something for Vagner, and I lost track of time." Khet was sad he let his friend down. He didn't want to be that kind of person.

Elesia's whole expression changed. "You forged Skrið, well, it had to happen sometime." Her speech was a little slurred.

Khet stood frozen in confusion. "How did you know?"

"Oh, shit. I always get a little chatty when I am into my cups. Well, into my bottles this time. You think I would have figured that out by now?"

"That doesn't answer my question."

"You know...this was meant to happen, but I just wanted to maybe have a couple of days with you unspoiled by it all. You're cute, and it has been a long time since I had someone like you in my life."

"Unspoiled? What does that mean?"

"Fine." Elesia shifted in her chair. Her drunkenness almost had her on the ground. "Here, have a seat. You might want a drink as well." Khet accepted the cup from Elesia with reservation and cautiously sat across from her.

The liquor was strong. He wanted to cough and make a face, but for some reason, he fought it. Warmth spread through his chest. "OK, go on." Alcohol burned his throat.

"Where to start, okay?" She grabbed another cup and took a long pull from it. "I know you forged Skrið, and I know you spoke to Narona, that stuck-up bitch." She drunkly giggled at that last comment. "You see, how should I put this? That book Vagner had you read. I am the one who found it."

"He said it was two thousand years old, impossible. Did he lie to me?"

"Didn't Narona tell you about me? She told the other two who I was and fucked them, apparently. By the look of you, you weren't so lucky." She chuckled.

The realization poured over him. "You're the one she brought back to life, you're Rin?"

"Hi, nice to meet you?" She reached her hand out in a friendly greeting.

Khet finished his glass and slid it to her for a refill. "How old are you?"

"Well, that is tricky to say. I have seen the world remade six or seven times. I remember when the sun would rise and set daily. A long time before those fuckin' Towers were made and the sun stopped moving. Don't get me started on that eyesore of a Wall."

Khet downed the cup. He hoped the liquor would make it make sense. "So you're immortal like the Dodecahedron?"

"No, those things are metal-made flesh. I am a real person that can't die."

"So why don't you take Skrið and kill Malak and the others?" His drunken honesty bubbled to the surface.

"I have no real useful powers. I can't die, but I can still feel all the pain. The number of times I should have died is countless. I spent years chained to a rock at the bottom of a river. Just to drown over and over again. I was only freed when Malak remade Sýna again. And that just got me out of the water. I was still chained to a large, fucking rock underground. I went a little mad for a while after that." She didn't cry, but her eyes did wet. "Not to mention getting stabbed, beaten to death, beheaded, quartered, burned alive, and I was hanged about twenty times. I felt it all. Three of your predecessors got me locked in the Temple's dungeons at Iridam. They acted dumb like you did when they saw the Grand Inquisitor."

"I am sorry." The confusion and sadness he felt for his friends made him feel worse.

"You didn't know. To tell the truth, you get a little numb to it after a while." She gave Khet a half-drunken smile. "Enough of the sad stuff. You had questions, ask them?"

"How did you know that I forged Skrið and talked to Narona?"

"That is easy. There was more than one book that fell out of that time thingy near Alfir's tower. Three actually, one I gave to the University, and the other two were for me, written by two different me's actually."

"What?" Khet's mind hurt from the thought.

"Yeah, each time they tried something different and apparently failed. At least that is what the books say."

He took the now refilled cup and sipped it. A thought was dislodged by the burn in his throat. "How did they do it?"

"Nope, can't go into that. If I told you, things might go differently, can't risk it. All I can say is we are doing something different. And since we are being honest, I think you are the most handsome hero." Her smile made his drunken mind lose focus.

For several long seconds, Khet was lost in her beauty. Her heavy-lidded eyes pulled him in with their hunger. Her lips looked soft; he desperately wanted to kiss them.

"That can't be all you wanted to know." She leaned back with a knowing smile; she had him.

Khet centered himself and attempted to push those thoughts aside. "Yes, the other two that forged their weapons. What happened to them?"

Rin's face changed to slight disapproval for the continued

questioning. "They died after they shattered the God Shard's on the Lost and Forgotten Towers. Centuries apart, of course. I wasn't there to watch. So I don't know, really."

"So you know the names of the Lost and Forgotten?"

"Not a clue. I think it had something to do with the magics, old and new, mixing. The Temple just explained it away."

"What are the Arankai planning to do with me?"

"You are just so full of questions. It is not my place to tell you. You will know soon enough. Now, can we discuss something else?"

Her smile brought Khet's questioning to a halt. The warmth of her hand as it slid playfully up his arm. Sensations pulsed through him. Her hunger infected him. All he could think about was her soft skin. The wood of the chair creaked as she moved closer to him; every second felt like an eternity of anticipation. Heat radiated from her body; he could smell it mixed with her soft perfume. He could almost taste her lips. The need to feel the caress of her hands, the shape of her breasts, the curve of her thighs, and the wonders in between consumed him.

Her breath was hot on his face, a potent mixture of alcohol and lust. He drank the moment in and fell into her embrace.

55

The lovers slept in each other's arms. Khet was the first to stir. Sunlight dappled through the trees. The room smelled of old booze and sex. Not exactly what Khet thought of for his first time. His head ached from the liquor more than it should have.

"Ah fuck. Dammit, Rin." She said blearily to herself.

"What's wrong?" The colorful room shifted in hue.

"This is wrong. So wrong. Why did I do that? Gods Damn It!" She cursed as she got out of bed to get dressed.

"Why is this wrong?" The room shifted towards a lifeless grey.

"I let my drinking affect my judgement again. You think being thousands of years old, I would learn." She hung her head. "And you are supposed to die."

"Vagner says we will do it differently this time. I won't die." Khet was a little insulted.

Rin still struggled to put her clothes back on. "Khet, you don't get it. The books that I have, how do I explain this to you? Each one of them has you dead, and the ones that came before, all dead. Yes, they were all different, but it all ended the same. The eighth hero dies. A ninth will rise in the future and finally free us."

Khet sat up in bed. "Why wouldn't Vagner have told me that?" His anger came to the surface.

"He doesn't know."

"If a ninth hero rises to free us, why am I so important?"

"You are a major part in the Gods' downfall. Just as the other two destroyed God Shards. You have a part to play, a critical part."

"Well, can you tell me what is going to happen?"

Rin sat at the end of the bed, her face full of anger. Anger at who, Khet had no idea. "War is coming. A long war. Magnus will command an army and feed off all the lost lives. Only a woman named Issahya will destroy him."

"Well, then why am I doing what I am doing? Why don't we wait for this Issahya to save us?"

"Because Khet, if you don't start it and do what the Arankai are planning, Magnus will be too strong, and Issahya will fail."

The joy he had from the night before was completely erased. All that was there was the rage. "No, I will defeat Magnus, and we will be free! You will see! I am putting an end to this!" Khet shouted in defiance.

"You are just a stupid boy! That does not know what he is dealing with." Rin's anger flared to match his.

They stood there in silence, no movements. Both hearts hammered inside their chests, faces red. Khet was hurt by Rin's words, wounded by them. He reacted in a way that most people do when they are wounded; he lashed out. "I don't care. Go and hide."

Rin held his gaze for a second longer. Her eyes held more meaning in them than anything she could say. She turned without a wasted word and left. The door remained open to mark the truth that she would not return.

A new anger burned within, one of defiance mixed with the hurt of lost friendship. The fact that Rin had two books with two separate stories showed Khet that he could change and make a new story. He would be the one to defeat Malak. To end Magnus's scheme for power. A story where the eighth hero frees them all and the war never comes.

56

Determination in his purpose fueled Khet through the hallways to the Prelate's office. The door to his office was slightly ajar. To let a breeze blow through the musty hallways, no doubt.

The small reception room was scant of any furniture, minus a small desk that sat vacant. Khet could hear mumbled words come from the Prelate's office. Vagner sat at a very simple, erudite desk surrounded by shelves upon shelves of books. In fact, every single table in his office was stacked high with books. The tables beneath them strained to hold the weight. Vagner sat at his desk, too engrossed in a book to notice Khet's arrival. The sound of Skrið as it thunked on the desk drew his attention.

"My dear boy...Is that what I think it is?" Vagner's eyes were the size of saucers. "You finished it already."

Khet stood there grimly and nodded. He had wanted since he was a young boy to be a hero of legend. Now he had a chance.

"Here, let's have a look, shall we?" Vagner wrapped his hands around the darkened haft. The head of Skrið had a cold blackness to it. The golden threads with their reddish glow were wrapped and twisted tightly around the head and haft. "Wow, this is quite heavy. How are you expected to wield this?"

Khet reached out with his golden thread and pulled Skrið to his hand. "It didn't seem that heavy to me." The hammer had heft in Khet's hands, but the rage they both held made the burden less. In his hands, the threads shone brighter.

"Maybe I am older than I thought. "Vagner chuckled. "Anyways, I am glad you are here. The Arankai will be convening here soon. We will need you there."

"Where is the meeting being held?"

"The council chamber, of course. All thirteen will be there." Vagner had a grin on his face that Khet didn't understand. "Get ready for an experience, my boy. Come, we will make our way there now."

Khet entered the council chamber, the creak of the heavy door announced his arrival. All conversations in the chamber ended as everyone turned to Khet. Even with all the stares aimed in his direction, Khet did not flinch. The anger and determination that set within his chest this morning still burned quite hot. Vagner guided Khet to a spot on the entry level of the chamber, while he went down to join the other eleven Arankai.

Khet glanced around at the twelve Arankai. There was nothing special about them. Just normal-looking men and women. At the center, a dark figure was seated. Khet could not make out what they were. Their form shifted constantly like a shadow on rippling water. A mask covered the upper half of the figure's face, and the only thing that held still. Strange runes carved into the mask. They glowed a deep, unsettling red. Unease pushed back against Khet's determination when he noticed that the masked figure's eyes were fixed in his direction.

Vagner joined the other Arankai and sat in his chair at the Valkai the Knowing's Tower. A strange thrum could be heard and felt deep in his chest. He made eye contact with Khet and winked. A strange, almost electric sensation swept through Khet. His vision had an alien glow cast over it. Khet scanned the room to figure out where the sound originated from. His heart stopped. All the people in the room were now shifting dark masses with a mask. Each one had a different rune, but all of them glowed a deep red.

"Khet, creation of the imprisoned ones, the hero that brings the dawn of our freedom, the Arankai welcomes you." The voice boomed. It was the figure in the center. The mask and shapeless form were gone. Now at the center stood a strong and powerful woman. Her wild hair and muscular features made the armor that she wore look unnecessary. A large sword was slung at her hip, and a menacing-looking spear was across her back. A large glowing crystal was set into a chest plate that only enhanced her fearsome appearance.

"Who are you? What are you?" The sound that came from Khet was not his voice. It was foreign and deep.

"My name is Arankai. What I am and who I am are none of your concern. We must speak on other matters." Arankai gave Khet a moment to see if he had further questions, then she continued. "We had debated many times in this chamber throughout the centuries, trying to find ways to end this, and we have made a decision." The whole time, she never took her eyes off Khet. The weight of her gaze pressed hard on him. "You have forged the hammer, Skrið, a weapon that can kill a god. Khet, I need you to go to the towers of Sidierion and Alfir and destroy the God shards."

Khet was not expecting this. "How? And why don't I just go directly to Malak and kill him?"

"As the Prelate here has explained, Malak is too powerful for you while he can harness the life crystal. On top of that, you have hundreds of Dodecahedron guarding the God Spire. You wouldn't survive. We need you to destroy the two towers and let the Gods battle each other. Then, when they are weakened from their battle, attack. Destroying the God shards is the only way to break the cycle. First, the destruction of the Sidierion shard will free all the contracted. Then, the Alfir shard will allow the sun to move through the sky. Giving the trapped gods a chance to attack." Arankai's eyes never moved from Khet.

"What cycle are you talking about?"

"This is not the first time this has happened. It is a cycle that has repeated time and time again. Different names, different faces, but the story is always the same. This time, we will destroy the time shard and keep the cycle from repeating. It is the only way."

"What if this plan of yours fails?" Panic filled Khet's chest.

"It must not fail. It cannot fail. Lives of our people for generations depend on it succeeding."

"How am I supposed to do this? The God towers are almost as tall as the wall. How am I going to get up there?" The weight of the task made Khet's determination falter. "And what of Issahya?"

The mention of Issahya gave Arankai pause. "I warn you not to invoke names you do not understand." The air about her shimmered. "A plan has been made. See to it. I have, we all have been awaiting your arrival. The heroes that came before you sacrificed greatly to set you on this path. You have a power greater than they ever possessed. Now go, all of us are counting on you."

The vision of Arankai faded from view. Khet and everybody else were back in the council chamber. Nothing was left of Arankai, except the mask that now rested on the chair at the center.

No words were spoken. All the energy had been pulled from the room. Everyone slowly made their way to an exit. Khet stood there absolutely confused by what he just witnessed. A hand rested on his shoulder.

"I was the same when I first saw Arankai. It was many years ago. Still to this day she moves me." Vagner's words did little to reassure Khet.

"Who or what is she?" Khet still had not moved his eyes from the mask in the center of the room.

"She? Well, I guess you could call Arankai that. I always thought of Arankai as a timeless entity. It, or she, has been with the University since we discovered the mask over two thousand years ago. Before we found the Book that Fell Through Time. What Arankai is, nobody really knows. Come now we have things to discuss and you need to meet your squad." Vagner made his way to the exit.

"My squad?" Khet had to force his feet to move so he could keep up with the scholar. The anger and determination that burned in his chest earlier was now merely embers.

57

They walked out a side door of the council chamber. Vagner led Khet to a small courtyard where a group of members of the Hand gathered. All had stern faces, all were youthful except two.

Vagner made a flourish with his hands."Commander Barnt ve Jost, Commander Gideon ve Greylock, this is Khet. Khet, you will be traveling with Commander Greylock and his squad. While Commander Jost will draw the Temple's attention away from your mission."

The two commanders nodded in acknowledgement of Khet. "Khet, let me introduce you to my team. There is Truse ve Knut, he is our Grun. Krina vi Korith is our Lightbringer. Belera vo Sivet is a Storm Wielder and finally there is Caspian ve Brigh, he is the best hunter and woodsman we have." Commander Greylock's dark features and heavy voice lent to his authority.

"Hello." Is the only thing Khet could utter. It was awkward to be so inexperienced and expected to be a part of this team.

"OK, I will leave you fine folks to it. Commander Jost, can we walk and talk, please?" Vagner and Commander Jost walked out the courtyard in a deep discussion.

All the Hand members stared at Khet. "How did they die? Abner, Raine, Grim, and Trip." It was Belera that spoke first. Khet heard faint thunder in the distance as she spoke.

Khet stood there. He couldn't find a reason within him to lie. So he told them the truth about Kase murdering them in their sleep and Trip sacrificing himself to save Khet. He also explained the reason he lied to Varith about how they died. He wanted to spare her as much pain as possible. "I am sorry." Is all Khet could really say after all that.

Several moments of silence passed before Commander Greylock cleared his throat. "We will honor their sacrifice by completing our mission. I am not asking, I am telling."

"Yes, Commander!" The others responded.

"Good. Now, Khet, I want you to see the route we are going to take." Commander Greylock unfolded a large map on the table. The map covered most of the southern half of Sýna. "We are here at the University. The plan is to travel along the Wall all the way to Dragon's Spine. We will have boats at the Saphos Sea to get us across. At the Dragon's Spine, we will travel underground."

"Wait, there is a tunnel that goes under the mountains." Khet was so shocked to hear it that he couldn't help but interrupt.

"Yes." The Commander's face was dark, and his deep grey eyes warned Khet not to interrupt him again. "After the Spine, we will be at Sidierion Tower. Khet, Truse, and I will scale the tower. Once you destroy that shard, all contracted will be free. That should keep the Temple mostly off our backs while we make our way to Alfir Tower. We currently don't know how the Arc Storms will react once the Sidierion shard is broken. So, we will have to wait and see if we can stick near the wall or go around the Blasted Plains to reach Alfir."

The Commander looked from person to person to verify they understood the plan. Until he made eye contact with Khet. "Now, Khet, our job is to get you to the Towers alive. You will do and go where you are told. If you wander off or don't follow mine or their orders, I will bind you and drag you to the Towers. Do I make myself clear?"

"Yes, sir." It sounded weak even in his ears.

"OK, we leave in one week. That should give us enough time to get to know each other and train." Commander Greylock stood quietly for a moment to see if anyone had any questions.

"How are we going to get to the top of the Towers? Also, in the Dunes of Bast, what are we going to do for water?" Khet thought those were important questions to ask.

All the Hand members gave Khet a flat look. "How we will get to the top of the towers is not a discussion for here. As for the water." The Commander held his hand aloft, and a perfect sphere of water formed and hovered just above it. "I am a Saphosi; having fresh water to drink will not be a problem." Greylock let the water fall to the ground. "I have been informed that you have abilities not like ours. Can you demonstrate for us?"

"OK." Khet reached into his bag and put on the Hell Hammer gauntlets. He poured heat into his fists and struck the air in front of him. The air thudded with each strike. The gauntlets glowed white-hot. The glare made it hard for any one of the Hand members to look directly at him.

"What is the difference between you and a forge-blessed?" Commander Greylock asked, obviously not impressed by the display.

"I can get much hotter than this. Also, I can…" Khet unfurled the golden thread. He wrapped a single filament around each of their weapons and another around multiple branches of a nearby tree. "Do this." With a thought, Khet relieved all of them of their weapons. "And this." He sent a pulse of fiery rage through the threads around the tree. Each limb was severed with bright flashes. All of it crashed down in a cacophony of snapping limbs. Confusion racked their faces as they all fumbled for their weapons.

The only one that didn't react was the Commander. "OK… OK, no need to show off. It is good to know that you are not helpless. You also have the hammer to break the shards, correct?"

Khet took hold of Skrið. The power inside it beckoned to him. In the distance, Khet saw a thick column of stone freestanding in the courtyard. He reared back and hurled Skrið at the column. There was a strange sound as Skrið flew towards the column. The very air thrummed with energy. It was as if an Arc Storm had erupted in the courtyard. The sound and the fury of the impact shook all of them to the bone. A great plume of dust filled the courtyard. Large pieces of the column flew in all directions. Khet used a thread to pull the hammer back to him.

It took them all a second to regain their composure. "Well, Khet, I am glad you are who you are, because that piece of stone was meant to be carved into the likeness of Commandant Aris. If you were not the one to break the God shards, your head would be on a pike before dinner." The Commander gritted his teeth.

"I am sorry… I had no idea it would do that." Khet was half panicked and half scared.

"Khet, I suggest you go with the others here for some time to train in the forest. Stay there until tomorrow morning at least. Belera, I leave you in charge. I must go explain this to the Commandant." He retrieved his weapon from the ground. The Commander made his way across the debris-strewn courtyard. A heavy burden lay upon his shoulders.

"Well, fuck me bloody, Khet." Truse uncontrollably chuckled at the impossible situation that just happened. "You know how to make a statement, friend."

"Can it, Truse! We need to get him out of here before everyone comes to see what happened." Belera ordered everyone. "Khet, follow us, unless you want the Commandant to skin you alive."

Fear gripped his spine and made his legs move unbidden. He followed them so close he was lost in the shuffling of the Hand members' cloaks.

The five of them moved through the University grounds with haste, keeping the Wall on their left. With each little twist and turn, they moved ever closer to it. Until Khet came face to face with the Wall. It made him pause. The dark stone stood in silent judgement.

Caspian ran into Khet's back. "What's wrong, Khet? We need to move."

"I have never been this close to the Wall." Khet's voice sounded almost frightened.

Belera and the others turned at hearing the conversation. "What is the problem, Caspian?" Her accent held an authority to it.

"Khet's shitting himself about the wall." Caspian emphasized that it wasn't his fault for the halt.

"It's just growing up in the south. The Wall was always talked about as if it was magical. And now I am here." Khet attempted to explain the swirl of emotions in his chest. A mixture of fear and awe.

"You're a southerner?" Krina asked.

"Yes, I am from a small farmstead three days south of El. I am not stupid." Khet's frustration with the way people treated him was on display.

Belera openly did not care. "No, being a southerner just means you are ignorant to how most of this world works. Travel to the south is blocked by the Dunes of Bast and Blasted Plains on the west side. Then the Dragon's Spine on the east. The Temple of the Twelve keeps tight control. So yes, you are ignorant."

"And our little Krina is a southerner as well." Truse interjected.

Krina's face bloomed red. "Fuck you, Truse. I hope your mother chokes on a bag of dicks."

"Alright, alright, that is enough." Belera tried to keep her laughter under control as she gave the order. "Khet, you need to get over this quickly. Go touch the wall and you will see it is just stone. There is nothing magical about it."

Khet approached the Wall with caution. At arm's length, Khet could only feel a slight breeze coming off the wall. Nothing magical, just dark stone warmed by the sun. He reached out to touch the surface. A loud thunderous boom shook him to his bones. Khet dove for the ground and braced for whatever was to come. Laughter erupted from behind him. Truse had slammed a large piece of metal to the ground and now was cackling on his back next to Khet.

"That's enough." Belera tried to tame her own laughter. "Are you satisfied now, Khet? We need to go." Belera didn't even wait for a response, turned with the others, and left.

Krina was the only one that stayed behind. She helped Khet up. "They pulled the same kind of shit when I first came here. They don't understand the level of indoctrination the Temple puts into us southerners. Don't worry, I think what you did in the courtyard will keep them from doing anything else to you."

Khet accepted her hand and stood, dusting himself off. "Thank you." The two walked in silence to catch up with the others.

58

The training area was more of a small camp. Two hard-structure buildings made of stone and several tents ranged from sleeping tents to a command tent took up a majority of the space. The dense forest around it made it feel secluded, even though not a 10-minute walk away was the University campus.

Belera issued commands upon their arrival. "Krina, Caspian, and Khet, you three come with me to introduce Khet to battle training. Trust you start a fire and prepare dinner."

"Why do I have to cook dinner?" Truse spoke as if he was insulted.

"Two reasons, one it is your turn. Second, I do remember last time we were out here training you disappeared for two whole damn weeks with that barmaid. The Commander made us hike to the Dragon's Spine and back for that. So it will remain your turn until you have learned your lesson. Is that clear?" Belera leaned into Truse's face.

Any fight within Truse ran and hid. "Yes, it is clear."

Belera turned and walked back towards the Wall. "The rest of you with me." She commanded.

They all jumped into action, not wanting to draw ire from Belera. Khet almost tripped over Caspian as he tried to keep up.

The four entered a clearing beside the Wall. A large wooden structure that gave the look of a giant ladder with uneven rungs stretched high on the wall. A couple of well-used ropes dangled from its top.

"Caspian, climb the ladder. Krina and I are going to see Khet's fighting abilities." Belera stood in her simple hand garb. Now this close, Khet was distracted by her beauty. Her black hair shined in the light of the sun. Her skin, a deep brown, spoke of growing up on the Timeless Plateau. Her rich brown eyes reminded Khet of chocolate.

"Khet, hello there. Lost you there, did I? I repeat, how much fighting experience do you have?" Belera's expression was a tired one.

Out of the corner of his eye, he could see Karina's pale face redden in embarrassment for him. "Not much. I have been in fights, though. I took on several Temple guards, and I have killed two Dodecahedrons."

If Belera was impressed, her face did not show it. "That was with your blessings. From the reports that I have seen, you just overpowered them."

"Yeah, so?" Khet felt a little taken aback by the way she dismissed his accomplishments.

"We have maybe a week to train you. Karina will spar with you first. Disarm yourself and do not use your blessings."

Karina had already dropped her gear and prepared herself. "Don't worry, Khet. I will be gentle." A grin that made Khet cold spread across her face.

He unloaded his gear on the side of the clearing. Khet really had no real clue how to fight, but he made a show of it. He rolled his shoulders and cracked his neck. He attempted to put a cocky grin on his face.

Karina stood about chest high to Khet. The pale skin of her arms was covered in small, thin scars. Her stance gave Khet a sense of fear that filled his chest. A relaxed stance, as if she was completely comfortable and confident in what was about to take place. Her eyes, a bright green, peered out between her red curls.

She flowed toward Khet with the grace of a dancer. He could barely recognize her strike before it was too late to move. Her blow just grazed his cheek as he jerked his head out of the way.

Khet reacted clumsily with a swing from his right arm. More of a flail than a proper strike.

Karina slapped it aside with such force that he felt the sting in his shoulder. This left Khet wide open on his right side. Her hand darted in and gently slapped Khet's face, soft like she was patting a baby's bottom. Another soft strike hit his chest. Another slithered around his guard and tapped his other cheek. She moved so quickly that Khet was completely overwhelmed.

He reached out to grab hold of her. He just wanted to slow her down some. She danced out of his reach, leaving him nothing but empty air to grab. His frustration at being made a fool simmered hot.

Karina set herself again. She flowed and twirled toward him. Another series of gentle taps came. He could do nothing to block her strikes. If this was a real fight, he would already be dead.

"Karina, enough." Belera ordered.

Karina floated away from Khet and took her original spot before the sparring match began.

Belera stepped forward. "Khet, you just witnessed what a truly exceptional Lightbringer can accomplish. Show him."

Karina stood in her fighting stance again. A second version of Karina peeled away from the original and stood beside her. The second gave a deep bow as if it performed some great feat.

"What?" His brain couldn't comprehend what he was seeing.

"It is a trick of the light. Very few Lightbringers are this skilled, but Karina can make you see things that are not there. Also, she is able to render herself mostly invisible." While Belera explained, the original Karina disappeared. The spot where she stood now just looked like a smudge on a glass window. "If you pay attention, you can still see her, but it is really hard to focus when you're being attacked."

Khet stood with his mouth slightly open as he attempted to understand. "How can you fight something you can't see?"

"She is still there. Objects react to her, watch." With a small flourish, Karina disappeared, replaced by a smudge in the light. Belera continued on. "You can still see a small distortion in the light. Look at the ground; there are footprints forming. And there is the air." Belera took a handful of sand from the ground and threw it in a wide arc. Specks of sand settled on Karina, now easy to see.

"Ah, fuck, Belera, my mouth was open!" Karina appeared back in full view as she spit sand out of her mouth.

"Couldn't I just get hot enough to burn her?" Khet asked.

Belera gave him a look he couldn't place. "You could, but then you would risk all of your comrades around you. They would be burned as well."

"OK, I never thought of it that way."

"Good, the southerner can learn." Now join Caspian on the ladder. I need to see your stamina holds up."

Khet could see Caspian sliding down the rope, his clothes soaked most of the way through with sweat. This was going to be a hard day.

59

The ladder stood almost flat against the Wall. Wide enough for about ten people to climb its rungs at the same time. Each of the rungs was spaced in a random pattern, some really close while others Khet would have to jump to.

"So Belera thinks your fighting is shit then?" Caspian took a deep drink from a water skin.

"Er... I really didn't fight at all."

"Hence the use of the word, shit. Don't take offense. Karina and Belera are our two best fighters. Now we go. You wouldn't mind a friendly race, would you?"

"That sounds great!" Belera called from behind them. "Khet, you keep going until you beat Caspian to the top. And Caspian, don't go easy on him."

A smile flashed on Caspian's sweaty face. "Well, my friend, I hope your climbing is better than your fighting; otherwise, we will be here for a while." He dashed for the first rung.

Khet completely caught flat-footed, lurched into motion.

The first rung was maybe chest-high, and Khet heaved himself up with ease. The wall was extremely close, and it made standing up precarious.

"With that amount of effort, I will be a corpse by the time you beat me." Caspian called out five rungs higher than Khet.

The comment burred him. He had to keep moving. Rung after rung,

Khet pulled himself up. Sweat stung his eyes. The heat from the sun and stone grew as he made his way to the top.

"I will be waiting for you at the bottom." Caspian said as he slid down the rope past Khet.

Khet looked to see where in the ladder he was. By his guess, maybe halfway. Every rung was at a different height, and some were more narrow than the others. Each time he mounted one, he would struggle to balance as he stood up. Winded, he pushed on.

At the top, the rope greeted him. The height made his guts twist. A fall from up there would surely kill him. A fear sank into his bones. His descent down the rope could not happen fast enough.

The ground slowly approached as he made his way down. Caspian stood at the bottom with a massive, well-rested grin on his face.

"Now that you are here, have a drink of water before we have another go at it."

Khet relished the cool water as it poured down his throat. It felt cool in his belly. Before he placed the stopper back in the water skin, Caspian was up the first rung. "Fuck." He bolted after him.

Caspian laughed as he pulled himself ever higher. The man moved like a squirrel up a tree. Khet would need to push harder.

With each rung, he threw more caution to the wind. Not waiting to regain his balance and just go for the next rung.

This time, his effort paid off well.

"Oh, shit. Looks like you have found your manhood this time 'round." Caspian commented as he slid down the rope. Khet was only five rungs from the top this time. The effort was still intense, but he managed it.

He slid down the rope much more confident this time. Caspian's smile was not as big as it was last time. Khet's breath was hard. His heart hammered.

Caspian didn't even give him a moment of rest. "At it again then."

Khet didn't stop for a drink this time; he pushed through the thirst. His clothes completely drenched through as he made his climb.

On the fifth rung, Khet stood too fast and slammed his head into the rung above. The shock of it made his back and left calf cramp. The seizing muscles threw him off balance, and he fell.

He impacted the ground before he knew what was happening. The air driven out of him, he gasped. Pain still had not made its presence known yet. Another deep breath, and pain exploded throughout his body. His yelp was quenched by his broken ribs.

He heard footsteps run towards him. From the locations where the pain was in his body. He guessed he had several broken ribs and a broken leg. His brain was thick with the pain. Blood was the only taste in his mouth. By instinct alone, his body called on his healing power.

A cooling sensation flooded his body and cleared his thoughts. The pain subsided fast. He rolled over to test his improved situation. His body was a little sore, but that faded fast. His fatigue evaporated along with it.

He popped up from the ground and met the stunned faces of Belera and Karina.

"Seem to have lost my balance. I will have to be more careful." He couldn't tell if his attempt at impressing them had worked.

"How are you standing? That fall should have broken something." Belera's face was full of amazement and skepticism.

"Yeah, I forgot to mention. A God also blessed me with healing powers. Still getting used to this whole thing."

"Khet, that doesn't count as beating me to the ground." Caspian announced as he slid down the rope. "How the hell are you standing? That was a big fall."

"Big hero here can also heal himself. He forgot to mention it to us." Belera folded her arms, not impressed with Khet's lack of sharing information.

"Healing, nice. Ready for another go?" Caspian grabbed the water skin and took a drink. Before he could finish, Khet was at the first rung. "Aw, you sly piece of shit. If that is how it's going to be."

Khet was proud of his accomplishment. He made it halfway up before Caspian overtook him. He was only two rungs behind when Caspian took to the rope.

Friendly competitive barbs and insults were said between the two as each round continued. Khet always nipped at Caspian's heels but never overtook him.

"Good but not good enough, friend," Caspian taunted as he grabbed the rope just before Khet could.

"Next time, I will get you next time." Khet slowed his descent down the rope; he needed time to think. His feet gently touched the ground. Caspian locked eyes with him. It was almost a dare for him to go first. The moment hung in the air.

Khet moved first. A thought struck him as he mounted the first rung. His threads; he could use his threads to secure his balance and pull himself to the next step.

The golden threads slithered up and around each rung as he climbed. His movements were now graceful. No more savage lunges to the next ledge. No more wasted movements.

He grabbed the rope and slid down in victory with a grin. Caspian stood breathless two rungs from the top. A simple thumbs up was given to congratulate him on his victory.

Belera stood with her arms crossed as he came to a stop at the bottom. Her face had a stern look to it. "You did well. It took you long enough to figure out how to actually use those threads of yours."

"What do you mean by that?"

"It is not my place to tell you. Just know we have been planning on you for a long time."

"Not going to get a straight answer out of you then?"

"Nope."

"Figured. So dinner?"

Caspian slid down the rope beside Khet. Exhaustion made up a large part of his visage. "About time you beat me. I almost took a tumble from the top just to end the torture." It was a weak chuckle, but the respect was there.

They traded friendly pats on the back. Since there was no need for Khet to keep his healing power surging through him, he stopped it. A wave of exhaustion swept him off his feet. His vision blurred, and the world spun around him. He was unconscious before his face hit the ground.

60

The next day, Khet woke stiff and sore. He lay there in his tent, replaying what brought him here. He remembered the ladder. He woke to eat dinner. *But how did I get into the tent?*

Khet heard footsteps come towards his tent. "Khet, wake yourself and meet me in my tent... Did you hear me?" Greylock's voice cleared the fog out of his mind.

"Yes, sir, I will be there in a moment." Khet scrambled out of his tent; muscles and joints pleasantly ached from a deep, motionless sleep. A small pot of porridge bubbled on the fire. The smell made Khet's mouth flood with saliva. Nobody else was around, so Khet ignored the hunger in his stomach and made way to the Commander's tent.

Commander Greylock stood behind a small table, dressed in a green tunic. The cut and fit of the tunic gave him an air of power and authority. It only added to his natural commanding presence. "So Belera has told me you can heal yourself. Is that true?"

"Yes, I can't heal anyone else, though."

"Good to know. Any other hidden abilities?" The Commander pulled out a chair for Khet.

"No."

Commander Greylock pulled a rolled-up parchment from a tube and unrolled it in front of Khet. "This is a sketch of the underside of Sideirion Tower." The rough sketch was of a cliff with a set of stairs floating some distance away. "From what I am told, the stairs are about 100 feet from the cliff side. After what you showed us yesterday, do you think you could make it across it?"

"Do you mean jump? No." Khet rebuked the idea.

"No, not jump. How you pulled our weapons from us. Can you reach over to the stairs and pull yourself to the stairs?" The Commander spoke as if he was well-practiced in explaining things to people who don't understand.

"I don't know if I could make them reach that distance." Khet relaxed now that he understood.

"I need you to try that today. We need to figure out how to cross this gap. I want you and Belera to work on how we can make a bridge to get across."

Khet nodded his head. "OK."

Commander Greylock shot Khet an aggravated look and instantly relaxed. "I apologize, Khet. I forgot you are not one of us. I have spoken with Belera, and she will be waiting for you at the ladder."

Khet left the tent at the Commander's dismissal. His mind was now full of ideas on how they would be able to cross the gap to the Sideirion stairs. The aspect of learning something new gave Khet focus. He made his way through the forest to the ladder.

Belera sat in the shady grass. A more relaxed posture today than yesterday. She waved Khet over as soon as she saw him. "Have you eaten yet?"

Khet's stomach growled so loudly he was almost embarrassed. "No, not yet."

"Here." Belera handed him some kind of food. It was a ball the size of Khet's fist.

"What is this?" Khet sniffed it. The smell was slightly sweet. A small bite revealed to be a pleasant mixture of salty and sweet.

"Rations, a quick and easy way to get a lot of the nutrients you need in a handy package." Belera took a bite of her own ration. "Normally, they are square-shaped, but the cooks at the University are trying a ball shape. They can be carried for months before they spoil, and one or two of them is good enough to feed a grown person all day. Don't ask me what is in them."

"Fair enough." Khet sat down beside Belera and enjoyed his ration in the shade of the trees.

"Did Commander Greylock speak with you about what he wants us to do?" Belera asked as she finished the last bite of her ration.

"Yes." Khet managed to say around a mouthful of the chewy food.

Belera stood and pointed towards the ladder. "After you are done, I want you to try to pull yourself to the top of the ladder."

Khet was only halfway done with his ration, but he already felt full. So he stored it in his bag for later. A slight apprehension filled him. Self-doubt tickled the back of his mind. The breeze felt cool on his skin. His mind searched for other things to distract from his doubt. The smell of Belera's perfume flowed into his lungs. His focus slid onto the smoothness of her skin, then the curve of her neck, and her dark curls that framed her beauty…

"If you are going to be that distracted, I suggest you visit a brothel." Belera smirked as she made a gesture towards Khet's groin.

Instantly, he was aware of the pressure built up in his breeches. "Er…I'm so sorry." His face reddened like a fresh tomato. Never had he wanted to run and hide so badly.

"It's fine. I am used to it. As long as you understand that I chose to be vo." Belera's tone had a practiced feel to it. Khet would bet that she had to explain that to many a man or woman.

"OK, sorry again. I will control myself better." He pushed those thoughts and urges far from his mind. With a deep exhale, Khet positioned himself at the base of the ladder. He focused on the task and sent a thread up towards the top. After thirty feet or so, the thread leaned right and toppled to the ground. Khet tried again, and the same thing happened. "No, I can't reach. It only goes so far and falls over."

Belera walked a distance away from Khet and held up a stick. "Take the stick from me."

Khet faced her and sent out a single thread. It only made it twenty feet before landing on the ground. "I am sorry, I can't." His tone was slightly defeated.

"Don't apologize, I have many ideas for us to try. How about we try a weighted throw, like you did with your hammer in the courtyard. Use that hook over there."

"What is the target you want me to aim at?" Khet asked for clarification.

"Wait, I have a better idea. Hold on." Belera went over and pulled a strange object from her bag. "This is a grappling launcher. The Hand uses it to throw hooks long distance, so we can scale walls or over gaps."

"If you have that, why don't you just use that?" Khet was confused now about why they wasted time when they already had a solution.

"One hundred feet of rope weighs a lot, so it affects how far the hook can travel. Your thread is much lighter. I think it will reach with your thread anchored to it. Here, let's try it. Wrap your thread around this anchor point on the hook." Belera held up the anchor point to Khet.

The small golden thread flowed out of Khet and wrapped tight around the small hook."Ok, I am ready."

"OK, 3...2...1." The launcher fired the grappling hook. It sailed up and over the platform much farther than expected. Khet pulled the thread taut, and the hook found purchase at the very top of the ladder.

Khet pulled himself up toward the hook. The Wall quickly came to greet him. He bounced off the Wall and thudded back to the ground. His head rang like a bell. "I am fine." He squeaked.

"Sure, you are. Next time, how about you move closer to the ladder before you go up?" Belera tried hard not to sound too amused at his plight.

"Sounds like a great idea, thanks." Khet failed to sound nonchalant about the whole situation. In the end, though, Khet did make it to the top of the ladder. It wasn't a hero's victory but a victory nonetheless.

Belera waited at the bottom of the ladder. "That went pretty well all things considered. Just remember when we show this to the Commander later, you get closer to the ladder before ascending." The slightest smirk was on Belera's face.

Khet reddened slightly. "Lesson learned, thank you."

The rest of the day went on without any issues. They tried different distances and different weights. Now that Khet thought a little more before he acted, it made it a lot less painful.

"Let's break for food. I am looking forward to a meal at the Great Hall. It feels like for the past three weeks all I have eaten was rations. I am craving some properly cooked food." The rumble of Belera's stomach made the announcement louder than her words.

61

The Great Hall looked as magical as it did before. All the vibrant colors streaming through the translucent stone ceiling bathed the dark-stained wooden walls. Students in their different-colored uniforms, scholars in their stately robes, some members of the Hand, and others of no affiliation milled about in conversation or enjoyed their meals.

Belera led Khet to an empty table. The spirited conversation at the table next to them was music to Khet's ears. He didn't understand all the terms they used, but Khet could feel the passion in them. Something about the variables of the transference of heat through a viscous medium. It might as well have been in a completely different language.

"What can I get you today?" A man appeared out of nowhere beside Khet.

Belera didn't hesitate a bit. "Could we get two meals and some extra meat for both, please? Also, a couple of glasses of ale would be appreciated, thank you."

The man was gone as quickly as he appeared. "Should we be drinking ale?" Khet was still a little off balance from the cacophony of sounds.

"Don't worry, the ale here will not get you drunk. The scholars at the University made it so it can't get you drunk. You must go outside of University grounds to get the real stuff. It tastes the same, though." Belera had to raise her voice slightly to be heard over the conversations around them.

Out of the corner of his eye, Khet saw a person waving at him. It was Vagner waving Khet over. Khet excused himself from the table and made his way over to the Prelate.

"So, Khet, I hear you are doing quite well with Commander Greylock's team. Even managed to destroy a little something meant for a certain Commandant?" The Prelate had a mischievous grin.

"Yeah...er...That was an accident." Was the only thing Khet could stammer out.

"No worries, my boy. From what I hear, Commandant Aris was furious at first, but when she found out it was you. She wants to enshrine the remains of the stone slab to honor you." Vagner laughed at the situation. "Sometimes it is good to knock her ego down a peg or two. You should feel proud. It is quite the accomplishment."

Khet didn't know how to feel about it. He had accepted what must be done, but the thought of being honored for it felt strange to him. Khet didn't like the weight of it on his shoulders. "OK, I guess." Khet didn't really have a response.

"Alright, I won't keep you from your meal and your lovely company." Vagner gave Khet a wink.

"Thank you, sir," Khet mumbled and turned to go back to his table.

Belera was already several bites deep into her meal when Khet sat down. "So, you are friendly with the Prelate Scholar of the University. You are more than just a pretty face." The playfulness in her rich brown eyes made his heart stutter.

Khet blushed at the compliment. "Look, I don't understand everything that is going on. It has been one crazy thing after another. I am not anything special. I am just me."

"I have spent most of my life as a part of the Hand. When becoming a member of the Hand, we are taught its history. For over a thousand years, the Hand has existed. Besides trying to counteract the injustices brought by the Temple of the Twelve, the Hand has been preparing for you. I have spent years training to be a part of your quest. Every member of the Hand has either been searching for you or training to aid you. You are more than something special. You are the beginning of our freedom. You are the gods' damn hero!" Cheers erupted around the table. Hand members banged their cups on the table to Belera's announcement.

Khet was overwhelmed by the cheering. Just over a month ago, he was a contracted blacksmith nobody, and now he is not just a hero, but the Hero. Just like a hero from one of his stories.

62

Sleep did not come easily for Khet that night. The weight of things made sleep near impossible. Eventually, he gave up and decided to go for a walk and get some air.

Walking through the forest, Khet tried to find ways to distract himself from the thoughts in his head. He walked to the clearing where the ladder was. His mind kept going back to Belera's words that he was the Hero. Thoughts of Rin and how the last words they spoke to each other were in anger kept repeating as well.

Khet pushed on along the Wall. He dragged his hand down it as he walked. The smooth stone felt so ancient to him, but all the magic that he once thought about the Wall was gone. It was just stone to him now.

"Couldn't sleep, out for a stroll, are we?" The voice startled Khet.

"Rin? What are you doing out here?" Khet tried to bring his hammering heart under control.

Rin stood there in the gentle shade of a tree. Her clothes were a deep green that blended well with the forest. "Could ask you the same. You are a ways from the University. I come out here to be alone sometimes, to clear my head."

"Look, I have been thinking a lot about what happened between us, and I am sorry for what I said."

"Khet, it is not your fault. The fault is mine, actually. You see, in my long life, I have been exposed to different types of magic. My emotions can spill over onto others when I lose control. And… I was drunk and really horny. Your urges that night were not solely yours. I know that is not an excuse. Just know that I am sorry for my part in that."

"No, that wasn't…"

Rin cut his words short with a raised hand. "In the morning, my anger in taking advantage of you affected you and forced you to say those words that you now feel guilt for. Again, I apologize for taking advantage of you and complicating our friendship." Rin's eyes held the ache of guilt.

"So, what now?" Khet had never had an experience like this with an immortal being or any being for that matter.

With wisdom and grace, Rin smiled. " In another life, I would have enjoyed having a lifelong friend like you. You really are something different."

"I have been told that more than once lately." The tension between them evaporated like a puddle on a sunny day.

"How about you come with me? There is a small stream near here that I like to dangle my feet in and think from time to time. We can start there."

Khet followed Rin silently to the stream. Her movements were dreamlike. He never thought he would see her again, and now she is sitting right beside him on the bank.

"I am sure you have questions bubbling around in that head of yours. Ask away." Rin asked.

Khet, not sure what to say, just said the first thing that popped into his head. "I remember you visiting Tarin's farmstead and giving me sweats. Did you visit other times?"

"Yes, I was always checking in on you from time to time." Rin was relaxed with her answer.

"What else do you know about me and this quest I am about to go on?"

"I am sorry, I can't tell you."

"Why not?"

"If I did, your mission, your quest will fail." She spoke with a known finality to the subject.

He wanted to avoid another argument with Rin, so Khet changed topics. "The forge where I got Narona's crystal. How did you know about it, and who made it?"

"Actually, I don't know who made it. It was just there. I placed the crystal on the anvil, and it was drawn down into it. The schema on the wall, or the weird darkness that clings to you, and don't let me forget the bottomless pit. It was there when Narona sent me there. That was before the founding of the University." Rin spoke the word like she was just recounting what she did yesterday.

"So, you don't know anything about it? Are there other weird places like that?" A passage from the Book That Fell Through Time played in his memory. " Have you seen the Living Wall?" Khet's mind was a jumble of questions.

An excited look came to Rin. "Yes, I have, no longer living though. The magic had seeped from it, and its caretakers were long dead. I did see the Fenris bones, carcass actually, before they carved the histories on them."

"Wait, the wall was dead? You said Fenris carcass?"

"Fenris was a mountain-sized wolf that was worshipped by a tribe of people in the north." Rin took a rock and threw it in the creek. "It was long dead by the time I laid my eyes on it."

"A mountain-sized wolf..." Khet tried to picture it, but it seemed so unreal. "What else?"

"One time, Narona wanted me to find some strange stone in the north. I never found what she wanted me to find, but what I did find still disturbs me."

"What was it?" Khet was tense with anticipation.

"It was in the Veil of Shadow near Narin's Tower. It is always perpetual twilight there. I was walking through the forest, and out of nowhere, there was a cave. I don't mean a cave inside of a hill. I mean out of nowhere. I was walking in between two trees and then inside a cave. I turned around and left the cave, and then the cave wasn't there. Walking back between the trees, I was back in the cave. That is not the weirdest thing." She could see Khet waited on every word.

"In the middle of the cave was a purple light suspended in the air. It just floated there, pulsing slowly and deeply. I was curious, so I made my way towards it. As I made my way, I felt a strange sensation and saw movement out of the corner of my eye. I turned to the side, and all that was there was my shadow. Thinking that's all it was, I kept on moving closer. The sensation grew stronger in my chest, and I could see my shadow out of the corner of my eye. I stopped about halfway to the light. When it dawned on me that my shadow was moving in front of me. It was the shadow from the crystal's light now in between me and the light. I turned around, and I could see that I was not casting a shadow. I turned and looked at the shadow. Now it stood in front of me. The shadow moved independently of me. It reached for me. I panicked and ran out of there."

Khet couldn't find what to say for several moments. "Anything else?" His brain was overwhelmed with the idea of a shadow that moved on its own.

"Well, there was that time I was trapped in a massive city underground for almost eighty years."

"What? How? What did you eat for eighty years?" Questions poured from Khet.

"After you have been alive for several thousand years, you get bored. So I wanted to see what I could find. I had spent some time around Alfir's tower before but never went near the mountains that circle the tower."

"You made it past the weird..." Khet tried to remember the term Vagner used to describe them. "time bubbles."

"Yes, that was a couple of centuries after finding the book. So, I did my best to stay away from them. I have not seen anyone fall into one, but I did see half a person fall out. They are very easy to avoid, really. All you do is look for a distortion in the air. Once you see it, you can't miss it." Getting her story back on track. "So, I made it to the mountains and found this massive cave at the base of Verðandi. Inside, there was the largest city I have ever seen. The largest buildings that were completely covered in glass. Fresh food of all different types was everywhere. I found rooms that had these metal doors that had nothing but frozen food inside. I explored for days and days. I climbed every tower. I explored every room. After I was there for a week or so, I decided I had seen enough and made my way for the exit, but it was gone."

"What did you do for the 80 years? How did you get out?" Khet was almost short of breath.

"Let's just say I went a little crazy. Being alone for that long will do that to you. As for getting out, I don't know. One day I went to sleep in a bed and woke up on the cavern floor with the light of the exit just in the distance. I met my sixth husband that day. He is the one that slowly brought me back to reality. I was a mess."

Curiosity tugged at Khet's insides. "Anything else?"

Rin smiled the most beautiful smile. "There is, but I must go."

"What?!" The abrupt change set Khet's mind spinning.

"I am sorry, Khet, I really am. I wish I could explain more to you, but I need you to understand that I can't." There was a tilt to Rin's voice that made Khet's heart ache.

"Will you ever be able to tell me?" Khet knew the answer.

"No, Khet, this is the last time we will speak. I can't tell you why. I just need you to trust me. What you are about to achieve will bring a dawn. You will free everyone. Your friendship in this short period of time in my life has meant a lot to me." Tears formed in Rin's eyes.

"But…" Khet didn't have words.

"I am sorry. I must go. I have to hurry; time is short now. I have to make it to They soon." Rin embraced Khet and held him tight. "I wish you luck, and I pray that you do put an end to all of this evil. I will find you after if you are successful."

"Wait, I don't understand…" A sharp wind peeled through the trees, blowing leaves and detritus into Khet's eyes. When he cleared his eyes, Rin was nowhere to be seen, like it was all a dream.

63

Khet was on the ground and leaned against a tree when Karina found him. "Khet, are you okay?"

He sat there for a moment, tried to pull himself out of his sadness. He had developed a true friendship with someone, and now they were gone just like the others. "Yeah, sorry, just dealing with things. It's a lot." Khet partially lied to Karina. He didn't want to explain all that he had lost.

"Yeah, it must be a lot. I couldn't even begin to imagine the weight of it all. Your actions, or possible sacrifice, will spare untold suffering for generations." Karina sat beside Khet and put a hand on his shoulder. "Did you know that for centuries we have been training to help you on your mission?"

"Belera explained that to me." Khet really didn't see the point in this. He displayed it openly.

"Did you know that this team is one of the greatest honors in the Hand?"

"No."

"We have competed and sacrificed to become a part of this team just to fight alongside you. Possibly even die by your side." Her voice held conviction.

"I never thought about it like that."

"From the very founding of this team, it was expected for us to not make it back. That is why it is such an honor. Our names will be lost in your legend, and we take great honor in that. You should too."

Khet contemplated her words. He always wanted to be a hero but never thought about dying as one or others dying to ascend him to a legend. To have a group of people that have believed in his purpose for centuries before he was ever born struck at Khet's core. The idea shifted his perspective. "Thank you for that. I need to hear it."

"Do you understand it though?"

"Yeah, we all have to die. Might as well die for a good reason."

"Exactly." Karina stood with a large stretch. "Let's go get some breakfast. I will tell the others I found you napping out here. No need to let them in on the hero having a breakdown."

A genuine smile showed on Khet's face. "Thank you. No need to add that to my legend."

Karina laughed. "Okay, legend, let's go eat."

64

The way back to the camp wasn't all that bad for Khet. The perspective that Karina had given him set his world mostly at ease. He still felt awkward that he was the Hero, like a piece of clothing that didn't quite fit. Khet could wear it fine and people could see it, but inside he wanted to go back to the farm kid. The person he was before all this started. Even though he was still the same person now, he just knew the truth about himself and the world.

"There you are, Khet. We thought you might have run off." Belera sounded a mixture of annoyed and relieved.

"I found him taking a nap underneath a tree about three hundred yards off that way." Karina chimed in.

"Really, a bedroll not comfortable enough?" Belera had a smile that hinted she knew some of the truth.

"I just needed some air. I just got a little too comfortable and nodded off. Sorry it won't happen again." Khet hoped Belera wouldn't question any further.

Belera leaned in towards Khet. "The Commander doesn't know and does not need to know. He would make us stand guard around your tent to make sure you don't wander off again. I don't want to do that and I don't think the others will appreciate it either. Do you understand?"

"Yes, I am sorry. It won't happen again." Khet lowered his head to show he was sorry.

"Think nothing of it. We have all been at that point once or twice." Belera gave Khet a smile that reassured him that she understood.

"Khet, Belera, come here." Commander Greylock ducked his head back in the command tent.

Khet froze for a second, did he hear the conversation he had with Belera?

Inside the tent a table was covered with different diagrams showing the ten active God Towers. Small annotations lined each diagram. Sideirion and Alfir were the diagrams sitting in the center of the table.

"Khet, Belera has told me that you are able to extend your thread long enough to reach the stairs under Sideirion Tower. Is that correct?" Commander Greylock rifled through other papers on his desk, not even looking at Khet as he spoke.

"Yes, that is right." Khet didn't feel as confident as he sounded.

"Belera, is there anything else you discovered about Khet's abilities?" The Commander stood at the center table and laid out several drawings.

" No, sir." Belera answered like a seasoned soldier.

"Sorry, sir..." Commander Greylock raised his hand to quiet Khet.

"Khet, you are not one of us, so don't try to be. Speak plainly, and we will have no issues." Commander Greylock locked eyes with Khet.

"OK, I am sorry. Can I ask you a question?" Khet tried to act natural.

The Commander donned a curious look. "Sure."

"When I was with the other members of the Hand. The ones that helped me get here. They didn't act like an army. The way you do."

"Abner and his squad are, I mean sadly were, a part of the scouts. Not any real rank in the scouts. We are a part of a force that will protect and defend after our mission is complete. My squad has the honor of aiding you. It is quite the honor to be in this squad, and many compete to get here. Each one of us is suited to aid your mission." Commander Greylock stood at attention with his fist across his chest. "We will not fail in bringing the dawn. On this, we swear!"

"On this, we swear!" Echoed Belera.

Khet stood in awe of the display. "I will do my best to complete my part in this." It was the best Khet could come up with to match their energy.

"Now, we have other things to discuss." Commander Greylock pointed at a picture of a Tower. "Have you ever seen a drawing of Alfir Tower?"

"I have seen pictures in the Sacrifice of the Twelve, that is it."

"We have had sketches drawn of the tower." Commander Greylock spread out three separate pictures, all drastically different. "These are all drawings of Alfir Tower. Done by different people looking at the tower from different angles."

Khet was confused. "What does that mean?"

"We don't know. It might have something to do with the mountains that surround it, causing a distortion. We don't know for sure. I just wanted to make you aware of the situation. After you destroy the Sideirion shard, things may get unpredictable. So I need you to be ready. Belera—" The Commander shifted his focus to his subordinate.

"Yes, sir." Belera acknowledged.

"I want you to take Khet to the Prelate and get as much insight into what we can expect once the Sideirion shard is destroyed. Go now; he is expecting you both."

"Yes, sir." Belera turned and moved out of the tent. Khet followed close behind.

Outside the tent, the others sat around the cook fire.

"I need you three to go and secure provisions for our trip. The quartermaster should have all of our supplies ready. Bring it all back here. I have a feeling we may need to leave sooner than planned."

"Yes, sir." The three replied.

Khet waited for the others to leave. "What makes you think we are going to be leaving earlier?"

Belera made sure that nobody else was within earshot. "I have been with Commander Greylock for several years, and he always gets antsy when something is happening and he can't tell us yet."

"What do you mean antsy? He seemed pretty calm to me."

"It was all the paper shuffling. The Commander is meticulous with his paper filing. He knows where every piece of paper is stored. The fact that he had to shuffle through paperwork is proof enough to me that something is up. I know it sounds like pretty flimsy evidence, but I know him pretty well."

"Maybe we should hurry up and go talk to the Prelate about the Towers. I have other questions I need to ask him."

"Good idea, the Prelate should be in his office today. I know a shortcut, follow me." Belera led Khet through the woods towards the university and to get some answers.

65

There was a major buzz going on throughout the University grounds. Most of the students were not wearing the standard uniforms for the University. Instead, they were all wearing variations of battle dress. There was chain mail, leather armor, and a couple of squads with plate armor. The University had changed to a fortress, preparing for war.

"What is going on?" Khet looked at all the commotion.

"Today is a drill training." Belera stated it as if it was normal.

"What is that?"

"A war could start after our mission is complete. The University is preparing for that possibility." Belera did not slow her stride when she gave her explanation.

Khet's pace slowed as he witnessed the firing of a large weapon. He stared in awe at the monstrous thing.

"That is a siege weapon. Think of a flatbow, but this one can fire giant bolts that explode." Belera's voice was nonplussed by the spectacle.

"How big is the beast you have to use something like that on?"

"You misunderstand, this isn't for just one beast. This is for taking out many enemies at once. If you mount it on a wall, it could keep back an army."

Khet once again reminded himself he knows so little, besides blacksmithing. He decided not to make himself look any more like a simple southerner than he already has. "OK, let's get to the Prelate. I could stay here all day and watch this."

Prelate Creshing's office was much quieter than the rest of the University. Varith was speaking with Vagner's assistance as they walked up.

Varith looked tired, with dark lines around her eyes. Like she hadn't slept well for several days. "Khet, I have been meaning to speak with you. Do you mind if we talk for a second?"

Belera snapped to attention with her right fist over her heart. "Ma'am, I served with your husband. He was a great man, and the Hand will miss him."

"Thank you for your kind words." Varith ushered Khet over to the side of the room so they could speak in private.

"Varith, I want to again say I am-"

"Khet, I want to apologize to myself. It wasn't your fault for Abner's death. He died helping people. I couldn't imagine a better reason to die for. Thank you for bringing back a piece of him. He loved being a part of the Hand."

Khet didn't know what to say. He had to say something. "I will make sure his sacrifice was not in vain." That was all he could come up with.

"I hope you do." Varith wore her mourning like a shroud as she left the room.

The air was thick with a morose tension. "The Prelate will see you now." The assistance words held a dull ring. It reverberated around the room, slowly brushing away the sadness.

Belera and Khet filed into Vagner's office. The Prelate Scholar was seated at his desk, surrounded by piles of open and closed books. Each pile seemed to be on the verge of a great collapse. That would bury him.

"Oh, Khet, my boy, come on in. Hello... Belera? I believe I am recalling that correctly." Vagner poked his head from around his piles of books. His eyes glowed blue.

"Yes, Prelate." Belera bowed her head in respect.

"I would ask you to just call me Vagner, but I know how you Hand types operate." Vagner walked over to a table in the corner of the room and grabbed a large, dusty tome. "I know why you are here. Look, I have read every book on the matter of Alfir's tower, and I can't make any sense of it. Neither has any other scholar, for that matter." He cracked open the tome and found what he was looking for. "From my best hypothesis and that of other scholars, it is that the time distortions in the area distort the tower's image. The same way heat can distort something at a distance. You see this drawing here." It was an old fold-out diagram in the tome. "It shows what the tower looks like up close and what it looks like when viewed in between the mountains of Urðr and Verðandi."

Khet tried to follow what Vagner said, but no luck. "So what does that mean?"

"I don't know, is the most honest thing I could say here. I do have a route that you should take to get there. Just be careful with the caverns in the area near the tower. We have reports of individuals disappearing and not coming back for many years, if at all."

Khet remembered the story about such a cave, the story Rin told him. "This path you want us to take, is it safe?"

"Again, I don't know. But if you go between Verðandi and Skuld, you should be fine. It is the same route Temple acolytes take." Vagner pointed at the two southernmost mountains. "There should be markings to guide through the hazards in the area. It is the most surveyed area near the Tower."

"What are the hazards?" Belera studied the map closely.

"Temporal bubbles mostly. Nasty pockets of distorted time. Don't fall into one of those. You may not come out again." Vagner pointed to the small crosshatches on the map. "If the stone markers are missing, just look for a shimmer to the air. It's quite obvious from what I am told."

"If it is so obvious, why have people fallen in them?" Khet figured the scholar didn't tell the full truth.

"Well, there have been reports of the bubbles moving. Also, the fact that dust storms in the area can be really dangerous." Vagner rubbed his chin. "I need to tell you this as well. There have been reports of strange figures appearing in the bubbles. The reports say the figures beckon you to come closer. None of this has been verified, mind you. Just wanted you made aware of it."

"OK... After we make it past the dust storms and temporal bubbles. How do we access the stairs underneath? Do you have an idea of where they are?" Belera folded her arms and waited for Vagner to answer.

His eyes lit up. "That you will find quite easy, Belera. Like the tower of the Forgotten. It seems Alfir's tower has stairs around the outside." Vagner pointed to all the diagrams of Alfir's tower, and each one had a set of stairs that wrapped around it. "Are there any other questions? I am in the middle of reading an interesting study on the possibilities of growing vegetables from a stone bed. It is quite fascinating."

"Yes, do you know if the destruction of the Sideirion shard will affect our ability to reach Alfir's tower? Also, does Commander Greylock have a copy of this map?" Belera pointed at the map that marked the pathway through the mountains.

"I have no idea what will happen. No records exist of the other two towers' destruction. Sorry, I can't help you." He shrugged sympathetically. "And yes, he should have it by now. I sent it to him just before you arrived. Khet, do you have any questions?"

"Yes, I wanted to know what the original plan was for me to do? What did the Book say originally?"

Vagner's eyes glowed a brighter shade of blue as if he was in deep thought. "Belera, could you be so kind as to wait outside? I need to talk to Khet in private."

"Yes, Prelate." Belera pivoted and left the room.

"I really do wish they would just use my name instead of my title. Anyway, where was I? Ah yes, the original plan, as you put it. You want to know about it?"

"You told me that this time we are doing something different. What was the original plan?"

"Let me tell you about the book a little. Besides the first two chapters, it is written more like a journal. Parts of it are written by a future me and somebody else beyond that and others. There are battle plans, successful ones and failures. Each battle plan has a set of ideas on how to do it better next time. Does this mean that version of me had a book they were learning from? He, or I, don't say. So we, the Arankai, have been adding to those plans and doing what we can to prepare." Vagner slouched down into a comfy chair. "But that isn't what you asked. You want to know specifically about your part in this."

"Yes."

"To keep it simple. The plan was, you being a part of a frontal assault on the God's Spire and killing Malak, but before you could destroy the crystal at the top of the tower. The trapped Gods attacked. You died as a result. The book goes on to say that the God named Magnus brings an army from outside the Wall. Then a war that lasts centuries is started. All the death-feeding Magnus and the others."

"But why? Why after Malak's death would the other Gods still care about us at all?"

"Maybe the Gods are a lot like us, or we are like them. They thirst for power for power's sake. It is a base instinct we all have. Some overcome it, some of us don't. It is probably the same for the Gods." Vagner noticed the distant look on Khet's face. "We have studied the Book over and over again and we have come up with the plan you have been told. The direct assault on the God's Spire leaves the Arankai and the Temple weakened. So this plan will leave us mostly intact to fight the battle to come. If it comes at all. I don't know if I should tell you this, but some of us think you have a chance to succeed and stop all of the Gods. With two more god shards destroyed and Malak's crystal gone, Magnus will have limited power. We think it won't be enough to bring his army from the other side of the Wall. In his weakened state, you will be able to defeat him. Bringing an end to this before it goes further."

Khet remained quiet for a brief period. Thinking about everything he had just been told and all that Rin had said. "So after I do this, we will all be free? If I am successful in defeating the Gods there will be no war?"

"Yes."

"Then I will do it." Without another word, Khet left the room.

66

Outside the Prelate's office, Belera waited for Khet. "Did you learn everything you need to, or are you still second-guessing yourself?" Belera stood in front of Khet as if she was challenging him to fight.

"I learned what I needed. I am ready."

"Good, I have to say I was a little worried there for a second. Your knees were getting a little shaky." Belera slapped Khet on his back as if he was now a welcomed member of the team.

After the two made their way out of the academic building, they were assaulted by the sounds of drum beats. No rhythm, just a cacophony of noise. Daggers of sound assaulted his ears.

"What is that?" Khet hoped Belera could hear him over the thunderous sound.

"Another battle drill. Look over there." Belera pointed over to a large group of people simulating a ditch battle. "You see, battle can be hectic. The sound disorientates, and the Commanders have to issue orders through everything. It is intense."

They both watched the drill for a little while longer. Belera could tell that the sound was getting to Khet and motioned for them to move along.

Just outside the courtyard, the sound faded away rapidly. This made Khet pause for a moment. "Did the drill just stop?"

Belera looked at Khet's confusion. "Oh, I am sorry. I forgot you are still new here. No, the drill is still going. If you take three steps back that way, you will hear it."

Khet took the three steps back, and the sound of the drums slapped his ears. Quickly, he moved back towards Belera. The sound was gone. "How?"

"That I don't know. You would have to ask one of the students. I just know that it does what it does. It could have something to do with the walls. I don't know." Belera turned and kept walking.

When they were close to the camp, they came across the others, and they had a horse cart loaded with supplies and three horses.

"Glad to see the Quartermaster made good." Belera inspected the loaded cart.

"Did the Commander say anything about us moving along soon?" Caspian asked.

"No, he didn't say it, but he was acting restless, and you know that means something is up."

Truse threw his thoughts in. "I was on patrol with the Commander a couple of years ago. We were walking down this forest road. The Commander was telling a story about a time when he was a child. Mid-sentence, a group of bandits ambushed us. He killed three by himself. After that, the other bandits ran; he just picked up the story right where he left it. The ambush didn't even faze him. So if he is restless, something must be going on."

Karina rested against the back of the cart. "What do you think it could be?"

Belera was quick to answer. "Don't know for sure, but I say we prepare. If there is anything you need to get done or goodbyes that need saying. Have it done before we bed tonight."

"Maybe I can talk up the barmaid for a good-bye kiss, maybe more than that." Caspian said with an impish smile.

"I am good to go. I made my amends with everyone I needed to when I joined the squad." Karina announced.

"Same." Said Belera.

Truse gave a sad bow. "I knew this would be coming sooner than later. Just the luck, ain't it? I just met the man of my dreams a couple of weeks ago, and now I must leave him."

Karina perked up. "Wait, didn't you meet the woman of your dreams a couple of months ago?"

"What about that farmhand you told me that every moment with him was bliss and you could never meet anyone better?" Added Caspian.

"I guess I am a simple soul that has many dreams." Truse said with a smile as he walked away. "I hope to have more before the end." He called from a distance.

The others looked to Khet to see if he had any business that needed tending.

"I am ready. I have nothing to attend to." Even though Khet felt courage in himself succeeding. A pang of sadness echoed in his chest from Rin's departure. He was determined to survive this so he could see her again.

The three remaining squad members drove the cart and horses to camp. Quiet in their own thoughts, steeling themselves for what is to come.

At camp that night, the three sat around and enjoyed stories of each other's adventures. Khet sat mostly quiet. Even with everything that had happened to him, he had no real adventures to share. He was still in the middle of his first one.

After a couple of hours, Commander Greylock came into the camp with a sullen look about him.

Belera, noticing the Commander's distress, asked, "Is everything alright, sir?"

"I have never shared this with any of you before. But I have a husband. I always knew that it would have to come to an end. But I never really wanted it to end." Commander Greylock spoke to the fire.

"You have a couple of nights left to be with your husband, sir. Why don't you go spend it with him?" Karina tried to ease her Commander's pain.

"I received word earlier today that we move out tomorrow. So I have said my goodbyes to him and tried to remind him what we do is for the benefit of all."

"Sir, go be with your husband, one last night. We will be here tomorrow." Belera tried to find a way to help.

"Belera, Karina, I thank you for your concern. We have said our goodbyes. Now I need to focus on our mission. Glad to see you picked up our supplies today. Do any of you need to take care of things before we leave?" Commander Greylock put back on his mantle of leadership, leaving the momentary weakness in the past.

"I spoke with the squad earlier, and those of us that had things to be taken care of are doing it right now. Do you need me to go get them now, sir?" Belera made ready to leave.

"Holdfast, Belera, let them have fun tonight. You would make an excellent Commander, Belera."

"Thank you, sir. I have learned a lot under your leadership." Belera's chest swelled with pride.

"I must go and pack some necessities for our mission. Remember, once we get to Saphos Sea, we will be only taking what we can carry on our backs. So anything extra will be left with the horses." He stood and gave a stretch. "I do hope these old bones handle this trip well. Rest well tonight; I don't think we will be having a lot of time to rest starting tomorrow."

"Good night, sir." The other three responded.

They sat there for a short while in the silence. The only one making any sort of conversation was the fire crackling away. It was a one-sided conversation while the others were alone in their thoughts.

Eventually, without any fanfare, the three said their goodnights and went to bed.

67

Sound of the camp in motion woke Khet from his slumber. He was grateful for the peaceful rest. No strange dreams or intrusive Gods to disrupt his rest.

Khet made his way outside the tent to be greeted by a half-dressed Belera. He quickly averted his eyes. "Good morning." He stammered.

"Khet, I forget you are a Southerner. They are just breasts, nothing to be embarrassed about. I will put on a shirt if that helps you." Belera spoke with a slight irritation in her tone.

Khet did risk one last glance at Belera's olive skin. She caught his glance and shot him a knowing smirk.

Khet's face reddened darkly.

"Do all you Westerners have no modesty?" Krina was stuffing something into a sack.

"The village I come from is on the eastern edge of the Dunes of Bast. It is always warm there, so we have little need for clothing. Sometimes I forget how people are awkward about nudity here. So not all Westerners are just people from my village." Belera finished dressing.

"Now that everybody is here and dressed." The last comment was aimed directly at Belera. "Yesterday I was ordered to start our mission. We leave as soon as possible. There are different farms along the way to Saphos that have fresh horses waiting for us. We are going to work in shifts until we make it to Saphos. We will not stop to camp. One person will drive the cart while one is on guard. The other two will sleep in the cart."

"What about me, Commander?" Khet didn't want to be a burden.

"Khet, I know you are capable of defending yourself, but I don't want to put you in harm's way unless I have to. If a member of the Temple sees those markings around your neck or bandits get ahold of you. All of our sacrifices will be for nothing. I want you by my side until we get underneath Dragon's Spine. We should be safe there." Commander Greylock didn't leave any space for Khet to object. "Now grab your things. We will only need one horse for the cart and another as a spare. We can return the other horse to the stables on our way out." Commander Greylock looked each one of them in the eye. "And another thing, we are going to leave without drawing much attention. Only a few people know we leave today. So act normal. Khet, you hide in the cart until we get a distance away from the University. Understood?"

"Yes, sir." They all replied.

The camp exploded into motion. Each one of them secured the last of their things into their packs. Khet double- and triple-checked that the Hell Hammer gauntlets and Skrið were secured to his belt. Lastly, he secured the knife he made at Graven's on his thigh. The pressure of the new scabbard he made for it was a comfortable memory.

After maybe an hour or so, all supplies were loaded into the cart, and they left the camp. It was a slow stroll through the University campus. Khet lay in the back of the cart, half covered in supplies. He just stared up at the blue cloudless sky.

"Commander Greylock, I am glad to have found you before you were off." The Prelate's voice shook Khet out of his daydreaming.

"Yes, Prelate, are you in need of something?" The Commander asked.

"I just had a little box of treats for you on your journey. I also want to say thanks." The Prelate's voice had a melancholic edge to it. Through all the positivity, it still cut to the truth. They were most likely not going to come back from this.

"Thank you, Prelate. Maybe after we get back, we could get some coffee." Khet could hear the Commander's smile.

"Will do, Commander. Good luck to you." The Prelate's voice was distant.

Khet lay there wondering what Vagner had handed the Commander. What could these treats be? A box plopped beside Khet's head. He heard the familiar sound of clinking bottles and the mouthwatering smell of pastries. Instantly, his stomach growled.

After what seemed like an eternity, Commander Greylock told Khet to come out of hiding. The air had never seemed fresher when Khet had sat up and tasted it. Free from his captivity, he surveyed the surroundings. They were not on a main road but a small forest trail barely wide enough for the cart.

"Why aren't we taking the main road?" Khet stood and had a long stretch.

"Less people to deal with." Commander Greylock waved for everyone to gather closer. "Everyone listen, from here on out, you will not refer to me as Commander. Do not use my rank. Just call me Gideon."

"OK, Gideon." Belera struggled with the words. It was like a poor attempt at a different language.

"Yeah, that didn't sound the least bit convincing, Belera," Karina chuckled.

The group erupted in laughter. Even Gideon had a smile on his face.

Hours passed, and eventually, the first shift started sleeping and the other driving. Khet and Gideon walked behind the cart while Caspian walked in the front. The spear's blade that Caspian held glinted in the sunlight.

Whenever fatigue would crawl into Khet's eyes, he would summon his healing power, and the fatigue would vanish. He had to do this several times before they reached their first stop to exchange horses.

After the horses were changed out, Gideon opened the box Vagner had given them. The box had seven green bottles and a dozen pastries inside. A small letter lay inside.

"

> *"May your journey ahead be successful. Know that your sacrifice will be honored and never forgotten."*

"

> *"Prelate Vagner ve Creshing"*

"

> *"P.S. The seventh bottle is a special rum. Save it for when it   is done."*

They all enjoyed the bottles of ale and the pastries. It was almost a celebration. Soon, though, reality of the task came back to them, and they set off again.

This time, though, Khet was in the back of the cart trying to rest for a while. Sleep was hard to come by, like a merchant running low on goods to sell. Khet wanted to stay awake just in case these were his last weeks. He wanted them to last as long as possible.

The rotations of sleep in the cart and guard duty kept on its monotonous cycle for days.

68

The fragrant smells are what first brought Khet out of his deep slumber. It was a rich, earthy smell like a bountiful crop after a fresh rainfall. He breathed it deeply.

Khet felt the movement of the cart as it moved along the road. Flashes of his experience with the slavers tore his eyes open. Panicked, he checked his surroundings.

The breath caught in his throat when he saw it. The beautiful Tower of Grunaive. The stone tower had a lush vibrancy to it. As if the Tower itself was made of plants. The Tower and everything in the vicinity had a healthiness to it that Khet couldn't describe.

"Pretty incredible, isn't it? Sometimes after hard months out on the road, we would come down here and soak in the pools and refresh ourselves." Gideon walked beside the cart. "Take your boots off and let your feet touch the soil. It is one of the most amazing feelings you're going to get." Gideon's voice sounded youthful and vibrant. Not the normal stern, commanding voice he is known for. His hard features had a soft glow.

Khet peered over the side of the cart, and indeed, Gideon walked barefoot in the soft soil. "OK, I think I will join you." Kicking off his boots, Khet stepped off the cart. The ground was soft and comforting. Walking was effortless; it felt better than his healing power. With each step, Khet felt rejuvenated, like he could walk forever. Any ache or pain that had slowly developed from day after day of sleep in the cart all melted away.

Once Khet got over the amazement, he noticed his surroundings more. Everywhere he looked, there were lush fruiting plants covered in the most inviting dew. Massive lakes of all different colors covered the land. The air felt cool on his skin. The sun even felt different this close to the tower.

"It's the algae." Belera noticed what Khet was gawking at: all the colors in the lake. "The healing properties of the Tower flow into the water, creating beautiful algae blooms. The algae will be harvested every couple of months and sold for its healing properties. They say the golden algae is as good as the most potent nectar." Her voice had a lustful tinge to it, and Khet was enjoying it. His mind wandered in that direction.

Khet turned his face to hide the slight flush in his cheeks.

"Don't get the wrong idea. Grunaive has that effect on everyone. Many babies were made after a couple's visit." Belera gave a slight chuckle. "I do think you are a pretty southern boy, but you're not my type."

Khet was fully embarrassed now. Even with his face burning, he couldn't take his eyes off of Belera as she walked away.

"Eyes forward, soldier!" Caspian's voice startled Khet. "Ah, it's okay, this place affects everyone that way. Eyes wonder, urges grow, stories as old as time really. A bit of advice though about Belera."

"What, no, it's not that." Khet made an attempt to get the words out.

"Look, I said it's fine. I just wanted to let you know that friendship is as far as you will go with her. She doesn't have a type. Not anyone, and she is comfortable with that. I just wanted to make you aware before you go and get your heart broken."

"I don't understand."

"It's not your job to understand her truths. All you need to do is respect them." Caspian gave Khet a friendly pat on the back and walked towards a man selling fruit off of a cart.

Khet walked behind the cart, feeling slightly embarrassed for Caspian's admonishment. Thoughts about what he could have learned if this destiny of his had not been forced upon him or others. He has learned so much in the past two months. Every day, he is still being taught something new.

Khet looked back at the Tower that is now a ways behind him. The lush, wet look of it glistening in the sunlight. He was glad he was able to see it in his life. Most people where he was from never left the area they grew up in. Nobody would believe all of the magical things he had seen. The lush, colorful plants. Flower blossoms everywhere you looked. Not a single person sick or tired. Nobody back home would believe this. If there was a home to go back to.

"Khet, time to put back on your boots. The effects of the Tower will fade quickly up ahead." Gideon stopped himself to put his boots on.

Khet could see everybody else with their boots. Now the ground felt less fulfilling through his thick boots. He wanted to go back and experience more of the magic, but he couldn't. All he could do was be happy for the time he had.

69

The next several days felt hollow to Khet. All the vibrance that was abundant around Grunaive Tower had faded. It was just dull drudgery, day in and day out. Until they came to the Sea of Saphos.

Saphos Sea was the color of sapphire. Its waves slowly rippled in the sunlight. The immensity of it was beyond Khet's comprehension. In the middle of all the liquid sapphire was Saphosi Tower. The shape of the tower flowed and curved so dramatically Khet could see the curves even from this great distance. Twin eternal waterfalls cascaded down the sides. Sending out gigantic plumes of water.

Khet was dragged from his amazement. Plumes of black smoke rose from the other side of the tree line off to the north. A small village was being attacked. Faint sounds of screams were carried on the wind.

"Everyone hold. I know we have our job to do, but those people need our help. Any objections?" Gideon turned to see if there were.

All were equipping themselves as an answer to his question.

"Here, sir." Belera tossed Gideon his long sword.

"Alright, Caspian, you and Karina go scout ahead. I need to know what we are dealing with. Go." Karina and Caspian disappeared into the forest. "Belera, I need rain to quench the fires."

"On it, sir." Belera spread her arms wide to the sky. The air around her thrummed with energy. The sky above filled with clouds that grew dark and ominous. It started as a few fat drops of water. Moments later, it was a torrent.

"When the fires are out, you join us. Trust, Khet, with me." Gideon led Khet and Truse into the trees.

Not far in, Caspian erupted through the brush. "Sir, it's the Temple. They are collecting people to contract into service. It looks like the village resisted. They are slaughtering everyone."

"We must hurry, no time for planning. Khet, don't do anything stupid."

"Sir, there are Dodecahedron with them. We counted three of them." Caspian, Truse, and Gideon all looked towards Khet.

"Khet, you are the only one who has ever killed one of those things. Can you handle three?" Gideon placed his hands on Khet's shoulders.

Khet could feel Skrið at his side. It pulsed with rage. His veins burned with it. "Yes, they will pay." The Hell Hammer Gauntlets eagerly slid on his hand. The rage pulsed stronger. He could hear it now. A dark laughter in his mind.

The blackened metal haft of Skrið radiated power as he grabbed hold of it.

The others backed away at the sight of it. "Khet, I need you to maintain control. There are innocent people down there. We need to protect them. Do you understand me?" Gideon sounded more like he was pleading with Khet instead of ordering.

"Yes." Khet knew that he couldn't promise anything, but he would try.

"Move!" Gideon gave the order, and they crashed through the forest.

The brush of the leaves and branches felt distant. All he could hear was his heart as it pounded in his ears. He burst through the underbrush, rage burned in his chest. *The Temple will burn!* echoed in his mind. Pure instinct took over. He became something else.

The four of them exploded from the brush like feral beasts. A Temple contracted soldier dragged a woman by the hair. His face went from confusion to a mask of horror as Khet buried his gauntlet into his face. Khet only felt the soldier's skull fracture as the soldier's body folded. His blood was too loud for him to hear anything else.

The Temple knight nearby couldn't raise his sword before Skrið made contact. A spray of blood and bone showered on people nearby. The once-proud knight now lay headless at Khet's feet. The pure joy of violence and blood lust fueled him.

A young Temple archer fiddled with his bow when Khet sent his threads out to him. The threads coiled around the archer's waist. With a solid pull, the young archer flew toward Khet. Skrið slammed into the archer's chest. He shrieked and flopped to the ground.

In the distance, Khet saw his target. At the end of a row of smoldering houses stood an acolyte surrounded by three Dodecahedron. A wicked smile came to his face. Power surged in his chest as he threw himself at them. The acolyte stood calmly without a care in the world. Safe in his little ring of protection. When the first immortal collapsed in a molten heap. Fear cut through him like a knife. Khet stood before him defiantly. His body glowed red-hot. The skin on the acolyte's face blistered. He shrieked as the other two Dodecahedron launched themselves at Khet.

Pain erupted in Khet's arm as he tried to block the swing of the immortal on his left with his gauntlet. The shattered bones ground and clicked as his arm fell uselessly to his side.

Skrið connected with the one on the right. Its chest blew open in a massive burst of power.

Khet lunged at the last Dodecahedron, just missing its sword swipe. It flailed. The armored limbs stuck Khet repeatedly. Each blow was worse than the last. Desperate, he unleashed his rage. The creature's armor softened as its body convulsed. All that was left was a pool of slag.

Khet collapsed, his healing power could not keep up with the damage. A shadow loomed over him. The burned face of the acolyte snarled as he raised his spear. Khet couldn't move.

The acolyte shrieked and dropped the spear as an arrow planted itself in his eye. He wavered slightly before Gideon's long sword took off his head.

"Good Caspian, are there any more of the bastards?" Gideon stood over Khet.

"The rest went running when Khet took care of those Dodecahedron." Caspian called out.

Lightning flashed as the sky ripped apart.

"OK, maybe none got away. Belera saw to that." Khet couldn't see Caspian, but his smile rang in his voice.

Gideon kneeled next to Khet. "Khet, are you going to be alright?"

"Did I do well?" It sounded weak even to him.

"You killed three Dodecahedrons and saved this village. You did great. Rest and heal yourself. We need to see if we can help these villagers." He gave Khet a smile that filled Khet with pride.

Khet lay there as his bones and bruises mended. The storm in the sky evaporated as if it never existed.

His wounds were still mending when he heard footsteps nearby. "I heard you can actually fight." Belera's voice sounded like music on the wind.

He tested his situation by sitting up. His left hand lightly ached. His jaw and neck still lightly throbbed, but it was melting away. Karina and Belera studied one of the dead Dodecahedron. Its body was a partially melted lump of slag.

Karina nudged the lump with her boot. "I would say more than just fight." She had a hungry look in her eye. Khet had heard of battle lust, but for the life of him, he couldn't see that happen right now.

He could feel himself flush slightly. "I heard a man say once, in battle, you never stop moving and never let go of your weapon. So I just did that."

Gideon came around the corner. "I think we have done everything we can do for them. Let us move on. I told them to make for the University. They will find shelter there."

The blackened remains of the homes lay in smoldering ruins. Not a single structure was left standing. The surviving villagers filed out of the village. Some carried the belongings, while others helped the wounded. A wagon full of corpses passed slowly by. "Another log on the pyre." Khet whispered to himself.

There was nothing he could do for these people, except ensuring it wouldn't happen again.

70

It wasn't much further to the Saphos Sea. As Gideon had said, there were boats and supplies waiting for them. Simple, finely crafted, maybe large enough to carry three people each.

Everyone loaded into the boats. Khet could feel their glances. Was it out of fear or respect? He didn't know, but he knew that things would be different now. *How could it not be different? I am the hero. I am the one they have been waiting for, and that battle in the village proved that I am real. I am the eighth hero of legend.*

Caspian looked under the packs. "I don't see any paddles. How are we going to use boats with no paddles?" He threw his hands in the air.

"We don't need them. Now it has been a while since I have done this, so give me a moment." Gideon stood at the bow of one of the small boats.

All three boats lurched forward; everyone jumped. "Sorry, like I said, it has been a while." Gideon steadied himself, and the boats moved again, smoother this time. "There we go. I suggest you sit back and rest. On the other side, it will all be on foot."

The boats slid across the sapphire water. Khet laid back and just marveled at the Saphosi Tower. The thunderous sound of the waterfalls steadily grew as they made their way swiftly across the water.

Belera was in the boat with Khet. "So, Khet, do you want to talk about what happened back there?"

Khet was so engrossed in the Tower that he had to look around to see who was talking. "Not really. I had a run-in with slavers not too long ago, and I was helpless then. I am not that helpless anymore."

"You are definitely not helpless. Still a naive southern farm boy, though." Belera had a playful smile on her face.

"I was contracted, not a farm boy either. I worked in a smithy."

"Oh, sorry to hear that."

"It wasn't all bad. They treated me well. Not like other contracted. It was almost like a family."

"Well, I guess that is nice. We will be near where you lived. I could talk to Gideon about stopping by to see them again."

"No, that is fine. They are all dead."

"Well, for fucks sake, man!" Belera laughed a deep laugh. "Aren't you just a tragic backstory? I guess you don't want to talk about that either?"

"No." Khet couldn't help it. Her laugh made him smile.

"Since you are not in the mood for sharing and I find the silence boring, I will tell you my tragic story." Belera made herself more comfortable. "Well, I grew up in a small village on the eastern edge of the Dunes of Bast. Life was pretty simple there. It was a village full of potters and artists. You see, the soil in the area was a clay that was perfect for making pottery. Also, on the banks of Lake of the Gods grew the most vibrant flowers out of rocks that were just as colorful."

"My mother was a gifted potter, and my father could paint the most breathtaking murals. Merchants would come to the village and buy all the different pieces of art they would make. Life was great until I got older." Belera drank from her water skin. "My parents kept pressuring me to marry. I was already looked at like a strange creature because I was never romantically involved with anyone. I just didn't find anyone attractive. Good and pleasant people, sure, but not a single one worth having sex with. My parents, being somewhat traditionalists, were going to arrange a marriage for me. They were literally going to force me to have to fuck someone for the rest of my life when I didn't want to fuck anyone. Isn't that messed up?"

Khet could hear the anger boiling in her chest. Still unable to understand her, he took Caspian's advice and respected her. "I don't see how they could do that to you."

"Exactly! Well, before they could make me go through with it. In the middle of the night, I snuck out and never went back. I was lucky enough to come across some members of the Hand when I first left. I became a member, and now I am here. I know it's probably not as tragic as yours, but we all have our own reasons to do what we do."

"Do you want to see them again? We could try to go by and see them on our way to Alfir's Tower."

Belera's face darkened. "Years ago, the Temple raided my village looking for someone. They left no survivors."

Khet couldn't stop himself. "Ha, you said I had a tragic story. Yours comes at a close second."

A smile spread across her face. "I guess you're right; we are all pretty tragic. I do wish that Jost wasn't doing such a good job. I would love to take down some more Temple bastards."

"What are you talking about?"

"Nobody told you? That figures. Jost is drawing the Temple's attention by starting a small conflict in the north. Haven't you noticed that we haven't seen many of the Temple?"

"I am a sheltered southern farm boy, remember? I have never been near a Tower in my life."

"OK, that makes sense. Well, we should be clear of the Temple until we reach Sidierion Tower. There are always Temple soldiers and their Dodecahedron there."

"Why there?"

"To protect that Tower. If that Tower falls, all the contracted will go free. The Temple has a lot of contracted. A lot of their army is contracted. When Sidierion falls, the Temple will be greatly weakened."

"What about the Dodecahedron?"

"Well, I have heard stories about a southern farm boy that has proven their title of immortal to be false."

"What can I say? I am a little special." Khet attempted not to sound boastful.

Belera shifted again. "So, enough of the tragic backstories. Let's talk about something else."

"What do you want to talk about?" Khet wanted to just relax for this trip, but he enjoyed Belera's company.

"If you weren't this 'Hero that will set us all free'. What would you be doing right now?"

Khet leaned back in his chair and thought about it. "Well, my plan was to walk the Pilgrimage, and after that, I don't know."

"That would have taken you years to finish. I know of many people who have claimed to have finished but only a few who actually have."

"What about you?"

"Instead of being forced into a marriage and being some man's sex toy? Then shooting out some kids for him?"

Khet swallowed hard. "Yeah... instead of that."

"I would still be a member of the Hand. I heard stories from merchants about them. I wanted to be one ever since I was young."

Khet took in his surroundings. The boats were almost to the other shore. He missed all the scenery that he wanted to see. Then again, he made a connection with Belera. To him, at the end of the day, that was worth more than the scenery.

71

The boats gently scraped against the shore. Everyone collected their packs and took shaky steps onto dry land. The ground felt different under his feet, not alive like the water. With one last look at Saphosi Tower and the beautiful sea, Khet turned and followed the others into the forest.

The group walked silently through the woods. A soft breeze rustled through the leaves. While not as lush as the forests near Grunaive, the leaves were a deep shade of green. Between the dark trunks of the trees and the leaves, the forest was almost black. They walked on mostly in silence. Small conversations would break out amongst them but quickly die. For hours, this cycle would continue.

The group was showing ever-increasing signs of fatigue before Gideon ordered a stop. "OK, somewhere up ahead is a set of standing stones. They are not located near the main trail. Reports say that a lot of animals go to the grove where the stones are. So, Caspian, I need you to scout ahead and find it. The rest of us will move off the trail and camp."

As the others moved off the trail, Caspian strung his bow. "How far do you want me to go? A couple of miles or until I find it?"

Gideon handed him two vials of nectar. "Take these, I hope you won't need them. If the map is right, we should be close. Go no more than 5 miles from here. If you don't find it, come to us, and we all will look for it after we rest."

"OK, sounds good. Be back in a while then." Caspian slipped through the woods. Khet stood on the edge of the trail and waited for Gideon.

"Yes, Khet."

"What is so important about the standing stones?"

"It is the entrance to the cave that will take us under Dragon's Spine. It is there."

"How long will it take to get through there, do you think?"

"From the information I had available before we left. The terrain is pretty flat. There is a small city we will have to navigate through. I estimate two and a half weeks."

"OK, two and a half weeks underground doesn't sound so bad."

"Well, it might come to pass that the people who will live on after us will have to be underground a lot longer."

Khet remembered the barrels next to the inn. "How long have they been planning for this?"

"Centuries, from what I was told. Who really knows when it comes to the Arankai? They are full of secrets."

Khet followed Gideon into the forest to look for the others. It wasn't too far in when they found them in a small clearing. Truse was busy starting a fire.

"Truse, it shouldn't get so cold tonight that we will need a fire." Gideon sat against a tree and pulled out a book.

"This isn't for warmth. I am hoping Caspian comes through with some venison or rabbit." There was an anticipation in Truse's eyes.

"I can't argue that; venison sounds really good right now." Gideon looked at his ration bag with light disdain. "OK, Truse, Karina, you two pull first watch. The rest of you get rest. I myself need rest. Belera, Khet, relieve them in five hours."

Khet slumped against a tree. Unable to get comfortable enough to actually sleep. He just sat there and looked at the mountains. This close to the Wall and the mountains, the mountains looked so small. The Wall's dark gray stone stretched so far into the clouds that Khet couldn't see the top.

It reminded him of the days leaning against the tree behind Tarin's smithy. Khet would spend hours looking at the Wall. On a couple of clear days, he could swear he could see the top of it. Occasionally, his mind would trick him into seeing a person on top of the Wall.

Khet mindlessly turned Narona's crystal between his fingers. The weight of it tied around his neck comforted him. She said it would protect him from a mighty blow. Maybe that is what will save him from the fate that some have accepted for him.

The smell of cooking meats brought Khet out of his slumber. He couldn't remember even feeling tired enough to sleep. Caspian worked with Truse to cook a small deer Caspian had hunted.

"Hey Khet, come here and try this. Caspian came through and bagged us some venison." Truse kept his voice low. He didn't want to wake Belera or Greylock.

Khet attempted to get his clumsy feet to move quietly. The position he fell asleep in left most of his lower half numb. After several steps and proper blood flow restored, Khet's steps were no more deliberate than a stumble. The smell from the cooking meats made Khet's mouth water. He indeed was hungry.

Truse cut a piece off and dabbed it in some seasoning. It was hot to the touch. Khet fumbled it for a moment. His first bite was an explosion of salts and herbs. He couldn't control himself; he gave a low, pleasurable moan. Khet had never tasted something like this before. The strange spices, both sweet and savory, told stories of strange lands.

"It's good, right? The spice blend is my own creation. Whenever I go anywhere with Caspian, I bring it. He always hunts down something delectable." Truse prepared another piece for Khet.

"Your spices are the reason I go out of my way to hunt something." Caspian patted his full belly.

Gideon propped himself up. "Did you find the standing stones?"

"Yes, sir, I did. If you go a hundred yards up the trail. Then head north for another about three hundred, you will see the trail that leads to them." Caspian took a bite of the venison. "It took me longer to hunt and clean this fella than to find the stones."

"Good… good, now get some rest. Khet, eat your fill then relieve Karina. Hey, Belera, are you with us?" Gideon bit down on a large hunk of meat.

"I am here. Let me piss first. I am about to burst." Belera said as she walked off into the forest.

"Truse, you try to cook and dry as much as you can. Then get some rest. After that, we will head out."

Khet grabbed a couple more pieces of meat and walked out to find Karina.

"That smells delicious. I was wondering when someone would come out to relieve me." Krina came out of nowhere.

Khet jumped so hard he almost choked. "Damn! Don't do that."

"Stay alert, stay alive, Khet." Karina chuckled as she walked back to camp.

Once Khet's heart slowed down after a bit. He settled down to keep watch. For a while, he could hear the chatter from the camp. Once everyone was asleep, the only sound was the breeze through the trees. Every now and then, Khet would hear a small animal scurrying through the fallen leaves.

"It is always strange when it is quiet."

Khet jumped at Gideon's voice right next to him. The large man could move silently when he wanted to.

"Sorry, I didn't mean to scare you. I just wanted to check on you and relieve you to get a couple more hours' rest before we leave."

"Are you sure? I am feeling okay."

"Take some advice from an old commander. Rest while you can because you may not be able to in the future."

"Okay, before I go, can I ask you a question?"

"Sure."

"Do you know where the entrance that leads to the base of Sideirion's Tower?"

"Yes, it is roughly ten miles north of the tower. Just about three miles north of the Temple's outpost."

"The Temple has an outpost there?"

"Yeah, a fortified one at that. Last reports I read only twelve Dodecahedron, but two to three thousand soldiers."

"And we are just going to walk by, and nobody says anything?"

"That is the plan. Now go rest. It is still several weeks before we even have to worry about that."

Khet turned and walked back to the camp. This time, he tried to find a tree more comfortable than the last one he slept at.

72

After several hours of rest, they packed camp and made way for the entrance under the mountains. The path to the standing stones was exactly as Caspian had said. They walked to the entrance of the alcove. There was a strange sense of foreboding coming from the entrance. A warning to all, stay clear and never return.

Khet's skin crawled at the sensations that rolled through him. "I hate this feeling. I don't want to be here!" It was just as bad as the time he went through the stones with Clair.

Truse mirrored Khet's sentiment. "Yeah, I am feeling like we should run from here!"

"Hold true, the feeling will pass!" Gideon walked through to the threshold.

Khet forced himself on. Each step, the fear and dread grew in his gut. Two steps beyond the entrance, the fear and dread evaporated like they were never there. "I hate that. Do you know what that does?"

"Scholars at the University say the stones emit a sound that keeps people away. Or some kind of magic. Really don't know." Gideon waited for everyone's head to clear.

"They have been out here many times trying to figure out how the stones are generating it. From what I understand, they don't know yet." Gideon took notice of everyone seeming ready to carry on. "OK, everyone, let's head in. Karina, get ready, we will be needing your light."

The group followed Gideon through the stones to a wall covered in dense growth. He reached out and pulled the growth to the side. It revealed a darkened cavern that seemed to go on forever. He held the growth so the others could easily enter. Once they were all through, he let it drop behind them.

Light only trickled through the growth in the cavern. A dark shape stood out. An ancient iron door with the strange eye embossed on it. A gentle light filtered through the seams of the doorway.

"Karina, hold on to the light for a moment." Gideon opened the heavy door. The door complained loudly from being disturbed. "I heard of stairs like these." The awe of mystery enveloped his face. "OK, everyone, follow me."

They filed quietly down the stairs. The same type of stairs Khet had traveled in the past. Ten steps, turn, ten steps, turn, and on it went.

The door at the bottom was the same as the others, dark iron with an embossed eye. The view beyond the door was comfortably similar to Khet's.

The doorway opened on a hilltop overlooking a vast, glowing city.

"Well, shit." Gideon breathed into the darkness. "They told me about the city, but by the Gods I didn't think it was going to be like this."

"Which way do we go?" Belera asked.

"We follow the stones through the city. After that, we follow a ravine to Vulcan's Tower. After that, there is only one path we can go." A long ribbon of golden light flowed into and was lost in the great city. "Let's keep moving. We can rest again after we are out of the city."

All of them stayed close to the golden ribbon of light that showed them the way. Above floated small flecks of light that lazily spiraled around the city. Just like what Khet had seen before.

Buildings came up out of the dark as they moved on. Wind could be heard rustling the tall grass and pushing through trees. All was just out of sight.

The road went from hard-packed dirt to stone as the city walls came into view. A dull glow seeped from the stone.

"Are we sure we can go through there?" Belera's voice shook with unease.

Khet chimed in before anyone else could. "You guys have never seen one of these?" Khet looked at them in the dim light. "Ha, the sheltered southern farm boy has been through one of the other cities. On my way to the University. Just follow the glow stones. We will be fine."

"OK, if you say so, Khet. But if a ghost appears, I am running home." Belera stated.

Khet led them now with his shoulders up, full of confidence.

"Well, the Hero says it is safe, let's go." Gideon fell in close behind Khet.

The city was the same as the one before. All the buildings had a gentle glow. Side streets would seemingly stretch on forever in the distance.

The golden ribbon of glow stones wove through the city. The path took them through streets wide enough for four carts to pass through easily, to narrow alleys. Only wide enough for them to travel single file.

After one such alley, the path opened to a massive causeway lined with giant statues. These statues were different from the statues in the other city. These were beasts that looked twisted and unnatural. Claws and large wings were on most of them. Luckily, the golden path turned before they got any closer.

"Has anyone seen any scraps of waste? This is the cleanest city I have ever seen." Truse asked.

They all paused for a moment and surveyed the area. No rubbish was anywhere to be seen. "Another question for the scholars to answer. Let's keep going." Gideon replied.

At the end of the city, the darkness crushed back in on them. The golden path and the small flecks of light above were the only light available. No dull blue glow on the cavern walls here.

They found themselves in a dense forest, the light above blocked by the leafy canopy. On they marched in the golden gloom. A brighter light shone in the distance.

A large glow stone stood at the end of a long pole. It illuminated a large clearing.

"Good, we made it." Gideon pointed to the pole. "We will camp near the way post. We don't need tents or a watch. We won't rest for too long. Karina, there should be a large pile of stones near the post. Gather some for us. The ravine we walk to Vulcan's tower is just beyond here, and there is no light trail."

All of them set about on the ground to rest for a short while. Very few conversations happened. Just some whispers. Khet found a spot and had himself a deep sleep.

73

"Everyone up! We have been followed!" Gideon yelled.

Khet jolted out of his deep sleep. His head was on a swivel as he scrambled for his gauntlets.

"Karina, light! We need more light!" Bellowed Gideon.

Khet stood and tried to get his bearings. Searing light erupted from Karina's hands. She hurled it in the direction Gideon pointed. Khet followed it with his eyes. Galins scattered as the balls of light came towards them.

"Galins, I count seven. Anyone see the leader?" Belera called out as the group lined up to face the creatures.

Karina quickly hurled other brightly glowing stones to light up more of the soon-to-be battlefield . The way the shadows crisscrossed from different directions, the scene looked unreal.

With a shriek, the galins charged.

"I see no leader!" Caspian called over the shrieks.

"Kill them all!" Gideon commanded seconds before the galins entered striking range.

Khet's gauntlets glowed brightly as he took swings at one of the galins. It kept its distance, just outside of his reach. With his heart hammering and blood pounding in his ears, Khet pushed on. Sweat stung his eyes. A claw raked across his bicep, a flare of pain erupted.

Another galin came from Khet's right. It tackled him to the ground. In a moment of sheer terror, Khet pushed all the heat he could into his body. An ear-shattering cry came from the galin atop Khet. As he burned through the creature's body.

Khet's body glowed with white-hot heat. He launched himself at the nearest galin. It shrieked as Khet turned it to ash. Other cries and shrieks filled the cavern. Khet continued to throw his molten visage at another galin. It shriveled to a burnt husk in his arms.

"Khet! Too hot! Enough!" Gideon yelled over the chaos.

Quickly, Khet pulled back on the flames burning inside him. Extinguished, Khet stood in the dark. Just a faint glow from the stones Krina scattered. A painful moan came from somewhere in the dark.

"Truse! Belera is down! She needs healing, now!" Commanded Gideon.

"Yes, sir!" Truse moved swiftly to Belera's side. "She is burned pretty badly, but I think I can heal her." Laying his hands on Belera, a soft light emitted from his palms. "It's okay, I will fix you up. Just relax now."

"Everyone else, sound off, name, and condition." Gideon called.

"Karina, good."

"Caspian, bleeding but breathing."

"Khet, good."

Gideon stood and strode towards Khet. "You control your fucking power!" Gideon struck Khet across the face. The force of the blow knocked Khet off his feet. "That could have killed all of us! We have the actual world counting on us! We can't afford any of us dying because you can't control yourself." Greylock pivoted and made his way back to Belera.

"She will be alright. A little sore for a couple of days, but alright." Truse reported to Gideon.

"Will I be pretty again? Tell me the truth." Belera's voice was weak.

A smile came to Truse's face. "Well, I have some bad news, you were never that pretty to begin with, and I am no miracle worker." He chuckled softly. "Now rest."

"For a healer, your bedside manner is shit." Belera said through a painful smile.

"She will be alright, here let me help you up." Karina extended her hand to Khet.

Khet took her hand and stood up. "I am sorry. I didn't know."

"Hey, it happens. Just be glad she will be alright. We all have hurt a friend when learning our abilities." Karina quickly turned away from Khet. "It seems you have burned off your clothes."

Khet was suddenly aware of the cool breeze on his nether region. He covered himself and made his way over to his pack. Khet quickly grabbed his pack and made for the shadows.

After putting his extra set of clothes on, he made his way back to the group. Everyone that wasn't injured either picked through the mess that was now camp. Or pulled the remains of galins outside the camp.

"They must have been starving, trapped down here." Caspian checked his bedroll for any damage.

"I don't think they will be coming back after Khet burned through three of them." Truse handed a vial of nectar to Caspian.

"Sorry, one of them tackled me, and I panicked. Then I just went after the other two." Khet tried to convey how savory he was.

"Next time, do better." Gideon made his way back to Khet. "Look, I apologize for striking you. That was out of line." Gideon extended his hand to Khet.

Khet flinched slightly but took Gideon's offer. "I am sorry as well. I will do better next time."

"Look, Khet, we all have had that experience. I almost killed my uncle after he insulted my mother."

"How?"

"Filled his lungs with water. My ability was still very new to me. So I understand." Gideon turned and went back to Belera.

Khet followed; he didn't want to face her, but he knew he should. "I am sorry."

Belera locked eyes with Khet. "You can make it up to me by warming up some water to make some stew for me." She smiled; her strength had somewhat returned. The burns had faded slightly. "All is forgiven. Just remember if you get struck by a random lightning bolt later, you had it coming." A bit of laughter came from the group.

"Belera, are you good to move?" Greylock stood in the middle of the camp.

"Yeah, I will be fine. I may never play the lute, but I will survive." Belera groaned and willed herself up.

"I never knew you played." Truse looked surprised at Belera's revelation.

"I don't, but maybe someday I might have a go at it. Can't a girl dream?" Her voice dripped sarcasm.

Khet gathered his belongings. His heart was not as heavy as it was.

They all made their way to the vast ravine. The black mouth of it opened wide and inviting. A low rumble could be heard in the distance.

"What is that noise?" Khet asked.

"That should be Iron Falls. The iron lake around Vulcan's Tower flows down here. We should be crossing it in a week or so." Gideon replied.

"A week or so and we can hear it already?"

"Seems like it. Karina, hand out some glow stones for everyone. And let's move."

Karina handed everyone a bright stone. Khet rolled it in his hands; it was such a smooth river stone. He placed the stone in a set of braided cord that was made to hold a light stone. They all had this braided cord on their belts.

Khet stood and watched the others secure their stones.

"Everyone ready?" Gideon walked around and checked each one. "OK, follow me."

The group walked into the vast blackness of the ravine, steadily moving towards the roar of Iron Falls.

74

The rhythm of the march settled in on them. They would march for a while. Rest and eat a little food. Then, they would repeat it all again. The only thing that really marked their progress was the sound of the Iron Falls. With each step, the falls grew louder and louder.

On their eighth day in the deep ravine, the thunder of the falls was so loud that you had to shout to be heard.

"WE SHOULD KEEP GOING! THERE IS NO WAY ANYONE OF US WILL BE ABLE TO SLEEP WITH THIS NOISE!!" Gideon strained his shout to be heard.

The others nodded in agreement and made their way forward. It wasn't long until they caught sight of it. A massive bridge with glowing blue crystals placed evenly down the walkway. It looked ancient and vast. Runes that glowed white were carved all along the bridge. The surface made impossible curves in and around the underside of the bridge. All the lines would twist together and spread to other knots. Just to flow to another. Reminded Khet of a tangled mess of black ribbon.

To the right of the bridge, in the distance, was a sight that Khet could not comprehend. A titanic molten iron fall flowed from somewhere above. It pooled and flowed through a giant hand. It spilled between giant fingers and flowed down an arm. Eventually, it made it to a giant shoulder and spilled down the giant's chest. A statue of some forgotten god bathed in the glowing iron. At the feet of the colossal statue was a complex of temples. Ancient and worn, with no sign of any worshippers. Rivers of molten iron flowed between the structures. It all glowed an eerie, dull red.

The iron flowed between all the temples. In small rivulets, it came together into a torrent of molten iron. With great spread, it rushed beneath the impossible bridge. Another drop flowed into a deep, dark void with no bottom in sight.

Karina tapped Khet on the shoulder to bring him out of his amazement. They walked onto the bridge. As Khet moved closer to the first blue crystal, the temperature dropped. By the time Khet was next to the crystal, he was chilled. A hoarfrost formed around the crystals. The roar of the falls below was deafening.

The view as they walked the bridge made it hard for Khet to stay focused on his march. He could easily make out that the size of the buildings in the distance was larger than anything at the University. The largest barely came to the giants' shin.

The molten iron itself made no sense to Khet. The way it flowed like hot honey down the colossus's chest. It gave the face a menace, to its stern look. All the while, the iron never cooled. *Magic can do some weird shit.* Clair's words rang in his mind.

What lived here and who built this were the only two things Khet could think about as they walked on. He was totally oblivious when the others stopped and looked to the other side of the bridge.

Truse had to jog to catch Khet's arm to get his attention. Truse pointed to the other side of the bridge. Floating in the air were stairs. Their dark colors were hard to see in the low light.

Khet walked over to get a closer look with the others. The stairs floated independently of the other stairs or anything else. Just floating there, detached from everything but solid in its place.

Gideon pressed on the first step, and it held firm. He moved his hands all around it, looking for wires or supports of any kind. There was nothing.

Caspian dared to walk up the stairs. He made it three before Gideon pulled him down. He yelled something at the others that Khet could not make out. But they all moved off.

Khet couldn't believe everything he had seen. How can magic like this exist? He couldn't believe all the stories and histories he had been told; not a single one mentioned magic or a place like this. Everything he had learned about the Gods and how Sýna came to be, stuff just wasn't adding up. At this point, he felt like somebody had lied when they told their story. Or maybe they all lied; Khet didn't know what to believe anymore.

The group walked on for hours in silence, exhausted and in need of rest. "OK, everyone, I think we are far enough. Khet, you pull first watch. Krina, light up the surrounding area. Everybody else, bunk down. Khet, come wake me when you need me to take over." Gideon gave out the orders and then just collapsed on his bag, asleep in seconds.

Karina quickly lit the surroundings and went to bed herself. Khet called on his healing power a little just to keep him sharp. He just paced around while he thought his thoughts. Confusing as his thoughts were.

75

Khet woke from his deep sleep as a foot nudged his ribs.

"Wake up there, hot stuff. Both literally and figuratively." The sound of Belera's sarcastic tone was a delight for him to wake to. He had been afraid she would treat him differently after the galin attack.

"OK...OK" Khet rolled onto his back. He was grateful that Caspian relieved him when he did for watch. He was beyond exhausted and he was afraid to rely on his healing power too much.

Everyone looked well rested if you considered the situation they were in. All were in various states of dress. Switching out more soiled clothes for the slightly less soiled. It is difficult to wash your clothes with no streams around.

Khet was acutely aware of his own stench. He was down to one set of clothes after he completely incinerated his only other pair.

Dingy and in need of a good scrub, they all ate breakfast and moved on with the march. With each step, now the thunder of Iron Falls receded. After only a couple of hours of walking that day, it became just a low rumble in the distance.

While they walked, the quality of the air changed. The dry air that had been their constant companion turned into a cool, humid air.

Greylock's head perked up. "Everyone, stop." He titled his head ever so slightly. "Karina, light an arrow for Caspian. Caspian, I want you to fire the arrow as far as you can."

"Anything we should be worried about?" Caspian handed Karina an arrow.

"Just a hunch. Now arc the arrow high, we need distance." Greylock's eyes were closed. He strained to listen for something that was unseen.

Caspian drew back the lighted arrow. Khet expected trouble and slid on his gauntlets. The arrow sailed high through the air. The bright glow revealed a glassy surface of an underground lake. The arrow sank below the surface in the distance with barely a sound.

"Time to wash up, everyone. I know I could use it. Karina, throw some stones in the water. I want to see how deep it is." Gideon already dropped his gear as he walked to the edge of the water.

The rocks revealed that in that area, the lake was only waste deep. With a small bridge that stretched over the water. Without a second thought, they all got in with clothes on. The water was cold but not too cold for Khet.

Submerging himself in the water, he felt better than he had in days. He took off his shirt and started scrubbing it to get it clean. Khet gasped at Belera's complete nudity.

"What? You will just have to deal with it. I want to be completely clean. Anyway, who knows what we will face when we get out of here? I am going to be as comfortable as I can be. You guys are free to join." Belera stood, not a single care was given.

"What the hell. You only live once, I guess." Caspian said as he stripped.

"You know, since we are all going to probably die in the coming weeks, might as well live it up a little." Karina joined in the revelry.

Khet stood there and watched all the others as they joined Belera in nudity. "Why not?" Khet finished and threw his clothes on the shore's edge.

It was freeing for Khet to just be there, floating nude in the dark. Everyone just floated quietly for a while, enjoying the moment.

After a while, Gideon broke the silence. "OK, we need to get moving. Wash what you need to wash. After you are done, put your clothes on the shore's edge, and I will pull the water from them."

They retrieved all they needed from their packs and set about to clean their clothes and gear. Each one completely nude and not caring. Khet wished he felt this comfortable sooner in his life.

When the wash was completed and Gideon pulled all the water out of everyone's gear. They all got dressed and stowed any extra gear.

Belera made her way over to Khet. "So, my southern farm boy. The whole nude thing wasn't all that bad, now was it?"

Khet could see her point now. "Yeah, wasn't bad at all. I don't think it would go over well everywhere, but I see your point."

She smiled, a satisfied smile. Her scar from the burns was barely noticeable.

With all the gear stored and spirits a lot higher. They made their way over the lake. The bridge was made of wood that showed no sign of being aged or scarred. Completely untouched by time.

Khet hoped they would all survive what comes next. He wanted to share these stories with others. Nobody would believe him, but he wanted to share them nonetheless. Also, maybe to see Rin again.

76

The group reached the mouth of the cave three days later. The light of the sun blinded them after over two weeks in darkness. They all stood at the mouth of the cave for a while to let their eyes adjust.

Khet walked over to speak privately with Gideon. "Can I ask you a question about what we saw at Iron Falls?"

"I don't know what that was. Everything I have read, all it mentioned was smoke and the falls themselves. Nothing in there mentioned a giant statue and a city." Gideon squinted as he dug through his pack. "Have you seen my book?"

"No, what book?" Khet joined the search.

"It's a... ah here it is." Gideon kissed the cover of the book. Extremely happy to find it. "When I first married Alner, I would get sent on these long missions and I wouldn't see him for months. We both would miss out on massive parts of each other's lives. So Alner came up with this idea. He had a book and I had a book. He would write letters to me in his. Telling me about his day and what neighborhood gossip he heard and I would do the same. When I would come home we would trade and read each other's books. This is all the letters he has written to me through all the years. I read it before I go to bed. It reminds me why I am doing this. To protect Alner and everyone else."

Caspian came from out of the woods. Khet was thankful for the distraction. "It is a ghost town. The walls of the fortress have very few guards. I only see a couple contracted and very few members of the Temple." Caspian reported.

"What about the Temple's garrison?" Gideon had a confused look on his face.

"I can't see everything but the gates are open and nobody's home."

"OK." Gideon paced for a moment in thought. "Everyone, change of plans. Caspian, Karina, and I are going to scout ahead. Belera, you take the others and go around the backside of the Tower. It looks like the Temple has abandoned their fort. Try to avoid contact. Meet us at the cave entrance north of the tower."

"Why would they abandon Sideirion Tower?" Belera said as she fastened her pack.

"I don't know. That is why we are going to find out." Gideon grabbed his gear and checked his sword.

"Good luck, sir." Belera offered her hand to Gideon.

He accepted it. "You too. And Khet, none of your flashy displays now. We don't know what is going on, and we don't need the extra attention."

Khet nodded his head and grabbed his gear. The group separated and went their own ways.

Belera led Khet and Truse down the hill away from the direction Gideon and the others took. The route was not an easy one. The brush was thick, and they had to backtrack several times to get around impassible areas.

When they hit the tree line, Sideirion Tower came into full view. Compared to the other three towers Khet had seen, Sideirion was awfully bland. It was enormous, like the others. The walls were flat with various runes carved into them. The others had life to them. Sideirion Tower was a cold, dead stone block with writing on it. Still, its presence stood out against the lush green surroundings.

"Khet, keep up. We need to stay together." Belera called after him.

"Sorry, I was lost in thought." Khet jogged to catch up.

"Look, I know you said you were contracted and you must have some hate in you for this tower, but I need you to focus." Belera warned.

"You know I never thought of it that way. My time as a contracted was actually good. They took care of us and raised me."

"They still bought you and owned you. I don't think we have the same definition for good." Truse added as they walked along.

"Truse is right, the simple fact that they bought and owned you makes them not good people. They may have been better than slavers and other people that own contracted. They still owned and held you to your contract." Belera led them into another thicket of trees.

"I know and understand what you are saying, but Tarin and Kase were not like that."

"And now they're all dead. I would love to continue this chat and unpack all of your childhood trauma, but we have company." Belera pointed to an acolyte of the Temple walking towards them with two burly-looking contracted.

"Greetings, children of the Twelve. May I ask what brings you to the Tower of Sideirion? All Temple business has been temporarily suspended." The acolyte and the contracted stopped a small distance away.

"Yeah, where is everyone?"

"Oh, I have the most glorious of news. The leaders of the evil Arankai have been found at the University. All marshal forces have been sent there to deal with the problem. Don't you worry, soon enough Temple services will recommence. It may be a couple of months, but we have the power of the Twelve on our side." The acolyte had the widest grin as he shared the news.

"When did this happen? How long did the garrison here leave?" Belera had a massive amount of concern in her voice.

"My dear child, they left two weeks ago. I am sure if you hurry, you can join them before they make it to that cesspit of a University, may it burn." The smile was still there.

"Good, we still have time." Belera spoke to Khet and Truse. "Thank you, acolyte, for the news." Belera gracefully walked towards the acolyte in a gesture of thanks, hand outstretched.

As the acolyte grabbed ahold of her hand, Belera smoothly pulled a long knife from her belt and pushed it through the acolyte's neck. "This is for my mother and father." She whispered into his ear as his body spasmed and hit the ground.

The two contracted stood there too stunned to move. Belera dug through the acolyte's robe until she found what she was looking for, two small stones. "I assume these are yours." She tossed each one to one of the contracted. "I don't know your word of breaking or whatever you call it. If you can free yourselves, I suggest you do it."

The two stood there in a daze and then looked at each other as if making an agreement. They brought the stones to their mouths and whispered something. There was a small cracking sound and the collars fell to the ground. "Thank you," the man on the left said.

"Don't thank me yet. Are either of you two God-Blessed?" Belera asked them.

The man on the right raised his hand. "I am a Grun."

"Well, that will be helpful. This area will be a bad place to be in the next couple of days. I suggest you grab any supplies you can and leave. There is a large cave that leads under the whole of Dragon's Spine." Belera pointed in the direction that they came from.

"What about the others?" the man on the left said.

"Take as many as you can. There is no food, water, and light is scarce. Pack enough for two weeks of hard marching. Now go."

"Thank you." They both said as they turned and ran down the slope towards the contracted living quarters.

"Well, no time for celebration; we need to hurry. Most of the Temple's army is contracted. We break this shard, and there goes the army." Belera took off at a run, down the slope, and the others quickly followed.

77

The three of them were quite winded when they reached the cave entrance. Belera surveyed the area and made sure they were alone.

"Eat, drink, and rest while you can. Once Gideon hears what is going on, I don't think we will be stopping much before we destroy this shard. Once this is destroyed and all contracted free, the Temple will be plenty busy while we make our way to Alfir's Tower." Belera sat herself down on a rock in the shade of a tree.

The others did the same. Finding shade and resting while they could. Khet took some deep sips of his water skin and nibbled on a ration. The peace only lasted a short while before they heard footsteps. They all drew their weapons and waited.

"It's me, Gideon." They all relaxed as Gideon came around a large tree. "Belera, what did you do? There is a contracted uprising in the fortress."

"We ran into an acolyte, and he didn't mind his own business. That isn't the important thing anyway. The Temple is on its way to attack the University." Belera took a bite of her ration.

"When? How many?"

"The full garrison, and they left two weeks ago."

"OK, we should have a couple of days. Good to know we are just a couple of hours from the stairs. Rest and drink, everyone. Sleep if you can. Once we leave here, there will be no stopping until we break that shard."

Everyone in the group was restless, except for Caspian. He gently snored beneath a tree. Khet's teeth were on edge. Everything had led to this. All this time they were trying to get here, and now it is about to happen. His body vibrated with anxiousness, and this was just the first shard. There was still Alfir and actually fighting Gods. The thought overwhelmed him.

"Are you ready?" Gideon sat in front of Khet.

"I think so."

"Good. We will be with you all the way. I was told once that no real hero tries to be a hero. That title is given to them by others. The hero needs to earn it. We have no way of knowing how tomorrow or the next day will turn out. Hell, once you smash that shard, there could be an explosion that kills us all. But I do know that when that Sideirion shard is gone. Everyone will be free to make their own way. Their own path." Greylock stood. "Let's go free some people. Give the Temple a nice black eye. Then we will go and shatter Alfir."

Khet came to his feet and followed Gideon before he was aware of it. When Gideon commands, people follow. All of them were up and strode defiantly towards the mouth of the shadowy cave.

The cavern's interior was different from the cave they were just in. Nothing but high walls and a smooth rock floor. It looked to be a natural cave, even though Khet knew it wasn't. They walked for about four hours before the faintest glow could be seen in the distance.

Khet caught up with Greylock. "Should we suspect something like the Iron Falls up ahead?"

"The only thing I know is a fog that glows, permeates the cavern the stairs are in. Nothing like Iron Falls."

Khet walked on and held onto the hope that Gideon was wrong. He wanted to see something that defied everything he knew again. It wasn't much longer until Khet saw that Gideon was mistaken.

Another massive cavern welcomed them. Its actual size was hard to determine given the darkness. Gideon was correct about the luminous fog. It poured from the very rock that made the cavern. All the colors Khet could think of slowly spun and mixed with each other.

All the fog, with all of its beautiful colors, was pulled to a single point that floated a distance away in the massive cavern. Khet followed the flow of the fog from the rocks around him. The closer and closer it moved towards the center, the faster it went. Until close to the center, it blurred out of existence.

"Before anyone asks, I don't know what that is. We have a job to do.

Let's go." Gideon walked to the cliff's edge. The stairs easily visible in the glowing fog. "Caspian, tie the rope around Khet and find an anchor point. Maybe this piece of bridge."

"Will do." Caspian pulled the rope out of his bag.

"Khet, I know we have already talked about this, but I want to go over it one more time. You will secure your thread to the grappling hook. Belera will fire it and hook the stairs. You will then pull yourself over to the stairs while we stabilize you. On the other side, you will secure the rope. Where I and Caspian will follow you over. The others will maintain guard and make sure we will have something to climb back on. Is everyone clear?"

"Yes, sir!" They all answered. Eerily, there was no echo. It was like the sound was pulled in the same direction as the fog.

Everyone set in motion to the tasks that they were given. Khet raised his arms so Caspian could tie the rope around his waist. Then he waited for Belera to ready the grapple launcher. He made a mistake and looked down the cliff. It was a gaping black void. He kicked a large rock into the void and waited. No sound of impact ever came back. It made his spine tingle.

Belera readied herself with the launcher. Khet spun one of his threads to the hook.

"Ready?" Belera looked at Khet dead in the eyes.

For a second, he lost himself. "Sorry. Yes, I am ready."

The grappling hook sailed across the chasm and gained purchase on the staircase. With a couple of test pulls, Khet was ready.

"Good luck, farm boy." Belera said. She tried to sound sarcastic, not worried, like Khet could tell she was.

"We got you, Khet. Don't worry if your line breaks; this will hold. You will slam really hard into the wall, but hey, you will be alive." Uneasy chuckles sounded at Truse's attempt at a joke.

"Here we go." Khet leaned over the edge. The rope around his waist sank in. Ever so cautiously, he pulled the line in. Khet wished they had practiced this a little more. Inch by inch, he made his way across. Cheers and laughter sounded when his feet made purchase on the stairs. Even though the sound was muted.

Securing the rope to the railing, Khet gave the signal for the others to cross. Gideon and Caspian sailed across on small pulleys.

"I see you guys had the easy way across." Khet smirked as they made it to the stairs.

"Easy, that was terrifying. Trusting your life to a man 'that you don't know that well's knot work. Looks good by the way." Caspian said with a little dance to his step.

"Alright, let's get this done. Khet, lead the way." Gideon made a motion to give Khet the lead.

The stairs were solid for not having any real structure to them. It was many flights before the stairs actually went inside the tower. Khet expected it to be pitch black on the inside of the tower. The walls were covered in the same runes that were on the outside. The light coming off of them was more than bright enough to light their way. The same pattern as the other mysterious stairs. Ten steps, turn, ten steps, turn.

The only sounds Khet could hear were his heart beating loudly in his ears, his breath coming hard, and their clunking footsteps. With every step, the air became heavier and heavier.

"Anyone else having a hard time breathing?" Gideon asked between gasps of air.

"Yes." They both answered.

"Push through, we are almost there." Gideon wheezed.

The minutes that followed were agonizing. Each step was a struggle. Then they made it to a door. Khet fell against it with exhaustion. The stone slab gently swung open. Fresh air slammed against their faces as they breathed fitfully for what seemed like their first time in forever.

Several minutes later, they gasped, trying to relax themselves. Khet was the first to regain full control of his breathing. He stood and began to investigate the top of the tower. It did not take him long to find what he was looking for.

The Sideirion shard was the size of a broad man's chest. It shone with a blueish-green ethereal light. The shard rested on a plinth with columns on either side. The stone that cradled the shard was dark black and highly polished. Drastically different from the dull grey stone that surrounded it.

Gideon and Caspian joined Khet. They all took in the view. The Wall still towered over them nearby. From this height, they almost could see the towers of Vulcan and Arcanus. A small black smudge stood out to the northeast. It was the hill Khet had rendered to slag. Khet stared for a moment and let the memories wash over him. *That was where this all started.*

"It's up to you now, Khet. Go free everyone." Gideon padded Khet on the back.

"Yeah, Khet, give those Temple bastards something to think about." Caspian added.

Khet pulled Skrið from his belt. The weight of the hammer was power in his hand. He stood before the shard, watching it shimmer. As he raised Skrið into the air. Thoughts of everyone he had cared for and lost flooded his mind. All the pain that this one shard had caused him and countless others throughout time. All that he held for just a moment. Then, with the weight of it all, he brought the hammer down.

78

Khet opened his eyes; he was sprawled on a set of strangely familiar stairs. He remembered being in front of the Sideirion shard and striking it. There was a flash of hot white light. Khet still had the sensation of his body being ripped apart and slammed back together. The pain of it echoed in his body.

The familiar stairs Khet stood upon were old and degraded. Old dried blood covered parts. At least that is what Khet thought it was. The two torches that burned on the wall offered little light in the darkness.

The torches sat on either side of a door that Khet knew but couldn't place. It was damaged and scarred as if something used a battering ram to open it from the inside. The door on the right side barely held on by a single hinge. It lay askew against the door frame. It allowed Khet a clear view of the inside.

Curiosity pushed him to peer inside. A voice could be heard. A familiar voice like something he remembered from a half-forgotten dream. The owner of the voice came into view.

Magnus stood in his gleaming armor. The armor was so bright and polished it looked aflame.

It all rushed back to Khet; this is the temple he would visit when he was younger. It was the temple he came to when he visited Magnus, Arrinia, and Rafir. The blood and damage was not here the other times he was here.

"Khet, is that you?" Magnus's voice boomed. "How did you get here?" He threw open the last door. The force of the blow snapped the hinges and sent the door bouncing down the stairs.

Khet stood back in awe of Magnus's size. The God towered over Khet. Fear gripped him. A shiver rippled through his spine.

"It is you." Magnus's smile was full of menace. "How did you get here by yourself?" His eyes lit up. " "Did you kill Malak?" Venom was in his smile.

Khet shook. This was not supposed to happen. Nobody said this would happen. Thoughts of Gideon and Caspian on top of Sideirion Tower flashed in his mind.

"Did your voice not come with you?" Magnus pushed open the other door, knocking it completely off the hinges to join the other. "Rafir, come here; you need to see this. We have a visitor."

Khet was close enough to the doorway that he could see a great deal inside. There was a woman's body staked to the back wall. She wore the same dress that Khet remembered Arrinia had worn. His stomach sank. Along another wall, other bodies hung; massive stakes pierced the old, dried corpses. One had a faded dress similar to the one Narona wore.

Khet's attention was brought back to his immediate surroundings when Rafir came around the corner.

"Khet, my, my, how did you get here?" Rafir stood the same height as Magnus, but he wore no armor. Just fine clothing in various shades of green. "Speak, what did you do to get here? Did you kill Malak?"

Khet couldn't stop himself; the words were pulled from him. "The last thing I remember, I destroyed the Sideirion shard, and I woke up here. No, I didn't kill Malak." Once the words left him, Khet almost collapsed; his heart raced.

"Magnus, do you remember many, many years ago when two of his kind showed up here out of nowhere?" Rafir rubbed his close-cropped beard in thought.

"Ah yes, I remember them. Because of them, the world spun just enough to build a stronger army. You shattered another one for us?" Magnus salivated at the thought. "Not exactly what we wanted out of you, Khet. We hoped you would kill Malak, and then we could just move in and take over. Use our army just enough to keep the energy flowing, not too much though. Don't want to draw the attention of the others until we are ready for them."

"There are others?" Khet's curiosity overran his fear.

Magnus had a surprised look on his face as if he had forgotten Khet was there. "Well, since you are about to die, I might as well tell you. Yes, there are the Thrones. Malak was smart and made this world in one of their blind spots. Then he got greedy and trapped the rest of us. But soon we will have our revenge. I will take that power of that crystal of his and reshape this world to my liking. Then when I have enough power, I will end those Thrones, and I will then be free." The malice reverberated in his voice. It stirred something deep within Khet, rage.

"Look, Magnus." Rafir's voice oozed excitement.

Khet turned to see. It was Sýna. He could see the Wall and what was inside it. As the world slowly turned, the God's Spire and its giant crystal silhouetted against the sun. It hung there, the entirety of his world now half in light and the other in darkness.

"That is perfect. We can reach Malak now with little effort. Well, Khet, your usefulness is over. We have what we need from you." Magnus summoned a blade to his hand.

The rage deep within Khet flared with a rush. It flooded through him. He wrenched Skrið free from his belt and brought it down on Magnus's unsuspecting hand. Magnus let out a painful scream as the blade clattered down the steps. Khet seized the moment of surprise and hurled Skrið at Rafir's face.

Rafir's face was complete confusion as Skrið made contact. Khet witnessed a massive spray of blood, bone, and flesh. As Skrið moved through Rafir.

Khet reached out with a thread and brought it back to his hand. Confidence and rage pulsed within him. The mixture purged out all fear. He knew they could die now. He knew that he could kill them. He could win this. Khet readied himself to attack Magnus.

"You impotent slime. You think you can kill me!" Magnus spread his hands to Khet. "Fall."

With great force, Khet was thrown from the steps.

79

Khet fell through the blackness. He hoped he would just wake in bed or somewhere else like he did in the past. But it never happened; he just fell. A great wind thundered in his ears as it tore at his clothes.

Khet turned himself, and he could see Sýna as it rushed underneath him. He just cleared the west part of the Wall, and he could see the University. Rin's beautiful smile flashed in his mind. He would never see that again.

The God's Spire and its giant crystal came into view. Khet saw an opportunity to maybe help his friends and all the innocents below. He readied Skrið. He put all he had into that throw.

Skrið made contact with the crystal. The explosion created large chunks, the size of small mountains. They hurtled in all directions. Magnus and Malak will both be weak now. *Maybe that will be enough.*

The ground was coming up quickly. Khet knew this was the end. The stories were right; he was destined to die. He just hoped he had done enough.

Khet could feel heat searing at his chest. He clutched at what burned him. It was Narona's crystal. He had forgotten about it. She said that it was to protect him from a mighty blow.

As the ground rushed up to meet him, Khet gripped the crystal and hoped it would protect him.

Pain racked his body. Each breath made everything hurt more. Khet opened his eyes. Blinking the dirt and dust out of his eyes, and he rose to his knees.

Dust was thick in the air. Khet coughed repeatedly. Each one as painful as the last. Narona's crystal had worked, and he was alive. Unsteadily, he stood up.

Khet padded his hands over his body, calling on his healing power. A smile came to him as he remembered Rafir's fate. Healing flowed through him, easing all his pain. Standing up straighter and able to take deep breaths again, Khet surveyed his surroundings.

From what he could tell, he had to be somewhere near Alfir's Tower. He could make out the three mountains that surrounded the tower in the distance.

A thunderous sound came from the west. A massive hole had been blown into the wall. Gigantic pieces of it were falling to the ground.

"NNNNOOOOOOOO!!!!!!" A booming voice sounded from everywhere all at once. The pain of it hurt Khet's mind. "Where is he?" The voice oozed malice.

80

An explosion rocked Khet off his feet. His world spun as he was thrown. He scrambled back upright, slipping on the Hell Hammer gauntlets that still hung at his side.

"There you are." Magnus stood in all his fury. "Because you have destroyed the one thing I needed, I am going to make your people suffer. I will bring my army through that hole in the Wall and enslave every last one of them. They will know that it was Khet that forced this fate upon them and they will curse you. They will remember you as a villain. And when I rebuild the crystal, I will kill them all."

Khet ran at Magnus with everything he had. Pouring all he could into his gauntlets. Magnus just stood there with a smirk as Khet made contact with his chest.

The force of the blow threw them both back. Khet tumbled as he hit the ground. His white howl of hatred for the God took over. It fused into his very being. He rose to his feet as the rage pulsed.

"Impressive." Magnus stood up, a significant dent where Khet made contact with his armor. "Using the power I gave you against me and still managed to damage my armor. You would have easily killed Malak. Too bad he was already dead when I got there."

"What?"

"Yes, Malak was dead. Looked like he had been dead for a long, long time. Now it is time for you to join him." Magnus strode confidently towards Khet.

Khet unfurled his threads in an attempt to restrain Magnus. Magnus swatted all but one out of the air. Khet wrapped the thread around Magnus's waist. Khet pulled hard. His feet lurched from the ground. Surprise filled Magnus's face as Khet flew at him.

The blow was so great that the great golden helm of Magnus flew off. Magnus stumbled as Khet continued to strike. Strike after strike, Khet could hear Magnus's armor break under the pummeling.

Pain erupted in Khet's side as he was sent airborne. He pulsed his healing power as he skidded along the ground.

"You fool! You have lost your weapon. You can't kill me. I am a God." Magnus's voice lacked the bravado that it once had. Replaced by doubt mixed with a little doubt.

Khet sprung to his feet. His rage pushed him on. "OK, I may not kill you, but I am going to make it hurt." Khet surged at Magnus. He rolled to the left, just avoiding a blow from Magnus.

Again, Khet repeated his strikes. He howled with rage. Great golden hands grabbed him and squeezed his throat.

Time slowed as the life was crushed from him. Khet guided threads around the damaged gauntlet of Magnus. He poured all his rage into the thread. All his hate. All his pain. All his suffering. It all flared into the thread.

Magnus roared in pain and sent Khet flying through the air. The impact forced the air from his lungs. Pain knifed through his shoulder. He gasped for any air he could take in. He stood, and his left arm hung lifeless from his side. His shoulder was shattered.

"You worthless miscreant. I watched your people crawl from the mud. I watched your cities rise and fall. You pathetic worm. You dare to fight me." Magnus clutched his bloody stump. A black, sickly blood seeped from the wound.

"So Gods do bleed." Khet smiled at the sight of him. The rage inside him smiled as well.

Magnus roared as he came at Khet. A golden spike appeared in his hand. Khet used his threads to pull himself to the side just as the tip of the spike passed by. He tumbled as he tried to regain his footing. Pain seared into his side as he was thrown from his feet again. A golden spike had pierced his side.

He wrenched it free with his good arm. Blood flowed out of the fresh wound. Khet's vision swam. His healing power was not compensating enough for his wounds.

"I am impressed you made it this far. Narona made you well." Khet

304

saw a shimmer of light form behind Magnus, a temporal bubble. "It seems you are at the end of your abilities now, filth. Time to lay down and die." A great golden axe took shape in Magnus's hand.

Khet flared his threads far and wide; he needed a solid anchor. He summoned all his heat until his body glowed white hot. Magnus just stood there with a smirk.

"Too bad you're so weak. I might actually be scared..." Magnus's remark was cut short by Khet's impact into his chest.

A gigantic pulse of energy sent Magnus reeling back into the temporal bubble. Khet's body crumpled to the ground. His broken bones ground against each other. He smiled as he lay broken on the ground. His bones were powder. He could barely breathe. His healing surged and flared, but there was so much damage already done. His vision blackened around the edges. His mind raced. *Did I do it? Did I save everyone? Was this the great plan? Were they safe?*

His vision shimmered as the light faded.

81

There he stood, Khet the Betrayer of Man, atop the rubble that was once a part of the Sacred Wall. The Wall that protected us from the evil Gods outside. Khet was satisfied with killing our god Sideirion and silencing his tower.

Now we have been made defenseless. Will the remaining nine gods return to us in our time of need? Will they defend us against the hoards of enemies that pour through the hole that Khet made for them?

We have to hold strong and keep the enemy at bay and pray for our gods' return…

Excerpt From "The Fall of the Hero"

"Hey kid, you shouldn't read that garbage; it will rot your brain." The woman leaned against the cave wall, enjoying her drink.

"My mother says I should read more so I can become smarter." The little girl replied, annoyed that the stranger interrupted her reading.

"Well, your mother is right; you should read more, especially at your age. Just pick a different book. The Fallen have lost their reason and are just grasping for power." The woman took a long sip of her drink.

The little girl placed her glow rock and the book on the cavern floor. "What kind of book should I read? How about the book you have? Can I read that one?"

The woman laid her hand on the ancient-looking book. "No, I am sorry; this is a special book that I have to keep safe for someone." The woman slipped the book back in her pack. "I am so sorry, sugar. My name is Rin. What is yours?"

The little girl perked up and offered Rin her hand in greeting. "My friends call me Issy."

Rin shook Issy's hand. "That is a cute name. Is it short for something?"

"Issahya, it is short for Issahya."

Rin smiled. "Interesting."

*****

The old woman closed the ancient tome and gave a tired sigh. "I don't want to have to do this again. So please make it stick."

The powerful-looking woman rocked back in her chair. "That is the plan."